Dangerous Games

USA TODAY BESTSELLING AUTHOR

T.K. LEIGH

DANGEROUS GAMES

Published by Carpe Per Diem, Inc. / Tracy Kellam, 25852 McBean Parkway # 806, Santa Clarita, CA 91355

Edited by: Kim Young, Kim's Editing Services

Cover Image Elements:

Merla © 2019

Watercolor_Concept © 2019

Used under license from Adobe

To my very own rockstar…

Chapter One

ONE OF MY earliest memories is that of my parents kissing. It may not sound like a poignant or remarkable event, considering they were married and kissed several times a day, but this particular kiss has always stayed with me.

I couldn't have been more than three years old. My father had a conference to attend in Florida, so my mother decided we'd all go. One day, when my father walked into the hotel room after a day of seminars, he kissed my mother, practically stealing her breath. When he pulled back, she murmured, "Welcome home."

At the time, I thought it odd. We weren't home. This was just a hotel room we were staying in for a few nights. When I asked my mother, she told me something I'll never forget.

"Home isn't a place. It's a feeling. And when I'm with your father, I'm home."

Since then, I've searched for that feeling of home, desperate to experience that same belonging my mother did every time she peered into my father's eyes.

I never thought I'd find it where I did.

* * *

A blast of wind whips my hair in front of my face. I smooth it behind my ear as I stare at the awning of a lounge near Bryant Park. Everything about it appears trendy and pretentious. I shouldn't be surprised this is the type of place Jessie requested I meet him. He was never the kind of person to head to a neighborhood dive bar for a beer.

I could easily turn around, tell him something came up at the hospital and I had to work overtime. But there was something that urged me to pick up my cell when I saw his name flash on my caller ID. Something in his voice that made me agree to his request. Guilt. Remorse. Desperation.

I'm not sure if it's on my part or his.

Maybe both.

When Jessie and I dated, then were engaged, he had a commanding presence. It may have seemed that way because his nearly twenty-three years felt mature next to my almost nineteen. He had this confidence that drew me to him, making me forget about everyone else who came before him.

Almost everyone else.

Regardless, in those few years we were together, he'd never sounded so lost, so uncertain as he did on the phone. Whatever he needs to talk to me about must be important if he called after not having so much as sent a text or email in the past nine years. I worry the secret I've been keeping is about to come out in a spectacular fashion.

Inhaling a calming breath, I smooth my hands over my wool coat, descending the short flight of stairs into the basement lounge on shaky legs. A wall of warmth assaults me the instant I step into the darkened room. It's not a typical Manhattan bar — big, noisy, overcrowded. This place is small, maybe enough seats for thirty people between the short bar counter and lush chairs. There's no loud music being piped in. Instead, ambient jazz sounds in the background.

"Do you have a reservation?" a petite blonde in a black dress asks as I attempt to unwrap my scarf, a few beads of sweat forming on the back of my neck, most likely from a combination of nerves and the drastic change in temperature from the frigid air outside.

"Actually, I'm meeting—"

"Izzy?"

I fling my gaze in the direction of that voice, my breath hitching when I see a man I haven't seen in nearly a decade. A man I'd hoped to never see again. Not because he'd sought comfort in another woman's arms before I'd officially returned his ring. But because I fear what he'll notice in my eyes.

"Jessie." I feel like I'm staring at a living memory, the act of peering into his dark orbs returning me to a time in my life when seeing him was an everyday occurrence. For over two years, it was.

Not a single strand of his chestnut hair is out of place, his jawline clean-shaven, making me think he probably has a weekly appointment with his barber. His tall, slender physique looks borderline intimidating in an impeccably tailored three-piece suit. Jessie always was the type to dress well, even when he was younger.

"Dress for the job you want. Not the one you have," he'd say.

Now, based on what I know, he has the job he always wanted — managing his brother's rising music career.

"Hey." He scrapes a hand through his hair. "I'm glad you're here. It really..." He exhales a shaky breath. "You had every reason not to, but I'm grateful you agreed to meet me."

I press my lips into a tight line, not responding. How can I? I fear the second I open my mouth, the truth will fall from me like an avalanche. The unease about his invitation has been eating me up to the point I've barely slept since I received his phone call. Anyone else in my position wouldn't have agreed, would have distanced themselves. But curiosity got the better of me. As did my compassion. Despite our past, this is a man I once imagined spending the rest of my life with. A man I once loved.

One I probably always will.

"Can I take your jacket, miss?" the hostess asks, cutting through my thoughts.

"Thank you." I remove my scarf and gloves before unbuttoning my coat.

As I shrug out of it, Jessie reacts quickly, helping me, as he always did. I offer him an appreciative smile. When he takes in the dress I selected for tonight, his eyes flare. It's a far cry from the jeans and t-shirts I wore every day of my undergraduate career. The last time he saw me, I was a girl, only a few weeks past my twenty-first birthday. A lot can change in that time.

"Enjoying the show?" I retort playfully, crossing my arms in front of my chest, which only serves to accentuate my cleavage that's already prominently on display, thanks to the plunging neckline of the sleek red dress.

"Um... Sorry, Iz. You just... You look... Wow."

My cheeks heat. Regardless of everything that transpired between us, the fact he still finds me beautiful is a much-needed confidence boost after having recently celebrated my thirtieth birthday.

"This way." He places his hand on the small of my back, leading me toward a secluded table in a darkened corner. When I slip into the lounge chair, he ensures I'm comfortable before taking his seat across from me. "What would you like to drink?" He signals for a server. "I'm assuming you've outgrown jungle juice and kamikaze shots."

My stomach roils at the mere mention. "You assume correctly. I can't even think about triple sec without wanting to hurl."

"Duly noted." There's a twinkle in his eye I never noticed before. He's always been charming and charismatic. It was what attracted me to him all those years ago. But now it's more pronounced, his maturity accentuating all the qualities I once appreciated.

"What can I get you?" a tall redhead in a tight-fitting dress asks, placing a cocktail napkin in front of me.

"Dry martini, please."

"Certainly." She turns her attention to Jessie. "Another club soda?"

With a curt nod, he responds. "Please."

"Of course."

I watch as she retreats, then turn back to him. "No jungle juice for you, either?"

"Nah. I'm not much of a drinker these days. At least not when I need to keep a clear head."

I swallow hard. "And what do you need to have a clear head for?" My voice trembles, my mouth growing dry as a chill trickles down my spine.

He brushes the pad of his thumb the length of his bottom lip. His contemplative stare causes goosebumps to prickle my skin, a sinking sensation settling deep in my stomach. "Obviously I didn't call to reminisce about the past." His eyes gleam with amusement.

"I figured as much." I run my clammy hands along the skirt of my dress, fidgeting with the hem in a desperate need to do something with my hands.

"I didn't see any other option." He narrows his gaze on me, much like my father did when he caught me sneaking in after curfew during high school.

But back then, I was simply having innocent fun with friends. This secret isn't innocent, especially where

Jessie's concerned.

"Here you go," our server interrupts, placing a martini glass in front of me and a small tumbler filled with a clear effervescent liquid in front of Jessie. As anxious as I am to get on with this conversation, I welcome the reprieve. Or stay of execution.

"Thank you," Jessie says.

The waitress nods. "Holler if you need anything else."

Once we're alone again, he lifts his glass. "To making amends." He raises his brow in expectation.

Hand trembling, I reach for my drink, bringing it toward his. "To making amends," I repeat. But amends for what?

After we've both taken a sip of our respective beverages, he returns his glass to the table, clearing his throat. "I want to start by thanking you for coming. I realize I was cryptic over the phone—"

"That's a gross understatement." I give him a coy smile, masking my nerves. "I can't help but think that was intentional so I'd have no choice but to show up to find out what you wanted."

"Can you blame me? If I were in your shoes, I'd be suspicious if my ex called out of the blue after eight years."

"Nine," I correct.

"Right." He hangs his head. "Nine years." He blows out a laugh, his eyes glistening with nostalgia. "In some respects, it doesn't seem possible that much time could have passed. In others, it does." He slowly lifts his gaze to mine. The remorse I see within is enough to bring me to my knees, my guilt festering even more, squeezing my lungs and tugging at my heart. "Izzy…" He reaches across the table, grasping my hand in his. He looks down as he toys with the barren ring finger where the symbol of his devotion once sat. "I kept it."

"Kept what?"

"Your ring. I could have sold it. Hell, the jeweler I went to had a buyback program the saleswoman was keen to make me aware of, more so when she learned how young you were." He laughs slightly, still caressing my skin. "But I couldn't. Even though I knew selling that ring would help pay off some of my student loans——"

"Why didn't you?"

He drops his hold on me, taking a sip of his club soda. "It didn't seem right. A part of me hoped you'd come back. But the other part knew that would never happen. Not after I betrayed you."

My stomach sours at the regret laced around every syllable. Every breath. Every small smile.

"You didn't betray me." I pull the olive from my martini and bite it off the cocktail stick. "I couldn't expect you to remain faithful when I gave you every indication that I was done. Like Ross would say, we were on a break."

His mouth kicks up into the same smirk that stole my heart once upon a time. "Still a *Friends* fanatic?"

"Some things will never change."

He peers at me thoughtfully. "That's actually comforting. Whenever I scroll through the channels and see *Friends* is on, I think of you. But our situation was a little different than Ross and Rachel's 'break'."

"How so?"

He nods at my left hand. "You were still wearing my ring, due to my insistence. If I wanted you to keep it so badly, why would I hurt you like I did?"

I hide my hand under the table. I wish I had the courage to tell him I hadn't been wearing it. Not in private anyway. Around my friends and family, I made sure to keep it on, not wanting to admit they were right.

That we *were* too young to get engaged. At least I was. Jessie was always mature beyond his years.

"I played a part in what happened, too. A big part. I ignored your calls, even after Asher…" I trail off, heat washing over my complexion at the mention of Jessie's older brother. It's the first time either of us has brought him up. Can he hear the affection in the simple way my mouth caresses his name? Can he see the longing in my expression? Can he feel the heartbreak from across the table?

Clearing my throat, I continue, lowering my voice. "Even after Asher reached out and told me you were in a bad place, begging me to talk to you, I didn't."

"We'd agreed to take a break from each other while you were home for Christmas. I didn't expect you to pick up the phone and call me every day like you usually did when we were apart, especially after that fight."

I stare into the distance, recalling the argument that started the storm to follow. It was my last night up in Boston before I was to head home to Connecticut for my Christmas break from college. I wanted to see Asher's band perform at a local club. Jessie wanted a quiet night at home. At the time, I saw his insistence we stay home as a way to control my behavior. It was ridiculous and irrational. Further proof we weren't ready to be married.

My friends warned me things would change once we were married. No more nights out. No more hanging out with friends. All my time would be devoted to Jessie.

In essence, this argument wasn't about seeing Asher's band. It was about my fear regarding the upcoming changes. My fear of Jessie pushing me away after he finally realized I wasn't the person he thought I was. So, in typical Izzy fashion, instead of trying to work things out, I ran. Or at least tried to. But Jessie wouldn't let me, begged me to take time to think it over. It was almost like he knew.

"I'm not asking you to forgive me for my lapse of judgment." His words force my attention back to him. I attempt to argue once more, but he holds up his free hand, interrupting me. "Do you have any idea how many times my finger hovered over your contact in my cell only to chicken out at the last minute?" His tone grows impassioned. "God, Izzy. So many times. I've wanted to apologize for years, tell you how ashamed I am of what I put you through. Tell you—"

"You have nothing to apologize for." Although I didn't make him believe so at the time. It was easier to use his supposed infidelity as the catalyst for our breakup instead of admitting the truth to anyone, including myself.

"Yes, I do."

"Same Jessie York. Still always has to have the last word."

"Same Isabella Nolan. Still always trying to see the good in everyone. Even someone who doesn't deserve it. Not after what I did."

As much as I doubt I'll ever be able to tell Jessie the real reason I walked away, I hate the idea of him shouldering the blame that seems to still eat at him.

"Fifty-fifty split?" I offer with a smile.

He furrows his brow, seemingly confused by my statement. Then realization kicks in, as I knew it would.

Whenever we had a disagreement, we'd inevitably apologize, both wanting to bear the majority of the blame for the argument. Although back then, it was usually over my family's love of the Mets and his love of the Red Sox. I could never bring up the year 1986 without it igniting intense emotions. That was the year the Red Sox got so close to winning the World Series, until an error allowed the Mets to take it. Regardless of the reason for the fight, we always agreed to share the blame equally. It was what made our relationship work so well.

Until it didn't.

Smiling, he extends his hand toward me. "Fifty-fifty split," he repeats. I allow him to shake my hand, as we always did to solidify our agreement.

I'm about to make a crack about Billy Buckner when he cuts me off.

"I know where you're going, and I don't want to hear it. It's still a bit of a sore spot, even though the curse is broken." A hint of his Boston accent shines through in his words.

I laugh, any lingering unease melting off as I joke with him. Like we used to. We always were good friends. I often thought we were better as friends than as a couple.

"I didn't think I'd ever get to hear that again," he remarks thoughtfully.

"What?"

"Your laugh." He smiles a pained smile. "Still as beautiful as you are."

I lower my eyes. No other guy I'd dated ever admitted their feelings so unabashedly. With Jessie, there were no games, no questioning where he stood. After what I've done, I don't feel like I deserve his compliment.

"You must be wondering why I called," he says after a beat.

"It wasn't to apologize?" I ask timidly.

"Well, yes and no."

"No?" A knot forms in my stomach, my trepidation increasing with each silent second. Every sound is heightened. The clink of ice against glass. The occasional chuckle. The melody of Ella Fitzgerald's voice as she sings about how much she loves the city of Manhattan.

A laugh rips from his throat. It's not filled with humor. But not quite sarcastic, either. It heightens my anxiety even more.

"I never thought I'd reach a point where I'd have this conversation with you."

"What conversation?" My words are barely audible, a weight bearing down on my chest.

"You're going to think I'm crazy. But I'm left with no choice…" He trails off.

My heartbeat echoes in my ears, the hairs on my nape standing on end. He knows. He must. Maybe his apology was a front. A way to lull me into a false sense of security before he pounces, forcing me to reveal the secret I knew I wouldn't be able to keep forever.

I wonder if this is how condemned prisoners feel when they're led to the execution chamber and are asked if they'd like to make one final statement. No wonder many don't. What is there to say? The people watching have already made up their minds. Nothing the accused says will change their opinion. Just like nothing I say to Jessie will lessen the sting of my actions. All I can do is beg for forgiveness.

"It's about Asher."

"I can explain," I interject. "It didn't—"

"He's blocked," he interrupts before I can incriminate myself.

Stilling, I blink. Once. Twice. Allowing my brain to process his statement. "Blocked?"

"He's missed the past three deadlines. I don't know how much time the label's willing to give him. This next album can make or break his career. Can turn him

11

from a one-hit wonder into a household name. Well, even more a household name than he's already become, considering you can't turn on the radio without hearing 'Amante'."

I swipe up my martini glass, gulping down the liquid. "What do I have to do with any of this?"

On a long sigh, he reaches into the inner pocket of his suit. "This." He tosses a folded piece of paper onto the table. But it's not just any folded piece of paper. It's folded into the shape of an origami dove. Something Asher and I always did as our way of apologizing after we'd gotten into an argument. Jessie and I had the fifty-fifty split. Asher and I had origami doves.

I look at the paper, able to make out a music staff and notes scratched on it, most likely discarded versions of a song Asher's trying to find. "I'm not sure I—"

"Every song he's written lately ends up as an origami dove. I know this was a thing between you guys. I didn't realize you two were still in touch."

"We're not." A sour taste fills my mouth. It's not a complete lie, but not forthcoming, either.

"Then why is he making these damn origami doves? He's refused to give me answers, so I figured I had no choice but to go to the source."

"How should I know?" I peer into eyes that are borderline accusatory. "Maybe he's feeling a bit nostalgic. Wishes things could return to the way they were before he had all this pressure on him."

He squints, seemingly toiling over this explanation for validity. My mouth grows dry and I take another large sip of my drink, but nothing settles my nerves at the prospect of Jessie putting the pieces together. Then his shoulders fall.

"I remember how you guys would stay up all night working on music. I guess that was one of the things I was always jealous about." He laughs slightly. "I hated the mere thought of him stealing you away, although he'd never do that. But all I saw was my brother and girlfriend sharing a bond I'd never have with either of you. I've never exactly been…musically inclined."

"You don't say," I tease in an attempt to lighten the mood.

While Jessie's always had a great ear for music, he couldn't hold a tune if his life depended on it, growing frustrated whenever I tried to teach him the basics of playing the piano or guitar. It's all further proof that he and his brother truly are complete opposites. Whatever Jessie excelled at, Asher struggled with, and vice versa. Together, though, they're a force to be reckoned with. Which is why Asher's rise to stardom over the past year has been rapid. He writes addictive songs and performs them with a soulful presence you can't help but be drawn to. As his manager, Jessie knows how to market his sex appeal and beautiful music to the masses.

As much as I've tried to avoid everything to do with both Asher and Jessie York, it's grown increasingly impossible, particularly once Asher's first album dropped and he made the rounds on the talk show circuit. Whenever I caught him on TV, I couldn't help but stop and listen to him tell the story of how he got his big break. How he was about to throw in the towel when he received the phone call that changed his life.

One of the members of Fallen Grace, the biggest boy band around today, had seen Asher perform at a local club. After playing Asher's stuff for the rest of the band, they approached him with a proposition. They'd been searching for a newer, less boy-band-esque sound, and Asher had exactly what they'd been looking for.

When they asked him to write the songs for their new album, Asher agreed, thinking it would be his only claim to fame. But once the band went public with the brains behind Fallen Grace 2.0, as they'd referred to it, record labels knocked down his door, begging for him to sign with them. In a matter of months, Asher went from nearly giving up on a music career to having all the major labels fighting over him.

"This is why I need you, Iz. All the songs Asher released on the last album were ones he'd written when you were in the picture. Trust me. I wouldn't be here if it weren't necessary. I get the feeling all these damn doves are a sign. An S.O.S., so to speak."

"S.O.S.? What are you talking about?"

He drags his fingers through his perfectly groomed hair, tugging at it. It's clear whatever's blocking Asher plagues Jessie, too.

"Asher plans to head up north in a few weeks to work on the new album. To Grams' lake house, where he wrote so many of his old songs. Where *you* helped him write so many of his old songs. I want you to…hang out with him, like you used to."

My face heats, limbs jittery as I listen to Jessie's proposal that I go up to the lake house and spend time with Asher. If he knew the truth, he'd be singing a different tune.

"I didn't do anything. I'm sure if he goes up there on his own, he'll find that inspiration. I have commitments here. I can't ignore those."

"We've tried that, but it didn't work. We recreated everything. Except there was one thing missing. You."

I'm about to protest, but he interrupts.

"I understand I'm asking a lot of you, considering our…past. I'm sure the last thing you want to do is hang out with your ex's brother at his grandmother's lake house in the dead of winter."

I remain straight-faced, not wanting him to read

between the lines of my expression.

"That's why I'm willing to compensate you for your time." He reaches into the messenger bag at his feet, withdrawing several papers and extending them toward me.

"What's this?" I ask, my eyes scanning the pages, which could be written in a foreign language as far as I'm concerned.

"A standard royalty distribution arrangement. I want to buy some of your time."

"I'm not sure I—"

"You'll get points on the album."

"Points?"

"Yes. In layman's terms, a point is a royalty percentage. I'll give you two points, or two percent of every album sold. Same goes for streaming royalties. Taking the numbers from his debut album, that would have already netted you nearly fifty grand."

My eyes widen as I choke on my own saliva. "Fifty grand?" I knew Asher was doing well for himself. He's been lauded as the next John Mayer, albeit with a more soulful and bluesy vibe. I didn't realize he's already *become* the next John Mayer. If two percent of sales equals fifty grand in six months, I can't imagine the money Asher is pulling in.

"And early projections look like this upcoming album will easily be four times that, possibly more."

My jaw drops. "So you're offering me potentially two hundred grand just to spend time with Asher?"

"More or less."

I blink, struggling to wrap my head around this. "This is an incredible offer, but I—"

"There's more. An extra...incentive."

"Incentive?"

"Like I mentioned, we're past deadline here. This

album was supposed to come out at the beginning of this year in order to help with notoriously low first quarter sales. The label gave us an extension, but it needs to drop in the second quarter. So I'm willing to offer you an additional twenty grand, payable at the end of his time up north, contingent on him writing a full album worth of songs by the time he's set to go into the recording studio."

"And when is that?"

"March first."

"It's already the middle of January, Jessie. You want me to find some way of inspiring him to write a dozen or so songs in a little more than a month?"

He shrugs. "He's done it before when you were around."

I shake my head. "It's been years. I don't—"

His hand covers mine, squeezing. "*Please*, Izzy." His words are laced with desperation. "I'm out of options. I need you. *Asher* needs you."

"This is crazy. What am I supposed to do?"

"Whatever it takes. Within reason, of course," he adds quickly. "I'm not paying you to sleep with him like some managers hire girls to spark their client's inspiration. Not that Asher would do that anyway. Not with our past."

"Of course not," I say with a tight-lipped smile, doing my best to keep my expression neutral. I feel his eyes skate over my face, the seconds seeming to stretch.

"Just… Do whatever you used to do whenever you guys burned the proverbial midnight oil. *That's* what I'm trying to recreate here. Those nights you both stayed up until all hours, which always seemed to result in him writing yet another song."

I focus on the papers, the words bleeding into each other. This entire scenario seems absurd. The last thing

I expected when I agreed to meet him was this kind of proposition. But no amount of money would make me agree to *this* proposition.

I close the royalty agreement and push it back toward him. "I don't think it's a good idea. Can't you hire some songwriters to compose the songs for the album?"

"I tried. Asher refused. Said he's a songwriter first. Performer second. It was part of the deal he made with the label. Only his material. He'd sooner give it all up before performing someone else's song because some fuckhead in a suit told him to. His words, not mine." He rolls his eyes. "According to Asher, I'd probably fit into that fuckhead in a suit category."

I laugh, able to picture Asher saying those precise words.

"*Please*, Iz," Jessie implores again, his voice turning serious. "At this point, I'm out of options. And time. If this album doesn't drop soon, Asher's career will be over. He'll lose everything. His contract prohibits him from being picked up by another label or releasing independently for two years. By that time, he'll no longer be current."

"So if he doesn't release this album, it's all over?"

He nods. "Most likely. This industry is cutthroat enough as it is. If he disappears for two years, he'll lose all his forward momentum. He'll be starting from scratch. You know how much he wants this. How long this has been his dream."

"I do."

"Listen…" Jessie pushes out of his chair and stands, leaving the contract with me. Retrieving his wallet, he throws several bills down, enough to cover our drinks and a rather generous tip. "Don't do it for me. Do it for Asher. Just…" He exhales a long breath. "Just look over the agreement and take some time to think about it."

He cracks a small smile. "But not too much. Time is at a premium. Can you promise you'll do that? That you'll think about it?"

I exhale a long breath. "Okay."

"Thank you." He turns, and I watch him make his way through the lounge, everything about his stride and the way he carries himself confident and mature.

"Hey, Jessie?" I call out before he can disappear.

Stopping, he glances over his shoulder with an arched brow.

"You were good to me. Just wanted you to know that."

A smile tugs on his mouth. "Thanks, Iz. I needed to hear that." Then he continues out of the bar, leaving me alone to consider his proposal.

But there is nothing to consider. I can't bring myself to fall into Asher's world.

Not after I made the mistake of sleeping with him a year ago.

Chapter Two

One Year Ago

"WELL, THANK GOD that's over." Chloe spun on her heels, hurrying toward the bank of elevators, as if it were a race.

I couldn't blame her. After the past several days of being stuck at the bachelorette party that never ended, I wanted to get as far away from the clanging bells of slot machines, too.

I never thought I would have been the type of person to be in Las Vegas for a bachelorette party. Certainly no one within my tight-knit circle of friends had any desire to celebrate their upcoming nuptials with such a cliché and overdone event. But that was before I'd received a phone call out of the blue from my childhood friend, Hannah.

I'd all but forgotten about the adolescent pact Chloe and I had made with her to be in each other's bridal parties if the day should ever arrive. Despite having grown apart from Hannah since then, Chloe and I honored our word and hopped on a plane bound for the tenth circle of hell.

"I swear, if one more guy approaches me thinking I'm a prostitute because my hair's a different shade, I'm going to lose it. I'm not the first person to color my hair gray and lilac, for crying out loud." She gestured to her wavy locks that fell to her mid-back.

I must admit, it took me a while to get used to the color, knowing I'd never be so daring as to change my hair to such a unique tone. But that was Chloe. Bold and a bit reckless. Plus, her natural shade of blonde made it easier to do something like that. There wasn't much I could do with my nearly jet-black hair. As far as our appearance went, Chloe and I were as opposite as could be. She was short and petite, the picture of an all-American girl, aside from her choice in hair color. I was on the taller side with curves and olive-toned skin, thanks to my Latina heritage.

"You know how this place can be," I responded when I caught up to her. "It's bachelorette party central. You saw how the girls behaved. They're away from home and responsibility, so they throw common sense out the window and flirt with anything with a pulse. Same goes for the men here for bachelor parties. And, as we all know, men aren't nearly as intelligent as women, so they say and do even dumber things."

Her laughter filled the elevator vestibule, overpowering the abrasive noise of the casino. "You've got that right." When a car arrived, she slung her arm over my shoulders, which proved slightly difficult due to our height difference, her five-two to my five-seven, but we managed. Like always.

"Lobby tomorrow at eleven?" I arched a brow at Chloe when the elevator stopped on my floor. "Or maybe I should tell you 10:30 so you'll be on time."

She playfully jabbed me in the side. "Don't worry. I'll be there. There's no way in hell I'm missing my flight out of this godforsaken town."

"Good. Or I'm leaving without you. Because there's no way in hell *I'm* missing my flight out of this godforsaken town."

"Goodnight, Izzy," she sang, pushing me out of the

car before the doors closed on me.

"Night, Chloe," I called back as I made my way toward my room.

Once inside, I took a minute to relish in the tranquility. My ears still rang from the constant barrage of noise in the casino, but other than a faint conversation I could make out from the room next door, it was peaceful, the whirring of the air conditioner the only sound.

An urgent need to wash off the remnants of tonight's festivities, namely the showgirl lessons that came complete with full makeup, overtook me and I headed for the bathroom, starting the shower. After a few minutes of rigorously scrubbing my face, I felt like myself again. Not this dress-wearing, club-going girl I'd been the past few days.

Emerging from the bathroom, I glanced at the clock to see it was just after eleven. I should have packed and gotten some sleep, but I wasn't even close to being tired. As a nurse, I typically worked the night shift. Since I'd stayed out until the early hours of the morning all weekend, my body had remained on that schedule. So, instead of throwing on some pajamas, I slid on a pair of jeans and a black top, then left my room to explore the Vegas nightlife on my own. And hopefully find a low-key bar. After a weekend of nothing but overpriced, pretentious clubs, I needed a simple bar and a good beer.

Most other women my age probably wouldn't want to venture off on their own at night in Vegas, but I wasn't most women. I liked being alone. Liked being able to do what I wanted when I wanted. Liked not having to depend on anyone else for my own happiness. That was the benefit of being an only child. An *adopted* only child. I became fiercely independent at an early age.

I meandered along the casino floor, the tables overflowing with people trying their hand at blackjack, poker, or roulette, probably gambling away their life savings in the hopes of winning big. Cocktail waitresses in skintight dresses that barely covered their ass carried trays holding drinks. Despite having one of the top air filtration systems available, a thin layer of smoke seemed to fill the space, the stench of nicotine permanently ingrained in my nostrils. It was going to take days to get the stink out of my hair once I got home.

As I wandered in search of a place where I could grab a decent beer, the sound of a live band cut through, a nice change from the typical thump of club music they blared all hours of the day. I looked in its direction, spying what appeared to be an Irish pub. I grinned at the familiarity. My mother would have admonished me for going to an Irish pub while in Vegas, considering I lived in New York and couldn't trip without falling on yet another bar just like this one. That was probably what called me to this place. It reminded me of home.

I stepped inside, everything about my surroundings seeming to go against what Vegas stood for. Yes, it was still a bar and the music was loud, but it wasn't ostentatious. Wasn't filled with women wearing as little clothing as they could get away with on the prowl for some poor schmuck to buy them overpriced drinks for the night. Wasn't crawling with men dressed in suits who bathed in far too much cologne.

I walked toward a long bar that sat along the wall and found a vacant stool. My eyes were drawn to the ceiling, dozens of bills of every currency pinned to it. A bartender approached and took my order for a beer, returning with a pint within seconds. I took a sip of the hoppy ale, exhaling at the flavor that seemed so foreign after the past few nights of only consuming mixed, saccharine drinks. This was exactly what I needed to feel normal again.

I surveyed the darkened space, nothing flashy or unique about it. Just like every other bar I'd been to in my adult life, the lounge was filled with heavy wood tables, patrons enjoying a variety of drinks and bar food while they listened to live music. A large crowd filled the area in front of the stage, dancing to the band as they covered a Coldplay song. They were pretty good, much better than some of the artists getting airtime on the radio these days. I'd take rock music any day over the latest auto-tuned boy band who wouldn't know how to hold a guitar if their life depended on it.

The song ended and applause broke out, a few girls cheering and clapping enthusiastically. Déjà vu washed over me, like I'd been here before. In a way, I had. I'd once been one of those exuberant fans cheering for the local band, hoping they'd someday make it big. But that was a lifetime ago.

"Thanks all," the lead singer's voice carried over the loud chatter and clanging of ice against glass. "We're going to take a quick break, but before we do, we have a special guest who's agreed to get up on stage with us tonight. Remember this name, folks, because in the next few months, you won't be able to turn on your radios without hearing his music. Ladies and gentlemen, give it up for Asher York!"

A gasp escaped, my eyes darting toward the stage. I froze, my brain unable to tell my lungs to breathe, my heart to beat, my body to move. All I heard was that name. It couldn't be him, could it? How? I'd never been great at statistics, but the likelihood of the two of us being in the same bar in Las Vegas had to be… What?

One in a million? A billion? It had to be someone else with the same name. Someone else who was also a musician. Someone else who was six-two, with dark hair and a smile that could melt panties.

I told myself I was imagining it, that I was still stuck in the memories of my college days when my roommate and I would go to whatever club Asher's band was playing and dance the night away. That must have been it. The reality of being in the same room as him seemed so far out of the realm of possibilities, especially considering the last I knew, he was a music teacher in the suburbs of Boston, playing the occasional gig on the weekends.

Then again, the last time I had spoken to him was eight years ago.

A lot could change in that amount of time.

And when a figure jumped onto the stage and faced the crowd, I realized truer words had never been spoken, or thought. A lot *could* change in that amount of time. And Asher York had certainly changed.

I watched with a mixture of intrigue and surprise as he grabbed an acoustic-electric guitar from a stand, plugging a cable into the end of the body. The man resembled the Asher York I once knew, but he was a far cry from the lanky man I remembered. And I definitely remembered him. Asher York wasn't the kind of person anyone could forget.

His broad chest pulled at the simple gray t-shirt, his biceps filling the sleeves quite nicely. His dark hair had grown out and had a sexy, disheveled vibe, the perfect complement to the scruff along his jaw. But that wasn't the biggest change. Oh no. As if he weren't rock god personified with the longer hair and muscular physique, he had to add tattoos to the fantasy.

I should have left. Paid for my beer. Headed back to

my room. The last thing I needed was to reopen old wounds. And seeing Asher did just that. But like the first time my college roommate dragged me to a club to see a local band that was gaining in popularity, I was drawn to the man's rough, emotion-filled voice.

I stared at my beer, concentrating on the melody. It sounded familiar, like a cloudy memory trying to return to the surface of my subconscious. The longer I listened, the more clear it became. By the time he sang the first chorus, it hit me. It was the same melody I'd heard him toil over endlessly during those late summer nights we stayed up together at his grandmother's lake house, while my then fiancé slept inside.

Who also happened to be Asher's brother.

During the two years I'd dated Jessie, I was welcomed into his family with open arms. That included spending a few weeks of the summer at the lake house. It was actually one of the things I missed most when we broke up. The card games. The smell of burgers on the grill. Spending the early morning hours listening to Asher pluck away at his guitar as he attempted to piece together a song.

This song.

Allowing my dark hair to cascade in front of my face in the hopes that Asher didn't recognize me in the crowd, I risked a glance at him. He seemed to have cast a spell on everyone here, just as he did all those years ago. People bobbed their heads in time with the song, one I'd heard more times than I cared to admit, the familiar chords akin to coming home after a long absence.

I was transfixed as I listened to him sing about feeling like he was made for a particular woman, but she never saw him until it was too late. I didn't realize my eyes were glued to his every move until deafening applause thundered around me. The girls who had preened before the lead singer of the other band mere minutes ago now fawned over Asher.

He smiled that breathtaking smile of his as he thanked the crowd, still as enigmatic a presence as always. His gaze floated over the throng, coming to an abrupt stop when he locked eyes with mine. I tried to look away, but the simple act of our gazes meeting turned me to stone, apart from the fluttering in my chest. It shouldn't have. I shouldn't have had any reaction to him. But I did. I had from the first time I saw him across a packed club in Boston.

Snapping out of my stupor, I refocused my attention on my beer and drained it. I grabbed a bill from my wallet and left it on the counter, not caring about getting any change. The excessive tip was a price I was willing to pay to keep the past buried. To keep my secret buried.

I was about to jump down from the stool when a hand on the bar next to me stopped me.

"Running off without even saying hi?"

My eyes darted up, coming face-to-face with Asher York. His voice was even smoother than I remembered. A husky sound that hit places on my body that hadn't felt excitement in an eternity.

I parted my lips, attempting to come up with a response, but I was rendered speechless when I caught a glimpse of his arm leaning on the bar, the position causing his biceps to flex and push against the confines of his t-shirt, stretching the fabric.

A woodsy scent surrounded me as I stared, the smell reminding me of large family dinners, playing guitar on the dock overlooking the lake on his grandmother's property, roasting marshmallows. Reminded me of a girl I used to be. One I'd tried to keep in the past.

Swallowing down the bittersweet memories, I pushed a strand of hair behind my ear, forcing a smile. "Asher. Good to see you." I held my head high, looking anywhere but directly into his eyes. I couldn't. He had the same eyes as Jessie. Born eleven months apart, their appearance had always been strikingly similar. But that was where their similarities ended, the brothers as opposite as two people could be. Regardless, I'd never met siblings as close as they were. Or maybe I'd found it so foreign since I was an only child.

"Phew." He blew out a breath, laughing shakily. "I wasn't positive it was you. I thought it was, but everyone in this town seems to look like someone else."

I shrugged, finally meeting his gaze. "It's me."

"Good. That would have been awkward otherwise." A flirtatious smile curved up the corners of his lips. He even had the same smile as Jessie. But Asher's looked more natural, like he was actually happy. "What are you doing in Vegas?" he continued when I didn't immediately say anything.

"I could ask you the same question."

He nodded at the stage. "Music." He didn't embellish. "Your turn."

"Bachelorette party. Hannah's getting married next month, and Bernadette was in charge of planning her bachelorette party."

A look of understanding crossed his face. "Say no more."

As uneasy as it should have been to see Asher again, considering his connection to a time in my life I would have preferred to keep in my rearview mirror, it was refreshing to talk to someone who already knew me, scars and all. Someone I didn't have to go into all the details of my life with because he already knew. Hell, he'd been present during some of them.

"Cash you out, miss?" the bartender's voice cut through.

I nodded. "Thank you."

"Actually," Asher interrupted before the bartender could retreat with my money, "she'll have another. And I'll have an IPA." He placed a finger on the cash I'd left on the bar and slid it back in front of me. "Put all her drinks on my tab."

"That's not necessary," I insisted, attempting to push the bill back toward the bartender. "I really should be going. It's been a long night and I—"

The heat coming off him as his hand wrapped around my arm stopped me mid-sentence. I flung my wide eyes to his, my insides vibrating at his touch.

"Stay."

One word, and my mouth went dry.

One word, and my heart pounded in my chest.

One word, and I forgot all the reasons I should leave.

"Okay." I slowly slunk back into my barstool.

What harm would one drink with an old friend be?

Chapter Three

Present Day

TURNS OUT, ONE drink *did* lead to a lot of harm. Not only to Jessie, but to my heart. And Asher's.

In my life, I've made my fair share of mistakes, but sleeping with Asher in Vegas tops them all. With his invitation to stay, the web was cast, each minute we spent together another string tethering me to him until it was nearly impossible to walk away.

But we had no choice but to do just that, considering who we were to each other.

"Earth to Izzy," a familiar voice cuts through. I meet Nora's sky blue eyes as we sit at a bar by Columbus Circle for our traditional Thursday evening get-together. I almost didn't come tonight, but after Jessie's proposition, I need a night with my girls, need some sort of normalcy.

"Sorry." I smile half-heartedly. "Must have spaced out."

"Are you okay?" She places a hand on my forearm. "You don't seem like yourself."

"Just thinking about one of the kids at work." I hate using my patients as an excuse when it's Jessie's proposition that weighs heavy on my mind. I shouldn't give it a moment's thought. There is absolutely nothing good that can come out of seeing Asher York again. But I can't forget Jessie's insistence that I'm his last resort…and Asher's last chance.

"I can't imagine doing what you do." A sympathetic expression crosses her face. "It must take its toll."

I swallow hard, nodding, sipping my vodka tonic. I shift my eyes to Evie, who sits on the other side of Nora. "Is Chloe still at the office?"

She furrows her brows. "She hasn't been in all week."

"She hasn't?"

"No. I assumed she would have told you. Lincoln surprised her with a trip to Vegas, since this week marked the one-year anniversary of them hooking up during that blackout."

I take another sip of my drink, trying to act as if that fact hasn't also been on my mind the past few days. Yes, it's the anniversary of Chloe and Lincoln hooking up when we were stranded in Vegas during a blackout, but it's also the anniversary of me sleeping with Asher, an event I was confident I'd put behind me once I left the city of sin. That was before Jessie walked back into my life.

"She won't be here?"

"No. She's coming." Evie looks at her watch. "She should be here any—"

As if on cue, a whirlwind of blonde hair flies through the doors, heading straight toward us. "Sorry I'm late," Chloe exhales, dropping her purse on the bar and signaling the bartender for her normal martini before assuming her seat.

"How was Vegas?" Evie asks, leaning toward her, her green eyes alight with anticipation.

"Yeah. How was Vegas?" I repeat, my tone almost accusatory.

Chloe looks my way, a silent apology in her gaze. I know why she didn't mention it to me. I may have spent the past year insisting I rarely thought of my one night with Asher, but she can see the truth. That even though it was only one night, it's been impossible for me to truly forget. Even more so now that Asher York has become a household name.

"Actually…," she begins, addressing Evie and Nora, "I have a newfound appreciation for that city."

"I did find it odd you'd willingly go to Vegas," Nora interjects, knowing all too well how much Chloe despises everything to do with that place. Next to me, Nora's known Chloe the longest, having been roommates their freshman year of college.

"Yes, well, I suppose it took meeting the right guy to change my mind. And he's changed my mind on a lot of things. Like this." With a blinding smile, she holds her left hand toward us, a large diamond on a very important finger. But that's not all. In addition to the ring sits a double band on either side.

We all simultaneously gasp.

"You're married?" Evie shrieks.

Chloe nods excitedly as we all take turns examining the stunning setting.

"That's amazing!" Nora adds, flinging her arms around her. "And I'm not even the least bit upset you got married without telling us." She pulls back, holding her at arm's length. "It's perfect. Exactly what I've always imagined your wedding would be like. Crazy. Untraditional. Private. Like you."

"I'm happy for you," I offer, although my words lack any enthusiasm.

With Chloe's marriage to Lincoln, coupled with Evie's wedding to Julian late last year and Nora's to Jeremy last summer, I'm now the odd one out. The only one in our circle who isn't married. The only one who's so far away from the sound of wedding bells I may as well pack my bags for the convent.

Chloe reaches across the bar, grasping my hand in hers, and we share a look. It's strange to think of her as married. She's always been fiercely independent, vehemently anti-relationship. Until Lincoln weaseled his way into her heart.

"Are you okay?"

I hate this question. Am I okay my best friend is married? Of course. I'm thrilled she found someone who values and respects her. Am I okay my best friend is married to one of Asher York's college friends? That's a more difficult question to answer. How will I react when I run into him at a party they throw? Will we pretend Vegas never happened? Will I ever be able to move on, like I've tried?

"Better than okay. I'm so happy for you. Truly."

She squeezes my hand, then pulls back, answering the myriad of questions Evie rapidly fires at her.

Over the next hour, Chloe shares every detail of her special day. The few pictures she has tell the story of a wedding as outrageous as one would expect a Vegas wedding to be. Hell, Chloe didn't even wear white. Instead, she opted for a tight-fitting red dress while Lincoln wore his typical tweed blazer and jeans. And around her neck hangs a strand of penises, like she wore the night she first met Lincoln. Anyone else wouldn't want photos of what's supposed to be the most memorable day of their lives marred with a penis necklace, but Chloe's never been one to play by the rules.

"But don't worry," she says as she finishes her martini. "We're going to do a little reception this summer." She looks at Evie. "Can we throw it at Julian's Southampton home? Well, I guess it's yours, too. Sorry. It's weird to think of you as a Hamptons socialite."

Evie smiles. "Don't worry. I still call it his house, to which he reminds me it's mine, too. And of course. You guys are more than welcome to have a reception there. We'd be honored to host it."

"Thank you." Chloe gives her an appreciative smile before glancing at her watch. "Crap." She pushes out of her chair, tugging her coat back on. "Sorry to drink and dash, but my *husband's* waiting. Love you girls." She blows us all a kiss, then retreats in the same flurry with which she arrived.

We all return our eyes forward, a silence washing over us as we process the fact that Chloe got married. The bar is still abuzz with activity, a mixture of commuters and tourists coming out of the cold for a minute to grab a quick drink. Polite chatter surrounds us, interspersed with a few cheers from people watching the hockey game on the large screen TVs hanging from the ceiling. Everything is exactly like it is on any other Thursday.

Except my anti-marriage best friend is now married. And to the man she hooked up with on the same night I slept with Asher.

"Well, that's something I wouldn't have put money on," Nora says after a beat, pushing a lock of her strawberry blonde hair behind her ear.

"My money was on her never getting married," Evie offers. "Just living with Lincoln. She's never been a traditional girl. At least from what I picked up in the six or so years since I started working at the magazine."

Both her and Nora look to me, considering I've known Chloe since childhood. "She humored her cousin, Hannah, and me whenever we would plan our weddings as kids. But I don't think she ever saw the point. Probably because there was always a strange dynamic between her parents. She didn't exactly come from a house filled with love." I pinch my lips into a tight line, then brighten my expression. "But I'm happy for her. She deserves this."

I truly believe that. Between caring for an alcoholic mother and dealing with a father who always looked at her as an inconvenience before finally smartening up, she's had one hell of a year. One hell of a life. She deserves to be with someone who will fight for her. And Lincoln does that. He has from the beginning.

"So now it's just you." Evie's voice is chipper, her expression bright as she peers at me. "When are you going to tie the knot?"

I roll my eyes. "I'd need to meet someone first."

"I thought you had something going on with one of the anesthesiologists at the hospital," Nora interjects.

"Who wouldn't love to marry a doctor?" Evie agrees.

"It's a casual thing when we both need to work off some stress. Trust me. Dating is difficult enough, especially in this city. Not to mention the fact I work a job with strange hours. I've yet to find any guy who'd be okay with my schedule for the long term. It's easier to go in detached with no expectations. Saves me from being pushed to the side when he realizes I'm not what he wants."

"It's okay," Nora assures me, straightening her spine. "Sometimes marriage isn't all it's cracked up to be."

This certainly catches our attention. Nora was the first one in our group to get married. What was supposed to be a no-strings-attached hookup, arranged through Tinder, turned into a whirlwind romance. Less than three months after their first date, she'd agreed to marry him. It struck me as odd and I questioned Jeremy's motives, how he could go from wanting a quick romp in the sack to proposing in what seemed like the blink of an eye, but Nora reminded us she did the same thing. That when you met the right one, you just…knew.

I can't fault her there. People questioned my own engagement to Jessie all those years ago. Claimed we were too young to get married, to make that life-altering decision. I used the same argument Nora did. I think a part of me worried he was my only chance at happiness, at finally having a family. At finally having a home.

"Is everything okay with you and Jeremy?" I ask in a low voice.

"Of course," she answers cheerfully, but doesn't look directly at me. Or Evie.

She fidgets with the hem of her black pencil skirt. It doesn't matter that she runs a yoga and meditation studio and spends most of her days in workout clothes. She still likes to look fashionable in public. Unlike myself, who has no problem wearing scrubs almost every minute of my day, although I did put on jeans and a nice shirt tonight.

"Everything's great. He's been traveling a lot for work. And…"

"Yes?" Evie leans closer.

"It's stupid," she states after a brief pause.

"What is?"

Nora worries her bottom lip, floating her gaze between Evie and me. Then she exhales a long breath. "The two-year anniversary of our first date was over the weekend. Or I guess the first time we slept together, because our first real date didn't happen until a few weeks after that. But he didn't even acknowledge it. I didn't expect things to maintain their excitement after being together for several years, but… I don't know…" Her shoulders fall. "Last year, he celebrated every anniversary, ones I couldn't even remember. And I'm the girl in our relationship. *I'm* supposed to be the one who remembers the date he first burped in front of me, or when I first made him his favorite meal." She sighs, swirling her wine around in the glass. "I just wish we could still have that spark, ya know?"

Evie places her hand on Nora's bicep, smiling sympathetically. "I get it. It's a pitfall of all relationships. You get comfortable. Maybe you need to rekindle the spark somehow."

"Have you had this problem with Julian?"

Evie hesitates, probably because she hasn't. I've seen them together. I've never observed two people as in love as they are... Until Lincoln and Chloe. And I thought Nora and Jeremy. Maybe appearances can be deceiving.

"No. But we do things to keep the spark alive. When I used to be in charge of the sex and dating column at the magazine before being promoted to assistant editor, this was a common topic, one I wrote about constantly."

"And what advice did you give?"

"Sometimes you need to go back to the start, remind each other why he called you up for a date after it was only supposed to be a random hookup."

Nora focuses her eyes forward. Then she jumps up from the barstool, tugging her wool coat over her. "That's it! You're a genius, Evie." She kisses her head, then hugs me before rushing out of the bar, much like Chloe.

"And then there were two," I comment as I bring my glass to my lips.

At that moment, Evie's phone chirps and she floats her eyes to it, her expression shining, a blush blooming on her cheeks. It doesn't take a genius to know who's texting her.

"Julian?" I ask.

"Yeah."

"Do you need to go?"

When her eyes fall on me, there's a flicker of pity within. "Do you mind? It's just—"

I wave her off. "Go. Enjoy your evening."

Her brows furrow. "Are you sure you're not upset? I feel like we're all ditching you for our husbands. Well, we kind of are, but—"

"It's okay. Dr. Ben texted earlier to see if I wanted to come over," I lie.

"Fun." She waggles her brows, withdrawing a few bills to cover her drink. "You enjoy Dr. McDreamy." She scoots off her barstool and buttons up her coat. "See you later, Iz."

"You bet."

I watch as she scurries toward the exit. Once she disappears from view, I settle back into my barstool, signaling the bartender for another drink.

"And then there was one."

Chapter Four

TV CAMERAS LINE the sidewalk when I arrive for my shift the following Wednesday evening. This isn't the first time I've bypassed news crews to get into the hospital. But as I strain to catch snippets of what the reporters say, a heaviness settles in the pit of my stomach.

Layoffs. Budget cuts. Board salary increases.

I walk through the front doors and into chaos. Another nurse I recognize pushes past, head lowered, tears streaking down her cheeks, holding a box of what I can only assume to be the contents of her locker.

Not wanting to stare, I keep my eyes forward as I make my way into an elevator, joining a mixture of visitors, doctors, and nurses. Normally, there's a bit of chatter about the day, weekend plans, the latest drama involving a staff member. But it's silent today, which doesn't help to settle my nerves, considering my supervisor called and requested that I come to the hospital a little early. I assumed it was for my quarterly review, although now that I think about it, I had my review not even six weeks ago.

When the elevator slows to a stop on my floor, I almost don't want to get off. Holding my head high, I smile as I pass the registration desk. The familiar scent of hand sanitizer, latex, and coffee greets me, as it has nearly every day for the past three years.

When Emma, the intake nurse, looks at me with

apologetic eyes, I know why I've been asked to come in early. After all, I *am* the newest nurse in the unit, the one with the least seniority. It doesn't matter I've probably clocked more hours than some of the nurses who've been here significantly longer. My anniversary date is the most recent. As the old saying goes, last one in is the first one out.

My heart echoes in my ears as I approach Donna's work area, a semi-private cubicle just off the registration desk. I knock gently on the partition wall, and she looks up from the file she was reviewing. Removing her glasses, she greets me with a warm smile, an underlying sadness visible.

"Izzy. Thanks for coming in early."

"I'm getting fired, aren't I?" I blurt out. "I saw the reporters out front. They're all talking about massive layoffs."

She stands from her desk, grabbing the file, before ushering me away. "We'll talk in private. Your union steward is already here."

She doesn't have to say anything else. There's only one reason for a union steward to be present at a meeting between myself and my supervisor. To protect my interests.

I follow her down the hallway, moving swiftly through the oncology wing and toward one of the administrative offices. When we enter, a dark-skinned woman wearing pink scrubs stands. I greet Justine with a nod. I haven't had much interaction with her, since she works in cardiology, but I've always respected her drive and tenacity to protect the interests of all nurses.

Donna lowers herself into the chair behind the desk, gesturing for me to sit in the free one across from her and next to Justine. I do so, albeit warily. She places her glasses back on, opening the file and perusing it briefly before returning her attention to me.

Expelling a sigh, she seems to be at a loss for words. "This is the part of the job they don't warn you about when you take it. It's one thing to have to fire someone who can't cut it, but another…" She trails off, collecting her thoughts before lifting her eyes to mine again. "You're right. The directive came down around Thanksgiving. Every department was ordered to cut their budget by varying degrees."

"Which translates into cutting staff."

She removes her glasses, shaking her head. "My hands are tied here. I was told to decrease my nursing staff by two."

"So that means Gretchen and I are getting the ax, right?"

"If I had any other choice, I'd keep you, Izzy. I'm just following orders, whether I like them or not." She retrieves a set of papers from the file. "The hospital has put together a severance package. Four months' salary paid on the first of every month, as well as health insurance for a year."

"Which would be great had I not had to depend on overtime hours to make ends meet." Since I'm the proverbial low man on the totem pole in this unit, there's nothing I can do to prevent this from happening, but I can't stop the panic from setting in.

"The hospital will also pay out any vacation or sick time you've accumulated," Justine adds. "Immediately."

"I truly am sorry," Donna says. "Trust me. I tried to fight this." She nods at Justine. "We all did. And the union's *still* trying to fight this. Unfortunately, those who make the decisions don't walk these floors, don't take care of patients, don't understand how worn thin the nursing staff is already. But I promise you, the second this passes and I'm able to hire more staff again, you're the first phone call I'll make. It kills me to have to let go of such an amazing nurse, but like I've said—"

"I know, I know. Your hands are tied."

* * *

A few hours later, I collapse on the couch in my tiny studio apartment, setting the box with all the belongings from my work locker on the coffee table in front of me. I have no idea what to do with myself. I can't remember a time I didn't work. My parents did well for themselves, but they wanted to teach me responsibility, so once I turned sixteen, I got a job. It was a condition of being able to get my driver's license. In the fourteen years since I entered the work force, I've rarely taken time off. Now that I don't have my work, I'm at a loss, not to mention unsure how I'll pay my bills.

As I contemplate my options, my phone rings. I pull it from my bag to dismiss the call, in no mood to talk to anyone. When I see it's my dad, I smile, my muscles relaxing.

"Hey, Papa."

"Hey, butterfly." It doesn't matter that I'm thirty. He'll always call me butterfly. I hated it when I was a teenager, but now that I've outgrown that phase of my life, I appreciate the affectionate nickname. "I heard the news about your hospital. Are you—"

"I've been let go," I answer quickly.

"Oh, sweetie… I'm so sorry. I know how much you loved that job."

"It's okay. There will be another job." I feed him the same line I've told myself repeatedly the past few hours. There's no doubt in my mind there *will* be another job. But there won't be another one like this.

"Do you need money? I can——"

"No. I'm fine. I'm getting four months' pay without having to lift a single finger. If you ask me, I made out in this scenario." I attempt to sound chipper so he can't hear the worry filling me.

"That's the right attitude."

When he pauses, I sense he didn't just call to check if I'm still employed.

"What is it?" I ask with hesitation.

"What do you mean?"

"I know you, Dad. There's another reason you called."

He blows out a breath. "I can't get anything by you, can I?"

"No, you can't. Tell me what it is."

"You've just been laid off. This can wait a few days. It's nothing that needs immediate attention."

"If it's more bad news, I'd rather hear it all on the same day."

"Are you sure?"

"I can handle it."

"Okay." He sighs. "I got a jump start on your taxes——"

"I told you I'd do them myself," I admonish.

"Which would take you hours. Whereas I can do this blindfolded."

"You're probably right. How much am I getting back?" It's still too soon to file, but the thought of getting that extra money will help ease the stress a little.

"Actually, sweetie, you're not. With the new tax law, things have changed. You can't deduct certain expenses like you used to."

I furrow my brows. "What does that mean?"

"It means you owe this year."

"Owe? How much?"

"A little over five grand."

Frustration builds in my throat. I want to scream, cry, something. I have a hard enough time making ends meet as it is. Now I have a substantial tax bill on top of being laid off? Apparently rock bottom has a basement.

"Your mother and I are willing to help if you need it."

"No," I say, stubborn as always. While most people would accept the help, that's never been who I am. "You don't have to. I'll take care of it myself. The hospital offered me a pretty good severance package. I'll be fine."

"We don't mind. You—"

"It's okay. I'm an adult. Paying taxes is part of it. But can I wait until April? By then, I'll have another job and will still be collecting my severance pay. Plus, I'm not in the habit of giving the government money before the due date when I could be earning interest on it."

"Like father, like daughter." He chuckles. "You can wait. That's why I called you now. Hell, it's why I asked for your final paystub from last year. I had a bad feeling in my gut, so I wanted to get ahead of the eight ball here, so to speak. Figured the more time you had to save, the better. But like I said, we are—"

"Don't worry," I interrupt. "I'll manage."

"Okay." He pauses for a beat, then states, "Since I'm delivering bad news, I should mention I received a phone call from Child Services today."

I chew on the inside of my cheek, not immediately saying anything.

"They just want an answer either way. A bunch of reporters are hounding them, still trying to be the first to run a story on the JFK baby. It *was* just the thirty-year anniversary."

"I know," I say with a sigh. "I saw the news stories they *did* run."

"You don't have to do anything you don't want to."

We have the same conversation around this time every year. The media reaches out to Child Services wanting to do a story on the baby who was abandoned in the ladies' room at JFK Airport. In turn, Child Services reaches out to my parents to see if I'd like to finally reveal my identity to the press. My parents ask me, telling me they'll support whatever I choose. I waver, a part of me wanting to go public just so I can find out who my birth mother was, another part unsure I'm ready to face that.

"Some of them do offer a small appearance fee," he reminds me.

"I just… I'm not interested in the media combing through my life and looking at me with sympathy because the woman who gave birth to me didn't want me. Not interested in the public offering their opinion on *why* she didn't want me."

"I understand. Your mother and I will always support your decision in this. If you do change your mind, we'll stand by your side every step of the way."

I allow his words to comfort me, as they always do. "Thanks, Papa. I'll come by soon for dinner."

"Your mother would love that. Greenwich isn't that far."

"According to some New Yorkers, it's a different country."

"Then make sure to bring your passport. Love you, butterfly."

"Love you, too, Papa."

Chapter Five

I SIT AT my tiny breakfast table, sorting through bills, prioritizing them by what I absolutely must pay. It's been so long since I've received a direct deposit without at least twenty hours of overtime pay that I've forgotten how little money I made, particularly in comparison to the high cost of living here in Manhattan. If I lived anywhere else, I probably would have been able to make it work. But now I can't even scrape by. After paying my rent and heating bill, the balance in my bank account is laughable.

Frustrated, I shove the bills away, watching them scatter onto the floor. I stare at them, venom in my gaze, when I notice the royalty agreement Jessie gave me. I push out of my chair, grabbing it, focusing on the twenty grand bonus if Asher makes his studio date. That money would certainly help. I'd be able to pay all my bills for the next few months and even put a little away in savings until the album released and the royalty payments started coming in.

Can I really do this? Can I really see Asher again? Is the money worth the eventual price my heart will pay from the simple act of being in his presence?

Perhaps I'm looking at this the wrong way. I *am* getting paid. Perhaps I should consider this as nothing more than a job, with Asher as my employer. Short-term employment while I search for something else.

Unlocking the screen on my phone, I scroll through

my contacts, my finger hovering when I come to Jessie's name. I once dialed this number so often he'd earned a spot in my favorites. Now it's been nine years since I hit this number.

I hold my breath as I listen to the line ring. I can end the call. It's not like I don't have options. I can ask my parents for a loan. Even Chloe, Evie, and Nora offered to help when they learned I'd been laid off. But my pride prevents me from asking anyone to support me. I like knowing I can find my own way. Maybe this is the way I need to go.

"I was wrong," Jessie's deep voice answers on the third ring.

"Excuse me?"

"About how long it would take you to call. I figured you'd call in a day to accept my offer. Instead, you made me wait on pins and needles for over a month. You really know how to torture a guy."

"What makes you think I'm calling to accept? I could be calling as a courtesy to tell you I'm not interested."

"True, but I know you well enough to know you'll do this. Despite what happened between us, you'd never hold that against Asher. You're too compassionate a person."

I chew on my lower lip. He'd be singing a different tune if he knew the truth.

"Well, luckily for you, I've recently found myself with some free time on my hands and am willing to help."

"Thank you," he breathes. "You have no idea what this means to me. And Asher. Would you like to go over the contract in greater detail? I can answer any questions."

"That's not necessary. I read it over," I lie, not wanting him to think I'm doing this out of pure desperation and would agree no matter what was contained in these pages. I don't need his pity. Don't need anyone's pity. "It all seems rather straight forward. I hang out with Asher. I get a percentage. If he makes the studio date with enough songs to record an entire album, I'll receive a bonus, payable immediately."

"That about sums it up." He pauses. "Except there's just one thing. Something I couldn't put in the contract, but I hope you'll agree regardless."

"What's that?" My skin prickles with heat, unease weighing down my stomach.

"I want this arrangement to stay between us. I don't want you to tell Asher I'm paying you to...inspire him."

"So... Asher doesn't know." My words come out as a mixture of a question and a statement.

"No. And I want to keep it that way. If he knew the truth, the whole thing might backfire. I want your interactions to be as authentic as possible. Like they were all those years ago. When you spent time with him because you genuinely liked being with him. That's what I'm trying to recreate. And you're the only person who can do that."

I take a few steps toward the opposite end of my apartment and peer out at the city below me. "Don't you think he'll be suspicious? How do you plan on explaining my sudden reappearance after all this time?"

"Don't worry about that. I've got it handled."

"How?"

"Grams," he explains. "She's been on my case to make things right with you for years. Says she can't meet her maker when there's still an imbalance in her world, or something like that."

His statement causes a laugh to escape. It sounds exactly like something she'd say. She always was good at laying on those guilt trips.

"I'll just tell Asher you're there for Grams' sake."

"And when I stay longer than a normal visit? How do you hope to explain that? He'll question it at some point."

"Don't worry about that. I'll take care of it. Even if it means telling everyone we're together again."

"No!" I shout.

It's one thing to keep Asher in the dark about the true reason I'm there. Hell, it'll be awkward enough as it is. At least we parted ways on somewhat amicable terms after our one night together. We both realized it was a mistake to sleep together, regardless of any feelings we may have had for one another. But the mere thought of Jessie trying to convince Asher we're back together makes it difficult to breathe. I couldn't betray Asher like that.

Too bad I had no problem betraying Jessie.

"I didn't realize the idea was that revolting," Jessie snips with a hint of venom.

"It's not that," I attempt to appease him, pulling my lips between my teeth. "I just… I don't like lying to your family. Any more than necessary," I add as an afterthought.

He doesn't immediately respond. Every second that passes causes my pulse to increase. I stare at the dull gray walls, praying I didn't just make him suspicious of me.

Of us.

"I understand the awkward position I'm putting you in," he says finally. "I'll just have Grams insist you stay after the weekend."

"And that's an invitation I'd never turn down. You know how much I love Grams." A warmth fills my heart at the memory of spending hours in the kitchen with her as she regaled me with another crazy story from her past.

"And she certainly loves you." He chuckles. "For months after you left, she always gave me that evil side eye of hers. The one that made me think she was casting some voodoo spell on me."

I join his laughter, all too familiar with that look. She'd given it to me a few times. Usually when I refused one of Asher's invitations to head out to the dock with him, opting to spend time with Jessie instead. Shouldn't she have been more upset if I *hadn't* chosen my boyfriend?

"So you're on board? You're okay keeping this quiet from Asher? I hate to be that guy, but without your agreement on this point, the deal is off the table."

I sigh, pinching the bridge of my nose. A premonition settles in my stomach that this has the potential to backfire, but does it matter? After my time at the lake house, I'll have no reason to see either man again. If Asher finds out the truth, that's on Jessie. Not me.

"You have my word. I won't mention our arrangement to Asher."

"I knew I could count on you, Iz. I'll arrange all your travel and send you the details. I'll try to get you into Logan Airport tomorrow around two and pick you up. That way, we can beat rush hour."

"Tomorrow?" I can't mask the surprise in my voice, my pulse skyrocketing. It was one thing to agree to this in the abstract, thinking I had time to mentally prepare. But now that I'm less than twenty-four hours away from coming face-to-face with the one man I've tried to forget, nerves wrack my body.

"Unfortunately, we're short on time. Every minute counts. It's already been a month since I came to you with my proposition."

I part my lips, about to tell Jessie this isn't a good

idea, when my gaze settles on the agreement. Twenty thousand dollars. I need that money.

"Of course," I relent. "I understand. I just lost track of the days."

"Thank you. You're saving his career. If you didn't agree to this, I don't know what I would have done."

I close my eyes, blowing out a breath. I can't back out now, not after the reminder of what's at stake. "I'll keep an eye out for my travel details. See you tomorrow, Jessie."

"See ya, Iz."

Chapter Six

A S JESSIE NAVIGATES along the steep, winding dirt road leading to Grams' lake house the following evening, I can't stop my heart from pounding, my hands from growing clammy, my stomach from becoming queasy. I try to hide my nerves from Jessie. In his mind, the hardest part of this adventure is over — spending three hours in an enclosed space with my ex-fiancé as he drove from Boston to a quaint house in the hills of New Hampshire. All I have to worry about now is reuniting with his brother.

Who I slept with, then avoided the past year.

Jessie drives around a bend, slowing to a crawl as he turns onto a gravel path, the uneven surface jostling me, before finally coming to a stop. He shifts the car into park and kills the ignition, glancing at me.

"Ready?"

I peer through the window at the two-story wooden structure. It looks the same as it did nearly a decade ago, except for a fresh coat of stain on the siding. Lights from within illuminate all the windows, and a bit of smoke billows out of the stone chimney. Blowing out a long breath, I nod.

"Just remember. You're here for Grams. Because you have an amazing heart and didn't want another year to go by without seeing her, despite any animosity you may still have toward me."

"Jessie, I don't—"

He holds up a hand, cutting me off. "It's okay. Lay on as much of a guilt trip as you want. Grams would probably appreciate that." With a deep chuckle, he opens the door, rushing around to help me.

When I open my own door and step down from the SUV, he gives me a playful look of admonishment. "Still the same stubborn Izzy, aren't you?"

"What do you mean?"

"You make it impossible for me to be a gentleman around you. In more ways than one." He flashes a devious smile, then strides to the trunk and retrieves our luggage, refusing to allow me to carry mine. "But seriously. Would it kill you to let a guy open the door for you once in a while?" He steers me up the path and toward the house.

"I'm fully capable of opening my own doors."

"You're fully capable of doing a lot of things. That doesn't mean you shouldn't be treated like the treasure you are. And that includes risking a fall on a sheet of ice to open the door for you."

The memory forces a laugh to escape. On our first date, I was confused when he attempted to rush to my side of the car. While I'd seen my father open my mother's door constantly, I never considered I'd date someone who would do that for me. By the time I finally got used to it, it had turned into a game. He'd dart from the driver's seat as quickly as possible to beat me to opening my door. Which was all in good fun...until he slipped on some ice and dislocated his shoulder.

"Okay. From now on, I'll wait for you to open my door. Just to avoid playing nurse while you recuperate."

He nudges me. "Actually, I kind of liked when you played nurse, especially when you walked in wearing that sexy little costume."

My cheeks blush, but it's not enough for me to steer the conversation elsewhere. It's refreshing to reminisce about the good times we shared. And we did share some amazing times together.

"Do you have any idea how difficult it was to find a sexy nurse's costume in January? I had to rush order one online so it would get here in time. But you were worth having to eat ramen noodles for a few weeks until I got my next paycheck." My admission slips out before I can stop it.

"And you were worth dislocating my shoulder. I'd happily risk it again to hear your squeals of joy when you won our little game." He smirks, then stops beside a large oak tree lining the drive.

"Do you remember what happened here?" He nods toward the tree, dropping our bags to the ground.

I head toward it, running my fingers along the bark, stopping when I feel the indentation. "J.Y. and I.N," I murmur.

"Do you remember what I told you right after we carved our initials into that tree?"

I straighten, meeting his gaze. "That you loved me."

"You thought I was crazy. That it was too soon." When he tucks a strand of hair behind my ear, my breathing quickens. "You always were on the practical side."

"So were you. That's why it surprised me."

"What can I say?" He adjusts his stance, closing the distance between us. "You brought out a side of me I didn't know existed. You still do." His eyes skate over my face, seemingly imprinting everything about it to memory. My nose. My cheeks. My lips. Which he stares at for an inordinately long time. But he doesn't push forward. Neither do I. I remain frozen in place. Too scared to advance. Too broken to retreat.

Then he exhales, releasing me from his hold. I should be relieved he didn't try to kiss me, but a small part of me wanted him to. Wanted to feel him. Wanted to replace the memory of Asher's lips on mine with a new one. One that isn't laced with lies and betrayal.

But I fear even if I kissed a thousand men, I'll never be able to erase Asher's kiss. Not with the way it's imprinted on my soul, in the very fiber of who I am.

"We should go inside," he states matter-of-factly.

"You're right. We should." I avert my eyes, pushing past the tree. Jessie catches up with ease.

"I'm sorry. I—"

"It's okay," I interrupt. The last thing I need is to listen to my ex-fiancé apologize for not kissing me when I never should have wanted him to in the first place.

"It's not that I don't want to kiss you, Iz. I do. Have since the second you walked into that bar and I saw you for the first time in years." He drops the bags at the foot of the stairs leading up to the porch. His firm grip on my arm forces me to stop. "When you took off your jacket and revealed that red dress…" His voice grows husky, wanton, reminding me so much of Asher's tone when in the throes of passion. The vein in his neck throbs, his jaw clenched, nostrils flaring.

I'd always thought Jessie and Asher to be complete opposites. Where one was night, the other was day. Where one was difficult, the other was easy. Where one was aloof, the other was attentive. Regardless, they still exhibited the same intense passion toward whatever drove them. Whether it be music, work…or me.

"It drove me fucking crazy, Iz. Still does. As much as I want to kiss you — and I am *dying* to taste your lips again — I want it to happen because *you* want it to. Not because you're in a place where you're surrounded by memories of us. I want your kiss to come naturally, quietly. Like the way we fell in love all those years ago."

"Jessie…"

I wish he were the asshole I'd painted him to be to all my friends when I told them of our breakup. But an asshole wouldn't drop to his knees and beg me to give him another chance. Wouldn't unabashedly cry as he tried to grasp onto me, knowing nothing would keep me there. Wouldn't go along with my story that he was the one to blame, especially when we were both at fault.

"I don't blame you if you'll never trust me. But I promise if you give me a chance, I will spend every day regaining that trust."

I peer at him through guilt-ridden eyes. "I don't even know what to say." It's probably the first honest thing I've said to him since we reconnected. The first phrase that doesn't have a hidden meaning, that isn't a cover for my lies.

"I get it. You're probably wishing you never agreed to this. But I'm glad you did, if only so I could finally tell you everything I've wanted to say for years. I should have kept my mouth shut, but I hate the idea of wondering what if. I've lived the past nine years wondering what if. What if I hadn't pushed you to give up your social life for me? What if I was more understanding? What if I listened to you more?"

"You *did* listen. We were at two different places in our lives. Like Grams always says…"

"Everything happens for a reason."

"Exactly."

I grab my bag and drag it up the few steps and onto the porch. Jessie scrambles after me, grasping the handle from me before I can reach the door.

"But you know what I can't understand?" he asks softly.

"What's that?" I flick my gaze to him.

"For the life of me, I can't come up with a reason for what happened between us."

Chapter Seven

THE LAKE HOUSE is almost as I remember it, despite the passing of nearly a decade. The living room just off the foyer still exudes a rustic chic vibe, a mixture of modern furnishings and wood accents filling the space. I inhale, able to make out the faint aroma of a fire crackling in the fireplace in the great room toward the back of the spacious house.

As I look around, I feel like I've been here before. Not just in the physical sense, but also in an emotional way. The nervous energy filling me is reminiscent of the way I felt the first time Jessie brought me here to meet his family. It was the same day I realized the hot lead singer of the band I'd been following was also Jessie's older brother.

Sensing my nerves, Jessie grabs my hand, squeezing. I bring my gaze to his, offering him a grateful smile.

"It's about time you got here," a deep voice rumbles.

I stiffen, my breath catching as I fling my eyes toward the kitchen, my pulse skyrocketing, skin on fire. It's official. I didn't give this plan the care and consideration it deserved. I should have taken a page out of Evie's book and made a list of pros and cons.

Pros — Money. Paying my bills. Not ending up homeless.

Cons — Asher York. Sleeping with Asher York. The fact I was once engaged to Asher York's brother.

Yup. The cons win.

Panic setting in, I search for an escape route that won't draw any attention. But it's too late. The second I stepped into the SUV with Jessie it was too late.

"You're usually the one who's on time. What held you…"

As Asher rounds the corner into the living room and our gazes meet for the first time in over a year, he trails off, coming to a stop. His jaw drops, eyes blinking repeatedly, as if unsure he's seeing correctly. When his stare focuses on my hand joined in Jessie's, I quickly step away, lowering my head.

"Up," he finishes, doing his best to pretend this isn't an awkward encounter. But it is. There's no way this wouldn't be. I'm standing in a room with two men I've slept with. Two *brothers*.

"Sorry, man," Jessie says. I push down the thought of Asher and Jessie comparing war stories. "Traffic leaving the city was rough. And this one has a bladder the size of a pea." He hooks a thumb at me. "Pretty sure we stopped at every rest stop between the airport and here."

I slowly lift my eyes, meeting Asher's gaze once more. I haven't been this close to him since I kissed him goodbye in Vegas after we agreed we had no choice but to go our separate ways. And dammit, he looks even better than he did then. His dark hair is a little shorter, but still falls almost to his chin, a sexy, disheveled look to it. A bit of scruff covers his jawline, and I squeeze my legs together at the memory of it scraping along my thighs. His muscles pull at his V-neck t-shirt, his jeans falling sinfully from his hips. I could be wrong, but I think he has a few more tattoos than he did last year, the ink covering his left arm now a full sleeve.

Remembering where I am and who I'm with, I clear my throat, putting a stop to my mental undressing.

"Asher, it's good to see you." I thrust my hand out, doing my best to prevent it from trembling as I wait for him to shake it. "Congratulations on all your success."

"A handshake, Iz?" Jessie comments. "You guys used to be practically inseparable. I thought you'd be thrilled to see each other again." He looks at Asher. "Thought you'd like this little surprise."

"I'm certainly surprised. I don't think I'd be more surprised if Santa Claus, the Easter Bunny, and the Tooth Fairy all walked in together." Eyes still trained on me, he arches a single brow, silently asking if I'm okay with a hug.

I nod, my motion subtle. As apprehensive as I am about feeling Asher's body against mine once more, especially in Jessie's presence, I need to act as normal as possible.

His gaze not straying from mine, Asher steps toward me. The instant he encloses me in his strong embrace, I exhale my held breath. His touch is hesitant, like that first dance with a member of the opposite sex during middle school. Awkward. Stilted. Forced.

But as I melt into him, my own arms wrapping around his body, which feels even more muscular than it was a year ago, he relaxes, pulling me tighter against him. I close my eyes, resting my head against his chest, wishing I could stay in this place, in this moment, in this bubble, the rhythm of his racing heart soothing me in a cloak of familiarity.

"Good to see you again, Iz." Asher's words vibrate through me, followed by the sensation of his lips against my temple. It's a simple kiss, one shared so often between friends. But nothing between Asher and me has ever been simple. I try to ignore it, but even a slight brushing of his skin against mine causes a rush of need to fill me. It takes every ounce of resolve I possess to peel myself from him and return to Jessie's side.

"You, too, Ash." I fight against the tears threatening to fall down my cheeks. I'd give anything to return to Asher's arms. To live there. To die there. "Really good." *Too* good.

He peers at me with the same passion he did during our one night together. Then, as if remembering we're not alone, he rips his eyes from mine. His expression hardens, spine straightening, flipping the switch from *my* Asher to the Asher who was forced to erect a wall around his heart after I broke it. After we broke each other.

"Does Grams know she'll be here?"

His voice is almost accusatory, any affection he held toward me gone. I shouldn't be surprised. After all, our night together in Vegas was one big game of push and pull. For every step we took toward each other, he'd remember who I was and take two giant leaps backward. I imagine the same will be true now.

Except I won't take any more steps toward him.

I learned my lesson last time.

"Of course."

"And Mom and Dad?"

I fling my gaze toward Jessie. "Your parents are here, too?"

"I must have forgotten to mention that," he replies. "It was a last-minute trip anyway, a belated celebration for Grams' birthday."

I blink. It was one thing to be around Asher again. But their parents, too? How many more surprises will there be?

"Is that Jessie I hear?" Mrs. York's voice echoes against the tall ceiling before her short, petite frame appears in the doorway, then stops abruptly. "Izzy?" Her tone rises in pitch, obviously taken aback. Her stare shifts from me to Jessie, then takes a quick detour to Asher before returning to me.

"Grams has been on my case to do whatever it takes to get her to come see her." Sensing my own irritation with the situation, Jessie flashes me that megawatt smile of his that I couldn't help but say yes to when he first asked me out. "So I did."

Mrs. York remains frozen in place as this turn of events registers in her brain, the situation only serving to increase my trepidation. "Well..." Her mouth curving into a genuine smile, she holds her arms wide and pulls me in for a hug. "This is wonderful. A bit of a surprise, but wonderful all the same."

"It's great to see you, Mrs. York."

She releases me, narrowing her gaze. The years have been kind to her. Despite the fact she's on the other side of sixty, her auburn hair shows just a hint of gray, a few laugh lines, as my mother refers to wrinkles, around her eyes.

"Remember, Izzy. You're family. And family members don't use such formalities with one another. Call me Reagan."

"Thank you, Reagan."

She beams, then turns to Jessie. He leans down, his six-three frame dwarfing hers by over a foot. When he kisses her cheek, I can't help but feel the love they share.

"Well..." Reagan steps back. "I'm sure you'd both like to freshen up. Dinner won't be ready for about an hour, so take your time."

"Thanks, Ma." Jessie passes her another smile, then retreats, collecting our bags.

Averting my gaze, I follow him toward the stairs, brushing past Asher, hyperaware of his overwhelming presence so close to me. Just as I'm about to climb the steps, I hesitate. My brain tells me to keep walking, to not look back, that I won't like what I see. But my heart wants something else.

As I draw in a deep breath, I steal a glance over my shoulder, locking eyes with Asher. While it probably only lasts a heartbeat or two, it feels longer, the emotions swirling in his chestnut depths making me want to wrap him in my arms, yet run as far away as I can. A dozen questions seem to be etched in those dark orbs. Why am I here? Why did I ignore his attempts to reach out to me? But the most important one… Am I back with Jessie?

I'd love nothing more than to give him the answers to all of those and more. To shower him with kisses and convince him he's still the man I want. Tell him he's still the one my arms seek out in the middle of the night, only to be left bereft when I find nothing but a cold pillow. But we're walking a dangerous tightrope as it is. I can't make it more treacherous.

With an apologetic smile, I continue up the stairs. The floorboards creak as I follow Jessie down the hallway lined with family photographs. I find comfort in the groaning of wood I once tiptoed around whenever I finally slipped into Jessie's bed in the wee hours of the morning after staying up all night with Asher.

He leads me into the room we once shared whenever I came up here, depositing my suitcase on an ottoman at the foot of a queen-sized bed. "Don't worry. I'll be sleeping in another room. I just figured you'd want this room since it's the one you're used to. And there's a private bathroom."

I stare blankly at the familiar surroundings, still trying to process the past several minutes.

"You should have everything you need," he continues when I don't respond, "but if there's anything missing, let me know. I'll be right next door." He turns, about to close the door behind him, when I finally find my voice.

"Why didn't you tell anyone?"

He stops and faces me, his brows scrunched. "What do you mean?"

"That I'd be here. Why didn't you tell anyone?" I repeat.

He shrugs, nonchalant. "I told Grams."

I hate how cavalier he seems over the entire scenario, that he didn't think it a big deal to show up out of the blue with his ex-fiancée.

"Yes, but there are *other* people here, Jessie! Do you have any idea how uncomfortable it was to stand in that living room with your mother and brother looking at me like I'm not welcome? You know how I feel about that. You know I avoid these kinds of situations for a reason."

He approaches, running his hands down my arms in an attempt to appease me. Like he always did. "What makes you think you're not welcome?" His voice brims with compassion and adoration. "Of course you are. You're always welcome here."

"Then you should have told them," I hiss. "Should have told everyone. This is awkward enough without you making matters worse."

"Okay. I'm sorry." He sighs, dropping his hold on me. "I didn't mean for you to feel unwelcome." He runs his fingers through his hair, tugging at it. But, as always, it seems to return to its place, not a single lock skewed. "But I had my reasons, Izzy. You should know that about me. I don't do anything without having a damn good reason."

"And what was this damn good reason?"

He chews on his bottom lip, his breathing increasing

63

as he peers at me. With quick steps, he closes the distance between us. The suddenness of it takes me by surprise, and I back up until I hit the wall, nowhere else to go.

"Because I still have trouble talking about you without wanting to break down, Iz," he growls, his nostrils flaring. I part my lips, but I don't know how to respond. As quickly as it appears, his frantic demeanor softens and he pulls back, sighing. "I guess I didn't want to sit on the phone with Ma and listen to the hope build in her voice. Didn't want to get her hopes up for something I ruined. Figured if I waited until you got here, she'd see for herself there's nothing between us, not with how uneasy you are around me. Despite any fleeting moments that may have occurred, they're not real. I'm still the guy who broke your heart. Nothing I do or say can erase the past. I have to live with that." The anguish and remorse in his voice is enough to rip out my heart.

"Jessie…"

Slowly, I approach him. In a show of comfort I sense he needs, I rest my hand on his chest. He wraps his hand around mine, strengthening our connection.

"You didn't break my heart."

I peer up at him, on the verge of telling him the truth so he'll no longer live with this burden weighing him down. But I doubt the truth will make matters any better. In fact, it'd make them worse. No person wants to learn you left them because you fell in love with someone else. And no person would want to learn you left them because you fell in love with their brother, their own flesh and blood. It's better this way.

"I still hurt you, Iz."

I bring my free hand up to his cheek, and he leans into my touch. A spark of something ignites in my core.

I drag my body closer to his, his smooth skin familiar. And right now, with this strange energy surrounding me, I crave familiar.

"We hurt each other," I remind him. "And ourselves."

He inhales a shaky breath, nodding as he touches his forehead to mine.

"I don't want you to carry this blame anymore, Jessie," I implore. "Please."

"But—"

"Izzy, Ma wants to know how you'd like…"

The second I hear Asher's voice, I jump back, whirling around to face the doorway. I'd hoped I was fast enough so he wouldn't walk in on us in any sort of compromising position.

"Your steak cooked," he finishes, words laced with venom as he looks between me and Jessie, then back at me again, his lip curling into a snarl.

"Medium will be fine," Jessie answers for me.

Asher broadens his stance, his stare unnerving me. "I asked Izzy. Is that how you want your steak? Still medium, like you used to enjoy? Or have you moved on? Tried something different and liked it enough to take a risk on it?"

My jaw drops, gaze widening as I attempt to come up with a response. This clearly isn't about steak. Out of the corner of my eye, I take a peek at Jessie, whose brows are furrowed, the wheels spinning as he surveys us. His analytical gaze takes inventory of my flushed complexion, my increased breathing, my glossy eyes. Then he turns to Asher, assessing his flared nostrils, tight muscles, narrowed glare, a formidable presence in this small space.

"Medium is fine," I blurt out in the hopes of ending this standoff and putting to bed any lingering suspicions

Jessie may have.

"Medium it is." There's a bite in Asher's tone. "I hope you enjoy the kind of steak everyone else eats." He spins around, his footsteps heavy as he storms away.

"I'll go talk to him," Jessie says quickly, retreating from me.

"Jessie, no. You don't have to," I plead, partly because it's not worth it, partly because I worry what Asher will reveal in his angered state.

"You're a guest here. *My* guest. He needs to treat you as such."

"No. Really. It's okay." I rush after him, stepping in front of him. "Let it go. Trust me. Nine years may have passed, but I guarantee by morning, he'll have left an origami dove outside my door." I playfully nudge him, my lips cracking into a small smile. "You know how he can be. Brooding musician and all that."

Jessie studies me for a moment, then expels a breath. "I don't like him talking to you like that."

I don't respond to his statement, looping my arm through his and pulling him back into my room.

"And so what if you like your steak medium? What's the big deal about trying something new? Taking a risk? It's steak! Not exactly a life-altering decision."

I avoid his eyes as I walk to my suitcase and busy myself opening it, searching for my toiletry bag. If he only knew the half of it. "Like I said, brooding musician."

"For a minute, I thought it was some kind of weird code between you two."

I keep my head lowered. When he doesn't say anything for what feels like an eternity, I risk a glance at him to see him looking pensively at me.

"But considering you haven't spoken to each other in years, I don't see how that would be possible.

"Exactly." I force a smile.

Chapter Eight

Nine Years Ago

I STARED UP at the two-story white Colonial, drawing in a deep breath. A premonition formed in my gut that this was a bad idea. That I shouldn't have taken the initiative and driven up here to surprise Jessie upon his return from spending Christmas in Florida with his parents. Maybe I should have waited to see him until the spring semester began, as we'd agreed. At the very least I probably should have called him to let him know I'd be here. But after weeks of ignoring him, not giving him any indication I still wanted to be with him, let alone marry him, I didn't know what to say when I finally did see him.

A knocking ripped me away from my increasingly tumultuous thoughts, and I flung my gaze to see Asher standing outside the driver's side door. I lowered the window, peering into dark eyes framed with thick lashes.

"Are you coming, or are you just going to sit in your car all day?"

"Right." I killed the ignition and grabbed my purse from the passenger seat, opening the door and stepping onto the street. "Thanks for meeting me. I didn't..." I trailed off.

"What?" His voice was harsh. "Didn't think I would, considering you've ignored Jessie?"

I shrank into myself. I'd hoped Asher would be more compassionate, as he always had been toward me. Then again, I wasn't family. Jessie was. When push came to shove, his loyalties would stay with his brother. Not me.

"It's...complicated," I argued in my defense. "We agreed to take a break from each other."

He widened his stance, making his already tall physique appear even more intimidating. "As my phone calls to you these past few weeks should indicate, I'm aware. Am I to now assume this break is over?"

I should have known to expect an interrogation when I'd asked Asher to help. I just hadn't realized it would be this difficult to discuss this with him. It felt...wrong. In the two years I'd dated Jessie, not once did I talk about our relationship with Asher. He never brought it up, either, like it was a permanent elephant in the room we were both content to ignore.

"To be honest, I don't know." I pushed past him, but he caught up to me easily.

"If you're still unsure, why did you come?"

I shrugged as I followed him toward the front door. "My mother convinced me it wasn't fair to carry on like this. That I needed to either agree to resolve our differences or walk away. So that's what I'm here to do." I chewed on the inside of my cheek, my shoulders falling. "I'm just not sure which path I'll take."

"When do you plan to figure that out? Jessie's flight is landing soon."

"I'll know when I look into his eyes."

He cocked a brow. "His eyes?"

I nodded. "My mother's advice. She said I'd know it's love, that it's worth it, if I looked into his eyes and saw a piece of myself staring back."

"That's it? You'll look into his eyes and hope it gives

you the right answer to a life-altering decision?"

"That about sums it up," I said, climbing up the front porch and coming to a stop by the door, lowering my head. "Of course, now that you say it out loud, it sounds ridiculous."

"Iz…" He exhaled, his voice softening as the atmosphere shifted from one of friends to something…different. "Look at me."

On a hard swallow, I lifted my eyes to his, time seeming to stand still. If my life were a movie, this would have been the scene where the background faded out and everything happened in slow motion. Where the seconds stretched into hours as we connected on a level we never had before.

I blinked as I peered into his deep pools. My breathing became ragged, my mouth grew dry, my pulse increased. A warmth spread through me, a sensation of euphoria making me feel like I could fly. Wasn't this how I should have felt when I looked into Jessie's eyes? Why was this happening with Asher?

"Iz…," he said again, closing the distance between us.

"Yes?" I replied shakily.

He raked his gaze over me, studying every breath, every heartbeat, every blink. His lips parted, as if on the cusp of telling me something he'd been keeping locked inside for ages. Then he shook his head, stepping back, the tension breaking. Or perhaps I imagined it was there to begin with.

"Maybe your mother's right. Maybe one look *is* all you need." Averting his eyes, he reached into his jacket and grabbed a set of keys, handing them to me. "Good luck with whatever you decide."

"Thanks." I took the keys from him, brushing off my unsettled emotions. I turned toward the door, inserting the key into the lock. The sooner I was alone, the better.

"Izzy...," Asher said once more, and I lifted my head, but didn't meet his stare.

"Yes?"

"I..." He licked his lips, clearly out of sorts.

"Yes?" I repeated.

Then he sighed. "I hope you get the answer you need." When he didn't immediately walk away, I chanced a glimpse into his eyes. There was a sadness within I hadn't noticed before, almost like he could sense this may be the last time we'd see each other. Then he turned, making his way down the driveway and back to his car.

Once he drove off, I opened the door and slipped into the house, breathing in the familiar scent. It brought back memories of my time with Jessie. Cooking together in the kitchen. Watching movies on the large projection screen in the back yard. Sitting together on the swing on the front porch. From the very beginning, he did everything to make me a priority. To shower me with compassion, admiration...love. Hell, he even moved back into his parents' house to save money so we could afford our own place once we were married.

I continued past the foyer and into the living room, snapping on the lights to make the house appear more lived in. Checking my watch, I noted that Jessie's flight had just landed, so he'd probably be home within an hour. Heat prickled my skin, my stomach fluttering at the thought. Not out of excitement. More out of nerves, still unsure of the path to take, whether I truly was ready to commit myself to him for the rest of my life, regardless of what I saw in his eyes.

With the minutes ticking by, I grabbed a notebook out of my purse and made myself comfortable on the couch. Opening to a fresh sheet of paper, I drew a line down the center. On one side I wrote "Pros", the other "Cons". I hoped this would give me the answer I needed.

Sadly, the only pro I came up with was that Jessie treated me well.

After staring at the page with a grocery list of cons and only one pro for an inordinately long time, I shoved my notebook into my bag, not wanting it to taunt me any further. Falling back onto the couch, I stared at the ceiling, wondering if I made a mistake in coming up here. Maybe it was impulsive to jump into my car and barge in on Jessie's life after weeks of no communication. I'd hoped by surrounding myself with memories of us, I'd know what to do. But it only served to confuse me more.

I toyed with where my ring sat on my finger, the simple band and stone more like a burden than a symbol of Jessie's love and devotion. I didn't want it to feel like that. I wanted to feel Jessie's love. *Needed* it.

Releasing a frustrated groan, I stood, pacing the room, when a framed photo on the mantle caught my eye. I came to an abrupt stop in front of it. To most, it would appear to be an innocent photo commemorating what should have been a joyous event — Jessie's proposal. Grams had wanted to capture the moment and asked us to pose for a photo. At the last minute, she'd ordered Asher to join us.

I closed my eyes, trying to return to that day, to experience that same bliss I was sure I had after I'd agreed to marry Jessie. I replayed everything in my mind. Watching Jessie lower himself to one knee. Gasping when he withdrew a ring box and presented it to me. Jessie fumbling over his words as he asked me to marry him. There was no elaborate speech or declaration of love, but those things didn't matter to me.

I squeezed my eyes tighter, attempting to remember. Most women could probably recall every detail of the moment the love of their life proposed. For me, it was a blur, apart from the fact that I now wore a ring. But as I forced myself back in time, another memory returned to the surface... Asher's eyes studying me, begging me to say no. Jessie had asked me to be his wife, yet in the split second before I'd agreed, I'd sought out Asher's gaze. Not Jessie's.

Worse, in that heartbeat, I'd wished it were Asher on one knee.

Not Jessie.

I flung my eyes open, gasping for air as the truth hit me with the force of a freight train. I couldn't breathe. Couldn't see. Couldn't think.

It wasn't true. I would have realized it much earlier if it were, wouldn't I? This was merely the result of my relationship with Jessie being in limbo this past month. But as I floated my eyes back to the photograph, to *Asher*'s image, to the way he peered upon me with sadness and adoration, I couldn't avoid the truth.

I loved Asher. I loved our easy conversations. I loved the hours I spent listening to him strum his guitar as we stayed up and watched the sunrise over the lake together. I loved the way he always looked at me as if I were the only woman in the world.

The sound of the door opening startled me, and I jumped, darting my gaze toward the entryway, my heart thundering in my chest. What should I say to Jessie? I had to tell him *something*. He noticed whenever I was a bit...off. And I was more than a bit off. I was petrified.

Suddenly, giggling interspersed with moans filtered into the room. I froze, staring as the man I was supposed to marry kissed another woman. And not just any other woman… *Candace*. His ex who never seemed to understand they'd broken up. I should have been upset. Should have been heartbroken.

And I was, but not because of Jessie.

Because of Asher.

Because I'd somehow fallen in love with Asher while dating his brother.

Because I'd fallen in love with a man I could never have.

Consumed by my thoughts, I didn't realize my grip on the photo loosened until it crashed to the floor, the glass shattering. Jessie tore away from Candace, searching the space until his gaze fell on me. His complexion paled, eyes widening.

"Izzy…" Panic overtook him as he rushed to me, his shoes crunching against the glass.

I looked at the photo. The irony that I was posed between these two brothers in the picture wasn't lost on me. How had I allowed myself to fall for both of them? To come between them?

He dropped to his knees, not caring about the shards of glass cutting into his skin. The stench of alcohol was strong as I met his eyes. In that moment, my heart broke *for* him. For what I did to him. For how my heart betrayed him. Should he have sought comfort in another woman's arms? Of course not. But I didn't believe he'd intentionally do that to hurt me. I knew the type of person Candace was — calculating, vindictive, manipulative.

Asher had repeatedly reached out to me over the past month, telling me Jessie was in a bad place after our break. Now I saw it. It didn't help that he'd probably consumed more than enough alcohol tonight to impair his judgment.

As I peered at him, the anguish covering him made me reconsider this course of action. But how could I stay with him when his brother owned a piece of my heart? If Asher weren't a part of his everyday life, maybe things would have been different. I could have immersed myself in our relationship, pushed all memories of Asher from my brain, forcing my heart to only think of Jessie.

But that would never be possible when I'd see him at dinner every Sunday night. When he'd stand next to Jessie as we said our vows to each other.

With shaky hands, I slid the ring off my finger, holding it out to him, tears falling from my eyes. But I wasn't crying for Jessie. I was crying because of everything else I was about to lose.

"No," he slurred. "Please, Iz. I'm not…" He tugged at his hair, making him look unkempt and desperate. A man at the end of his rope. "I'm not thinking clearly. I haven't been able to since you left. Fuck! I didn't even notice your car was parked out front. That's how off I am. Please, Izzy. Let's just try again."

I shook my head, my voice trembling. "I can't do that."

Now that I realized my feelings for Asher, I couldn't wear Jessie's ring. Couldn't go to his bed without wondering what it would be like to be with Asher. Couldn't savor his touch without wishing it were Asher's calloused fingers skating over my skin instead.

His sobs echoed as Candace looked on with smug satisfaction, probably thinking she'd won, that he'd chosen her over me, something she'd been hoping for since the first time we'd met. But there was no winner or loser in this game.

I brushed by him and collected my purse. Just as I was about to push my way past Candace, I paused, glancing back at Jessie's broken frame, his eyes pleading with me. I would have given anything to go to him and offer him the comfort he deserved. He didn't deserve this. Neither one of us did. But there would be other girls. He only had one brother.

"I'm sorry." I held his gaze a moment longer. Then I walked away, with no intention of seeing him again.

Or Asher.

Chapter Nine

Present Day

I RUN MY fingers over a familiar image, surprised to see it back in a frame and placed prominently on the dresser in Jessie's room at Grams' lake house. It brings back so many memories. Not just of the day Jessie and I got engaged, but also of the day I ended things with him. It's remarkable how one photograph can bring forward memories of two polarizing events. A beginning. And an end.

I wonder why Jessie kept this photo, why he chose to display it up here. Then again, maybe he didn't. Maybe someone else did, knowing the memories it would evoke. The *feelings* it would evoke.

"It worked, I see."

The unexpected voice causes me to all but jump out of my skin. In my surprise, I drop my hold on the frame, which clatters to the floor, the glass cracking.

I whirl around, my pulse racing. Not at the invasion into my semi-private space, but at what Grams would think when she saw the photo I'd been admiring.

"What worked?"

She approaches me with little difficulty, despite her ninety years. She certainly doesn't look her age, her petite, slender body dressed in a pair of jeans and a simple cream-colored sweater. Her hair is a vibrant shade of platinum. Her skin wears the evidence of her age, but not to the extent one would think. In truth, she doesn't look a day older than she did when I last saw her.

"My plan, of course."

"Your plan?" I throw her a sideways glance, still confused.

"To reunite you with my grandson."

"Jessie and I aren't reunited. Not like that."

She gives me a mischievous look. "Not *that* grandson."

"Grams...," I warn.

"It's curious, isn't it?"

"What is?"

"How the frame broke." She nods to the shattered glass on the floor.

I scramble to pick it up, collecting the pieces in my hands. What is it about this damn photo? I'm beginning to think it's cursed. "It was an accident. I'll replace—"

"That's not what I mean, my darling Isabella." She holds my gaze for a moment, her blazing green to my dull brown. "I meant *where* it broke. Some might say it's a sign of what's to come."

I look down at the frame. The glass is fractured between Jessie and me, a spider web of cracks obscuring him from being visible. All that's left is me. And Asher.

"I don't know what you're talking about," I fumble. "This—"

"I always wondered about the two of you." A smirk tugs on her lips.

"Who? Jessie and me?" I ask, my voice nearly pleading with her.

"I think we both know I'm not talking about Jessie." She places her hands on my biceps, her comforting touch like coming home after a long absence.

"There's nothing going on between Asher and me."

I set the broken frame on the dresser, stepping away from it, as if it holds some contagious disease.

"Are you sure about that?"

"Of course."

"Then why are you here?"

I open my mouth, then quickly snap it shut. Why *am* I here? I can't tell her it's because I'm getting paid to be here, although that's my main motivation for agreeing. At least that's what I keep insisting, despite my heart telling me there's a bigger reason. A *deeper* reason.

"Does your silence mean you don't know? Or are you too scared to admit it to yourself?"

When I dated Jessie, Grams was one of the few people I could always confide in. In fact, she was the first person I raised my doubts to regarding my engagement. At first, it was exciting. But as summer turned into fall and I began my junior year of college, the fact we were at different stages of our lives came into sharp focus. The semester had only just started, and I already felt myself slipping away from my normal circle of friends because Jessie wanted me to attend his work functions with him.

So instead of donning a t-shirt and a pair of jeans before heading to check out the local music scene with my roommate, I was forced to wear a dress and stand at Jessie's side while he schmoozed potential clients for the management company he'd begun to work for.

When I mentioned this to Grams, the only advice she gave me was, "What's meant to be will be. No matter what path you choose, the second I met you, I knew in my heart you were meant to be a York."

Now, all these years later, I can't help but wonder if she saw something I refused to.

I peer into her kind eyes, searching for any sort of guidance, something I know she'll tell me must come from within. "I'm just really confused."

With a smile, she wraps her arms around me, kissing my cheek. "Giving a piece of your heart to two men is never easy. Trust me. I know."

"You do?" My voice rises in pitch as I pull back.

"Same thing happened to me. A few months ago, actually."

I blink repeatedly. "A few months ago?"

"What?" She gives me a playful look. "Just because I've spent nine decades on this planet you don't think I can date?"

"I didn't say that," I flounder. "I just—"

"Trust me, dear." She leans in. "You're never too old for love."

I stare at her for several protracted moments, trying to wrap my head around the idea of her dating. Then again, she was never one to adhere to society's expectations. Just because our culture says someone her age should take it easy and spend the last few years of her life relaxing, maybe knitting from a comfortable rocking chair, that's never been Grams. She's always lived life, would never want to leave this world in a nursing home. She'll go out doing something she loves.

"So how did you choose?"

"You're assuming I have." She winks.

"Do you mean to tell me you're still seeing both men?"

She shrugs, looping her arm through mine and leading me out of the bedroom and down the hall. "My darling, when you're my age, some things no longer matter. And you want to have as many orgasms as you can since you don't know when your last will be."

"Grams!" I exclaim, my face heating. I'd like to say I'm surprised by her forwardness, but I'm not. This is quintessential Grams.

"The trick is to date a younger man," she whispers as I help her down the stairs, although she doesn't appear to need it. "Many men my age aren't able to…perform. Then again, there aren't many men my age around."

"How young are we talking?"

"Carl is only sixty-five." She waggles her brows as we continue into the kitchen. "But when you reach ninety, twenty-something years isn't that big of a difference."

"Great," a deep, gravelly voice interrupts.

We both look in its direction to see Sean, Asher and Jessie's father, standing by the island, opening a bottle of wine. It's evident where Asher and Jessie got their height from, Sean measuring around six-two or six-three. He has a slender physique, one I imagine he still maintains by his daily five-mile runs. His hair has grayed over the past decade, but it makes him appear distinguished. As Chloe would put it, Sean York is most definitely a silver fox.

"Glad to see Mom's sharing all her dating stories with you, too." He winks, then approaches, kissing my cheek, as if no time has passed since he greeted me this way. "Good to see you again, Iz."

"You, too."

"There's nothing wrong with dating at my age," Grams states.

"I didn't say there was, Ma. But as your son, there are certain things I'd rather be left to the imagination."

Grams places a hand on her hip. "I'm not sure what your father, God rest his soul, taught you about how these things work, but you're only here because I had sex."

I stifle a laugh. With each passing moment I spend with Grams, I become more and more at ease.

"Certain urges don't go away because you get a few more wrinkles. But if you'd prefer, I can find someone else to spend time with. I hear there are some amazing dating apps out there." She looks at me. "What's that one called? Tingle?"

"Tinder?"

"That's right." She grins mischievously as she glances back at Sean. "I could find a new companion on Tinder, one I'm sure wouldn't be interested in anything more than my company."

"Please don't. I doubt anyone close to your age would be on there anyway." He blows out a long breath, shaking his head. "Come on. We're in the great room."

He places the bottle and several glasses on a small tray, then heads from the kitchen, making his way down a short flight of stairs and into a large room with vaulted ceilings overlooking the back of the property that abuts the lake. But with the sun having set, nothing but darkness surrounds us, the moon casting a slight glow over the snow-covered ground.

Grams loops her arms through mine once more. As we descend the stairs, she leans toward me. "He's wrong. There *are* people my age on Tinder. How do you think I met Henry?"

I fling my eyes to hers. "You met a guy on Tinder?" I whisper.

"I'm old. Not dead."

The instant we step into the great room, Jessie and Asher jump to their feet.

"There are my two boys." She allows Jessie to hug her and kiss her cheek before turning her attention to Asher. There's an affection between them that wasn't there when she peered at Jessie, even though he's named after her, which accounts for the feminine spelling of his name. Then again, Asher and Grams have always had a unique bond.

She brings her hand up to his cheek, and he briefly closes his eyes. I don't know many men who have this kind of connection to their grandmothers. Hell, to their entire families. It confirms the fact that the fame he's enjoyed this past year hasn't changed his devotion to these people.

I hope it never will.

"Let's all sit and visit for a while before dinner," Reagan announces in the same pacifying tone I remember. She smooths a lock of her dark hair behind her ear, her brown eyes shining with excitement. "It's not often we get together like this anymore, especially up here at the lake house. And to add Izzy on top of it... I'm not sure when we'll all have the chance to do this again."

"Come on, Grams." Asher grabs her hand, leading her toward the couch where he and Jessie were sitting on opposite ends.

"I'll take the reading chair." She pulls away from him. "Isabella can sit on the couch." Not allowing him a moment to protest, she lowers herself into the high-back chair. A self-satisfied smile crosses her face as she looks between Asher and me, both of us uneasy with indecision.

I do my best to pretend this isn't a big deal, that there isn't some hidden meaning behind me sitting between Jessie and Asher. It's not the first time we've sat on this couch in this arrangement. But it's the first time since I slept with Asher.

His eyes locking with mine, he extends his arm toward the couch. "Shall we?" My stomach flutters with the wings of a thousand butterflies, the sound of his voice causing desire to flood through me.

Feeling all eyes on me, my cheeks heat as I make my way to the middle of the couch, lowering myself next to

Jessie, who greets me with that same charismatic smile he always does, none the wiser to any awkwardness about this situation. When Asher sits down, I face forward, meeting Reagan's and Sean's content expressions.

Sean pours wine into each of the glasses and hands them out. Once we all have one, he raises his own, waiting until we do the same.

"To things being back to the way they were."

"The way they were," everyone replies in unison, which I do half-heartedly.

I doubt things can ever truly return to the way they were. Not with this mess I've made.

Chapter Ten

"SO YOU'RE USING your time up here as a writing retreat?" Reagan asks Asher around a mouthful of steak as we all sit at the large dining table enjoying the delicious filet mignon Sean prepared. I always found it endearing how he loved cooking, a trait he passed down to his sons. I often joked that I needed to marry Jessie so I wouldn't starve, his kitchen skills far superior to mine, although I've improved since then.

"I hope to," Asher responds, his voice devoid of any excitement or enthusiasm.

"He's been blocked," Jessie adds from beside me.

I try to stop myself from wondering if another woman ever sat in this chair. The idea of Jessie with another woman doesn't upset me like I thought it would. But a woman sitting in the chair beside Asher? I can't stomach the notion of him sneaking his hand under the table and squeezing her thigh. Of him leaning into her, whispering how beautiful she looks. Of him peering at her with all the love he once had for me. Now all I get from him is awkward indifference.

"I thought you'd written a bunch of songs," Sean offers. "What did I hear you strumming earlier?"

"I can still write. I doubt I'll ever be at a point where no melody or lyrics come. But everything I've written..." He slowly lifts his eyes to meet mine across the table. "It's missing something. Almost like a piece of my soul has disappeared."

I swallow hard at the honesty with which he speaks. It's so heartfelt and pure, a stark contradiction to the games most other men play. But Asher has never been one to play games. He speaks from the heart, regardless of how much it may hurt him.

"That's why I proposed coming up here, even in the dead of winter," Jessie interrupts, reminding me of his presence.

I tear my eyes from Asher's, grabbing my wine glass with a trembling hand and taking a large gulp. I glance around the table, no one the wiser about whatever just transpired between Asher and me…except Grams. She looks upon me with a mixture of intrigue and superiority, as if watching a carefully orchestrated chess match play out before her.

"You always did find this place perfect for allowing those creative juices to flow," Reagan offers with a smile. "And what luck that Izzy's here, too. It'll be like old times. Isn't that great, Ash?"

I try not to look directly at him, but I can feel his eyes still trained on me. Hell, I doubt they've left me since the second I walked into the great room with Grams.

"Absolutely," he replies curtly, the softness in his tone now nothing but a distant memory. "Like old times. Like nothing's changed." He stabs a piece of steak and shoves it into his mouth.

"What's up with you?" Jessie hisses, leaning toward him. "You've been a prick since we got here. You'd think you'd treat Izzy with a bit more decency after all these years. She never did anything to hurt you."

I blanch at his words. Jessie's statement couldn't be further from the truth. I did hurt Asher. We hurt each other. But what choice did we have? We'd fallen under the spell of the bubble we created around ourselves. But bubbles can only survive for so long before they burst.

When we crossed that line between friendship and something more, we knew it wouldn't last. I don't think either one of us was ready to crash to the ground with such finality.

"You're right. She didn't." He clears his throat. "I'm feeling a bit off." He smiles a fabricated smile, pushing the Brussels sprouts around his plate, but Jessie's inquisitive stare remains focused on him. "I ran into an old flame recently," he fumbles, chancing a glimpse in my direction. "But she's still with the same guy she was all those years ago."

"Forget her," Jessie encourages. "You're Asher York. If she doesn't see what thousands of screaming women at your shows do, then she's not worth it." He turns to me, nudging me with his shoulder. "Tell him, Iz."

"Tell him what?" I ask with a shaky breath, the irony almost laughable. This dinner couldn't get any more awkward if we all sat here naked.

"That this girl isn't worth it. That he'll find 'the one' when he least expects it." When I don't immediately say anything, Jessie continues. "There are plenty of fish in the sea. And your sea is about to become infinitely bigger." He cuts into his steak, bringing a piece up to his mouth.

"She probably realizes she doesn't deserve you," I blurt out, much to everyone's surprise. Much to my surprise, too. All eyes dart to me as heat rolls across my nape. "It's probably why she keeps pushing you away. Why she's settling for the path she chose. Because she doesn't think she deserves your love."

"Why would she ever think that?" he chokes out.

"Maybe it hurts too much otherwise. Maybe she doesn't think it would ever work out. Maybe she doubts you'll ever choose her."

"Maybe she needs to stop trying to control every

decision." He leans toward me, his voice becoming increasingly impassioned with each word. "Maybe if she stopped thinking everyone would eventually hurt or abandon her, she'd see the truth that's been staring at her for years."

"And what truth is that?" Grams asks in a pointed voice. She gives me a knowing look before returning her attention to Asher.

"That I'd choose her if she'd let me."

A self-satisfied smile tugs on Grams' lips. "Trust me. True love always has a habit of coming back. It's like a boomerang." She levels her eyes on me. "You can run as far from it as possible, but it *will* find you. And if you're not careful, it will knock you out cold."

Sean rolls his eyes. I always found their relationship charming. Whereas Grams is on the eccentric side, Sean is pragmatic. An admirable quality, especially for an investment banker. I often wondered if he took more after his father, but I never met him. He'd passed away when Asher and Jessie were young. Regardless of the differences in personality, there's no mistaking that Sean is Grams' son. They both have the same blazing green eyes.

"But make no mistake," she continues. "True love *will* come back. Some things you can't fight, no matter what."

"Exactly," Jessie interjects, seemingly oblivious to the mounting tension between Asher and me. I have no idea how. Probably all the whiskey he's consumed tonight. "Like the way I couldn't fight the need to know who you were." He flashes me a lazy smile, confirming my suspicions that his judgment is most certainly compromised. Good. Hopefully he won't remember this strange conversation tomorrow. "Which is why I pretty much stalked you until you agreed to go to dinner with me."

Reagan sighs, placing a hand over her heart. "When he first told us about you, I knew I'd like you. Especially since you made him work for it."

"And she's making me work for it again," he announces. I fling my eyes to his, a silent question in my glare. He ignores me, the alcohol loosening his lips.

"You two are getting back together?" Reagan's voice brims with excitement. "When I saw you here, I hoped you'd decided to give it another chance, but I thought—"

"We're *not* back together," I interject quickly, able to sense Asher's muscles tightening across the few feet separating us. I don't have to look at him to know that vein in his neck pulses with controlled irritation.

"Exactly." Jessie smiles at Reagan before floating his eyes back to mine. "But I think Asher put it perfectly." He leans into the crook of my neck, and I can smell the liquor coming off his breath. He always was an overly amorous drunk. "I'd choose you if you'd let me."

The words don't carry the same meaning as they did when Asher said them. Don't cause my knees to weaken, my heart to pound, my skin to ache with the promise of his touch.

A chair scraping against the hardwood flooring cuts through, the sound loud and jarring. All eyes turn to Asher as he stands, chest heaving, glowering at Jessie, who still doesn't seem to notice. Or his brain's too foggy to register the obvious animosity in his brother's stare.

"Is something wrong?" Grams asks, feigning confusion.

Asher opens his mouth. I can physically feel his need to tell everyone what's eating him up. Instead, he blows out a labored sigh, scrubbing a hand over his face. When he returns his attention to the table, the fury and heartache are gone, his eyes almost vacant.

"I'm on a tight deadline. I should head back into the music room. See if I can find some inspiration."

"Would you like some company?" I ask before I can stop the words from spilling from my mouth, the question a natural one. At least it was a decade ago.

"I wouldn't be very good company right now."

I nod subtly. "Of course."

"Well, when I wake up tomorrow, I hope you'll have something I can present to the label," Jessie announces. "One song would go a long way as a good faith gesture."

"I'll try my best."

Asher makes his way around the table, everyone standing to wish him luck. He pulls Grams in for a sweet hug, kissing her cheek, then doing the same to Reagan. Sean gives him a slight hug, as does Jessie. When he reaches me, there's a brief hesitation before he places a chaste peck on my cheek.

"'Later, Iz."

I don't know why that gesture leaves a sour taste in my mouth. I shouldn't care that he bid me goodnight in the same manner he did his mother and grandmother. Shouldn't care that his kiss lacked meaning, emotion.

But I'd rather he not kiss me at all if the only thing I feel when he does is forced complacency.

Chapter Eleven

One Year Ago

A WIDE SMILE tugged on my mouth as I stood in front of the massive vanity mirror in the even more inordinate bathroom, toweling off my hair after a shower. I didn't have much longer until I needed to get out of here and catch my flight back to New York. After last night, I wouldn't have minded if it were canceled. Sadly, despite a blackout that left all of Vegas without power or cell service for a little over twelve hours, that power came on this morning, flight operations having resumed at the airport, including my own.

I reminisced about the past forty-eight hours, an electricity filling me at how unexpected it all was. Running into Asher at a bar where he got up on stage and performed a song I hadn't heard in nearly a decade. Learning he'd been hired by one of the top bands in the country to help write the songs for their next album and was staying at their ridiculously posh house on the outskirts of the city. Watching the sunrise together before he drove me back to the hotel so I could get to the airport, only to find out my flight was canceled. Calling Asher, who offered a place to stay for the night. The sexual tension increasing with each passing hour, coming to a breaking point when the power went out.

As much as I didn't want to blur the lines between us,

something I fought against because of his relationship to my ex-fiancé, I couldn't help but feel like this was the path we were always meant to take. Maybe meeting Jessie was a steppingstone on my way to Asher.

"Hey."

Asher's voice cut through my thoughts, and I straightened, my heart skipping a beat at the way he looked in a pair of jeans and a simple t-shirt, leaning against the doorjamb. His arms were crossed, causing his biceps to flex, which only served to make me want to drop my towel and feel him one last time.

"Hey."

"So, I need to tell you something, but I don't want you to freak out."

"Okay…"

He pushed off the wall, his eyes averted. From this alone, I sensed I wasn't going to like what he was about to say. He ran his hands through hair that was still damp from our sex-filled shower.

"That was Jessie on the phone."

"And?" Considering the history between his brother and me, I doubted he'd bring him up unless it was important.

Asher didn't say anything right away, simply staring at me. Then he sighed. "He's downstairs."

"What?" My heart plummeted to the pit of my stomach, frantic eyes searching his for an indication this was a joke. That this wasn't real. But all I saw was the same honesty I always had from Asher.

I pushed past him, darting toward my suitcase. I hastily threw all my items back into it, a need to get out of this house overtaking me.

"Do you think he knows?"

"Of course not. Pretty sure he would have greeted me with a broken nose instead of a hug."

"Then why—"

He placed his hands on my biceps in an attempt to placate me, but nothing could. This all just got real. A little too real. I'd known what I was getting into last night. Had known the ramifications and ignored them. The blackout bubble had seduced me into thinking we wouldn't suffer the consequences of our actions. At least not anytime soon. For once, I'd chosen to live in the moment. And now we'd both have to pay the price.

"He heard about the blackout and came out to check on me."

"From Boston? How did he get a flight if the airport just reopened?"

He licked his lips, his gaze steady, expression calm. "Because he doesn't live in Boston anymore." He swallowed hard. "He lives in Los Angeles. He's..." He hesitated. "He's my manager."

My body froze, his words a punch to the gut. "Your manager?" I squeaked out, blindsided.

Granted, I'd never asked who his manager was, or if he even had one, but considering my history with Jessie, I would have thought he'd mention that little tidbit of information. It wasn't just a familial relationship I was dealing with here. Asher and Jessie had a professional relationship, too. It was like learning the guy I'd just had amazing sex with was my ex's new boss. But it was worse with us, because I should have known better. There was so much more at stake than I ever could have imagined.

"Yes." He didn't embellish further, but he didn't need to. It made sense. Jessie was a business major, a natural salesman. He could charm the squirrels out of the trees in the dead of winter, even though they knew it was their only means of protection against the elements. There was no one else Asher would trust with his career. It was always their plan.

I shook off his touch, shrinking into myself. "Why didn't you tell me?"

"It didn't seem like it mattered."

"Didn't seem like it mattered?" I repeated, my voice rising in pitch. I quickly lowered it, unsure where Jessie was. For all I knew, he could have been eavesdropping outside the door. "It matters. It matters a lot. So… What? You let Jessie in and then came up to fuck me one last time before dropping this bomb?" My disbelief at this situation growing, I grabbed the first pair of pants I found in my disheveled suitcase and yanked them on, not caring about my lack of underwear.

"It's not like that, Iz. I'm as surprised as you are. I bought us a little time and have him in the studio, listening to some demos I've written for a solo album I have in the works."

I slowed my motions, finding solace in the fact that Jessie was locked away in the opposite end of the house. Then memories from last night floated back and my eyes widened.

"Asher! My pants and tank top are in there! They have my perfume all over them. The same perfume I wore back in college. The same perfume he bought me repeatedly. If he picks them up and—"

"Relax," he soothed, running his hands down my arms. "I brought them back up here before letting him in." He nodded at the pants I just tugged on. "You're wearing them."

"That still doesn't make this okay." I pushed out of his hold, grabbing a bra and slipping it on, turning from him. After tugging on a shirt, I added, "You should have told me."

"Would that have changed anything?"

I whirled around to face him, my mouth agape,

about to insist it would, but stopped myself. *Would* it have changed anything? Would I have wanted Asher any less than I did last night?

When he reached for my face and brushed his fingers against my skin, I couldn't help but melt into the contact. One touch was all I needed to reassure me that his intentions were noble, even if the outcome was less than desirable.

"I understand I should have mentioned it. But I didn't want to burst our bubble. Wanted to prevent you from enduring any heartache." He brought his lips toward mine, and I sighed at the promise of his kiss. "Just like I tried to do all those years ago."

I melted into him, digging my hands into his hair, his words wrapping around me like a blanket. But as the meaning in his statement sank in, I stiffened, pushing against him.

"What did you say?"

Disoriented, he blinked repeatedly. This time, *he* was at a loss for words. "I—"

"What heartache did you want to prevent all those years ago?" I stepped back, eyeing him with suspicion, a knot tightening in my stomach.

"I...," he stammered, his breathing quickening.

"What heartache did you want to prevent?" I asked again through clenched teeth, my temper flaming.

He didn't say anything. He didn't have to. The answer was etched in the worry lines on his face. In his pleading eyes. In the hard bob of his Adam's apple.

"Oh, my god. You knew. That's what you mean, right? When you said you tried to prevent my heartache, you're talking about that night, aren't you?"

Again, he remained silent. What *was* there to say?

"How could you keep that from me? You knew what I was walking into, yet—"

"No." He darted his eyes to mine, that vein in his neck throbbing. His fists clenched, every muscle in his body vibrating with a passion I'd yet to see in another person. Even him. "I had no idea what you were walking into."

"But—"

"Maybe you've forgotten, because the story you told last night left out quite a few things."

"I didn't think it necessary to go into all the gory details."

"Really?" Defensive, he folded his arms across his chest. "Is that why Chloe didn't even seem to know what happened? Why she appeared just as interested in the story as someone who'd never heard it? Because you didn't think it necessary to go into 'all the gory details' with one of your dearest friends when it happened? Don't you always say that keeping the truth is as bad as lying?"

"That's not the same, and you know it. The details didn't involve Chloe."

What could I say to him? That the reason I'd left out so many details about the night I ended my engagement to Jessie was because of what I feared it would finally reveal. That the real reason I'd broken up with him wasn't because he sought comfort in another woman's embrace.

It was because I realized I'd fallen in love with his brother…

"You kept something from me that affected *me* directly," I continued.

"According to what both you and Jessie told me about the fight you had before Christmas break, it seemed you'd written him off, even if you claimed you weren't sure about what your plan was. Hell, he said you tried to give back the ring, but he begged you to keep it."

"All the more reason he shouldn't have sought out his ex," I snipped back.

"Agreed, but you also can't stand there and blame me for this."

"You still should have told me what you knew about Jessie."

"Goddammit, Izzy!" He slammed his hand into the wall, frustration radiating from his fist, spreading up his tense arm and through the rest of his body. "I'm not saying what Jessie did was right, but he was in a really bad place. I wanted to tell you Candace had started circling like a hawk again." His head hung as he expelled a breath.

"Then why didn't you?"

It wasn't the fact that he kept this from me that had betrayal flowing through my body. Once I'd realized my feelings for Asher, I knew I could never be with Jessie again. It was the realization of the truth that had been screaming at me ever since I first felt myself falling victim to Asher's hypnotic spell.

He would *always* choose Jessie.

"He's my brother." His voice was choked as he brought his eyes back to mine. "I couldn't betray him like that."

All I could do was nod at his confirmation of my suspicion, the lump in my throat bordering on painful, cutting off my oxygen. This was the reason I walked away all those years ago. And the reason I should have walked away the other night. There was no possible way for us to have a happy ending. Not when it meant hurting someone we both loved. And despite it all, I still loved Jessie. At least the Jessie he was when we dated.

A loud chiming cut through the tension, causing Asher to flinch. I had no reason to believe it, other than a feeling in my gut, but I knew the alert was a text from Jessie. I didn't say a word, just glanced at the outline of a cellphone in Asher's pocket. I could tell he struggled between staying in the moment with me and seeing what his brother wanted. When it chimed again, he groaned, yanking it out.

"You should go," I said softly, turning from him. "Distract him. I'll finish packing and be out of your way."

"Please, Izzy. I don't want to leave you like this. What can I do to make up for it? I'll do anything."

I glanced over my shoulder as I was about to disappear into the bathroom. "We both know there's nothing you can do. Jessie will always come between us. We were fooling ourselves to hope otherwise."

"He doesn't have to. We don't have to let him."

I forced a smile, although my heart was breaking. I stepped toward him, a breath away. "I think you already have."

He parted his lips, but I placed a finger over his mouth, silencing him. Then I hoisted myself onto my toes, kissing him one last time. A lone tear slid down my cheek at the finality of it all.

"Goodbye, Asher."

Chapter Twelve

Present Day

I BLINK AWAY my tears as that day replays in my mind, the emotions as strong and vibrant as if it happened yesterday. It serves as the reminder I need right now. Despite Asher saying he'd choose me if I'd let him, it's most likely an empty promise. When it really matters, he'll realize I'm not worth him risking that relationship, that bond I can't even begin to comprehend.

On a long sigh, I look around the tranquil bedroom. It's exactly as it was last night when I fell into bed, yet it seems different, the dawning of day casting everything in a new light. When I reach for my cellphone and see it's already after nine, I toss the duvet off me.

My feet hit the cold, hardwood floor, and I quickly step into my slippers before shuffling into the bathroom. After I splash some water onto my face, I readjust my dark hair, smoothing it back into a tight ponytail. Content with my appearance, I grab an oversized cable knit cardigan and pull it on over my tank top and pajama pants, then leave my bedroom.

Silence greets me when I emerge onto the first floor, the house lacking the vitality and life it had last night. I continue past the living room and into the kitchen, expecting Sean or Reagan to be sitting at the island,

Sean looking at a newspaper, Reagan with a book in front of her. Instead, it's empty.

I make my way toward the dining area, peering over the railing and into the great room, which is also vacant.

"Peaceful, isn't it?"

I spin around to see Grams, leaning against the kitchen counter, surprising me once again. I'm not sure what to make of her outfit — black capri yoga pants, an off-the-shoulder black t-shirt with the Rolling Stones logo, and a Tibetan scarf wrapped around her head, the remains of the material flowing over her shoulder.

"I think that's why I've been spending more and more time here, instead of living with Sean and Reagan at their house near the city. No constant noise. You can really get in tune with yourself."

"I suppose." I smile as I walk past her. When I pop a pod into the one-cup brewer, the aroma of coffee fills the kitchen, comforting my soul.

"So have you?"

"Have I what?"

"Gotten in tune with yourself."

"I'm already in tune with myself." I grab the milk out of the refrigerator, keeping my back to Grams as I pour some into my mug.

"If you say so. But I sense a struggle within. Like you're at a crossroads."

I face her. "I'm not at a crossroads."

"It seems you are." She lowers herself onto one of the barstools by the kitchen island and pats the one beside it for me to sit, which I do. "You have a choice to make."

"There's no choice to make. Everything is fine. No crossroads. No battle. No nothing."

She squints, her analytical stare raking over me, lips

pinched. "Did Jessie or Asher ever mention a girl named Emilia Morgan?"

"Not that I can recall."

"She was a friend of theirs." She floats her gaze from mine, peering into the distance. "Moved into the district when Jessie was in seventh grade. But she was involved with the music program, so Asher knew her, too. Throughout middle and high school, the boys spent a lot of time with her, usually in big groups, as is so often the case during adolescence. Jessie certainly had a thing for her."

"And Asher?" I ask timidly, not sure I want to hear a story about Asher and his long-lost love.

"I think he saw her as someone he shared a certain level of comfort with. There weren't any romantic intentions there, but Jessie didn't see it that way, especially when Asher told him he planned to ask her to prom."

"Why didn't Asher explain they were just friends?"

"He did. But Jessie always felt like he grew up in his brother's shadow. At an early age, Asher exhibited a talent for music. Jessie always put on a smile and said he was proud of his brother's accomplishments. I think there's a part of Jessie that will always be envious of him. Even if there was nothing romantic between Asher and Emilia—"

"Jessie saw it as another thing his brother had that he didn't," I interrupt, putting the pieces together.

"Precisely."

I pause before asking my next question. "What happened?"

When she brings her eyes to mine, they're sad. "She disappeared. Almost twenty years ago now. Asher was seventeen. Jessie sixteen. One day, she never showed up for school. When the administrative office called to inform her mother, she said she hadn't been home all weekend, thought she was spending it at a friend's house. When that friend was questioned, she said she hadn't seen her since the previous Friday. By the time she was reported missing, it was hard to pinpoint when she'd been taken. Or from where."

"Did the police ever find her?"

She blows out a sigh. "No. During the course of the investigation, the police found out she'd gone to a clinic after school that Friday. She was pregnant."

"Was it…"

"Jessie's or Asher's?"

I nod.

"No. The police questioned both boys, since they were friendly with her, but both denied so much as kissing her. They believed them. In fact, according to all the kids at school, she was quiet, reserved, withdrawn, didn't have a boyfriend. That was why Asher had planned to ask her to prom. He was always a popular kid, could have had his pick of any girl, who would have gladly gone to prom with him. He said there was always something sad about Emilia, said he wanted to make her feel like she belonged. And it wasn't just an invitation out of pity. As I said before, he truly did enjoy her company. Liked that he didn't have to pretend to be interested in her, as he did with so many of the other girls who sought him out. Plus, they had a similar taste in music. She was a fan of the blues."

"Like Asher," I breathe.

"Exactly."

"So she disappeared without a trace?"

"No body. Nothing in nearly twenty years."

I shift my gaze forward. No wonder neither of them spoke of her. I doubt I'd be able to if I'd lost someone and never got any closure.

Returning my eyes to Grams, I furrow my brow, confused. "That's a tragic story, but I'm not sure what it has to do with me."

She pinches her lips together in contemplation. "I'm not quite sure, either," she admits after a brief pause. "I guess I just wanted you to know that you're not the first girl to come between those boys."

"I'm not—"

She holds up her hand, cutting me off. "Don't underestimate the bond they share. You may think Asher will destroy his relationship with Jessie if he were to pursue something with you—"

"He would. How could he not? It's been nearly ten years, but Jessie's not over it. He still regrets it. He'd be crushed if he learned his brother and I started dating."

She grabs my hands in hers, squeezing them tightly. "Don't forget who Jessie is. He's made a career out of doing everything to help Asher achieve happiness. In the end, that's all Jessie wants for his brother. I truly believe with every fiber of my being that once Jessie realizes just how happy you make Asher, he'll understand. In fact, he'll probably be your biggest cheerleader, just as he's been for Asher all these years."

"But what if you're wrong? What if this *does* destroy their relationship? There will always be another girl. Asher will never have another brother." I repeat the same argument I've made to myself more times than I can count.

"Didn't you hear him last night? He'd choose you if you'd just let him. So maybe you should stop trying to protect your heart and just let him choose you."

I part my lips, on the brink of insisting it's a fool's game, when she continues.

"If you can't do that, you can at least bring the boy a cup of coffee." She nods toward the window over the sink that boasts a stunning view of the lake. The sunlight glimmers on it, casting a beautiful sheen on the snow covering the rest of the property. But that's not what catches my eye. It's the familiar figure sitting in our spot at the end of the dock.

"If I bring him a coffee, will you stop trying to play matchmaker?" I groan, feigning annoyance.

"I'll never stop trying to help two people who are meant to be together find their way back to each other."

Playfully rolling my eyes, I push out of the barstool and head to the counter, getting to work on preparing a coffee the way Asher likes it. "Pretty sure Jessie wouldn't take too kindly if he found out what you've been scheming behind his back."

"Keep Jessie out of this."

"I don't quite think that's possible."

"Anything's possible, my dear girl. Now go." She shoos me away. "I need to do my morning meditation exercises anyway."

I arch a brow. "Meditation exercises?"

"Yes. No use starting the day unless I'm in tune with myself and the celestial beings." She presses her hands together in front of her and bows. "Namaste, Isabella."

I chuckle, wondering how many people get in tune with the celestial beings wearing a shirt with a giant tongue on it. This woman is certainly one of a kind. "Namaste, Grams."

Chapter Thirteen

A WALL OF frigid air assaults me the second I step outside, a shiver rolling through me. I consider heading back into the house to put on a coat, or at least something other than my thin slippers. But it took me long enough to work up the courage to come out here and talk to Asher. If I go back to my room, I'll probably convince myself not to do this.

I trek through the snow and toward the dock, keeping my head lowered to fight off the wind that whips sporadically. I try to remain as quiet as possible, but when Asher hears the groan of the wood under my feet upon my approach, he glances over his shoulder, his expression blank. There was once a time he'd greet me with a warm smile. That was before we muddied the waters.

"Figured you could use some coffee." I hold up the steaming mug, the aroma inviting.

After yesterday, I fully expect him to tell me he's fine, that he just wants to be alone. To my surprise, he nods, albeit subtly.

I slowly make my way to where he sits on the edge of the dock, extending one of the mugs toward him. He takes it, shifting to his left, an unspoken invitation for me to join him. I lower myself, place my mug beside me, and reach into my pocket, retrieving the origami dove I'd made before heading out here.

When I toss it onto his lap, he flashes his gaze to it,

then hangs his head.

"I'm the one who should be apologizing, Iz."

"What do you possibly have to apologize for? I mean, other than you being a bit of a prick last night." This elicits a slight laugh and I smile. "But I can't fault you for that. I probably would have acted ten times worse if the shoe were on the other foot. If *you'd* shown up out of the blue and I learned we were spending the weekend under the same roof."

"Trust me. I have plenty of other things I should be sorry about. Especially when it comes to you."

He locks eyes with me before returning them to the frozen lake, snow-capped hills visible in the distance. In the summer, this view would be of fish circling in the muddy water, the occasional duck waddling about, and turtles sunning themselves on the rocky shoreline. Now everything is desolate, the normal inhabitants gone.

"Do you remember the first time you came up here?" he asks, breaking the stark silence.

A small smile tugs on my lips as I nod. "It was the weekend before Thanksgiving, but your family was celebrating early because your parents were heading to their Florida house for the winter. They wanted to be gone before the snowstorm hit."

"They love the fall foliage, but the second they hear the word snow, they book the first flight out they can get. Or they used to before Grams got older."

"I remember."

"Jessie had told me about you before you even agreed to that first date." He laughs slightly, then takes another sip of his coffee. I grab mine and do the same, holding my mug between my bare hands. "I'd never seen him so...happy. So when he said he'd invited you up here for our early Thanksgiving celebration, I couldn't wait to meet the girl who finally made my brother smile

106

again. I knew she had to be someone special."

He pulls his lips between his teeth, his expression strained. "When he walked into the house and I saw the woman at his side was the same girl I'd been checking out the past several weeks at a bunch of my gigs, the same girl who served as the inspiration for so many of the songs I'd written, my heart sank."

"Asher…," I barely manage to say through the lump building in my throat.

"You want to know the funny part?" His voice is pained, the vein in his neck throbbing with tension.

"What's that?" I ask timidly, not sure I want to torture myself any further with this story.

"I actually told him about you. Told him all about this amazing, beautiful woman who had these killer hips I couldn't stop watching whenever she danced."

The wind picks up, almost howling through the barren trees, and I pull my cardigan tighter into my body. The cold doesn't seem to faze Asher, even though he's dressed in only a pair of jeans and long-sleeved black t-shirt, work boots on his feet. The sole warm item of clothing he wears is a gray beanie, his dark hair jutting out from underneath it in all directions.

"I've always done well with the ladies." He blows out a nervous laugh. "Unfortunately, all they saw was a guy with a guitar. They weren't interested in anything serious. I was getting tired of the random hookups. I wanted more." The corners of his mouth quirk up. Something about the way he peers at me makes me think he's been wanting to tell me this for a long time. Maybe since that very first Thanksgiving celebration. "I wanted you."

"Then why didn't you ask me out when you first saw me?" I can't help but think all this heartache could have been avoided if he'd approached me sooner. If he'd asked me out before Jessie. Then again, there's no way of knowing for certain. We probably would have found another way to torture ourselves. We seem to excel at that.

"I can't explain it, but from the instant I noticed you, I knew you were different. Knew you wouldn't be the least bit impressed by some random guy approaching you at a club. I'd only get one opportunity with you. I needed to make sure the timing was right. So I waited. But, unfortunately, I waited too long." His expression falls. "I guess that's why I acted the way I did yesterday. Walking into the living room to greet Jessie and seeing you beside him brought me back to the moment I had to swallow the hard truth that the woman I'd begun to fall for could never be mine. I knew there was a chance you'd have a boyfriend. But I convinced myself if that were the case, you wouldn't hit the local music scene as often as you did without him there."

"Jessie wasn't exactly a night owl."

"The second I saw you with him, I knew why you wouldn't be together at the bar or club." He chuckles, a momentary break in the tense atmosphere. "He probably told you the same thing he told me whenever I asked if he wanted to come to one of our gigs."

"I actually never invited him. He was understanding of my time with my friends. It wasn't until…" I trail off, lowering my eyes as I continue. "It wasn't until we were engaged that it seemed to become an issue. Or maybe it wasn't until we were engaged that I realized we weren't all that compatible. That we were two parallel lines. We could get close, but we'd never truly intersect. Not like we needed to in order to survive."

"Kind of like us." He lifts his somber eyes to mine. "We'll never intersect, either. Not like I wish we could."

Seeing the way his shoulders slump forward makes

me want to wrap my arms around him, tell him that maybe we could. But we've been in this place before. I already know how this story ends.

"You probably don't remember, but during that first dinner, he asked me how things were going with that girl I'd told him about."

My mind rewinds to that day. I never thought much about the conversation between Jessie and Asher. Simply thought it was two brothers helping each other out, something I admired and respected. Now that I know the truth, I see it through a different lens.

"And you told him you found out she had a boyfriend," I reply in a distant voice.

"Funny thing is, I had every intention of finally asking you out the next time I saw you. Had this whole speech planned. I didn't know anything about you, but I knew whatever I said to you had to be good. Had to be well thought out. Something about you made me think you wouldn't be easily persuaded by some cheesy pickup line. You deserved more." His Adam's apple bobs up and down in a hard swallow. "At least more than I could ever give you." He briefly closes his eyes, drawing in a long breath. "You were right."

"What do you mean?"

"That morning in Vegas. When Jessie showed up and burst our bubble. Remember what we argued about?"

My lips form a tight line as I nod. "About the night I broke off our engagement. Officially."

"And do you remember what you accused me of?" His voice cracks.

A ball of dread forms in my stomach at where this conversation is going. "That you knew Jessie had been fooling around with Candace. You denied it."

He hangs his head. "And do you remember what you

told me earlier that day when I met you and gave you the keys to the house? Before he brought Candace home and you saw them?"

I slowly nod. "That I wasn't sure what I would do. That I needed to look into his eyes before I made that decision. That I'd know the answer then."

"And how did you say you'd know the answer?"

"Because I'd see a piece of myself staring back at me."

"And do you want to know what I did?"

"I—"

"I went to the gig I had that night and hoped…fuck, *prayed* you didn't see a piece of yourself in Jessie." He floats his wild gaze to mine. "Do you want to know why?"

I swallow hard, no words coming.

"Because I wanted you to see that when you looked at me."

"Asher…," I breathe, on the brink of telling him I did, that the reason I ended the engagement was because I realized I loved him, but he continues before I can get another word in.

"After Jessie landed, he stopped at the bar where my band was playing. I'd never seen him look so damn depressed, all because he still hadn't heard from you. I could have told him right then and there that you were waiting at the house, that it might not be over, but I didn't. We started our set, and the next thing I knew, I saw Candace sitting on the barstool next to him, licking his proverbial battle wounds. I watched them leave together. I could have warned him, since it was more than apparent they were going somewhere more private. Yet I kept my mouth shut. Didn't warn my brother he was about to bring a girl back to the same house where the love of his fucking life was waiting for him. All because I wanted you to leave him.

"So I'm sorry, Iz. I'm sorry I didn't try to talk some sense into Jessie. I'm sorry I didn't warn you. I'm sorry I didn't tell you the truth earlier. And I'm sorry I didn't grow a set of balls and approach you before my brother did. But you know what I'm *not* sorry about?"

I shake my head. I couldn't guess even if I wanted to, everything Asher's saying completely unexpected.

"I'm not sorry you broke up. I'm not sorry I slept with you in Vegas. And I'm not sorry for all the times I've thought of you since then. I'll never apologize for that, for how I feel about you."

He stands, his long strides taking him down the dock and toward the house.

"Asher, wait!" I shout, jumping to my feet and chasing after him, leaving our coffee mugs. He doesn't stop until my hand wraps around his bicep, forcing him to face me.

Our chests heave as we stand in the snow, my slippers no protection against the wet and cold. "During that same argument, you let it slip that you tried to prevent me from enduring any heartache. What were you talking about?"

His face blanches.

"I know it's not that night. It couldn't be. You just confessed you didn't try to stop Jessie. I get the feeling you wanted me to think it was so you didn't have to tell me what you were actually referring to."

He stares at me for what feels like an eternity, then exhales. "We hung out lot once you started dating Jessie. Sometimes we spent more time together than Jessie and you did."

I nod in agreement.

"All those hours spent together confirmed what I felt in my heart before I'd even spoken a single word to you.

So I decided to finally come clean, tell you I noticed you in the club, that I was going to ask you out... That I loved you. That I wanted you to choose me. Had it all planned out. We were all up here for the Fourth of July. I decided that night, after everyone went to sleep and we were hanging out, I'd let it all ride." He shrugs as a sad smile builds on his mouth. "But right before Jessie went to bed, he pulled me aside and showed me the ring, told me he was going to propose the following day.

"So I kept my true feelings locked inside to prevent you from enduring any heartache over having to make a choice. Because despite the fact you were with him, I knew once I told you, it would change things. So in order to protect your heart, I broke mine." He turns from me, continuing back up toward the house.

"What would you have said?" I call out. He pauses and slowly faces me. I take a few steps toward him. "That night before Jessie proposed, what would you have said?"

His features soften as his gaze skates over my face. His mouth curves in the corners, and I see the Asher I once watched pluck away at the strings of his guitar for hours.

"I would have spoken from the heart." He closes the distance between us, stopping an inch from me, separated by an invisible line both of us are too scared to cross. "That the instant my eyes first locked on yours from across that club, I felt something. Something I'd written about in songs but didn't think was real."

"What was that?"

"A spark. There was this electricity that zapped my heart." He chuckles. "It sounds crazy, but I've always believed in love at first sight. And when I first saw you, I knew."

"Knew what?"

He leans down. I crane my head back, still as drawn to him as I've always been. His lips inch closer, his warm breath dancing on my mouth causing my insides to coil.

"That you would be the last woman I'd ever love. That even if you turned me down, nothing would stop that. That I may date other women, but they would never be you. My heart would never beat like it does for you." Licking his lips, he starts to erase the last bit of space between us.

I place my hand on his chest before he can seal his declaration with a kiss. "Asher, I—"

"Please don't. Don't push me away. Not yet. Just let me stay in this place where I can taste the promise of your kiss on my lips. Where you haven't turned me down." He swallows hard as he finishes in a choked voice. "Where I still have hope for what we almost had."

I sigh, closing my eyes. "You'll always be my favorite almost."

"You'll always be my favorite almost, too, Iz." His cold fingers trace the curve of my face, along my cheek, settling on my bottom lip.

I expect him to keep going, as he so often did when brushing the pad of his thumb along my lip, but he freezes. I open my eyes and am met with an Asher deep in thought.

"My favorite almost…," he repeats, his eyes glassed over. I watch as he bobs his head, almost like he hears a song in his mind. Then his expression brightens. "That's it!"

Before I know what's happening, he links his fingers with mine and tugs me back toward the house, my legs struggling to keep up with his excited strides. Dozens of questions swirl in my head about what's going on, but none of that matters.

Not when I can finally savor in the sensation of his skin on mine once more.

Chapter Fourteen

ASHER HURRIES INTO the basement, not stopping until he's seated at the piano in the music room. I'm still confused about what's going on, about what epiphany my simple statement caused, but when his fingers slide over the keys as he experiments with a bluesy beat, I know.

He's found his song.

There's a frenzied air about him, focused and intense. It brings back memories of spending those long nights with him, sometimes in this very room, as he toiled over various melodies and lyrics. Not much has changed since then. The walls are still padded with egg crate foam to soundproof it as much as possible. A piano sits against one wall, various guitars on stands spread throughout the rest of the room. Cables and microphones fill a crate off to the side, put to use when Asher needs to record something.

His low voice fills the space, his brain pulling lyrics out of thin air. Then again, that's probably not entirely true. They've always been in his mind. In his heart. In his soul. They just needed a little urging to come out. A little inspiration.

As he plays the melody, I can almost hear the full band arrangement in my head. The beat is driving, the lower notes maintaining a steady rhythm under the lyrics about a woman and man stealing moments together. A kiss here. A touch there. All culminating in what you'd think would be an explosive encounter, but the story stops just shy of that.

> "I've waited years to kiss you goodnight.
> I've waited years, and we've come so close.
> I've waited years to make you mine.
> Instead, you'll forever be my favorite almost."

Time stands still as I watch him work, repeating the same melody as he susses out the right notes and lyrics. I bob my head in time with the addictive beat, a smile tugging on my lips as I lose myself in the energy he exudes. I've always felt drawn to this man and the music he creates. Even more so now, knowing I inspired this song. Then again, he just admitted I inspired him to write a lot of his songs, probably *all* of his songs.

He belts out the chorus he appears to have settled on, his raspy voice touching parts of my body that haven't felt anything in a long time now. A quiver rolls over me, every last nerve ending tingling. When he plays the final note, I expect him to start from the beginning again. Instead, I feel the heat of his stare on me as I sit beside him, his heavy breathing echoing in the stillness.

I face him, swallowing hard at the fervor in his gaze. His chest heaves. His nostrils flare. His jaw clenches. Desire pools in his dark eyes as they trace over my features. He cups my cheeks, his grip harsh, fingers burrowing into my skin. It's so warm against my chilled flesh. My breathing increases, the roughness of his calloused hands lighting a fire that's lain dormant for a year now. But with this one touch, that match is struck. This time, I don't want anything to extinguish it.

"Tell me to stop." His words come out like a growl. "Tell me we can't do this. That this is wrong. That this isn't what you want."

I peer into his fevered eyes, shaking my head. It *is*

wrong. We *shouldn't* do this. But that doesn't diminish the truth. "I want this. I want you. So much."

"So much," he repeats. His grip on me tightening, he edges closer. My gaze is transfixed on his full lips, my need to savor them tuning out everything else. The risk of getting caught. That I wanted to keep my distance for a reason. That I know this won't end well. None of that matters right now. All that does is losing myself in the taste of his kiss after starving myself for too long.

He runs the pad of his thumb along my bottom lip, the gesture causing my body to quiver. "You like when I do that, don't you?"

All I can manage is a barely noticeable nod.

"It's a simple touch." He inches closer still, his breath intermingling with mine.

"There's no such thing. Not when it comes to you. Every single one of your touches holds a power over me."

"And you will always own me. Always."

He erases the final distance between us, and I surrender to him.

"Was that a new song?"

At the sound of the booming voice, Asher instantly releases me and we both sit upright, flinging our eyes toward the doorway just as Jessie rounds the corner into the room.

"Mom said she thought she heard music coming from down here." He flicks his gaze between us. Not one hint of accusation lines his expression, only genuine excitement.

An awkward beat passes before Asher clears his throat, standing. "She did."

"Can I hear it?"

"You should play it for him. It'll be great on the album." I raise myself to my feet, pulling my cardigan closer to fight off the intense chill that seems to consume me, my limbs shaking at the idea of how close we were to getting caught. What the hell was I thinking?

Asher floats his gaze to mine, a single brow raised in question, silently asking if I'm okay. I nod subtly, and he returns to the bench, drawing in a deep breath before the now familiar baseline surrounds me.

When he sings the opening verse, goosebumps prickle my skin. I focus my gaze on Jessie as he taps his foot in time to the beat, worried he'll put the pieces together and realize *I'm* Asher's favorite almost.

Chewing on my fingernails, something I rarely do, I discreetly back away, convinced Jessie is bound to discover the truth. How could he not when Asher sings about a girl he's always wanted but could never have because she belongs to another man?

As he continues singing, his parents and Grams peek in to listen in on his latest creation. His parents look upon him with nothing short of pride. Grams is different, though. Whereas his parents and even Jessie may not have picked up on the story behind the lyrics, Grams does. She shoots me a mischievous smile, another advance in her game of chess.

"That was *awesome!*" Jessie exclaims excitedly when the song comes to an end. He rushes to Asher, patting his back. "I knew coming back here would help you get past this block." He steals a glance at me, winking, before returning his attention to his brother. "Think you can work on a demo so I can get it to the label?"

Asher stares blankly ahead. "Yeah. Sure." His voice is even, a complete contradiction to Jessie's enthusiasm over the prospect of a new song

"I can already hear this one being played nonstop on the radio. Hell, I can practically feel the rafters shake in the arenas when the opening measures fill the place and the audience loses their minds. Especially your female fans. This song is sexy as fuck."

"Jessie!" Reagan admonishes. "Language."

His complexion flushes. It doesn't matter that he's thirty-four. He still cringes whenever his mother scolds him for swearing. I find it endearing.

"Sorry, Ma." He looks back at Asher. "But it's still sexy. The label will love it. This is the exact thing they're looking for. Sex appeal with soul. You fu—" He stops short, glancing at his mother before returning his gaze to Asher. "Freaking nailed it. Let's get a demo to them. Think you can do one here? I doubt there are any studios even remotely close to this place."

Asher waves his hand around. "This will be fine. It's not professional grade, but it'll do for a demo."

"Great." Jessie beams, his eyes alight with excitement. Then his expression falls as his gaze lands on me.

I shrink into myself. Did he figure it out? Did the lyrics finally sink in?

"Why are you flushed?"

"Flushed?" I ask.

"Yeah." He steps toward me, analyzing me. "Your cheeks are red. And you're breathing heavy. Are you okay?"

I part my lips, blinking repeatedly as all eyes in the room zero in on me. "I—" I stammer, suddenly feeling lightheaded.

"What is it?"

"I—"

"I asked Izzy to bring Asher a coffee earlier as he sat out on the dock," Grams interrupts, coming to my rescue when my brain refuses to fire. "I guess I didn't take into account that she wasn't dressed appropriately." She gestures to my slipper-clad feet.

119

I hadn't noticed how frigid I was, the rush of adrenaline from watching Asher work making me oblivious to everything. Now my entire body shakes.

"Your lips are turning blue," Jessie exclaims, rushing toward me, pressing his hands against my cheeks. "You're freezing, baby. What were you thinking going out there like this?" Before I can react, Jessie swoops me into his arms in a cradle hold.

"I c-can walk," I attempt to say through the strong chattering of my teeth, my body quivering almost violently. I've never felt so cold. Even my insides feel frozen.

"Not a chance in hell. You shouldn't have been out there in the first place." He shoots daggers at Asher before passing Grams a look of disapproval. "The way you're shivering, you'll barely make it up the stairs."

I try to glance back at Asher, but Jessie's steps are quick, the entire house a blur as he runs me up to the second floor. How could I have gotten so cold so quickly? I was only outside for twenty minutes, max. Then again, I was outside in wet slippers in temperatures no warmer than ten degrees. Then an additional twenty or thirty minutes in a chilly basement room.

"What am I supposed to do?" Jessie asks, kicking open the door to my room.

"W-what do y-you mean?"

"You're the nurse. How to you treat hypothermia?"

"I d-don't have hy-hypothermia," I argue, barely able to say the words through my trembles.

"For argument's sake, let's say you have a mild case. What do I do?"

"G-get me out of my clothes."

"Okay." He sets me on the bed, reaching for my cardigan to slide it off.

"I c-can do that," I insist, trying to push the sleeves down my arms, failing miserably.

"Oh really? You're doing a bang-up job, Iz. Just stop. Let someone help you for once, okay?"

I close my eyes, hating that I have to depend on Jessie. I consider telling him to have Asher come help, but doubt that would go over well, although Grams would probably declare a checkmate if that were to occur.

I nod, momentarily giving up my fight, allowing Jessie to take off my cardigan. When his fingers brush against my hands, he inhales a sharp breath at how icy they are. He grabs them in his, rubbing furiously.

"No. The m-movies lie," I manage to say. "No massaging or r-rubbing."

He instantly stops, keeping my hands in his for a beat before pulling away. "Got it." He gets back to work peeling off my slippers. I steal a glimpse of my feet, noticing they're a brighter shade of red than they should be.

"I have to get under these c-covers. And I'll need more blankets, too."

With a nod, he lifts the duvet, about to help me under when I stop him.

"I have to t-take off the rest of my clothes. At least my p-pants."

Jessie blinks, mouth slightly agape. "Oh." He swallows hard. "I can ask Ma or Grams to come help if you'd rather. I'm sure they won't mind."

I should take him up on his offer. But I'm driven by the need to get warm, something I don't think I'll ever feel again. "You're here. They're not. And I'm f-fucking freezing, Jessie, so take off my goddamn pants," I order out of pure desperation.

"I need to help you into a standing position."

He wraps his arms around me, carefully hoisting me to my feet. I rest my head against his chest, a tiny breath escaping at the warmth of his embrace surrounding me. It's so welcome, so inviting, so familiar. I can't help but find comfort in the way he holds me with the same affection he did all those years ago.

"Can you hold on to my shoulders?" Jessie asks in a husky voice.

"Okay."

He helps me rest my arms around his neck, then hooks his fingers into the waistband of my pajama pants, lowering them over my hips. "You can sit again." With a hand on my lower back, he helps me lay back on the mattress, peeling my pants off me and dropping them onto the floor.

After helping me lift my legs onto the bed, he fluffs the pillow behind me, pulling the duvet over my body. "Are you okay to keep your underwear on?"

"I'll be fine. I just need a few more blankets. And tea with no caffeine, if you have any."

"Of course." He brushes my hair out of my face, placing a kiss on my forehead. I close my eyes, reveling in the warmth of his lips on my skin. Then he pulls back, heading toward the closed door to my room. He's about to open it when he pauses, meeting my stare once more. "Izzy, I…"

"Yes?"

He chews on his lower lip, rolling his words over in his head. "I'm really worried about you."

"You don't need to worry about me. I'm fine."

He smiles a sad smile. "I'll always worry about you."

Chapter Fifteen

A N ARM ENCIRCLES my midsection, pulling me into a warm, firm body. I know this body. I've experienced this body. And it's one I crave to experience just one more time.

"What are you doing?" I rasp out, my eyelids heavy from exhaustion.

"Shh…" Asher tightens his hold, his bare chest warming me. "Body heat can help raise your internal temperature." His tone is lighthearted and spirited, a complete contradiction to the intensity from earlier today when he shared his truths with me.

"Is that right?" I joke back, unable to reel in my smile. This is the Asher I fell in love with all those years ago. This carefree, vivacious man who always made me laugh without even trying. I've missed this man.

"I read it on the internet. So it must be true."

"I wouldn't trust everything you read on the internet. If I did that, then according to some gossip websites, you're gay."

"Would a gay man be this turned on by just the feel of you?" He grinds his hips against me, making me whimper.

I should stop this right now. After all, we're at his grandmother's lake house where anyone could walk in. Where *his brother* could walk in. But none of that fazes me. Not when I've craved him for the past year…even longer. I couldn't tell him to stop any more than I could survive without oxygen.

His hot breath nears the nape of my neck, making every inch of me tremble in anticipation.

"Cold?"

"Quite the opposite," I exhale as he adjusts his body, pulling me closer into him until I can barely decipher where he ends and I begin.

"Is this okay?" he asks, lightly brushing his mouth against my shoulder blades. My muscles relax at the contact, all the tension rolling off me.

"Yes," I murmur, fire spreading through my veins.

"Good." His lips continue to skim against my nape, his touch achingly light, before finding that spot where my neck meets my shoulder. His teeth clamp on to me.

"Asher…" I writhe against him, my chest heaving.

"Is this okay?" His tone this time is more gruff and demanding.

"Yes…"

"Good." He delicately kisses the spot he just bit, the perfect combination of pleasure and pain.

He gently pushes me onto my back, and our eyes finally meet. Ravenous desire greets me as he crawls on top of me, pressing a knee between my legs, nudging them open. I reach up and push his hair out of his face, needing to look into his depths with no obstruction.

He lowers his mouth toward mine, every second ratcheting up my appetite more and more, my heart thundering against the walls of my chest. His lips barely graze mine, and I quiver.

"Is this okay?" he asks yet again.

"God yes," I moan, closing my eyes as he erases the last remnants of space between us. A second passes. Then another. And another.

When I don't feel his lips on mine, I slowly open my eyes, blinking repeatedly at the sudden disappearance of Asher's gaze. In fact, Asher isn't in bed with me at all. The room is mostly devoid of light, heavy blankets weighing me down as I lay on my back. Alone.

Disoriented, I prop myself up on my elbows and take in my surroundings, yelping when I notice Asher sitting in the reading chair in the corner, a tray of food on the table beside him.

"Jesus Christ!" I clutch my chest in an attempt to slow my racing heart. "Do you always make a habit out of sneaking into people's bedrooms and watching them sleep?" I avert my eyes, praying he can't see my flushed expression in the dim lighting.

I look around the room, noting the sun has almost set. I don't even remember falling asleep. The last thing I recall is asking Jessie for more blankets. Judging by the layers upon layers of blankets on top of me, he must have brought them to me at some point.

"Not exactly," Asher muses as I push the extra blankets from my body and lean against the headboard. "Do you always make it a habit to moan my name in your sleep?"

"I did no such thing," I bite out, cheeks heating. "You're making that up."

"By the current shade of red on your complexion, you know I'm not." He waggles his brows. "You should be happy *I* was the one who witnessed it, not Jessie. If you'd woken up fifteen minutes earlier, it would have been. That would have sparked a few questions."

I smooth the blankets on my lap, still trying to avoid his mischievous eyes, but it's nearly impossible, especially when he has that same spirited attitude as in my dream.

"Why *are* you here? And why was Jessie here before?"

"He was worried. So was I." He stands, lifting the tray and carrying it toward me. "I brought you something to eat. Figured you might like some soup." He sets it on the bedside table.

"Your mom didn't have to go through the trouble of making soup. Jessie overreacted." I lean over the steaming bowl and inhale the comforting aroma of chicken noodle soup.

"He didn't overreact. You shouldn't have been out in the snow. I was an idiot for not noticing how cold you were earlier." He sits on the edge of the mattress toward the foot of the bed. "And Mom didn't make the soup," he adds as an afterthought.

"She didn't?" I ask around a mouthful, the hot broth warming my insides. There's no way this is store bought. "Then who did?"

"Me."

I choke as I swallow, coughing several times before grabbing the water and taking a sip, setting the spoon back down on the tray.

"Gee, thanks," Asher jokes. "Glad to know you're *that* shocked over the idea. I *do* know how to cook. If I recall correctly, I made some of my father's world-famous burgers for you in Vegas. What was it you called them?" He pinches his lips together, tapping his chin, deep in thought. "Ah, yes. You called them 'positively orgasmic'."

"I know you can cook. I guess…" I shake my head. "I don't know."

"What?"

"I didn't think you'd want to drop what you were doing to make me soup, considering how time-consuming it can be."

He leans toward me, squeezing my leg through the duvet. "For you, Iz, I'd drop everything."

I meet his eyes and offer him a smile. Today has been a wild ride, but there's no one I'd rather be with right now, despite all the unresolved issues between us. "Thank you, Asher. The soup really is delicious. I'll have to put you on speed dial for whenever I get sick so you can come over and make me some."

"I would if you'd let me."

I nod, swallowing through the lump building in my throat. "I know." I hold his gaze another moment, then clear my throat, lifting the bowl of soup and eating another spoonful. "So, did you cut a demo?"

He scrubs a hand over his face. "I did. Jessie is sending it off to the label."

"He is?" I ask over the bowl. "How?"

"Grams put in Wi-Fi."

"Wow. Never thought that would happen."

"She *did* add parental controls. Said if she notices Jessie paying more attention to an inanimate object than a living, breathing human who isn't long for this world, she'll block his devices."

I bark out a laugh. "That sounds like something Grams would say."

I eat more of the soup as we sit in comfortable silence. Asher keeps his eyes trained on me, but not in an overly amorous way. It's more analytical, like he's making sure I really am okay.

"You know what this reminds me of?" I ask when I place my now empty bowl back onto the tray.

"What's that?"

"That time I caught a stomach bug the same day everyone planned on a day-long outing on the lake. You stayed behind and took care of me, even when I was bent over the toilet and retching everything in my stomach."

He blows out a laugh. "I remember. You puked over everything. The floor. The sink. Your clothes. I spent hours cleaning all of it while you slept it off."

I hesitate before making my next statement. "You undressed me that day. Remember?"

His ears redden and he smiles shyly. "That's a day I'll never forget. If I wasn't jealous of Jessie before, I certainly was when I saw how amazing you looked in just your bra and panties." The vein in his neck throbs as his jaw tightens, his eyes flaming. "The sight of you…" His hands clench and unclench as he hisses out a breath. "It was a good thing you were sick because if you weren't, I couldn't have been held responsible for any of my actions."

I smile, relishing in his compliment. "You wouldn't have done anything," I say after a beat.

"What makes you think that?"

"Making a move on a girl you know is seeing someone isn't really your style."

He shrugs. "Generally not, but people do crazy things for love."

I sip my water. "They most certainly do."

"So…" He clears his throat, his tone brightening. "Think you're up to socializing? Grams made a bit of a…request."

I arch a brow. "A request?"

"Family time."

"And what did she have in mind for this family time?"

He chuckles as he shakes his head. "You won't believe this. She wants to have a game night."

My eyes widen. "Game night?"

"Yup."

To anyone else, this wouldn't seem like a crazy idea, but Asher and I have a unique history with game night, considering it was a game night turned risqué that led to us finally kissing during that Vegas blackout.

That led to us doing a lot of other things, too.

"Well," I say brightly, "I doubt Grams will want to play Never Have I Ever and spice it up with a pair of sexy dice."

"You never know," he shoots back sarcastically. "Grams can be...unexpected."

"The best things often are."

Chapter Sixteen

"**H**OW COULD YOU not get that?" Reagan exclaims once the sand in the hourglass drains to the bottom.

"Get what?" Sean shoots back in a lighthearted tone. "You drew a blob with glasses. How was I supposed to come up with 'one smart cookie' out of that?"

"It's obviously a cookie. I even put frosting and sprinkles on it because your favorite Christmas cookies are those little anisette ones."

"Like I said, a blob."

"Dad, just apologize and move on," Asher interjects.

At first, I was edgy when Grams paired Asher with me in this game of Pictionary, worried what we might reveal, but I think she forced us together for a reason. If nothing else, being on the same team, having to decipher one another's horrific attempts at drawing, has eased the tension. There are a few sly glances and playful winks, but I don't feel awkward. Even better, I don't feel awkward being with him while Jessie's in the same room.

"Ma's a lot more stubborn than you are," Asher continues. "Plus, you should know to never argue with a woman unless you're prepared to sleep on the couch."

Reagan straightens her spine, a smug expression on her face as she looks from Sean to Asher. "I knew I raised you right." She winks. "Looks like it's your turn," she says to him. "Roll at least a four, guess the drawing, and you guys win."

"You should do the honors," I say, scooping the die off the table. "That way, if we don't get to the finish line, I can blame you for throwing the game."

"I appreciate that," he retorts, his voice heavy with sarcasm.

"I figured you would."

I extend my hand toward his, and he reaches for the die. When his fingers graze my skin, a rush spreads through me. I quickly pull away, acting as if I didn't just react this strongly to a simple touch. Finally, Asher rolls, forcing everyone's attention, including mine, back to the game. When the die lands on six, I cheer while everyone else groans.

He turns to me. "You should draw."

"Are you sure?"

"You're better at putting words into picture form," he insists with all seriousness. I stand, heading toward where a whiteboard sits on an easel. I'm about to pull a card from the stack when he adds, "Plus, if I can't decipher it, I can blame you for throwing the game." He crosses his arms in front of his chest, a self-satisfied grin on his face.

I place a hand on my hip, feigning irritation, but it's a lost cause, especially when I can't help but stare at how nicely his biceps fill out his t-shirt. His muscles aren't huge, but he's not scrawny, either. His arms are...perfect. *He* is perfect.

"Okay, Iz. Let's win this one."

Asher's voice forces my eyes up. When he waggles his brows, it leaves no question in my mind that he caught me checking him out.

Not wanting him to rattle me, I refocus on the game, grabbing a card out of the box. I look at the phrase for the permitted five seconds, then nod to Grams, giving her the go-ahead to flip the timer.

I uncap the marker and get to work drawing something that hopefully resembles a prize ribbon. Almost immediately after I start sketching, Asher shouts out anything remotely applicable.

"Ribbon. Circle. Blue. Number one."

At that, I turn around, motioning for him to keep going, that he's getting close.

"Winner. Medal. Best in Show."

I point to him, doing more hand motions I doubt anyone would understand the meaning of.

"Best?"

I quickly nod, then turn back to the whiteboard, sketching two circles, hoping they appear like the planet earth.

"Best planet. Best planets," he attempts.

I shake my head, stealing a glimpse of the timer to see the sand is more than halfway gone.

"Best globes. Best boobs."

I give him a disapproving look, my lips pinched, eyes narrowed. He shrugs playfully before continuing guessing. I glance between him and the board, trying to figure out another way to sketch this idiom.

"Best world."

I spin around, eyes wide, encouraging him on since he's so close.

"Best of both worlds!" he shouts out as the last grain of sand falls to the bottom of the hourglass.

"Yes!" I exclaim, jumping up and down.

Asher bolts from the couch, hoisting me into his arms and spinning me around before putting my feet back onto the floor. His enthusiasm infectious, we do our own version of a touchdown dance, wiggling our butts and waving our arms. With the way we act, you'd think we'd just scored the winning touchdown in the Super

Bowl, netting us a healthy bonus.

"Okay, okay," Jessie says, his voice even. "You won Pictionary. You didn't find a cure for cancer. Sit down and stop gloating."

"Someone's mad they lost," Asher teases, tousling Jessie's hair as he passes him on the way back to the couch. Jessie quickly slaps his hands away, smoothing his hair back into position.

"I'll get you back."

"So, what's next?" Asher asks as he begins to clean up the Pictionary pieces.

Jessie stretches as he stands. "Actually, I think I'll call it a night."

"It's only ten."

"For most people, that's a reasonable bedtime." He turns his attention to me. "Iz, you okay?"

"I'm fine. I'm not that tired, considering I slept most of the day. I'll stay up and visit a little while longer, make up for lost time."

He squeezes my shoulder. "Let me know if you need anything, no matter the time of night."

I touch my hand to his. "I will."

He leans down, kissing my cheek, then retreats.

"We're going to head up, too," Sean announces as he and Reagan stand. "We *also* go to bed at a normal hour."

"I suppose I may head to my room, too," Grams states.

"Don't even try to tell me you go to bed at a normal hour," Asher teases, standing to say goodnight to his parents and grandmother. "I know for a fact you're as much a night owl as I am."

"You're correct about that, my darling boy." She caresses his cheek, gently running her thumb along the scruff of his beard, then pulls away. "But nighttime is

133

when all the crazy people message me on those dating apps, and I like to mess with them. Are you aware there's a trend among some intellectually deprived men to send a picture of their penis?"

I stifle a laugh as Asher's face turns a bright shade of crimson. No one wants to talk to a family member about dick pics, especially your ninety-year-old grandmother.

"I've heard of such a thing."

"I don't understand it. I might be impressed if they were hung. But at my age, I've seen my fair share of penises. You have to try harder if you want to impress me. And four inches ain't going to cut it."

"Okay then!" Sean interrupts, taking Grams' arm and helping her up the stairs. "Time to get you to bed so you can sleep off some of that whiskey."

"You two stay out of trouble." She laughs, then turns around, meeting our eyes from atop the landing. "Actually, maybe you two should get into a little trouble. It could be good for the soul." With a wink, she disappears into the kitchen.

"She's something else," Asher comments, a hint of nerves audible in his voice.

I glance at him as he runs a hand through his hair, the confident rockstar nowhere in sight. It's no longer Asher York, the man who earned a spot on this year's list of sexiest men alive. Now, it's just Asher.

"She certainly is." I bite my lower lip, fidgeting with the hem of my sweater, a strained silence filling the air.

"I should—" I start.

"Do you—" Asher begins at the same time.

We both stop, then laugh nervously.

"Okay, this is stupid," he states. "It never used to be this way between us."

"That was before…ya know."

"I know," he sighs, shaking his head as he lowers himself beside me. "If I'd known it would end with me not even knowing how to act around you, I'd like to say I wouldn't have crossed that line." He lifts his fiery eyes to mine. "But I probably would have. I knew it was a risk. But I also knew the reward would be amazing."

A voice in my head tells me to retreat. To not ask the question on the tip of my tongue. To excuse myself and keep my distance. To do the job I'm here to do, then walk away. But if I listened to that voice, I never would have experienced this man's kisses, this man's arms, this man's love. The brain may be more logical, but the heart can be more powerful. And right now, my heart is infinitely more powerful.

"And was it amazing?" I ask huskily, eyes resolute.

"It was." A sad smile tugs on his mouth. "It could be again."

A strange feeling of honesty washes over me, almost like we're in our bubble again. "That's why I'm struggling so much with this, with being around you. Because it could be amazing. But it will most likely destroy us, too. That's the power you have over me."

"You hold that power over me, too. But remember what Grams always said?"

"Grams says a lot of things." I laugh. "Are you talking about 'an arrogant bug is a cocky roach'? Or maybe 'every hooker is pretty under candlelight'?"

Asher's chuckles fill the room, his eyes shining with love for his grandmother. "I wasn't talking about that. Although, based on some of the prostitutes I saw in Vegas, I can attest to the fact that some of them are *only* attractive under candlelight."

"Is that so?" I give him a disapproving look. "I didn't take you for the type of man who needed to pay someone for sex."

"And I don't. Never have. Never will. I mean, sex is great." He floats his gaze back to mine, steady and even. "But sex without love is as hollow and ridiculous as love without sex."

"Hunter S. Thompson," I state, recognizing the quote.

"Precisely."

"So… Grams?"

"Right." He licks his lips. "I've been doing a lot of thinking. Maybe *too* much, especially after our conversation on the dock earlier."

I push a strand of hair behind my ear, lowering my head. But Asher won't let me avoid this, placing his finger under my chin and tilting my eyes back to his.

"And do you know what I realized?"

"What's that?"

"I just want you. However I can get you. So if all I can have are brief moments of awkward interaction every once in a while, I'll take it. If you want to be friends, although we both know we'll never truly be able to remain just friends, I'm happy to try that, too." He edges toward me as he drops his voice, his tone throaty and addictive. "But I'd love if you'd stop thinking of all the reasons we shouldn't cross that line again and focus on the one reason we should."

"What's that?"

"Like Grams says, true love has a way of finding its way home. And in the past twenty-four hours, I've been reminded of probably the most important thing in all my thirty-five years."

"And that is?"

He traces a line along the curve of my face, sparks following his touch, igniting a fire in me. "*You're* my home." Slowly, his lips inch closer to mine, the seconds stretching. My pulse increases, my breathing becoming ragged from a combination of hunger for this man and fear of Jessie walking in on us. I flick my eyes toward the kitchen to ensure we're alone.

"Don't." Asher's stern command forces my attention back to him. "Stay with me, Isabella. Stay in this bubble."

I sigh, tension rolling off me. "I've really missed our bubble."

"Me, too." With a smile, he erases the distance between us once more.

I close my eyes, bracing for his lips to brush mine. But after several long moments pass with nothing happening, I return my gaze to his, almost worried this is another dream. Thankfully when I open my eyes this time, he's still here, his expression even, thoughtful.

"What's wrong?"

"Nothing."

"Then—"

"Do you want to kiss me?"

His question catches me off-guard. It should be an easy one to answer. I'm here, in his arms, a breath away from his kiss. But at the same time, I'm here, in his arms, a breath away from his kiss. As much as I've dreamed of this, fantasized about it, I've also been here before, on the precipice of crossing the invisible line we've drawn between us.

"Answer the question. Don't think. There should be no thought involved. Do. You. Want. To. Kiss. Me?"

"I… I don't know."

He nods, then drops his hold on me. "Good."

I scrunch my brow. "You're not upset?"

"Why would I be?" he asks dismissively. "I'm not in the habit of kissing women who don't want to be kissed."

"But—"

He clutches my cheeks, bringing my face within a breath of his. "But the second you figure out what you want, the second you realize you can't keep running from this, come to me. My lips will be waiting for your kiss." He runs the pad of his thumb along my bottom lip, causing a tiny moan to escape. "My arms will be waiting for your embrace. My heart will be waiting for your love. Whether it takes two hours, two years, or two decades, they'll always welcome you home. You need to finally realize this is where you belong. I can't force you to do that. You need to figure it out yourself."

Chapter Seventeen

I STARE AT the ceiling, studying the tree bark texture, as I have all night. The sun's been up for several hours, but I haven't slept a wink. Possibly due to the fact I slept most of the day yesterday. Most likely because my mind has been consumed with yesterday's events, culminating in Asher leaving the ball in my court about whether we continue what we started in Vegas or attempt to be the friends we both know we'll never be.

Maybe if Jessie were the asshole I made him out to be to my friends, this would be easier. But he's not. He never was. Apart from a momentary lapse of judgment when he was in a bad place because of me, he truly is a great guy — kind, compassionate, gracious. That makes the guilt of what Asher and I have done even more painful to bear.

Glancing at the time to see it's nearly ten, I push the covers off, resigned that sleep isn't in the cards. I pad into the bathroom, turn on the shower, shrug out of my pajamas, then step under the refreshing stream, washing off the past few days. After a longer than normal shower, I reach for where I remember the towel rack to be, my hand coming up empty.

Peeling back the curtain, I peer at the wall. Sure enough, there's a towel rack, albeit empty.

"Shit," I groan, stepping onto the tile, searching the room for any sign of a towel. Given this is an older house, the tiny space can't fit much more than the bathtub, toilet, and pedestal sink. Certainly no cabinets or linen closet, so Grams kept the extra towels on the top shelf of the bedroom closet. I hope she still does.

I hug my naked, droplet-covered body and awkwardly dash into the bedroom, doing my best not to slip on the trail of water I leave in my wake. As I open the closet and find a towel, a knock sounds on the bedroom door.

"Hold on," I mumble, securing a flimsy towel around my body. When the door unexpectedly opens, I fling my surprised eyes to it. Asher comes to an abrupt stop mere inches away when he sees me in only a towel that barely covers what it needs to.

"What part of *hold on* did you not understand?!" I shriek, bringing one hand to the top of my towel, the other to the bottom in an attempt to tug it down. I'm not sure what's worse — giving him a peek at a nipple or my hoo-ha.

"I thought you said come in!" he argues in his defense, ears red, gaze wide. "That's what it sounded like!"

"Well, it wasn't!" I start to storm away, but skid on the puddle I left on the floor. In the hopes of breaking my fall, I drop my hold on the towel and reach for the first thing I can. Which happens to be Asher. The unexpected force obviously taking him by surprise, he falters, his own feet giving out from beneath him. We crash onto the floor with a thump, him on his back, me on my front.

On top of Asher.

Without a towel.

Several long moments pass as I remain frozen in place, not so much as breathing. Heat flashes across my neck as I squeeze my eyes shut. "Tell me this is just a dream."

It's silent for a beat. Then Asher's throaty laugh rumbles from his chest, the sound more full of life than anything I've heard in a while. I hesitate, wanting to berate him for laughing at my expense, but the vibration of his laughter enthralls me, and I join in. If Jessie were to walk in, I wouldn't be so cavalier about this, but he's not here. It's just us. Sharing a moment of embarrassment we'll both laugh over for years to come.

At least I hope we will.

I bury my head in his chest. "I'm naked. On top of you."

His laughter only increases, his body shaking, the sound addictive and mesmerizing. God, I love his laugh. Not because it has this sexy baritone that hits me deep in my core, but because *I* make him feel this way. *I* make him happy.

"Not the first time," he reminds me, his voice having a flirtatious quality. "But at least we were *both* naked then."

I playfully pinch him in the side, and he yelps. "Close your eyes. I need to get off you."

"You don't have to." He waggles his brows, lasciviously licking his lips, which earns yet another pinch. "Ouch!"

"Close. Your. Eyes," I insist through a clenched jaw, trying to reel in my smile, an impossible feat when I'm staring back at Asher's sinful smirk.

"You know, I *have* seen you naked, Iz. It's not a big deal. I can probably draw your body from memory." His voice turns seductive as his hand grazes my hip.

His touch is light, barely there. Regardless, my veins flood with warmth. This time, it's not out of embarrassment, but unyielding desire, my hunger for this man increasing with every second I remain with my

141

body pinned to his.

His lips edge close to my neck, the brush of them against me causing goosebumps to prickle my skin. "Every dip. Every curve. I know them all."

"Asher… Please." I meet his eyes, begging him to stop. I *need* him to stop. If he doesn't, we'll pass that point of no return. Hell, we'll crash through it with fanfare.

He studies me for a moment, then sighs. "Okay." He makes a show of closing his eyes, keeping his hands by his head. His lack of touch leaves an emptiness inside me. "My eyes are closed, so I can't see that adorable birthmark on the bottom swell of your right breast."

"Whatever." I roll my eyes as I carefully push myself off him, mindful not to slip in the water yet again. Once I've re-secured the towel into place, I dash to the dresser, grab the first pair of jeans and sweater I can find, then lock myself in the bathroom.

Heart hammering in my chest, I lean against the door, doing everything to calm my out-of-control libido, but it's a losing battle. The feel of Asher's body against mine, his hands on my flesh, and his husky voice have brought back all those feelings I've tried to forget. But as I've learned, there's no forgetting Asher York. Something about him spoke to me before I even knew his name. And with each second we spend together, he embeds himself deeper and deeper into my soul to the point where I'm no longer certain of the path I'm on. The path I *should* be on.

I dress quickly, then run a brush through my hair before throwing it into a messy bun. When I step back into the bedroom, Asher's still here, but is now sitting on the edge of the bed, his gaze focused on the imprint my body left in the mattress. He smooths his hand over it longingly.

"You still sleep on the same side," he remarks.

"I always sleep on the same side."

"I switched, ya know."

My brows scrunched, I step toward him, stopping a foot away. "What do you mean?"

"I used to sleep on the same side as you. But after..." He licks his lips, shaking his head. "Well, after Vegas, I started sleeping on the other side." He runs his hand through his hair, making me want to reach out and feel his locks against my fingers. "It's stupid, but I liked pretending you were still next to me." He lifts his eyes to mine.

I'd love nothing more than to wrap him in my arms, tell him I did the same thing. Tell him about the countless nights I dreamt he was beside me, holding me, making love to me, only to wake up and realize he wasn't. But I can't. Don't want to give him hope.

"So, what did you want when you knocked?"

"Oh. Right." He stands, clearing his throat. "Jessie took Grams to church."

"Grams went to church?" I scrunch up my nose. "I thought she'd always been vehemently anti-established religion."

"Apparently, after ninety years, she found Jesus...or so she claimed when she informed me this morning. They left early. She insisted on going to a church near my parents' house in Melrose."

My eyes widen. "She made Jessie drive back to the city? That's three hours away."

"You know how she can be. When she gets an idea in her head, there's no talking her out of it. We figure one of her 'gentleman callers', as she refers to them, goes to the church."

"Are you suggesting Grams went all the way to Melrose for a Sunday morning booty call?"

He pinches the bridge of his nose. "*Please* don't use Grams and booty call in the same sentence. There should be a law against that."

"Okay, okay. Got it. When will they be back?"

He shrugs. "Not sure. There's a snowstorm coming, so they may not make it back before then. Mom and Dad left early this morning, too. Dad's flying out on a business trip tomorrow, so he needed to go. They were going to wake you to see if you wanted a ride, but I said I'd drive you back to Boston, if Jessie isn't able to get back in time. That's why I knocked. We need to leave soon to beat the snow. I'm sure you need to get home for work."

I chew on my lower lip, averting my eyes. "Actually, I lost my job."

"You lost your job?" he repeats, concern evident in his tone. "How? Why? I—"

"It's always a risk working for some of these big hospitals. The board of directors thought they deserved a raise, but in order to pay for that, they needed to take the money from somewhere else, like the nursing staff." I shrug. "I was the nurse with the least seniority in my unit, so I got the ax."

"Izzy…" When he reaches out and runs a hand down my arm, I don't back away. "I'm sorry. I know how much you loved that job. How hard you worked to get there."

"It's okay." I force a smile, trying not to think about all the kids I don't get to see anymore. "I'm a nurse. I'll find another job. Plus, I'm not sure I want to work for an organization that would dispense with their staff to pad their pockets so they can buy another yacht."

"The healthcare industry in this country is messed up."

I blow out a laugh. "Don't even get me started on

144

that subject. So much for the edict to 'Do no harm'. The healthcare industry does a lot of harm. At least those making the decisions, not those of us trying to get people the help they need and deserve."

"Are you okay? Financially, I mean. Do you need anything?"

"I'm fine. The hospital offered a decent severance package." *Plus, your brother's giving me a share of the royalties just for being here. Not to mention the twenty grand I'll get if you make your studio date.*

"Will you stay?" His voice is soft, expression even.

It's reminiscent of the night he approached me at the bar in Vegas. He'd begged me to stay then, too. I knew I shouldn't, knew I should walk away, but I didn't have twenty grand on the line. I could walk away now if I wanted to, ask my parents for help. I *should* ask my parents for help, tell Asher to take me back to Boston before things get more complicated. But like that night over a year ago, I don't care about that. I'm cast under his spell, desperate to be near him, no matter the cost.

And like that night over a year ago, I offer him a smile. "Okay."

His eyes brighten, muscles relaxing as absolute joy covers his expression. He frames my face in his large hands, and I tilt my head back, peering into his chestnut depths. I see so much in them. His pain. His victories. His struggles. But most of all, I see his love. There are many things I've questioned in my life. I've never doubted this man's devotion to me.

"Look." He releases his hold, nodding at the window behind me.

I spin around and peer outside, noticing a few flakes falling from the sky. "It's snowing. It's so much prettier here than in New York." A warmth spreads through me at how peaceful and serene this place is. "Back home, all I thought about during a snowstorm was how I might have to sleep at the hospital so I wouldn't miss my shift."

"No need to worry about that here." He slings an arm around my shoulders as we both admire the landscape. "You have nowhere else to be, darlin'."

"I like the sound of that." I nuzzle into his embrace.

"Me, too."

He tightens his hold, inhaling a deep breath as he feathers a soft kiss on the top of my head. I close my eyes, reveling in this moment. Asher's arms around me. Snow falling outside. A house to ourselves. It's like we're in our bubble again.

"Come on," he says after a beat, dropping his arm. "I'll make you breakfast."

"Breakfast?" I arch a brow.

"I make a killer *huevos rancheros*."

"Who am I to turn down an offer like that?" I take his outstretched hand, allowing him to pull me from the room. "Better watch out, though. A girl could get used to this."

"You shouldn't have to get used to it. You should be treated this way all day, every day."

Chapter Eighteen

"IT'S REALLY COMING down out there," I remark a few hours later, standing from the couch in the great room and sauntering past the grand piano in the center, where Asher currently sits. I stop in front of the window, marveling at the near white-out conditions. "I have a feeling Grams and Jessie won't be making it back today. You must be glad you didn't offer to accompany them."

"That definitely wasn't going to happen. Jessie is more open to the idea of organized religion than I am."

I spin around, placing a hand on a hip. "You'd think for a good Irish lad, you'd have spent more time in church."

"It was never my parents' thing."

He fools around with a melody I recognize as Queen's "Love of My Life". He doesn't even have to look at the keys, able to play and hold a conversation at the same time. To Asher, the act of playing piano or guitar is as innate as breathing. It doesn't require any concentration. It's something his body knows how to do. At least for a song he knows as well as this one.

"They weren't big fans of organized religion, either. Told us they'd let us make our own decision, instead of trying to force us to believe whatever they did. How about you? Did you go to church as a kid?"

I retreat from the window, plopping back down on the couch. "Occasionally. Mom's not overly religious, but I think there's a bit of guilt that still makes her go." I grab a blanket and cover my legs, settling in to watch the snow fall for the next day…maybe longer, according to some weather reports.

"Guilt?" He arches a brow before returning his attention to the piano as he plays a more difficult passage.

I almost want to stop the conversation and ask him to sing this song while strumming his twelve-string guitar. I used to love watching his fingers work the strings as he sang one of my absolute favorite Queen songs. The difficulty. The expertise. The beauty. It's what spoke to me the first time I saw him.

When he looks back at me, I explain. "Mom grew up Catholic. And my *abuela* was *really* Catholic. Like, went to church every day. Sometimes twice. And it seemed she was *always* at confession. I remember thinking she must do some pretty awful things on a regular basis to go to confession as often as she did." I laugh at the memory, my eyes shining. "I even asked my mother once if she was a witch."

"You thought your grandmother was a witch?"

"In my six-year-old mind, that was the most reasonable explanation for her need to go to confession nearly every day. Mama told me she just liked to carry everyone else's troubles on her shoulders. Called it a Mexican thing. And I think a little of that rubbed off on my mother, because once my *abuela* passed away, Mama started to go to church more. Said it was the one place she could talk to her."

"Some of that seems to have rubbed off on you, too."

I snort. "Me? The last time I stepped foot in a church was for my confirmation. And the only reason I did that was because my mother asked me to."

"I'm not talking about the whole Catholic guilt thing.

148

More of wanting to carry everyone else's troubles on your shoulders."

"I don't—"

He pulls his hands away from the piano and stands, taking several long strides toward me and sitting on the opposite end of the couch. "You can't claim you don't, Iz. Hell, look at the profession you chose. You've made a living out of carrying the burdens of complete strangers on your shoulders, even if for a short period of time. Something tells me you treat every one of your patients as you would your own son or daughter."

I look away, chewing my lower lip. "No kid should have to battle cancer. They've barely begun to live. So if I can help ease their pain, make them forget about everything they're missing out on because they're sick — trick or treating, making handprint turkeys on Thanksgiving, receiving Valentine's Day cards — then I'm happy."

"Like I said, you just want to lift their burden." He leans toward me, his gaze tracing over my face, studying my eyes, the soft point of my nose, the curve of my cheeks, the heart shape of my full lips. He reaches for me, and I don't pull away when he cups my cheek. "You have a beautiful soul. I felt it before I even knew your name. You—"

A chiming cuts through, but Asher doesn't move, staying in the moment with me. I glance at his phone on the coffee table.

"It's Grams," I say softly. "You should answer."

He hesitates, seemingly not wanting to break this connection. Then my cell chirps. I peek at it, Jessie's name on the screen.

"I get the feeling they're not coming back today." Grabbing his phone, Asher stands, taking a few steps from me.

I flash him a smile as he answers his cell, then bring mine to my ear.

"Hey, Jessie."

"How are you feeling?" Sincerity laces his words. No complaints about the snow. No bitching about having to drive Grams three hours away. Just concern for my well-being.

"I'm fine," I assure him. "Back to normal. How are you? I heard you took Grams to church."

"Don't get me started on that." He feigns irritation, but the love he has for his grandmother comes through clearly. "Hasn't gone in years, yet decided *now* was a good time to find Jesus. Come to find out, it was because of the new choir leader. Apparently, she met him at the senior center a few weeks ago. According to her, he's 'quite the looker'."

"Can't fault her for living her best life."

"And I don't. So, as you can tell by all the snow, we won't be coming back to the lake today."

"When will you be back?"

"Hard to say. Forecast is predicting a Nor'easter with blizzard-like conditions for the next twelve hours. I'll probably stay around here since I have to fly out to LA Wednesday anyway."

"You do?" This is news to me. When he'd invited me up here, I assumed he'd be here the entire time, too.

"It's a last minute thing, but I have to work out a deal for another client."

"You have other clients?" I whisper, stealing a glimpse at Asher, who seems to be partly paying attention to my conversation. I grab my mug and head into the kitchen to prepare a fresh cup of coffee as a front for leaving the room so I can talk to Jessie in private.

"Of course. I work for a talent management

company. I have other clients besides Asher who need my attention now that it looks like he's on his way to getting this album done. So, how's it going? Has he written anything else today?"

"No. Not yet." I can sense Jessie's disappointment over the phone. I always could pick up on his mood changes. "But I'm sure he will," I offer brightly.

"Time's ticking, Iz."

"I understand that." *More than you know.*

"Just... Don't forget why you're there. I'm thrilled you guys have rekindled your friendship, and I'm even more glad the stick that seemed to be shoved up his ass the other night has disappeared. But remember what's at stake. You're my last resort. My Hail Mary, if you will."

"I'll do whatever I can."

"That's all I ask. Hey, listen. I've got another call coming through. I'll talk to you later. Be good."

"I will," I respond, but he's already disconnected.

I blow out a breath, resting my hands on the counter, closing my eyes. It was one thing to have a few hours alone with Asher. But now that we're on our own for the foreseeable future, I smell trouble, bad decisions...and heartache.

"Everything okay?"

I whirl around, meeting Asher's gaze as he stands just inside the kitchen, arms crossed. I grit out a smile. "Perfect."

His eyes skate over my features, brows pulled together as he studies me. The last thing I need is for him to realize something's amiss, that I'm only here because Jessie's paying me. But is that even true anymore? I could have asked Asher to drive me to Boston earlier, yet I didn't. I *want* to be here, regardless of the money.

"Just needed to freshen up my coffee." I turn back around and pop a pod into the one-cup brewer.

"What did Jessie say?"

"Probably the same thing Grams told you."

"They're staying by the city."

"Yup."

"When did he say he'd be back?"

"He didn't. Said he has a meeting in LA in the middle of the week, so I wouldn't expect him anytime soon." When my coffee finishes brewing, I prepare it the way I like, then face Asher. "How about Grams?"

He playfully rolls his eyes. "Told me it would depend on her schedule back home. She called her plow guy."

"Plow guy? Please tell me that's not code for something inappropriate."

He chuckles. "For once, it's not. This street is private property, so she has to arrange for it to be plowed in the winter. She claimed he was so busy with the roads in town that there's no way he'll be able to get up this way for at least four days." His voice oozes sarcasm. "If you ask me, Grams is full of shit."

"Why would she lie about that?"

He joins me, leaning back against the counter, re-crossing his arms. "Why do you think? I know I'm not the only one who noticed Grams' strange behavior these past few days. At least stranger than normal."

I laugh. "You're not. It appears as if she's trying to play matchmaker between us."

"I'm pretty sure that's why she insisted on going to church. When I spoke with her, she claimed she had no idea about the snowstorm, but that woman watches the weather like a hawk."

"I remember. And not just in this area. Everywhere. She could tell us when there was an arctic blast in Florida, downpours in the Pacific Northwest, tornados in Oklahoma."

"Which is why I get the feeling this was all part of her master plan."

"Did you tell her about Vegas?" I ask in a low voice.

He stiffens, wide eyes meeting mine.

"It's okay if you did," I add quickly. "I'm not mad or anything."

He shakes his head. "I haven't talked about that night in over year. Not until yesterday with you."

"Then how does she seem to know?"

"There are some things on this planet you can't explain, and Grams is one of them. If I asked, she'd probably claim she had a vision."

"I'm not sure whether to be intrigued or embarrassed by the idea of Grams having a vision about what we did in Vegas."

He rakes a nervous hand through his hair, a boyish grin crawling across his lips, making his dimples pop. That's all it takes for the butterflies to flap their wings in my stomach. I adore his dimples. Love how carefree and unaffected they make him look.

"Especially if she had a vision about what we did in the shower."

My cheeks heat at the memory. Sex with Asher was insanely hot. I'd never had an orgasm as intense and mind-numbing as I did with him. But the next morning, when he pinned me against the wall of the shower and thrust into me like a man starved, he did things to my body I didn't think possible. To this day, it's still one of the most erotic moments I've ever experienced. Hell, everything about being with Asher is still one of the most erotic encounters I've ever experienced.

"That was pretty hot," I offer.

"Glad I could satisfy you. Feel free to leave a five-star review on Yelp." He winks playfully.

I lightly jab him in the side, to which he feigns pain, then eventually straightens. "So, what should we do first?"

"What do you mean?"

"Today." He nods toward the window over the sink, the lake in the distance barely visible through the heavy curtain of falling snow. "It's a snow day. How should we spend it? What did you do during your snow days growing up?"

I pinch my lips, mentally rewinding to my younger years. "I'd usually drag my mom outside to build a snowman."

"That's not an option right now. It's coming down hard. And that wind is pretty fierce. What else did you do to occupy your time?"

"Drank hot chocolate." I beam, a nostalgic gleam in my eyes.

"What else?"

"Watched movies."

"What movies?"

"*The Wizard of Oz*," I answer without a moment's hesitation.

"Really?"

"Or *The Sound of Music*."

"Well, then…" He pushes off the counter, walking away. "I've got some work to do."

"Heading back to the music room?" I ask, trying to hide my disappointment. I get that he has an album to work on, but I'd hoped he'd work at the piano in the great room, like he had all morning.

"No."

"But—"

"Hot chocolate." He opens the pantry, pulling out a jar of what appears to be hot chocolate mix. "And I'm pretty sure Grams owns both those movies, so we can

154

have the perfect snow day."

"It would still be a perfect snow day without all that," I say sincerely, my heart swelling that he's giving up his time to do this for me.

He glances over his shoulder as he ignites the burner on the stove, putting the kettle on it. "I'm glad you think so."

Chapter Nineteen

"WHAT DO YOU need me to do next?" Asher pushes the potatoes he'd just sliced off the cutting board and into the pot, then faces me.

After the third day of being snowed in at Grams' lake house, Asher and I have developed a routine. He'd make breakfast around ten, then we'd lounge on the couch — me with a book, him with a notepad as he attempted to jot down potential song lyrics. At some point in the afternoon, I'd put together a light lunch, usually just some cheese, meats, and fruits that we'd snack on while talking about everything and nothing. He'd occasionally break out his guitar, toying around with a melody. But since the day he wrote "My Favorite Almost", he hasn't written anything. I'm not sure if it's because he can't, or because he's enjoying his time with me.

"Add water and put them on the stovetop. Medium-high should be good."

"You got it." His arm brushes against mine as he lights one of the burners. I flash him a smile, then remove the ground beef and vegetable mixture, which will be the base of the Shepard's Pie, from the heat, setting it aside until the potatoes are done cooking.

The fire in his gaze warms my skin as he leans against the kitchen island, arms crossed in front of his chest, a gentle smile tugging on his lips. "I like this."

I stand across from him, mirroring his stance. "I like

this, too. I…" I cut my thought short.

"What?"

"Nothing." I quickly shake my head. "It's nothing."

"Just tell me."

"You'll think it's stupid."

"I'll never think anything about you is stupid."

I worry my bottom lip, then slowly lift my eyes to his. "I just… I always imagined the guy I ended up with would do this with me."

"Do what? Cook?"

"It sounds corny, but… I don't know…" I blow out a long breath. "During my childhood, my parents always cooked together. Hell, they *still* cook together. Mom's the chef in the family, but my dad stays by her side, always willing to lend a hand, whether it be making a salad or chopping potatoes." I smile at Asher, then look past him, my gaze distant as I talk about my parents and the love they still display for one another, even though they've been married nearly forty years. "Every so often, they steal a sly glance at one another. Or a kiss. And there are a few ass squeezes I try to ignore because, well… They're my parents."

Asher chuckles, his gaze brimming with affection.

"In those simple moments when they're doing an everyday, mundane task, there's so much love between them." I avert my eyes, pinching my lips together. "I guess I've always wanted that, too. Wanted to find someone who makes the ordinary seem extraordinary."

When I peer into Asher's eyes, they swirl with the same love and respect I witness between my parents on a daily basis. He doesn't say anything at first. Just admires me in a way every woman wants a man to look at her. Like Prince Charming regarded Cinderella when she walked into that ball, not caring she was a maid. Like Humphrey Bogart hungered for Ingrid

Bergman right before he put her on that plane out of Casablanca, and his life. Like Cary Grant revered Deborah Kerr when he visited her apartment and learned the reason she never showed up at the top of the Empire State Building, as she promised.

"Maybe you already have," he whispers, his gaze never leaving mine, almost begging me to agree. To give him this chance. To cross that line.

I part my lips, shaking my head, searching for the words I need. But, as seems to be the case lately, they're nowhere to be found at this crucial moment.

He swiftly pushes off the island, caging me against the counter in two long strides. When he places his hands on the surface and leans his weight on them, it takes all my resolve not to shift my gaze to his flexing biceps. But the intensity in his deep pools of brown won't let me. It steals my breath. The hairs on my nape stand at attention, my nerve endings stirring.

"I'm not going to pretend I haven't thought of the same thing," he begins, impassioned. "That I haven't fantasized about what life could be like with you, especially these past few days when we've been playing house, as you call it. Because I have. And a part of me doesn't want to just 'play' house with you anymore, Iz. A part of me is desperate for the real thing. To work toward building a life together, as crazy and impulsive as that sounds. But that's who I am, who I've always been. Crazy. Spontaneous."

"Asher...," I plead, but it falls on deaf ears.

"I've thought how I'd love nothing more than to slip out of bed before you woke up every morning to surprise you with breakfast in bed. How I could get used to rubbing your feet while we both relaxed on the sofa."

His hands go to my hips. Before I can react, he lifts

me up, setting me on the counter. He presses against my legs, and I part them, whimpering as he grinds against me. When he brings his mouth toward my neck, I close my eyes, tilting my head to give him better access. But his lips never touch my skin, making the ache in my core grow more vibrant and pronounced with every passing second.

"How I'd look forward to every evening," he croons, his voice husky, wanton, reckless. "To cooking with you in the kitchen. But I won't be happy with a few sly glances or ass grabs, Izzy." My eyes flutter open, and I watch as he moves his hand up to my neck. He still doesn't touch me. Instead, his hand hovers so close as he roams along my collarbone, over the swell of my breasts, and down my stomach. "Because being around you makes me hungry. Turns me into a man starved."

His chest heaves as he focuses on my lips, shameless in his need for me. I should push him away, not feed into this fantasy. But we're back in our bubble. And I don't want it to burst. Not yet.

"What would you do?" I ask in a barely audible voice. "In this fantasy of yours... What would you do?"

A slow smile curves his mouth as he inches toward me. But like before, his lips stop shy of caressing my skin. "You'd be standing by the island, peeling carrots." His words come out soft, even, yet still filled with lust.

"That's rather specific."

"I've had a lot of time to think about this over the past year." His mouth is poised above the curve of my neck, his nearness making me lightheaded. "I'd walk into the room but wouldn't alert you to my presence yet. I'd take a few minutes to appreciate the view. Adorable tank top. Short skirt. Heels that make your legs go on for miles."

I open my eyes, giving him a sardonic look.

"Cooking? In heels?"

He places a finger over my mouth, silencing me. "This is *my* fantasy. Not yours." He glares at me, his finger lingering on my lips before he gradually pulls it away. Then he scoops me off the counter, positioning me as he mentioned in his fantasy, my back to him as I stand in front of the island.

I keep my eyes forward, but the heat on my nape alerts me to his presence mere inches from me. I lick my lips, my skin flushing, breathing increasing.

"I'd finally approach and swipe your hair over one shoulder." He does as he states, a breath escaping my lungs as his fingers delicately brush against my shoulders. Even through the t-shirt covering my skin, I relish in the slight touch of his hands on my body, regardless of how fleeting.

"Then what?" I whimper.

"I'd bring my lips up to that place where your neck meets your shoulders. Which is right..." I hold my breath as the warmth of his mouth inches closer to that spot. "About..." My heart thunders in my chest, core clenching, muscles tightening. "Here."

I close my eyes as I brace to feel his lips on me, to revel in his kiss. It never comes.

"But I won't kiss you."

Dizziness overtakes me, my legs turning to jelly. "Jesus Christ." I place my hands on the island, needing it to support myself.

"Not yet anyway."

"Why?" I whine.

"Because I don't think you're hungry enough. Not yet."

"How do you know?"

"Because I can read your body better than you can." He forces me around. "I can tell when you're happy, sad..." His lips quirk into a smirk. "Horny." His arms trap me against the island. "Most importantly, I know when you're at your breaking point. Know when you're about to fall over that edge and into sweet oblivion." He studies me for a moment, assessing my flushed complexion, my labored breathing, my desperate gaze. Then he shakes his head. "You're not quite there yet."

"A little taste never hurt anyone." I crane my head, my lips seeking his.

With a harsh grip on my hips, he lifts me onto the counter again, forcing my legs apart. This time when he thrusts against me, he's not gentle, making it more than apparent how desperate he is for me. I gasp, which turns into a moan when his hands roam my body, his touch resolute.

"I would never be satisfied with a taste. I'd need to savor every last drop of you. I couldn't do that if I made a habit out of snacking on you throughout the day."

"I think you still could. I have faith in you."

"Is that right? Should a taste be on the menu?" He arches a brow, edging toward me. My gaze remains transfixed on his every move, urging him forward, but he stops with his lips poised mercilessly close to mine, permitting me to make the final decision of whether to cross this line.

"Perhaps it could be," I murmur, about to erase the last whisper between us, when the sound of something sizzling cuts through. We both fling our wide eyes toward the stove.

"Shit." I push against him and he steps back, allowing me to jump off the island. With quick movements, I rush to remove the pot of potatoes that had boiled over, turning off the gas. Asher dons an oven glove and lifts the grate off the burner, then carefully soaks up the spilled water with a dish towel.

I move the pot to a different burner, igniting it and setting it to medium-low. I focus on the potatoes as I stir them. I don't look at Asher, don't say anything, both of us staring at the stove for what feels like an eternity.

I can't stop thinking about Vegas, about the first time I was on the brink of kissing him when all the lights clicked off, leaving the entire city in complete darkness. Back then, I took it as a warning. Could this be the same thing? Is this a warning that, if we continue playing this dangerous game, disaster is around the corner?

Before I have a chance to give that too much thought, Asher's husky laughter reverberates through the room. My eyes float to him. Just like the other day when I slipped and slammed my naked body against his, bringing him to the floor, I can't help but join in, the ease and contentment covering his expression warming my heart. They say laughter is the best medicine. And right now, it's the perfect elixir to the doubt filling me.

"We really know how to steam things up, don't we?" he remarks.

"I guess we do."

"Come on." Turning from the stove, he swipes the two wine glasses off the island, heading toward the great room. I follow behind. "I'll play you a song. It's probably best I find something to keep my fingers occupied. I can't be trusted alone with you in the kitchen." He lowers himself onto the bench behind the baby grand piano, setting our glasses on the top.

"I'm not so sure this is any better."

"What makes you say that?"

With a sly smile, I saunter up to the rim of the piano, swaying my hips a little more than I normally would. "You may have fantasies about kitchen sex…" I fold my body over the closed lid, then turn to face him, propping my head up with my hand. "But my fantasy is piano sex."

He closes his eyes, every muscle in his body seeming to tighten. "That's it. It's official."

"What is?"

"I'll be jerking off later to the idea of fucking you on a piano."

"You're sick," I joke, pushing myself off the lid.

"What? I told you in Vegas. You used to be the queen of my spank bank." He drops his voice to a whisper. "But I'll let you in on a little secret."

"What's that?" I whisper back.

"You still are." He winks, then flashes me that same debonair smile, which causes me to giggle.

"Then maybe *I'll* let *you* in on a little secret." I grab my glass, taking a healthy sip of wine.

"What's that?" He peers at me with seductive eyes.

"You've been the king of my...nub hub for years."

He chuckles. "Nub hub?"

I shrug. "It's the best I could come up with on such short notice. I'm not a goddamn poet like you are."

He gets up from behind the piano and steps toward me, slinging his arm around my shoulders. "I like it. And I like that I'm the king of your nub hub. I'm officially putting that on my epitaph when I die. *Asher York. Beloved son. King of Isabella Nolan's nub hub. And once a top 100 musician.*" He pulls me onto the piano bench, positioning his fingers on the ivory keys. "Do you know what else I like?"

"What?"

"That we can joke about these things. That the tension and strain that seemed to drown you a few days ago is gone. That I have my Isabella back."

I smile. "And I like that I have my Asher back, too."

Chapter Twenty

"**D**ID YOU PACK any boots?" Asher asks the following morning when I emerge downstairs after a shower. I slow my steps, eyes floating over the living room to see him dressed in his normal jeans and t-shirt. But he's tugging on a pair of heavy work boots, a down jacket covering his shirt.

"I did." I cock a brow. "Why?"

He glances out the window at the large expanse of snow before turning his wicked grin to me. "Thought we could have some fun."

"In the snow?" My voice is heavy with skepticism.

"Why not? The winds have finally died down, so we won't get buried in a snowdrift."

When I turn my eyes to the window, surveying the conditions, I notice something different. "The road's clear."

"The plow truck came through early this morning." He smiles a sad smile. "If you want to go home, you can. You're not stuck here anymore. Say the word and I'll drive you to Boston, or New York. Wherever."

"New York is a six-hour drive from here."

"Still…" He shrugs. "I'd do it for you."

"I appreciate that." I lick my lips, meeting his gaze. "But I'd like to stay. If you don't mind." This time, I don't ask to stay because Jessie wants me here. I ask to stay because *I* want to be here. Want to be near Asher.

"I'd love for you to stay." His eyes shine with

affection, his gaze steady. Then his expression brightens. "Now, go get your boots. And I have some waterproof gloves for you. Don't want you becoming hypothermic again." He winks.

I groan as I move toward the stairs. "I didn't have hypothermia," I argue with fake irritation.

"We can pretend you do. Have some skin-to-skin time?" Asher waggles his brows, his mouth quirked up into a sexy smirk.

"In your dreams."

"You're right about that," he calls out as I continue up the steps and onto the landing. "I definitely do dream about skin-to-skin time with you, Iz. And you know you do the same."

"I plead the fifth," I sing.

"I'll take that as a yes," he intones back.

I can't help but laugh as I walk into my room, grabbing the snow boots I luckily packed. Then I head back downstairs, where Asher proceeds to bundle me up in a heavy ski jacket, hat, scarf, two pairs of socks, the boots, and gloves.

"Are you sure you're warm enough?" Asher studies me with concern, wrapping my scarf around my neck one more time.

"Pretty sure if I had balls, I'd be sweating them off right now."

He chuckles. "Well, I'm glad you don't. That would have to be a hard limit for me." He grabs my hand and leads me through the house, then out the back door.

The sun had caused a bit of the snow to melt, but the banks still come up to my knees. The only saving grace is that Asher stayed on top of it, doing his best to keep the path down to the lake clear.

"I think right here is a good spot," he says, stopping before the dock.

"For what?"

"For our snowman."

"We're going to build a snowman?"

"Why wouldn't we?"

"That's usually something only kids do."

"If you can't act like a kid once in a while, what fun is life?" With a wink, he steps off the cleared path and into the snow, then reaches down to form a small ball.

I should do something to persuade him to go back inside and work on his music, something he hasn't given much attention to the last few days, but I like spending this time with him. I pause to admire how relaxed and carefree he seems building a snowman, something he probably hasn't done in years.

He looks up, his brows pulling together when he sees me staring at him. "What is it?"

I smile. "Nothing."

He stomps through the snow toward me. "It's not nothing. Tell me what's going through your head."

"I like this side of you."

"And what side is that? My front. Because my front really likes you, too." He tugs me against him, circling his hips.

"That's not what I'm talking about... Perv." I swat him away, rolling my eyes at how shameless he is. But I know it's all in good fun, that he won't cross that line unless I make the final move.

"I can't help it around you."

I blow out an exaggerated breath, feigning irritation. "I like that we can joke with each other. That I feel comfortable around you. That you're not this tortured, brooding musician I'd painted you as for years." I avert my eyes, lowering my voice. "I like that you're smiling."

His expression softens as he brushes a glove-covered hand along the cool skin of my cheek. I bring my gaze to his. "You've given me a reason to smile again. For that, I'll always be grateful, even if this is all I can have of you."

I open my mouth to tell him we don't have a choice, but he silences my protest with a finger against my lips.

"I know all the complications. Right now, though, I want to pretend this is my life. That *you* are my life. Because even if you walk away without giving me another taste of your lips, you still will be my life. Let me have these moments, these memories I can hold on to. Can you give me that?"

I swallow hard, a tear escaping. I want to lose myself in him, promise to give him everything, every part of me. Even that piece of my heart I'd kept from him. The one I'd given his brother. But I can't. Jessie still holds that. I fear he always will.

"I can do that."

"Good." He smiles, but it doesn't reach his eyes. Neither does mine, our reality too depressing to find happiness in this scenario. "Now, let's build that snowman."

I take his outstretched hand and follow him toward a section he'd cleared. We work together, neither one of us saying a word for several minutes. I try to focus on our project to keep my mind from wandering to other things, namely whether I want to walk away from Asher without feeling his lips on mine one more time. I shouldn't even be thinking about kissing him, but it's been on my mind since our erotic encounter in the kitchen. Since he nearly kissed me my first morning here. Hell, since I walked into the house and our eyes locked for the first time in over a year.

"Know what this reminds me of?" Asher cuts through my thoughts.

"What's that?" I help him roll the snow across the

yard, adding to the bulk.

"The time you dragged Jessie out here, kicking and screaming, and forced him to build a snowman." He straightens, brushing the snow off his gloves as he faces me. I do the same. "I thought he was an idiot for not wanting to do this with you. After a few minutes, I had enough of his whining about the cold and came out." He blows out a soft laugh. "It was immature, but I—"

"Made a snowball and threw it our way."

"I'd hoped it would knock some sense into him."

"Instead, it hit me."

His eyes narrow on me, his complexion flushed from the cool air, his breath visible as he exhales. "I was so worried you'd be pissed. That you'd never want to hang out again. Jessie tried to be chivalrous and defend your honor. But instead of letting him—"

"I told him to step aside. That this meant war."

He slowly nods. "The snowball fight that erupted afterward is one of my fondest memories."

I arch a brow. "Even though you lost?"

He steps back, aghast. "What do you mean I lost?"

"I *definitely* won that fight."

"No way. You might have gotten in a handful of blows, but under no circumstances did you win."

"It was way more than a handful. You didn't notice them because you have more padding than I do."

"More padding?"

"Exactly."

"That's the story you're going with?"

"Damn straight." I place my hands on my hips, keeping my head held high.

His stare remaining trained on me, he bends down, scooping up some snow and forming it into a ball. "Perhaps we should have a rematch."

"A rematch?"

"To settle the score once and for all."

"And what are the rules?" I press, my lips pinched.

"No rules."

"There need to be rules."

"Fine," he says after a moment of contemplation. "We'll keep it simple. First one to get hit in the kill zone loses."

"Kill zone?"

"Here." He places his hand over his heart.

"Okay." I scoop up some snow, forming my own ball, packing it tightly. "Let the games begin."

Without giving him a chance to react, I throw it hard against him, but all these heavy layers disrupt my aim and I hit his shoulder. He grins a sinister smile, and I squeal, bolting in the opposite direction.

I expect to immediately be hit, but I'm not. In fact, I don't even hear him following, the only sound that of a snowmobile in the distance. I slow my retreat, looking over my shoulder. He hasn't moved. Instead, his eyes are focused intently on me as he repeatedly tosses his snowball into the air, catching it again.

"Why aren't you chasing me, trying to nail me?" I instantly slap my hand over my mouth. "I mean…"

"I think I've made it more than clear I am *definitely* trying to nail you, Izzy." He slowly meanders toward me, still tossing the same snowball. I gape at him, no words coming, his prurient glare causing my heart to spike, my knees to buckle. "But the reason I'm not chasing you," he continues, "is because there's no way in hell I want to miss the view of your ass. It's a fucking work of art, and I'd be crazy not to take a minute to appreciate how incredible it looks, especially in those jeans."

As he approaches, a chill spreads through me, and it has nothing to do with the frigid temperature. My breathing increases, eyes locked on his, unable to look away from the unrelenting want in his gaze.

"Oh, and one more thing," he says, his voice husky.

"What's that?" I whimper.

He stops less than an inch from me, his lips curving into one of the sexiest smirks I've ever seen. "You lose." He crushes the snowball against the chest of my coat, his eyes dancing with delight.

It takes me a moment to process what just happened. Finally, I snap out of the trance Asher's words placed on me.

"You're a cheater!"

His chuckles echo against the stillness surrounding us. "We agreed. First one hit in the kill zone loses. You're the first who got hit in the kill zone. No rules about *how* you got hit."

"But you cheated!"

"How?"

"You… You…" I flounder to come up with something, then blurt out, "You bewitched me."

His laughter grows even louder, the lines around his eyes crinkling with amusement. "It was only fair."

"How? How was that fair?"

"Because."

"Because why?"

In a heartbeat, his expression falls, his pupils dilating as he loops his arm around my waist, pulling me against him. I don't fight him when he leans down, his lips skimming against my cheek. "Because you bewitched me. So hard, darlin'."

I'd never been one for pet names or terms of endearment, but there's something incredibly sexy and invigorating about the way he says "darlin'" in his soulful voice. Like he's singing a song he's written just for me.

He brings his hand toward my face, about to cup my cheek when his phone rings. He stills, no longer advancing, but not retreating, either. Then he curses, stepping away.

"Give me a minute." He pulls his phone out of his back pocket. When his shoulders fall, it doesn't take a genius to figure out who's calling. "Hey, Jessie." His voice is exuberant, a complete shift from the seductive tone he used mere seconds ago. "Good, good. Things are good." There's a pause, and Asher chews on his lower lip. "Not yet... I will... Don't worry. We'll still make that date..."

He glances at me, playfully rolling his eyes, feigning irritation with his brother's pestering. I wish I could be as blasé about it as Asher seems, but I can't. After all, Jessie did offer me a large sum of money to spend time with him in the hopes of inspiring him. As of now, I haven't exactly fulfilled my end of the bargain. I haven't so much as pushed Asher to go into the music room, too wrapped up in pretending this life we've lived the past few days could be our reality.

"Sure..." Asher faces me, extending the phone toward me. "He wants to talk to you," he whispers.

"Me? Why?"

He shrugs. "Probably to make sure you're okay." He doesn't sound annoyed by that. But he doesn't sound unaffected, either.

On a long inhale, I take the phone, turning from him as I bring it to my ear. "Hey, Jessie."

"What the hell is going on up there?" he snips out, but keeps his voice low so Asher can't overhear.

"We're building a snowman. Like old times." I flash Asher a smile to assuage the suspicion I see swirling in his eyes. "You know, if you were wondering how I'm feeling, you could have texted."

171

"I did. Five times. You haven't responded."

"Oh." My shoulders fall. I'd forgotten about that. He *had* texted me. I simply ignored them. I've ignored all my texts lately.

"Has he written anything since I left?"

"No, but—"

"Obviously this isn't working," he interrupts, his tone short. "I have a meeting this afternoon, but I'll grab the first flight back. I think—"

"No!" I shout, eyes flinging wide. My response is uncontrolled, but the last thing I want is for Jessie to be here, to burst our bubble. I lower my voice, glancing at Asher, trying to play off my reaction as if it's nothing. "I mean, you don't have to do that. I told you, I'm fine. No need for any follow-up," I grit out, hoping he picks up on the fact that I'm probably within earshot of Asher.

He releases a labored sigh. I picture him pinching the bridge of his nose as he decides between giving his brother another chance and doing something to control the situation. That was always the problem with Jessie. His need to control everything.

"You do remember the benefit to you, correct?"

"Of course." How could I forget the "benefit"? That money's been weighing on my mind, especially whenever I've checked my email and received another notice that one of my bills is overdue.

"Then do something. At this point, I don't care what. Just…" I can physically feel his frustration through the phone. "Please, Iz. I'm sure you're having a blast reconnecting with an old friend. I would be, too, if I were there with you. But there is so much at stake. I can't have you be a distraction. I need you to be an inspiration." The slight ache in his voice is evidence of how difficult that must have been for him to admit. "I'll give you two more days. If there's no forward progress, I'll need to think of something else."

"It won't be necessary."

"I hope it's not."

I linger on the line a moment longer. But when he doesn't say anything further, I glance at the screen, seeing he's ended the call.

Blowing out a breath, I stare at the frozen lake. I can't blame Jessie for being concerned. It *is* Friday. In less than ten days, Asher is supposed to hit the studio to record an album filled with songs he's yet to write. That means he must write at least a song a day, preferably more. It's not impossible. When he's really inspired, I've seen him pen two, sometimes three songs in a day. Maybe it's my fault. Maybe I've been selfish, wanting Asher to focus all his attention on me instead of what's important — this album. It's why I'm here. Jessie's call reminded me of that.

"Did my brother tell you to stop playing with me?" Asher jokes, approaching from behind.

I turn around and hand the phone back to him. "More or less. Asked me to stop distracting you so you can write. He's worried about the album. He's worried about *you.*"

He closes his eyes, nodding slightly. "Then I suppose I should probably get back to work."

"You probably should." I hate the idea that this is the end. That this carefree Asher I've been treated to will disappear now that Jessie snapped the proverbial whip.

"But once you make some headway, I'll drag you back out here and we can have another snowball fight." I nudge him. "Or maybe finish building our snowman." I gesture to our abandoned project, only the bottom of our snowman built.

That earns me a smile. He drapes an arm over my

shoulders, leading me back to the house. "It's a date."

Chapter Twenty-One

I LIE AWAKE, eyes focused on the ceiling, the soft sound of the piano filtering its way up to me from the great room as Asher experiments with a melody. Jessie said he'd give him a few days before he intervened. But will he? Or is he booked on the first flight out of LA tomorrow? Will he show up unexpectedly like he did in Vegas, bursting our bubble? What if this is my last opportunity to be alone with Asher? Do I walk away from him and always wonder what could have happened if I let go of my fears?

Torn, I grab my cell from the nightstand, checking the time. Five minutes after midnight. I doubt Chloe will pick up, but I'm desperate for advice from someone who's been in a similar position. After all, Lincoln and Chloe faced quite a few hurdles in their own relationship.

Pressing her contact, I wait as I listen to the line ring. To my surprise, she answers.

"Is everything okay?" she asks frantically, not taking a breath before continuing. "Where have you been? You tell me you got fired. The next thing I know, I can't get a hold of you and your neighbor says she hasn't seen you in, like, a week. What the hell is going on?"

"Nothing," I respond, doing my best to assuage her. "I mean, *something's* going on, but I'm okay."

"Where are you?"

"At Grams' lake house," I admit after a brief moment

of hesitation.

"Grams?"

"Yes."

"As in, Jessie's grandmother?"

"Yes."

"And Asher's grandmother?"

"Well, they *are* brothers."

"I assume this has something to do with your meeting with Jessie a few weeks ago."

"It does."

"What did he want to talk to you about?"

I make out the rustling of blankets and imagine her getting out of bed and padding into the living room to allow Lincoln to sleep.

"Asher."

She inhales a sharp breath. "Did he find out about you two sleeping together in Vegas?" she whisper-shouts

"Thankfully, no."

"Then what did he want?"

I look out the windows at the bright moon shining on our abandoned snowman project from earlier. "My help. Asher has a studio date coming up to record his next album, but he didn't have any songs written, so Jessie thought surrounding Asher with all the people from the so-called glory days of his writing life would help."

"And that happens to be you."

"Whenever I came up to the lake house with Jessie, Asher and I did stay up almost all night together."

Another pause falls over the line. It doesn't matter that Chloe's a few hundred miles away. I can feel the wheels spinning in her mind.

"So let me see if I have this straight. Your ex-fiancé invited you up to his grandmother's lake house to inspire his brother, who you slept with in Vegas, which he doesn't know about."

"That about sums it up, although Jessie can't take the credit for the idea. It was Grams. She somehow knows there's something going on between Asher and me."

"There is?" I can hear the inquisitiveness in Chloe's tone.

"*Was*," I correct, then exhale deeply. "Is... Hell if I know right now. That's why I called. I'm so confused."

"So you're up there. With Asher. After all this time. How did that go?"

"How do you think?"

She laughs sarcastically. "Fucking awkward at first, I'd guess."

"It didn't help that Jessie conveniently left out the fact that I'd be here."

"Are you serious?" Her voice rises in pitch.

"Sure am. Which I had no idea about, so you can imagine *my* surprise when I saw that Asher was surprised to see me. Let's just say we were all really freaking surprised."

There's a pause, and I picture Chloe pinching her lips together as she processes this information. "And how did Asher react to seeing you with Jessie?"

"It definitely brought out the jealous monster inside him. There were a handful of tense moments. But Grams forced us to talk to each other, something we hadn't done since Vegas."

"What did you say? Better yet... What did *he* say?"

I wrack my brain to explain what we'd discussed that day out on the dock. "He told me the truth. About everything."

"Like what?" Her voice oozes with curiosity. To Chloe, who was once a gossip columnist for a women's magazine before being promoted to the current affairs editor, this kind of thing is her secret pleasure.

"Like the fact he had a thing for me from the first time he saw me walk into the club where his band was playing."

"That's no big surprise," she replies dismissively. "Anyone with two eyes could have told you that."

"He also admitted he was about to ask me out all those years ago when I walked into Grams' lake house on Jessie's arm."

"That must have crushed him," she exhales.

"So when I walked in on Friday…"

"It brought back those memories," Chloe finishes.

"That's why Asher was a bit…off."

"What else did he tell you?" she presses, sensing there's probably more.

This secret is a little harder to share. Because I'll also have to divulge the secret *I've* been keeping. "We talked about the night Jessie and I broke off our engagement."

"Which he deserved for what he did," Chloe snips out.

I pinch the bridge of my nose, drawing in a deep breath. I've kept the truth from Chloe for so long. I have no idea how she'll react. But if there's one thing Asher's ability to come clean has taught me, it's that I need to do the same with my friends, even if I haven't told him the truth. I'm not sure I'm ready to tell him I love him, that I've always loved him. It would make this situation even more difficult, make it even harder for him to let me go.

And vice versa.

"What if I told you Jessie didn't do anything wrong?"

The line is silent as Chloe seemingly assesses what I could be implying. "How is cheating on you with another woman *not* wrong?"

I swallow hard. "Because, technically, he didn't cheat

on me."

"But—"

"We had… Well, I guess you could say we took a step back to decide if we really wanted to be together."

"You did?" She can't mask her utter shock at this revelation.

"Long story short, we'd gotten into an argument before Christmas break. Since I was headed home to Connecticut and Jessie to Florida to visit his snowbird parents, it gave us the opportunity to figure things out. I didn't even want to agree to that, just wanted to give him back the ring, but he convinced me to take a minute and consider everything I was throwing away. So I agreed to hold off on making a decision. All during break, I ignored his phone calls, texts, everything. Even when I listened to his voicemails and heard how heartbroken he sounded, how desperate he was. Still, I gave him no indication I hoped to reconcile, that I *would* go back to him when the semester began."

"But you went up to Boston to surprise him after he landed in town. That's what you told us. How you made him his favorite lasagna. How you took a page out of *Pretty Woman* and waited for him with just a tie on. At some point, you must have decided you wanted to keep wearing that ring. Right?"

I cringe. "I may have embellished. I never did any of those things. I just… I was worried you'd figure out the truth."

"And what truth is that?"

I expected her words to come out biting. Instead, there's only curiosity. "That the real reason I left Jessie was because I loved Asher. I didn't have it in my heart to tell Jessie that, so I made him believe I left him because he'd brought home his ex. And you want to know the kicker? Asher knew. Jessie had stopped at the bar where Asher's band had a gig that night. He saw Candace fawning all over him, knew I was waiting at the house. And you know what he did?"

"Nothing…," she exhales.

"Exactly. He didn't stop Jessie. He's carried that guilt with him for years."

The line falls silent, as I expected it would. When Asher shared this with me, it was a lot to process. It's even more so for Chloe now that she knows my truth, too.

"Did you tell Asher why you really left Jessie?" she asks finally.

I shake my head. "No."

"And you're still at the lake house?"

"Yes."

"Are Jessie and Asher both there?"

"Jessie had a meeting in LA, so he's out there now. Their parents left on Sunday. Grams left Sunday, too, but under the guise of going to church three hours away, fully aware that a snowstorm was coming and she wouldn't be able to get back up here. Even though the roads are now cleared, she still hasn't returned."

"So you're alone. With Asher. At the lake house."

"Yup."

"And?"

I expel a long breath. "And I'm so fucking confused, Chloe. We have these moments when we're friends, when we can joke and laugh with each other like we used to all those years ago. He makes me breakfast. We cook dinner together. We watch movies on the couch with a fire crackling in the hearth. It's been…"

"Magical," Chloe finishes.

"Yes," I exhale on a long sigh. "But now I'm worried it's all about to end. That our bubble's about to burst again."

"Have you slept together?" she asks in a low voice.

"No."

"Kissed?"

"There were a few near misses, but he said I have to make that call."

"Which you haven't done because you don't think it'll ever work, so why put the effort into something that won't last, not without hurting someone you both care about," she rattles off.

"Sounds about right."

She doesn't say anything for a few moments, but I can sense her mind reeling, taking all the information I just fed her and filing it away in the appropriate compartment.

"I always was suspicious of the cheating story. Granted, I did think you were too young to get married, but I couldn't discount the way Jessie looked at you. It seemed...odd he would cheat on you. He shouldn't have run into another woman's arms while there was still the open question about your status, but I guess I can't hate him for doing it."

"So you're not mad at me for lying to you?"

"I couldn't be mad at you for that. I kept what was going on between Lincoln and me a secret for probably the same reason you kept this from me."

"And what reason is that?"

"That I was scared of the way I felt about him. That it still didn't change the fact that we couldn't be together."

I look around the same room I once shared with Jessie, but am somehow surrounded by only memories of Asher. "I'm just torn."

"About what?"

"What do you think? Asher... And Jessie."

"I don't think you should worry about Jessie. He

shouldn't factor into this equation."

"But he does," I insist, my voice growing louder. "How can he not? I'm sitting here, after midnight, contemplating sleeping with Asher while I'm lying in the bed I used to share with his brother."

"You're focused on all the negatives, like always."

"I'm not—"

"Yes, you are. You always do that. It's just who you are. You look at all the reasons a decision is bad. You rarely consider the possible positive outcomes of a course of action."

"Because the negatives *always* outweigh the positives, at least where Asher and I are concerned."

"How?" Her voice is firm and demanding. "How is being happy outweighed by the fact you'll have to tell Jessie what's going on?"

"Because Asher will lose the relationship he has with his brother," I insist.

"You don't know that. I understand what you're going through. I went through the same thing with Lincoln. I didn't think there was any way for us to be together, either. For a while, I thought I was right. People will surprise you. You just need to decide if you're ready to take a risk, let someone love you like you've always deserved. But you have to be willing to face your fears."

I consider her words, wishing there were a clear-cut answer. That's what I like. A clear path with no gray area. The gray area scares me. You can lose everything in it. Hopes. Dreams. Wishes. I've always been an all-or-nothing kind of girl. But everything with Asher has always lived in that gray area.

"What made you decide you were ready to face your fears with Lincoln?" I ask.

"Because the idea of life without him scared me

more. So you need to ask yourself what scares you more? Jessie learning the truth? Or never having this connection with Asher again? That's all it comes down to. Living in the past or looking toward a future. Once you decide that, your answer will be clear."

Chapter Twenty-Two

A SIMPLE MELODY pulls me out of the bedroom, like a beacon leading a wayward ship to shore after being tossed around by the tumultuous ocean. After I ended my call with Chloe, there wasn't a second of hesitation on my part. She said I had a decision to make. I knew what that needed to be.

My feet pad lightly as I make my way down the stairs, through the living room, and into the kitchen. As I round the corner and the great room comes into view, I pause, taking a minute to admire Asher as he sits at the baby grand, bent over the keys, deep in concentration. Shadows dance on the walls, only a few low-light lamps and a crackling fire providing any kind of illumination.

I listen to him as he sings softly about a future with a woman he can't have yet, but in his heart, he knows it'll work out. About resting his hand on her shoulder as she sleeps peacefully during a secret rendezvous. About being her anchor in the storm of her life, never faltering or wavering.

"You wrote a new song," I murmur when the final note rings out against the high ceiling.

He tears his gaze to mine as I slowly descend the stairs into the room. "It's still a work in progress." Standing, his eyes briefly float to my bare legs. "Did I wake you?"

I shake my head, coming to a stop mere inches from

him. "No."

"Is everything okay?"

"Better than okay."

"Then wha—"

I clutch his cheeks, my grip fierce as I bring his lips within a whisper of mine. I pause, neither of us moving. Instead, we breathe in each other. In a way, this is more intimate than the most erotic and soul-fulfilling of kisses. We're in that place where we still have hope. Where there's the promise of a kiss. This place is magic. My *El Dorado*. My wonderland. My somewhere over the rainbow.

Asher's intense gaze remains locked on mine, waiting for my next move. With painstakingly slow movements, I finally close the last bit of space separating us, my lips touching his for the first time in over a year, testing the connection. His body stiffens as he inhales sharply. I can't blame him. After all, we've almost made it to this exact place several times over the past few days. But each time, I pulled back. I'm done with that. Done depriving myself of this amazing sensation.

A growl rips from his throat as he burrows his fingers into my hair, his hold firm and resolved. He deepens the kiss, his tongue swiping against my lips, begging for entrance. Without hesitating, I open for him, our tongues exploring, searching, savoring.

He yanks my body even harder against his. The way his arms consume me gives the impression he fears I'll disappear if he permits me even the smallest window of opportunity. But I have no intention of disappearing. Not while we're still in our bubble.

The ferocity of our kiss stealing his breath, he tears away, peering down at me, his chest heaving. Dark eyes trace over every inch of me, as if he's still unsure whether this is real or a dream. Then he smirks.

"Took you long enough. I would have lost money if I bet on how long I thought it would take for you to come to your senses."

"And how long did you think?"

"I'd hoped a minute."

I playfully punch him in his chest. "Cocky bastard."

He chuckles before his expression turns serious once more. "In all honesty, I hoped you'd come to your senses after about a day."

I chew on my lower lip. "Sorry I made you wait."

"Oh, darlin', trust me…" His hands frame my face, bringing my mouth back to his. "Even if it took you ten years, you'd be worth the wait."

He's about to kiss me when I place my hand on his chest, stopping him. "Did you mean what you said the other night? About taking whatever I'm willing to give?"

"Well… Yes. I suppose."

I nod, straightening my spine. "Then this is all I can give you. These moments when it's just us. When we're in a bubble."

I pray Asher understands why it needs to be this way. I suppose I'm asking him to stay with me in the gray area I always try to avoid. But this is the only way.

"I can't give you forever. It's not fair to me. Or you. Or anyone else," I add, not wanting to mention Jessie by name. "If you're not okay with that, I understand. But I need you to know that I'm not ready to go all in. That I'm not ready for *you* to go all in, either. That I'm still stuck in the middle, but I'd love nothing more than to be stuck in the middle with you. And I'm not saying that so you'll laugh at my reference to a Stealers Wheel song, but because that's all I'm comfortable with."

He doesn't move for several excruciating seconds. Simply stares. Analyzes. Decides. Then he draws in a deep breath, blowing it out on a long exhale, dropping his hold on me. Turning, he walks toward the mantle covered in family photos, focused on one in particular.

I squint, trying to decipher it. My heart warms when I realize it's a photo of Asher and me sitting on the dock, our feet dangling off the side. I can make out the neck of his guitar jutting out to his left, my head leaning on his right shoulder. The color is breathtaking, the sky the brilliant pink I recall from watching the sunrise with him in the summer. And that's what this photo depicts. One of the many sunrises I've watched with him.

"Right then." He spins around and advances toward me. The sudden movement catches me off-guard, my breath escaping when he encloses me in his arms. "I guess I better find a way to convince you to change your mind. That we *can* have it all."

Permitting me no chance to protest, he claims my mouth, his kiss devouring me, taking everything I have to give. But even after he takes every last breath, I doubt he'll be satisfied. He's made it clear time and time again. He'll always want more. He'll always *need* more.

I fear I will, too.

With a hand on my hip, he leads me toward the sitting area, his lips never straying from mine, the caress of his tongue powerful and forceful. When my legs hit the couch, he lowers my back onto it, nudging my legs apart and climbing on top of me.

"What?" I manage to say between kisses. "No piano sex? I thought this would be the perfect opportunity."

"And it would be..." He trails kisses along my jawline, and I crane my head, reveling in the jarring sensation of his beard against my flesh. "If all I wanted from you was sex." He nibbles my neck, eliciting a moan.

"That's not what you want?" I pant, wrapping my

legs around his midsection, subtly thrusting against him.

"No. Not tonight." His hands explore my torso, frantic yet measured. "I made a promise to myself." He returns his mouth to mine, but the kiss is too short, too simple, too weak, making me desperate for more. Asher knows this.

"And what's that?" I skate my fingers up and down his back, pulling up his t-shirt slightly, exposing his skin. When I dig my nails into his flesh, he arches into my touch, the look of pure ecstasy on his expression more satisfying than even the most potent of drugs. He is my addiction.

"That if I were ever lucky enough to return to this place, to be with you again, we wouldn't have sex. I promised myself I'd make love to you, Isabella." His lips curve into a sexy smirk. "At least the first time." He winks. "But don't worry. Piano sex is most definitely on the agenda tomorrow." He buries his head in the crook of my neck.

"There's an agenda?"

"Oh, absolutely. Eight o'clock: bedroom sex. Nine o'clock: shower sex. Ten o'clock: kitchen island sex. Eleven o'clock…" He pulls back. "Well, I may need a little rest by then."

I laugh, loving this side of Asher. Loving that even during the most carnal and erotic of moments between us, we're still the friends we once were. "Is that right?"

"Don't worry. It'll be a short rest. I won't be able to stay away from you for long." He covers my mouth with his, stealing yet another kiss, although I'd be hard-pressed to call it that. Not when I'd willingly give him every last one of my kisses until he bled me dry.

As he leans back, I loosen my grip on his waist. He runs a firm hand down my stomach, lifting my oversized t-shirt to expose a sliver of flesh over the line of my panties. Lowering his mouth, he traces his tongue around my belly button. I throw my head back, my breathing growing ragged.

"By noon, I'll be desperate to bury myself inside you again." He slithers farther south, gripping a thigh and hooking it over his shoulder. My pulse increases when he settles between my legs. "But first, I'll need to taste you. To consume every last drop of you." He presses his mouth to me.

I cry out, my panties a rather unwelcome barrier. I've never been this wired, this on edge, this frantic to succumb to whatever this man wants.

When he pulls away, I pant, squirming beneath him. "Don't stop." I reach for him, gripping his t-shirt and yanking him back to me. "Tell me more."

"One o'clock will call for a relaxing bath, where I'll wash every incredible inch of you." He moves his mouth to my neck, tugging on my earlobe, the addition of his swirling tongue causing a fire to rush through my veins. I fear the instant he pushes into me, I'll shatter into a million pieces.

"By two o'clock, I'll probably need some sort of nourishment. So, naturally, that means kitchen island sex again." He meets my eyes, winking.

"Naturally." Giggling, I rake my hands through his hair, and he groans, his eyelids fluttering closed for a brief moment.

"But once we've had some food, I'll take you back to the bedroom and live out a fantasy I've had for a very long time."

"And what's that?" I flirtatiously bite my lower lip.

"On the off-chance you'll be wearing any clothes, which is highly doubtful, I'll strip you naked. Then we'll crawl under the covers and spend hours in bed, with nowhere to be, no one to answer to, nothing to burst our bubble and force us back to reality."

He traces the curve of my face. The way he looks at me makes me feel more coveted, more cherished, more loved than any man who's come before him.

"I'll hold you as we share our hopes, our dreams. As we plan a future for ourselves, even if there's no chance of it becoming reality. But it won't matter. Because in our bubble, anything can happen." He pushes a tendril of hair behind my ear, his eyes shining with emotion. "I truly believe that, Iz." His lips brush against mine. "In our bubble, anything can happen," he repeats. "Anything is possible."

I swallow hard, wanting to agree, to give him the hope I sense he needs. But what good would that do?

"What happens next?" I ask finally, not wanting to sour my mood with a dose of reality.

He peers at me for a moment, a single brow arched. Then he blows out a breath, not pushing the topic I'm obviously unwilling to discuss. Not yet anyway.

"We'll come back here. I'll light a fire in the fireplace, then grab some blankets and make a spot for us on the floor right in front of it. We'll make love until we're physically exhausted and fall asleep in each other's arms, feeling like we finally made it home." He cups my face in his hands, everything about the way he regards me full of power and sincerity. "You're my home, Iz. Have been since the first time you smiled at me. And despite all the obstacles, in my heart, I know you always will be."

Overwhelmed by how passionate and honest he is, I wrap my arms around him, crushing my lips to his, wordlessly giving him everything he wants, everything he deserves. My body. My mind. My heart. They're no longer mine. They belong to him. His to hold. His to possess. His to keep.

He moves from my mouth, taking his time to savor everything he's craved this past year. My neck. My ear. My lips again. He inches the hem of my t-shirt farther and farther north, his hand skimming the swell of my breasts.

"Take it off. I need your mouth on me."

"Anywhere in particular?" he asks coyly, teasing my nipple.

"Right there," I exhale. "I need you to do that thing. When you suck on it and nibble at the same time."

"You like that?" He seals his mouth over my covered breast.

I moan, gripping the cushion below me, ready to come unhinged. "God yes."

"Well then…" He leans back, bringing me with him into a sitting position. "I'm here to please, Miss Nolan." With a wink, he lifts my t-shirt over my head and tosses it to the floor. His attention focused on me, he brushes a thumb against a nipple. His light touch only serves to increase my insatiable thirst for him.

"More," I whimper, my eyes fluttering closed.

"Gladly." He starts to lower me back onto the couch when he stops. "Wait a minute."

I fling my eyes open. "What is it?"

"I need more space. To make sure you're properly taken care of."

Standing, he scoops me into his arms, his steps quick as he rushes up to the second floor. Kicking the door to his room shut, he places me onto his bed, and I inhale the woodsy scent surrounding me. It should feel strange to be in a different room in this house, but it doesn't. It feels…right.

Crawling over me, he lowers his mouth to my breast, tracing the circumference, teasing and torturing.

"More," I beg again.

The instant his tongue finds my nipple, I release a sigh, tension rolling off me as I arch into his touch. "God, that feels incredible."

He chuckles softly. "Good. Because I fucking love the taste of you. Every inch of you." His teeth scrape against my sensitized flesh and I yelp, then lose myself in the mixture of pleasure and pain.

"Again," I say once the initial shock wears off.

His tongue draws a line from one nipple to the other, giving it the same treatment. He clamps his teeth onto it, pushing my body higher and higher, my moans of ecstasy echoing around us.

A hand grips my thigh as he hitches up my leg, the circling of his hips against my core causing moisture to pool.

"I want you," he groans.

"Have me. I'm yours. Always."

"Always," he repeats as he continues his journey down my body.

He releases his hold on my leg and settles between my thighs. In this moment, there is nothing sexier than Asher York peering up at me, an unmatched yearning in his eyes as his fingers hook into my panties. His brow cocked in question, I quickly nod, giving him permission.

He drags my panties down my legs, tossing them onto the floor. "I need to taste you." His voice comes out almost like a growl, the animal residing within making itself known.

"Yes."

His eyes never leaving mine, he drags a finger along my inner thigh. It ghosts my center, making my pulse spike.

"Please."

He chuckles as he spreads my desire around, pushing a finger inside, then another. When his tongue presses against me, it takes all my self-control not to fall into oblivion. But I don't want to rush this. Don't want the moment to be over before it has begun. I want to savor every thrust of his fingers, every swipe of his tongue, every vibration from his throat.

"So sweet," he comments between licks. I reach down, digging my fingers into his scalp, losing myself in what this man does to me. When he pulls away, I dart my eyes to him and am met with a devilish smile. "I hope it's not crude of me to say, but I've really fucking missed this pussy."

I can't help but laugh. "And this pussy has really fucking missed you." I push his head back down. "Now, remind her how incredible you are."

"Yes, ma'am."

His tongue returns to me as he slides his fingers inside again, stretching and filling me. I move with the rhythm he sets. I want it to last, but it's too good, my orgasm taking me by surprise as my screams of ecstasy surround us, fragments of light obscuring my vision.

"That's it, baby," Asher hisses through his own labored breathing, not breaking away from me. "Remember that. When you think we won't survive outside of this, remember what I do to you. What I alone can do to you."

"Asher," I plead, my body refusing to come down from my orgasm. And maybe that's okay. Maybe I deserve to live in this constant state of rapture. "Get inside me. Now."

Propping myself up, I force him away from me, his chest heaving, lips coated with my desire. When he stands from the bed, I kneel on the mattress in front of him, my body still tingling, and yank his shirt over his head.

He cocks a brow. "Eager?"

"Aren't you?" I pant.

"You have no fucking idea."

I pull on his belt buckle, and he takes the hint, sliding it from its loops. He rids himself of the rest of his clothes, tossing them to the side. I take a minute to appreciate everything this man is. Broad shoulders. Sculpted chest. Chiseled abs. Tasteful tattoos covering his muscular arms and spreading along his strong back. I'm sure each one has a story. I want to hear all of them. I want to know everything that's threaded into the fiber of who he is.

I bring my hand up to his chest and place it over his heart, relishing in the pounding rhythm that matches mine.

"It's yours," he offers in a soft voice, the atmosphere shifting from one of animalistic need to unyielding devotion. "Without you, it's useless. Just an organ in my body." He wraps an arm around my waist, tugging me against him.

We both sigh at the feel of skin against skin. Flesh against flesh. Heart against heart.

"But with you, it finally beats again. It finally has a *reason* to beat. You're my reason."

"And you're mine."

With gentle motions, he lowers me back onto the mattress and crawls on top of me. "Mine," he repeats, his hips circling, reigniting my body.

"Yours," I moan, scratching my fingers down his spine.

He kneels between my legs, bringing his erection up to me.

"Wait," I say as he's about to thrust inside.

He tears his eyes to mine. "What is it?"

"Are you sure you want to do it like this?"

"What do you mean?"

"It's just…" I blow out a breath. "I don't know about you, but I've been with other people since you." My words are hesitant. The last thing I want is for him to tell me he's changed his mind, but I can't ignore this discussion.

"How many?" His tone is impassive, more curious than upset.

"One. A doctor at the hospital. We're not together or anything. Just an occasional hookup when either one of us needs it. We used protection every single time."

His expression is even as he assesses my confession. Then he nods. "Okay."

"And you?"

"No one."

"Really?"

"Really."

I tilt my head. "You haven't slept with anyone this past year?"

"I had plenty of opportunities."

"I imagine you did."

He leans down. "But something told me it wasn't over between us. Not yet. So until I knew it was, that there was no longer a chance, my heart remained faithful."

"My heart remained faithful, too," I offer in consolation. "Even if my body didn't."

His lips caress mine. "I can live with that. While I hate the idea that another man has had you, I can't stomach the thought of anyone else owning your heart."

"Never," I breathe into his kiss. "That's yours. Always has been. Always will be."

"Always," he repeats as he inches inside me, a moan

195

falling from my throat. He pauses when he fills me to the hilt, not moving. Then he shudders, shivers running over him. "God, you feel even better than I remember."

He gradually retreats before pushing back in, his motions measured and restrained. There's no over-exaggerated breaths or cries, as was so often the case when I was with Dr. Ben. There's no need. Asher may have perfected the craft of playing the guitar and piano, but he's also an expert at playing me. He knows exactly where to touch me to make me cry out those high notes most musicians couldn't even fathom reaching.

"Asher, I…" I trail off, shaking my head, this act so beautiful it brings tears to my eyes.

"I know." His lips find mine as he slides back in, hitting that spot that drives me crazy, then retreating.

When my fingernails dig into the flesh of his back, an animalistic roar escapes his throat, pushing me to increase my rhythm against him.

"Goddamn, Izzy." Sweat beads on his brow as he matches my pace. "I'm trying to go slow, but I—"

"Don't. I love that I do this to you. Love that you can't control yourself around me." I grab his earlobe between my teeth. "Love that you have no problem showing me how much you want me. So let go," I whisper. "I want you to come inside me."

He pulls back, chest heaving. "I can't do that." A devilish glint shines in his eyes as he smirks. "Not until you come again."

Encouraged by his own playfulness, I give him a sardonic smile. "Do you think you're…up for the challenge?"

"Oh, baby…" He circles his hips before thrusting harshly into me, causing me to release a surprised yelp. "I think we both know I am."

"You're out of practice. Maybe your technique needs work."

"Do *you* think my technique needs work?"

I cup his cheeks and force his lips to mine. "I fucking love your technique, baby."

He kisses me fully as he increases his pace, his motions a mixture of reverent and desperate. "Suck," he orders, bringing his thumb to my mouth.

Goosebumps prickle my skin at the severity in his tone. Yet I oblige, circling my tongue along his digit before wrapping my lips around it.

"Fuck, Iz. You gotta stop that or I'm going to come."

I smile, releasing his finger. "Is that right?"

He glides his hand down my body, his thumb landing on my clit as he drives into me. My muscles clench, my lungs constrict, my pulse skyrockets.

"Harder," I beg, and he accedes to my demand, driving with more force, his ragged breaths echoing in the room. That's all it takes for me to shatter, my clenching muscles pushing Asher over the edge, our mutual cries and moans the perfect symphony to our reunion.

"I've missed this," he says after a few minutes as we attempt to get our breathing under control.

"I've missed this, too." Tilting my head, my lips find his.

"So?" He arches a brow.

"So…what?"

"Have I convinced you we can have more than the bubble yet?" He grins mischievously.

I swat at him, pushing him off me. "It'll take more than hot sex. You should know by now that I'm incredibly stubborn." I'm about to head to the bathroom when his arm around my stomach forces me back against him.

"And you should know by now that I love a challenge." He playfully pulses against me.

"Is that what I am to you? A challenge?"

He peppers kisses along my shoulder blades, and I melt into him, just as addicted to him as I was last year. As I was the first time I heard him sing. "You know you're so much more than that. But a challenge makes it fun."

Chapter Twenty-Three

SOFT LIPS FEATHER against my shoulder blade, and I moan, basking in the comfort of being wrapped in Asher's arms. As promised, yesterday was filled with a lot of sex, more than I can remember having in any previous twenty-four-hour period. It took everything I had not to lose myself in the fantasy of this being our life, of having this once we returned from the clouds.

The day wasn't all sex, though, despite what Asher tried to convince me of the other night. To my surprise, he wrote an impressive three songs, putting onto paper the music he heard in his head, the lyrics he felt in his soul. Maybe Grams was onto something when she encouraged Jessie to invite me up here. However, I doubt they expected it to take us sleeping together again to truly inspire him.

"Where did you get this scar?" Asher asks as he brushes his thumb along my hipbone.

"According to my mom, I was born with it."

He pushes me onto my back, peering at me with lazy eyes. I rake my fingers through his disheveled hair. I doubt I'll ever tire of waking up next to this man, of staring into his amorous gaze first thing in the morning.

"Do you know what caused it?" He rests on his side, propping his head in one hand, tracing the tiny scar with the other.

"Not sure. Without knowing who my birth mother was, it's impossible to say. But my guess is I was born with a lesion. Some babies are born with them on their scalp, but they can be present at birth on other parts of the body, like your limbs or torso. Could be a side effect of my birth mother taking medication for an overactive thyroid gland. Or could be due to an injury during development."

He nods, a lone finger tracing the outline of the tiny star shape right above my hipbone. I relish in his touch. He's not doing so as a precursor to something more. He simply caresses me because he can't seem to stop.

"Do you know much about your birth mother?"

"Not really. Aside from a few lackluster attempts, I haven't exactly looked, but it's kind of hard to find someone without a name."

He perks up, brows furrowing. "You don't even know her name?"

I didn't think it mattered. Regardless of how I got my start in life, the woman I've called Mama these past thirty years is the only mother I care about. But I still sometimes wonder why my birth mother didn't want me, didn't love me, didn't choose me. Learning you're adopted changes your outlook, despite the amount of love my family has showered upon me. It makes you question things you normally wouldn't. Makes you think you don't have value.

Makes you think you're not worth the risk.

"When I was about a week old, I was found wrapped in a bundle of blankets in one of the women's restrooms in the international terminal at JFK. That's all I know."

Asher inhales a sharp breath, sitting up, staring down at me in wonder. "*You're* the JFK baby?"

"You've heard the story…"

He chuckles, eyes shining. "It sounds crazy, but it's one of my strongest memories from my early childhood. Everyone's hearts went out to the poor little girl who was abandoned in an airport on Christmas. I was only five, but I remember thinking how Santa wouldn't be able to find her if she wasn't home. So I begged Mom to send the baby one of my gifts."

This brings a tear to my eye. I can't imagine a five-year-old actively deciding to part with one of his gifts. But he did. This is further proof that Asher has a beautiful soul.

"That's really sweet. When Mama told me where I came from, she mentioned how the Child Services office was flooded with gifts, cards, monetary donations used to set up a college fund for me. She kept some things, but donated a lot of it to area shelters and foster homes."

"How did your parents end up adopting you?"

"I was placed with them as a foster."

"How did Child Services choose them? I imagine it must have been difficult to decide who to place you with because of how high profile your case was."

"My parents were fairly well-off. Still are. Papa worked on Wall Street before he retired. Mama's never had to work, but she has a restless soul, so she worked as a flight attendant, like she was when she met my dad. My case manager was worried about placing me with a potential foster family who was only interested in me because of the large donations received after the story broke. So when my parents came up as a potential placement, it was the perfect fit. Wealthy family, a woman who was of Hispanic descent, like me. They probably figured it would be good for me to have that influence."

"But they eventually adopted you."

I nod. "After about two years. At that point, they donated all the money to an adoption charity. They didn't need it. In fact, they set up their own trust fund for me and matched the donations. It paid for my undergrad and master's degree programs."

Asher stares into the distance, absorbing this news. Then he lays back down, pulling me into his arms. He kisses the top of my head, wrapping me in his tight embrace. "I always wondered what happened to the JFK baby, but every article stated the family who adopted her was extremely private. And for your safety, they wouldn't disclose their identities or yours."

I roll over, meeting his eyes. "My parents kept my background quiet from everyone. The only other person who knows the true identity of the JFK baby is the woman who was my case worker. And now you, of course. Hell, my mother didn't even tell *me* the full story until I was eighteen. I knew I was adopted, but they just said they didn't have any information on my birth mother, which was the truth. They didn't. They still don't. No one does."

"Have you ever considered searching for her?"

"Who? My birth mother?" I prop myself up.

"Yeah." He returns to a sitting position himself. "Don't you want to know why she left you in an airport bathroom?"

"I've tried, but eventually gave up. You can't just run an internet search of the JFK baby's birth mother." I squint, pinching my lips together. "Well, actually you can. The results will say Rose Kennedy."

"Wasn't there a police report?" he presses, his gaze intense. "Witnesses? Video? You were found in an airport, for crying out loud. There has to be something."

"It was thirty years ago," I remind him. "Over ten years before 9/11. The police have footage of my birth mother in the terminal before she walked into the bathroom. But she never looked directly into any of the cameras. It was impossible to know what she looked like, other than she was approximately five-six, slender, with dark hair, wearing a black hoodie that hid her features."

"If you really were interested in finding out, I bet Lincoln could help you."

"Lincoln?" My brows scrunch together, wondering how Chloe's husband could help in this thirty-year cold case, as it's been touted on the news. "I don't—"

"He's the new chief general counsel for the *Times*. I'm sure there are quite a few reporters on staff who would love nothing more than to break the story behind the JFK baby. Hell, to put a name to the JFK baby in the first place." He lowers his voice. "Does Chloe know your background?"

I shake my head.

"People would love to know how the JFK baby turned out. And I think the JFK baby should learn where she came from, too." He narrows his gaze, giving me a knowing look.

"Why do you feel so strongly about this?"

"Because I *care* about you, Iz." He pushes me back against the mattress, hovering over me. "This is the kind of thing that can have long-term effects. I still volunteer with an organization that promotes arts education for high-risk kids in the hopes it will steer them on the right path, give them an outlet outside of drugs, alcohol, or anything else that could end with them in prison or an early grave."

I nod, more than aware of his philanthropic work. During the time I dated Jessie, I always found it noble that Asher gave up his Saturday mornings to work with kids from low-income neighborhoods, teaching them the fundamentals of music and eventually how to play an instrument of their choosing. It didn't fit into the persona of the brooding musician I'd painted. Then again, I was just as surprised to learn he was a high school music teacher. Perhaps if my high school music teacher looked like Asher, I would have stayed with it longer.

My curiosity getting the better of me, I'm about to ask why he got involved in this program in the first place, then it hits me. "Emilia…" The name escapes my lips before I can stop it. "That's why you feel so strongly, isn't it?"

He shoots up, eyes wide. "How…" He blinks repeatedly, staring at me. Then he hangs his head. "Grams."

"She told me about her. How you and Jessie were friends with her. How Jessie wanted to be more than friends, but one day, she disappeared."

"She came from a troubled family. Said music was the only thing that kept her relatively grounded. Then she quit out of the blue. I don't know…" He blows out a sigh. "I always wondered if things would have been different had I pushed her stay with it. It was obvious she hated to be at home. So, in a way, I see parts of Emilia in a lot of kids." He shifts his gaze to mine. "I see parts of Emilia in you, too. There are times I look at you and see that same distant expression in your eyes."

"I'm not her," I say through the lump in my throat. The pain of losing someone at such an impressionable age has obviously stayed with him. It doesn't help he never got any closure, that he's had to spend the past nearly twenty years wondering what happened to her.

"I know you're not. But I've worked with a lot of kids who were in the system. Who've been abandoned and never adopted. Who've spent their entire lives in foster care. Some of them don't know where they come from, which shows in their reluctance to form strong relationships with anyone. Sure, some of them have gone on to turn their lives around, but there's still something missing." He traces a line down my face. "I'm worried I'll never have all of you when there's still a piece of *you* missing."

I part my lips. Do I really want to put myself through all of this? To learn why my mother didn't want me?

I shift my gaze to his, the love shining through almost knocking the breath from me. It's so strong, so vibrant, so powerful. When he looks at me this way, I can't help but give him the hope I sense he needs.

I brush my mouth against his, savoring in the light caress of his early morning kiss. "For you, I'll think about it."

He angles back, cocking a brow. "Just think about it?"

"It's the best I can give you right now," I admit. "It might open old wounds. I need to be emotionally prepared for that."

"I can understand that. And I'll be by your side the entire time…if you'll let me."

I simply smile in response. Don't nod. Don't agree. I can't promise him a future when I'm still struggling with what that future holds. What I *want* it to hold.

When I went to him the other night, I was so certain this was the only way we could be together. That all we could ever have were these stolen moments when it was just us. But with each passing beat of my heart, I fear I'll no longer be able to walk away. That I'll want everything he's offered. That I'll want this fantasy with him.

Then again, I fear I already do.

Chapter Twenty-Four

A S A GIRL, I often looked forward to the day after a snowstorm, simply so I could admire the beauty of our property, the sun shining brightly off the blanket of white. But today, as I peer at the sunlight reflecting off another snow-covered expanse of wilderness, nothing about it seems bright, the ache in my heart too excruciating. This is the precise thing I'd hoped to avoid. I had a warning after my one night with Asher in Vegas. I knew how difficult it was to walk away after just one night. But did I listen? Of course not. Now I've made matters worse. Now I've spent several nights with Asher.

An arm encloses me in the warm embrace that has become my sanctuary, my respite...my home. A heaviness settles in my chest at the thought that this is the last morning we'll wake up together. The last morning we'll have...whatever this is.

Despite spending all this time together, we haven't discussed what would happen today, other than the fact that we'll drive to the airport. But that's where we'll part ways. He'll get on a flight to LA and hit the studio, now that he's written enough songs for an album. And I'll board a plane to New York, where I'll return to whatever semblance of a life I have left. At least I now have a little cushion with the money Jessie wired into my account, my payment for Asher making his studio date.

I glance at the clock on the wall of his bedroom, a lump forming in my throat. My flight leaves in a little more than five hours, which means we don't have much time before we need to hit the road. I squeeze my eyes shut, a lone tear trickling down my cheek. Now that the end is here, I want to go back in time, have one more hour, one more minute, one more second.

Asher pulls me closer, desperate fingers exploring my body, like a blind man reading Braille. When his lips brush the sensitive skin on my neck, I moan, losing myself in his seductive touch. Right now, I want to live in the present, live in Asher. I don't want to think about what's to come in mere hours when we have to burst our own bubble. It's too painful. Too final.

He pushes me onto my back, a lock of hair falling in front of his eyes as he peers down at me. His gaze traces over my face, seeming to focus on every mark, every line, every freckle. I want to look away from the pure intensity in his stare, but I can't, still cast under his spell. Even more so now that it's about to break.

For the first time, I question whether it *needs* to break.

His lips curve into a sad smile as he swipes a tear from my cheek. "I love you," he confesses, his voice filled with wonder.

I expel a short breath, struggling to come up with any meaningful response. His declaration doesn't come as a surprise. It's the fact he so willingly admits it that catches me off-guard. Despite the doubts that have plagued me the past few days, I haven't wavered from my original decision that I couldn't give him more than these rare, stolen moments.

"I know it's probably the last thing you want to hear since it will only make matters more confusing," he continues when I don't immediately respond. "But I do, Isabella. I love you so fucking much," he chokes out.

I search his eyes, wracking my brain for something, *anything*, to say in response, but I fear no words will ever be enough to properly convey the way I feel about him.

"I meant what I told you in Vegas right before we made love the first time." He pushes a tendril of hair behind my ear, his voice gruff. "I never wanted anything my brother had until you. I never *loved* anything my brother had until you."

The vein in his neck throbbing, he frames my face in his hands, his grip steady and determined. The way he holds me, the way he admires me, the way he worships me causes my heart to pound, the hair on my nape to stand on end.

"You may not believe in love at first sight, and maybe it's not love at that point." His fingers dig harder into my skin, pupils dilating, chest heaving. "But I truly believe two souls can feel a connection. Maybe that's all love at first sight is. One soul finding a piece of itself in another." He lowers his mouth to mine. "Because that's what I felt the second I saw you. I found the missing part of myself. And from that moment forward, I knew you'd be the only woman I'd ever love."

He presses his lips more firmly against mine, his kiss so much more charged now that his love is out in the open. There's more meaning, more purpose, more everything, the power in this one kiss erasing every last doubt in my mind that this is the path for me. That *Asher* is the path for me.

I wrap my legs around him, needing him closer, even a breath between us too much. Soon, there will be an entire country between us. Is that really what I want?

He softens the kiss, the intensity waning as he gently brushes his tongue against mine before pulling back.

I bring my hand to his cheek, running my thumb along the scruff of his unshaven jaw. "Asher…" I chew on my lower lip. How can I possibly respond to his declaration? In truth, there's only one way *to* respond. "I lo—"

"No," he interrupts quickly, silencing me. "Don't."

I blink repeatedly, confused. "But—"

"Not yet."

"Why not? I thought—"

"I don't only want your love inside this bubble. I need it everywhere. Inside. Outside. Today. Tomorrow." He skims his lips against mine. "Forever."

"I do. I will." The words leave my mouth before I can stop them, but they're true. I'll always love this man, no matter what the future holds.

His gaze is measured. "Then prove it."

"How?"

With a furrowed brow, he contemplates my question, squinting. When he looks back at me, his eyes sparkle. "I'll be in New York to talk with the label a week from Wednesday. They have me booked at the Four Seasons. Meet me in the lobby bar. Eight o'clock." The corners of his mouth lift into a small smile. "And bring those three words with you. Okay?"

I nod without a single hesitation. "Okay."

"Okay?" he repeats, his voice rising in pitch, his surprise apparent.

"Okay."

Growling, he crushes his body to mine, consuming me, his kiss fevered and frantic as his hands roam the contours of my frame in sheer desperation. "You just made me the happiest man alive."

"You've made me the happiest woman alive this week." I throw my head back as I savor in the feel of his mouth on every inch of me, the scruff along his jawline biting and bruising. "I don't want this to end."

"It doesn't have to." His lips cover mine, his kiss deep

and fulfilling as he circles his hips, bringing his arousal to my core. "It never has to end."

"Never," I whimper as I surrender to him once more, finding peace in my pledge that it won't be the last time, that we can survive outside our bubble, despite the obstacles facing us.

* * *

"Ten days." Asher's words come out as a mix between a promise and a question.

Busy travelers rush around us, pulling suitcases, while an overhead announcement calls for passengers to board before they lose their seat, which will be me soon if I don't hurry up. I thought saying goodbye would be easier with the knowledge that I'll see Asher again soon. But it's not. In fact, I think it makes it hurt even more, since I've realized this is the path I want.

"That's just 240 hours. 14,400 minutes. 864,000 seconds."

"Did you just do all that math in your head?" I choke out.

He shrugs. "I'm a musician. Essentially, music is just math."

I blink back my tears, my vision blurring. "I suppose it is."

"We just have to get through the next ten days. Then it'll be smooth sailing."

I blow out a laugh. "I have a feeling in ten days, things will get a lot more complicated."

"That may be so…" He adjusts his stance, bringing my body closer to his. He briefly lifts the sunglasses, which mask his appearance in case any passersby were to recognize him and blast his photo all over social media. "But I'd rather have complicated with you than easy with anyone else."

"Promise?" I barely manage to say.

"Promise."

His lips caress mine, sealing his vow with a kiss. Despair takes over, and he tightens his hold, kissing me with more passion, more magnitude, more longing. I wish I could stay in this moment forever, stay in his kiss forever. I fear the second I break away, it will all be over, despite the assurances we've made to each other.

When he brings the kiss to an end, he rests his forehead on mine. Neither one of us cares we're in public where anyone can bear witness to our agony, our heartache, our grief. Let them watch. Let them see what true love looks like. And I'm absolutely certain this is true love.

"You have to go," he murmurs after a beat.

"I'm scared," I admit.

"So am I. But I have to let you go. Only for a few days." He pulls back, cupping my cheeks in his large hands. "And then I'm coming for those three words, Izzy. You can be damn sure about that."

I pull my lips between my teeth to stop my chin from quivering. "Then why do I feel like this is the end?"

He shakes his head. "You can't think like that. It's not. I have to believe it's not. We have a plan. And it'll all work out. It has to. There's no reason it won't. Okay?"

"Okay," I respond, but I still can't shake this feeling in the pit of my stomach.

"Okay." He captures my mouth one last time, then steps away.

Sucking in a quivering breath, I reluctantly turn from him, heading toward the security checkpoint. As I'm about to get into line, I hear him call my name. I glance over my shoulder, heart warming as my gaze falls on my Asher, his soft guitar case slung over his back, hair askew, shoulders drooped.

I love you, he mouths.

I swipe at a new wave of tears sliding down my cheeks. He wants me to wait to utter those three words, but I can at least tell him I feel the same way.

"Ditto."

Chapter Twenty-Five

I DASH OUT of the cab, the frigid winter air blasting me with a harsh wind. I tug my jacket closer to my body and drop my head as I make my way toward the Italian restaurant in Hell's Kitchen. The instant I step inside, a wall of warmth hits me, the aroma of tomatoes, basil, and garlic filling my senses. It reminds me of Asher. Hell, *everything* has reminded me of Asher since I said goodbye to him at the airport five days ago. But this memory is particularly poignant. On our last night together, he made one of my favorite meals — gnocchi in a vodka cream sauce. It only makes me miss him even more. We've exchanged the occasional text over the past few days, but they've been innocuous on the off-chance Jessie might catch a glimpse of one.

"Good evening, miss. Do you have a reservation?" a polite voice pulls me back to the present.

I smile at the pleasant hostess dressed all in black. "I believe my mother reserved the private room. The last name is Nolan."

"Yes, of course. This way." She leads me through the restaurant, the tables crowded together, as is often the case in Manhattan. Patrons dine on beautifully prepared pasta dishes, steaks, and seafood as they sip on wine. It makes my stomach growl. "Right in here." The hostess comes to a stop past the long bar lining the wall, gesturing toward a doorway.

"Thank you." I offer her a smile, then walk into the

private room, surprised to see only Chloe sitting at the long table.

"Where is everyone?"

"Evie's running a little late. So is Nora." She pushes her chair back from the table and stands.

"And Lincoln?" I arch a brow.

"He's not coming."

I blink repeatedly, my heart dropping to my stomach. "Did something happen?" I whisper.

She laughs, shaking her head. "No. But I realized something after the last time we spoke."

"You did?"

She slowly nods, running her hands down my arms. "I lost sight of what's important. You needed me as a friend, and I wasn't there." She pinches her lips together, her expression laced with sincerity. "I don't want to become someone who forgets about her friends because I got married. And I'm sorry if I made you feel that way. If we all made you feel that way."

"You didn't," I insist. "I—"

"We did," she interrupts. "Hell, how much time passed before you finally caught my ear long enough to tell me what happened when you saw Jessie? I should have asked you the first time I saw you."

I shrug. "You'd just gotten married. That was more important than my meeting with my ex."

She peers intently at me with her steel gray eyes. "But it shouldn't have been. And I promise, I'll do my best not to lose sight of what *is* important. We all will. Okay?"

My lips quirk into a smile. "Okay."

She raises herself onto her toes and wraps her arms around me, hugging me tightly. I bend down to make it easier for her five-two frame to meet my five-seven height. Then she pulls back, grabbing my hand in hers, pulling me to the table.

Once we're both seated, she turns to me. "So, what did you end up deciding?"

I chew on my lower lip, trying to reel in my smile, but I can't. I'm actually glad no one else is here yet. It gives me a chance to update Chloe on everything that transpired at the lake house.

Meeting her eyes, I admit, "I chose my future."

"Your future?" She cocks a brow.

"Asher. I chose Asher. At first, I was uncertain."

"What do you mean?"

I grab the bottle of wine from the table and pour some into the glass in front of me. After swirling the red liquid, I bring it up to my lips, savoring the robust Cabernet. "I knew I wanted Asher but couldn't ignore all the reasons it would never work. So I told him all I could give him was what we had in our bubble. When it was just us."

"And he was okay with that?"

A grin lights up my face at the memory of his reaction. "Cocky bastard saw it as a challenge."

She snorts out a laugh. "I bet he did."

"So he said he'd have to find a way to convince me we could have everything *outside* of the bubble, too."

"And did he?"

I pause, milking the anticipation covering my friend's expression, her gaze bright, body leaning toward mine, breath held. "I believe he did."

Her expression widens, mouth agape. "He...did?"

I can understand why she'd be so shocked at my response. I was surprised myself. "He did."

She stares at me for several long moments, then she practically tackles me to the floor with the strength of her hug. "Oh, Izzy. I am so fucking happy for you. You deserve this. You deserve happiness, and we both know

215

Asher has *always* made you happy, even when that was supposed to be his brother's job."

She pulls back, excitement oozing from every inch of the woman who, a year ago, didn't get excited about anything. I suppose love changes you. "I can't believe you're dating Asher York." She lowers her voice. "Are you dating him…openly?"

"Not yet. We still have some…things to discuss."

"I can only imagine." She clutches my hand. "It will all work out. It has to." She crosses her legs, then leans toward me once more. "So, tell me, what made you change your mind?"

I replay my final morning with Asher. How I woke up convinced it was our last one together. Then how everything changed in the blink of an eye. "He told me he loves me."

Chloe clasps her hand over mine, squeezing, her eyes brimming with happiness. "We all knew he did. He has for a lot longer than you realize. And we all know how much you love him, too. So does he. I'm so glad you guys have decided to take this risk. You're soul mates!"

"I think so, too. But that's the funny thing."

"What is?"

"When I went to tell him the same, he stopped me."

She straightens, cocking her head to the side. "Why?"

"He said he didn't want me to tell him inside our bubble. That I needed to wait until we were in the real world."

A furtive stare crosses her face, then she nods, pushing a few strands of her blonde waves behind her ear. If there's anyone who's proof of how love can change your perspective, it's Chloe. A year ago, she sported gray and lilac ombre hair, a way to mask who she was behind the façade she'd erected. But Lincoln made her realize it was okay to be herself, to be vulnerable. In a way, Asher's done the same thing. He's made me realize that maybe there are some things worth taking a risk for. And maybe *I'm* worth the risk to him.

"I can see why he'd do that."

"Me, too."

"What happens next?"

I lean back, lifting my shoulders before allowing them to fall. "Once he wraps on the album, he'll come to New York to meet with the label."

"When?"

"This coming Wednesday."

"And?" She gives me a sideways glance.

"And I'm to meet him in the bar at the Four Seasons and bring those three words with me."

"That's it?"

"What more is there? Does anything else matter?"

She covers my hand with hers again, giving me an encouraging smile. "It doesn't. I'm glad you've finally realized that."

"Me, too."

"Sorry we're late!" Evie declares, out of breath.

Chloe and I pull apart from each other, but not before sharing a look. She arches a single brow, to which I shake my head. That's all she needs to know to keep quiet about Asher. At least for now. I don't mind telling Chloe, but I don't want this to be public knowledge yet.

I turn my eyes to the doorway as Evie and Nora rush into the room carrying gift bags. Rising, I scoot around the table and am instantly assaulted by Nora's enthusiastic hug.

"Happy Adoption Day!" she squeals.

"I told you guys. No gifts."

"When have we ever listened to that?" Evie asks, hugging me when Nora steps back.

"Never." I roll my eyes. "Although I know how you all are with gifts. I doubt these are appropriate for me to open in front of my parents."

My friends share a look, Nora cringing slightly. Then she announces, "Probably not, but I'd sure get a kick out of watching you blush."

"I hate all of you."

"No, you don't," Evie sings. "You love us. You'd be lost without us."

I feign irritation, but it only lasts a few moments. "You're right. I would be."

"Isabella, *mi amor*," a husky, accented voice cuts through. I return my attention to the doorway, beaming when I see my parents standing there.

"Mama." I walk into her outstretched arms. After these past several weeks, this is exactly what I need. A night with the most important people in my life — my parents and my friends.

"Happy 'Got Ya' Day, sweetie," she whispers, kissing my cheek.

"Love you, butterfly." Papa hugs me next, squeezing me tightly.

Even as a child, we never celebrated my birthday. My parents explained it was difficult to do anything because of how close to Christmas it was. Instead, they chose to celebrate my birthday on March fifth. It wasn't until I learned I was adopted that I realized the significance of the day. It was the date the judge signed off on my adoption and I became theirs officially. To them, that was more important than the day I came into this world. And it is to me, too.

I pull back, taking a minute to admire my parents. They couldn't be any more opposite if they tried. Papa is the typical all-American boy. Or at least he was when he was younger. Fair skin. Red hair. Tall. Muscular body he's maintained, even though it's been decades since he played college football.

Mama always said she had a thing for gingers, that she was a goner the second he opened his mouth and asked what she was doing after she got off work. It doesn't sound strange, but considering she was a flight attendant and he was one of her first-class passengers, it's not as commonplace as one would think.

I float my gaze to my mama, who doesn't look a day over forty, despite the fact she's over sixty. Her olive-toned skin is still relatively wrinkle free, her dark hair only sporting a few gray hairs. She still has a body any thirty-year-old would kill for, evidence she's stayed active throughout her life. She claims she needs to in order to eat all the food she wants, but I know better. She has a restless spirit. I suppose I got mine from her.

"We don't have to celebrate this," I admonish them, as I've done every year since I turned eighteen.

"Oh hush." She playfully nudges me. "We absolutely do. It's the day our family was complete." She holds me at arm's length. "And I plan on celebrating it as long as I live, *mi amor*. Even after I'm gone, I hope to enlist Chloe, Nora, and Evie to carry on the tradition." She glances over her shoulder, winking at my friends.

"And you know we will, Mrs. Nolan," Evie offers.

"I told you, Guinevere," Mama says, refusing to use Evie's nickname. When she'd learned her real name was Guinevere, she insisted on using it. Said it was far too beautiful a name to shorten, which is why she refuses to call me Izzy like everyone else in my life. "Call me Victoria."

"Okay, Victoria," she replies with a smile.

"Let's sit, sweetie." Papa clasps my mother's hand in

his and leads her to the table. He holds out her chair, then takes the seat next to her.

Once we're all situated, Mama looks around, her brows scrunched. "Where are your husbands? They're more than welcome. Especially yours, Chloe angel." She leans toward her. "I must say, when I got your wedding announcement, I thought I'd made my martini a little too strong. I love you with all my heart, but I never thought I'd see the day you got married."

"We all felt the same way when we saw her wearing a wedding band," Nora pipes up.

"You didn't know?" Mama presses.

"They eloped," I explain. "He took her to Vegas and they got married."

"It was a spur-of-the-moment decision," Chloe explains.

"Well, I'm thrilled for you. But you could have brought him."

"We decided to keep this a girls' day." She meets my eyes. "Like it's always been. We don't want to lose sight of how important our friendship is because some of us are married. Friends first. Always."

Mama smiles fondly upon my friends. "I'm so grateful you're all in my Isabella's life. She couldn't have asked for a better support group." She raises her glass. "Happy 'Got Ya' Day, Isabella."

"Thanks, Mama."

"No. Thank *you, mi amor.*"

The evening passes quickly as we all stuff ourselves with what my father claims to be the best Italian food in the city. I'd be hard-pressed to disagree. It's no surprise why we return to this restaurant every year for this celebration. It's where my parents first told me I was adopted. At the time, I wondered why they'd tell me something like that in public, not knowing how I'd react. During my childhood, there was no such thing as a trip into the city without coming here. In a way, it's always brought me comfort. It still does.

"How's the job hunt going?" my father asks as we sip our wine, our dessert plates barely containing any crumbs from the cannoli or tiramisu we scarfed down.

"I have a few prospects. A number of hospitals have contacted me, but they're not in the city."

"And you're okay with the severance package?" He lowers his voice. "You're still able to pay all your bills?"

Heat washes over my face as I avert my gaze. "I'm fine, Papa." I can't shake the feeling he knows I'm not being completely honest. If there's anyone who can get the truth out of me, it's this man. Hell, he's the one I told when I had sex for the first time, not my mom. He just...knows.

Clearing my throat, I straighten my spine, needing to change the subject. He doesn't need to know the only reason I'm able to pay my bills is because of the money Jessie paid me to spend time with Asher.

"There's something I wanted to talk to you about," I say nervously, my eyes floating around the table. "To all of you."

"Of course, *mi amor*," Mama replies. "What is it?"

I draw in a deep breath, praying she doesn't take this the wrong way. That neither of my parents take this the wrong way. This is something I need to do, especially if I hope to have a future with Asher. I need to fill in the missing pieces. And what better day to start this search than the anniversary of when I finally got my forever family.

Placing my hands on the table, I steel myself. "I want to find my birth mother."

The room is still as my words ring out around me. For a moment, it seems like the entire restaurant is quiet. No scraping of forks against plates. No polite conversation. No clanging of ice against glasses.

Then my mother stands and rushes toward me, wrapping me in her embrace. "Oh, Isabella, this is wonderful news." She pulls back, cupping my cheek with her hand. I look at my father, who wears a proud expression. For years, they've encouraged me to find answers. Hell, *everybody* has. I just didn't want my parents to think I didn't appreciate all the sacrifices they've made for me.

"I hope you find the answers you're looking for, butterfly," Papa offers.

"I'm not really looking for answers," I respond, although my voice lacks the conviction I wish it had. "It's more…curiosity than anything."

Mama smiles at me affectionately. "There's a part of your past that's missing. Part of your story. It's like picking up a book and starting at chapter three or four." She drops her hold on me, heading back to her chair and sitting. "You can probably still enjoy the story, but you'll never fully understand the characters, their motivations, their struggles. You need those missing pages."

"I realize that now, but to fill in those missing pages…" I turn toward Evie and Chloe, "I think I might need your help."

They peer at me, confused. "*Our* help?" Evie asks.

"Yes." I run my hands along my dress, smoothing the lines. "I've tried to do some research on my own, but it's difficult for me to get very far. Not to mention it was thirty years ago."

"Did you reach out to the adoption agency? Or Child Services?" Chloe presses. "I'm sure they have information that can help." She looks at my parents. "Don't they?"

"That's part of the problem," I explain. "The circumstances surrounding my adoption are a bit…unusual."

"Unusual?" Nora lifts a brow.

I glance at my parents, who give me a reassuring nod, before meeting my friends' gazes once more. "You were probably all too young to remember, but have you ever read stories about the JFK baby?"

Nora's brows scrunch together as she shakes her head, which I expected. After all, I was born before her, so she wouldn't have been around to see the headlines splashed across the front page of every paper, the reports on every news station. I only have because of all the research I've done over the years.

I shift my attention from Nora, peering at Chloe and Evie. No confusion there. Only realization mixed with utter shock. I had no doubt they'd know the story. After all, they both work at a magazine.

"*You're* the JFK baby," Chloe exhales, jaw slack, eyes wide.

I nod slightly. "I am."

"Holy shit," Evie breathes, her voice growing excited. "The magazine has tried to write a story on you nearly every year. We *really* wanted to this past December, since it was the thirtieth anniversary of you being found. But Child Services turned down every request. They said you preferred your privacy."

"And I did. But if I want answers on who my birth mother is, I need to do this. Need to go public with my identity and hope there's someone out there who can help. I just… I want to know who she is, why she did what she did. I think it will help me finally move on, feel accepted."

Realization falls over Chloe's expression as she puts the pieces together about why I feel strongly about this, *why* I need those missing pages. She reaches across the table and takes my hand in hers, squeezing.

"You deserve to know where you came from."

"I agree," Evie offers, placing her hand over ours. "We'll do everything we can to help you get those answers."

Nora joins in, her hand on top of all of ours. "And I'll do whatever I can, too. I'm not a journalist, but I know some killer meditation techniques that can help you push through the stressful moments."

We all break out laughing, my heart warming with how supportive my friends are.

"Thanks," I say with a kindhearted smile. "All of you."

Chapter Twenty-Six

MY HEART POUNDS in my chest as I hurry past Central Park, practically running toward the Four Seasons. All day, I haven't been able to stop smiling. I feel like a kid waking up on Christmas morning, rushing down the stairs to see what presents were left beneath the tree. But tonight, I know *exactly* what gift I'll be unwrapping. A very muscular, seductive gift I plan to enjoy all year long.

I make my way through the hotel lobby, everything upscale and shiny. It's still surreal to think this amount of opulence is now a part of Asher's lifestyle. That he's no longer the struggling musician who was happy to get a gig at a hole-in-the-wall bar or pub. I always told him he'd eventually share his music with the world. Now he is.

As I step inside the dimly lit lounge, my eyes float around for any sign of Asher, coming up empty. A few tables are occupied by hotel guests, but other than that, it's not overly busy.

I approach the bar and sit in one of the soft barstools. A bartender with slicked-back blond hair approaches immediately, his smile congenial. "What can I get you?"

"Vodka tonic, preferably with a Polish vodka."

"Belvedere okay?"

"Belvedere is perfect."

I feel a buzz from my clutch and pull out my cell, unlocking it to see a message from Asher.

> *Meeting ran late. Stuck in traffic. I promise I'm on my way. Hold on tight. GPS says twenty minutes. Sorry, Iz. I love you.*

My heart warms, a wide grin tugging on my lips. During our few conversations these past ten days, he's refrained from uttering those words. At first, it made me question whether he still felt the same way. But now, it makes sense. He's saving it for tonight. Just like I am.

"Do you love him?" a deep voice slurs as the bartender returns with my drink, setting it in front of me.

I look up from typing out my response to Asher, meeting the eyes of a man sitting two seats over. I estimate him to be in his thirties. Despite his designer suit, he's unkempt, dark hair askew, tie loosened, first few buttons of his dress shirt undone.

"Excuse me?"

"The guy you're texting…" He nods toward my cell. I quickly click off the screen, abandoning my message. "By the wide smile on your face, I surmise you're talking to someone you're interested in. So, tell me…" He angles toward me, the stench of whiskey strong. "Do you love him?"

I smooth the lines of the red dress I chose to wear tonight. The same red dress I wore when I met with Jessie mere weeks ago. But Asher deserves the same effort he did. Hell, he deserves more.

"I do."

He leans back, swaying in his seat. "That's beautiful. That's…" He lifts his glass. "Love is a beautiful fucking thing, isn't it?"

"I believe it is." I look forward again, bringing my drink to my lips, taking a sip. It's strong with a hint of sweetness from the lime. Exactly how I like it. I shift my eyes to the large screen television hanging above the bar. I pretend to be interested in the Rangers game, but I have no interest in hockey. Not right now anyway.

"Let me ask you something…"

Inhaling a calming breath, I turn back to my drunken companion. "What's that?"

He peers at me through slanted eyes. "If you found out your brother was dating someone off-limits, what would you do? Wait a minute… Wait a minute," he garbles, practically falling off his stool. "Let me rephrase that since you're of the opposite sex."

"Thank you for noticing."

"Say you found out your *sister* was dating someone she shouldn't, how would you react?"

I shrug. "I don't have a sister. Or any siblings, so…"

"This is hypo…hyper…"

"Hypothetical?" I arch a brow.

"That's it!" He points to me, his motions slow and lazy due to the amount of alcohol he's consumed. "Hypothetical," he stutters, having trouble pronouncing it. "Say you had a sister who started dating someone she shouldn't. What would you do?"

"I think I'd need more context before I draw a conclusion."

"Okay." He pulls back, nodding. "I get it. Context. Sure. I can give you context. How about this? Say you learned your brother had fallen in love with your ex?"

My heart plummets, my lungs constricting.

"And not just that he'd fallen in love with an ex, but your ex-goddamn-fiancée. And now the ring she wore was no longer yours, but his? What would you do? Would you be okay standing behind him during their wedding in a few days, telling him it doesn't bother you that he stole your goddamn life?"

I bring my glass to my mouth, swallowing a larger gulp than usual. "Is your brother marrying your ex-fiancée?"

"Ding! Ding! Ding! We have a winner!" he announces so the entire bar can hear. Then he blows out a labored sigh, his shoulders slumping forward. His Adam's apple bobs up and down as his brows pinch together. "Saturday. In just three days. Three...fucking...days." His grip on his glass tightens to the point where I worry it will shatter in his hands. "Three days, and my brother gets to marry the woman of *my* dreams. Gets to begin the life *I* was supposed to have." His voice becomes strained. "Is about to start the family *I* was supposed to start."

I listen to his story, unable to ignore the absolute agony in his voice. There are probably extenuating circumstances he's not telling me. After all, there are always two sides to every story. He *is* at a bar and is rather intoxicated. Perhaps he's struggling with alcoholism. Or something else that would justify his ex breaking up with him and marrying his brother.

"What happened?" I ask in a timid voice, although my heart screams at me not to, to walk away right now. "If you don't mind my asking."

He shakes his head, swiping at the few tears escaping. "That's the fucked-up thing. I don't even know. Sure, we had our disagreements. What couple doesn't?" He pulls his bottom lip between his teeth, the vein in his neck strained. "But I thought she was happy. She showed no sign she wasn't."

"So this must be recent then," I remark.

"No." He swallows his last sip of whiskey, then signals the bartender for another one, to which he obliges. I would have considered cutting him off, but based on the occasional thoughtful glances, I get the feeling the bartender sympathizes with him. Maybe he's gone through the same thing. Maybe in a cruel twist of fate, I'm surrounded by men whose brothers have run off with their girlfriends. "We broke up about six years ago."

That's good, I tell myself. *Six is less than nine. So it's not the same, right?*

I hold onto every difference I can, not wanting to admit I'm sitting next to the future version of Jessie.

"You and your brother must not be close then, huh?"

He exhales a long breath. "We're actually *very* close. He's my goddamn twin. We were born less than five minutes apart. And this is what happens. You want to know the worst part?"

I don't, but my curiosity gets the best of me. "What's that?"

"He's a great fucking guy. He makes her happy. But so did I." He punches his chest, the muscles in his face tensing. "At least I thought I did."

My eyes are unfocused as I stare at the dozens of bottles lining the back wall of the bar in tiers, the purple and blue mood lighting from overhead tinting the glass.

"You and your brother...," I begin, clearing my voice to steady it. "How are you? With each other, I mean."

"How do you think we are?" he shoots back.

"I don't know," I answer honestly. "Do you think you'll be able to move on from this? Learn to support him because he's happy? If he's your brother, that's all you want, right? For him to be happy, even if it comes at a cost to you?" My eyes beg him to give me the answer I'm desperate for.

He pinches the bridge of his nose as he shakes his head. "He's my brother. Of course I want him to be happy." He draws in a trembling breath. "But he stabbed me in the back. Any other girl…" He raises his voice. "He could have chosen any other girl, yet he chose the one he *knows* I still love. The girl he *knows* I'd still do anything to give my last name to." A sarcastic laugh rips from his throat. "Well, I guess she'll still have my last name. It just won't be because of me."

He throws back his glass, finishing his drink in one gulp. Then he slams the tumbler onto the bar, pushing out of his chair. He staggers before correcting himself. Once he's more sure of his footing, he buttons his suit jacket, doing his best to appear composed.

"Thank you for listening. I'm off to a family dinner where I have to pretend this entire scenario isn't ripping my heart to shreds."

He pulls several large bills from his wallet, then spins on unsteady legs. He only makes it a few steps before I call out.

"Excuse me?"

He slowly faces me, barely able to keep his eyes open. I want to tell him he should probably skip the dinner. I have a feeling it won't end well.

"Yes?"

"How's your family with all of this?"

"We were close, but now…" He exhales deeply. "This has destroyed our family. We'll never be the same again."

"You don't think you'll forgive him? That you'll become a family again?"

"I don't see how. The only reason I'm here now is because my grandfather is in his nineties and this is probably his last opportunity to be with the entire family." He shrugs. "I figure it's best he go out on a high note, thinking we still get along."

"But you don't?"

"We don't."

I nod as I process this story that hits a little too close to home. When I don't immediately say anything, he turns, waving as he heads from the bar. I try to convince myself this encounter doesn't mean anything. That the fact he was sitting in a bar where I was about to meet my own ex-fiancé's brother is irrelevant. It's just a coincidence. It's not a warning of what's to come. There's no hidden meaning. Right?

I tap my fingers against the bartop, my leg bouncing, heart racing. When my phone buzzes, I dart my eyes to it, a spike of adrenaline pumping through me when I see Jessie's name on the screen. We've barely spoken more than a few words to each other since I left the lake house, mostly because of the guilt I felt once I'd slept with Asher. Why would he be calling now?

With shaky hands, I bring the phone up to my ear. "Hey, Jessie."

"Iz! There you are. You've been impossible to get a hold of lately."

"Sorry," I reply in a soft voice. "I've been busy. Family stuff."

"Everything okay?" The authenticity in his tone makes my stomach churn.

"Great," I grit out. "Everything's great." When he doesn't say anything for several excruciatingly long moments, I ask, "Is there a reason you called?"

"I'm in New York."

"I know."

"You do?"

Crap.

"Well... Asher mentioned something about coming to New York," I fumble. "Something about the label?" It's not a lie. Asher did mention Jessie was here.

He's silent for a moment, and I swear my heart can be heard over the club music playing in the bar.

"We had a meeting earlier today to discuss his promo tour. I thought since I was in town, I'd see if you wanted to get together. There's a great bar in the lobby of the Four Seasons. I can meet you there in a bit."

I shoot out of my chair, frantically looking around. "Where are you?"

"Just getting back to the hotel, but if there's somewhere more convenient…"

My pulse skyrocketing, I hail the bartender and signal him for the check. I can't be here if Jessie walks in. What the hell was Asher thinking? Why would he ask me to meet him here if he knew there was a risk of Jessie seeing us? Maybe he doesn't care if Jessie finds out. And maybe I shouldn't, either. But I just had a glimpse into my future. Into Asher's future. The risk is too great. I've now seen that with my own eyes, seen what we'll do to Jessie if we continue down this road.

"Is Asher with you?"

"Nah. Said he had a few errands to run after our meeting. Said something about getting a haircut. I'm pretty sure that's code for a booty call. We both know Asher's not one for cutting his hair. So it'll just be us." He lowers his voice, the sound of the busy New York sidewalk audible in the background. "I'd really like to see you."

The bartender leaves my check, and I yank several bills from my wallet. "I appreciate the offer, but I have a lot going on."

"I knew it was a long shot. Just figured I'd give it a try. I'll always try with you, Iz."

I focus my attention at the hotel lobby as a familiar silhouette dressed in a crisp suit strides through the front doors. His steps lack the confidence they normally have, his shoulders slumped.

"Maybe some other time?" I offer as consolation,

although I have no intention of following through.

"Sure. Sounds good."

"Have a nice evening, Jessie."

"Bye, Iz."

I wait until the elevator doors close with him inside, then frantically pull on my jacket.

"Taking off?" the bartender asks as he dries a martini glass with a towel.

"Yes," I say breathily. "I... I have to go."

"Thought you were meeting someone. At least I assumed you were."

"I was."

"Was?"

"I...," I stammer. "I don't think it's going to work out."

I spin on my heels. I know this is childish and immature, but Asher has a knack for convincing me to stay, to give him a chance. I can't face him. Can't fall under his spell.

"Want me to give him a message?" the bartender calls after me.

I halt in my tracks, facing him. "Excuse me?"

"A message. In case someone walks in looking for you."

I press my lips together, contemplating. I'm about to tell him no when an idea pops into my head. "Do you have any notebook paper?"

"I do."

I head back to the bar, taking the piece of paper he holds out. I grab a pen and scribble down one word before folding it into an origami dove.

Once I'm content with it, I hand it to the bartender. "If you see a man with dark hair, beautiful brown eyes, and an unshaven jawline, can you..." I trail off, my voice catching. "Can you give him this?"

"Any message?"

"This is the message."

"Are you sure?"

Is it that obvious I don't want to go down this path but don't have any other choice?

Choice…

My conversation with Chloe a few weeks ago replays in my mind. *"That's all it comes down to. Living in the past or looking toward a future. Once you decide that, your answer will be clear."*

By going to Asher, I thought I was choosing my future. In a way, I was. But I'd forgotten about *his* future. So tonight, that's what I choose, even if it breaks my heart.

"I am." I give him a sad smile, then hurry out of the bar, holding my breath until I'm safely in a cab. I only make it a few blocks before my phone lights up with an incoming text.

Where are you? I'm in the bar.

Pain shoots through me, the lump in my throat agonizing. I never should have agreed to entertain this fantasy of his. Hell, I never should have slept with him in the first place.

A few more text messages appear, all growing more and more urgent. When my cell rings, I know the bartender must have given him the dove, especially when he continues to call throughout my cab ride to Chelsea, relentless in his need to talk to me.

After paying the driver, I step onto the sidewalk and toward Chloe's building. I press the buzzer for her apartment, praying she's home and will answer. I need her tonight. Need to be with someone who will understand why I did what I did. I type out a quick text to make sure.

It's me. Let me up.

Within seconds, the door clicks. I grab it, dashing into the elevator and riding up to the apartment she now shares with Lincoln, ignoring the constant dinging of my phone. When I emerge onto her floor, she's waiting in her doorway, brows wrinkled. The instant her eyes fall on me, understanding washes over her. She opens her arms, and I walk into them, sobs wracking through me as I relish in my best friend's embrace.

She holds me while my cell continues vibrating with a mixture of calls and messages, each one causing my heart to crack even more until all that's left are millions of pieces.

"Come on, Iz." An arm wrapped around me, Chloe brings me into the apartment, closing the door behind us.

When Lincoln sees us, he gets up from the couch, a questioning look on his face. Chloe shakes her head, silently telling him not to press the subject. Thankfully he doesn't, excusing himself to his office, giving us some privacy. I probably shouldn't have come here, considering Lincoln and Asher were college friends and still stay in touch. I know Chloe, though. She'll make sure Lincoln doesn't say anything if Asher were to reach out to him.

She leads me to the couch, and we sit in silence, staring blankly at the black screen of the TV, tears steadily falling down my cheeks. Finally, Chloe's voice cuts through.

"You look like you could use a drink."

I laugh through my sobs. "I absolutely could."

She squeezes my thigh. "You got it." Standing, she heads into the kitchen just as my phone pings yet again.

I chance one last look at the screen, my heart shattering when I see the anguish in Asher's last text. It

235

doesn't matter it's just words typed out. I can feel his desperation.

> *Please, Isabella. Don't do this. I'm begging you. It's not supposed to end this way. You're my heart. I can't go on without my heart. I love you.*

With a trembling hand, I bring up Asher's contact in my cell, staring at it. "Ditto," I choke out. Then I block his number.

I wish I could have given him a clean break, but we both knew there would never be anything clean about this. It's better I make him hate me before we get in too deep. Before we hurt someone we both care about. This is the right path. It has to be.

Because if it's not, what did I just do?

Chapter Twenty-Seven

"**E**ARTH TO IZZY."

Chloe's voice registers in my brain, snapping me out of my daze. I rip my eyes away from the TV in the corner of Lincoln's home office, returning my attention to the papers spread across the table in front of us.

Over the past few months as we've worked on discovering who my birth mother was, we've turned this into a war room, so to speak. Evie and Chloe had hoped to put the puzzle pieces together and find my birth mother before publishing the article on the JFK baby. That didn't happen. As expected, they hit dead end after dead end. Even enlisting Lincoln's help, who recruited some of the top investigative reporters at the paper, hadn't uncovered anything. It's like my mother vanished.

Feeling like we were out of options, we went ahead and ran a public interest piece three weeks ago. *The JFK Baby — Thirty Years Later.* We'd hoped by plastering it all over the internet, it might encourage people with information to message an email address the magazine set up. Unfortunately, most of those tips turned out to be baseless, just someone looking for their fifteen minutes of fame.

"Are you okay?" Chloe narrows her gaze on me before floating her eyes to the television.

I can't help but look at it again, watching Asher

perform on one of the afternoon talk shows. With the release of his album last month, his star grew bigger and bigger. Now I can barely go a day without hearing or reading his name somewhere. His music is everywhere, as it should be. It doesn't make it any easier, though. Doesn't make me reconsider whether I made the right decision in walking away. Doesn't stop me from imagining what my life would look like had I stayed in the bar that night.

"Fine. Great. Perfect," I answer quickly, grabbing a bunch of papers and pretending to read them, although all the words seem to blur together. I sip on my coffee, hoping it will help clear my mind, but nothing seems to. It hasn't in months. Despite this focus on finding my birth mother, as well as my new job at an outpatient cancer clinic here in the city, Asher still consumes most of my thoughts.

Will it always be this way?

"You know, you can come tomorrow."

Coffee spews out of my nose and I cough several times before flinging my wide eyes to Chloe. "What are you talking about?" I choke out.

"Tomorrow night. His concert. You should come with us. It's the start of the tour. You deserve to be there. He wouldn't have had an album to tour if it weren't for you."

I avoid her eyes, grabbing a napkin and dabbing coffee off the papers. "He would have eventually."

"You don't know that."

"Just like I don't know he wouldn't have. It's okay. It's better this way."

"For whom? Asher? Or you?"

This is the first time Chloe has pushed the topic of Asher since the night I appeared at her door a crying mess. In the months that followed, he'd attempted to

238

reach out to me through email. When that turned futile, he'd sought Lincoln's help, who'd remained neutral, not wanting to get involved. If Asher knew where I lived, he probably would have shown up at my apartment. Thankfully, it never came to that. I surmise he must have accepted that I didn't want to talk to him, the calls to Lincoln and emails to me having dwindled, becoming nonexistent once his album dropped.

"For Asher," I argue with a hushed tone so my voice doesn't carry into the hallway and throughout the apartment. "I did what was necessary for Asher."

"Mmm-hmm."

"What? I did."

"If that's what you need to tell yourself, Iz."

"Do you think I wanted to walk away from him again? There had to be a reason he asked me to meet him in *that* bar where I'd run into a man who'd been through the same thing we were about to do to Jessie. It put everything into perspective. Made it all too real. And Asher would eventually realize it wouldn't work. He'd go on with his life, enjoying fame and fortune, while I struggled to put the pieces of my life back together. I can't do that to myself again."

"And there it is." Her tone is laced with a hint of superiority.

"What?" I cock a brow, staring intently at her.

"Your real reason for walking away."

"I told you. It was so Asher wouldn't make a decision he'd come to regret."

Chloe shakes her head, angling toward me, eyes on fire. "You can't bullshit a bullshitter. Don't forget. I went through the same thing with Lincoln, convinced myself I did what I had to in order to protect him. But you know the real reason I pushed him away?"

"Because your feelings for him scared you shitless.

You worried when all the obstacles to your relationship were removed, it wouldn't be the same. That he'd no longer want you."

Chloe places her hand on my bicep, and I raise my gaze to hers. "More or less." She smiles before her expression turns serious once more. "But trust me. You have nothing to worry about. I saw the way he looked at you in Vegas."

"That was over a year ago."

"I also saw the way he looked at you while you dated his brother. Jessie certainly never looked at you that way."

"It doesn't matter. He can look at me like his heart physically can't beat without me—"

"And he does."

"That doesn't change anything. I will always be his brother's fiancée. Not ex. But fiancée. I can't change that. I can't go back and rewind the clock. If I could, you know damn well I would. Maybe I would have grown some *cojones* and walked up to the hot lead singer I couldn't get enough of. But I didn't. I stayed in my corner and worshiped him from afar. I tried to be happy with Jessie, although I knew something was missing."

"Then why don't you go after that something missing? Tell him you made a mistake? That you're finally ready for whatever this is? That you're ready to take a risk?"

I consider her question. Why *don't* I go to him? Jessie *did* send me passes to the concert tomorrow night. I could very easily go, talk to Asher. But I'm not sure that's how our story is supposed to go, not with everything that's at stake. I need some sort of assurance or divine intervention telling me this thing with Asher is worth the eventual destruction we'll cause.

"I need a sign," I explain.

She gives me a questioning look, eyes scrunched together. "A sign?" Then she blows out a laugh. "You've been spending too much time with Nora."

"We only got together in Vegas because of chance. And chance brought us back together a few months ago. Granted, it was in the shape of Jessie, or Grams, but still. Had they not intervened, we never would have seen each other again. And I walked away because of chance, because of the strange coincidence of meeting a man whose ex was about to marry his brother. I could be wrong, but with everything that's at stake, I need a sign we're meant to be together."

"If we all left everything up to chance, we'd never live. Sometimes you have to take the wheel and go the direction *you* want to go."

"That may be true." A smile curves my lips, my eyes shining with nostalgia. "But do you know what Grams said my first night at the lake house this winter?"

"What's that?"

"That true love is like a boomerang. You can run, but it will find you. Maybe that's what I need in order to know this is real, that it's worth the risk. I need the boomerang to come back."

Chloe expels an exasperated sigh. "Sometimes I wish you weren't so goddamn stubborn. If it were me and there was amazing sex on the line, I'd be lacing up my running shoes and waiting for them to fire that dang starting pistol."

I shake my head, grateful for the break in tension. "And that's a big deal for you. You hate running."

"Good sex is worth it." She winks.

"Worth what?"

A deep voice cuts through, and we look up to see Lincoln hovering in the doorway. His tall frame fills the space as he leans against the doorjamb, his arms crossed. He wears his usual jeans and blazer, his dark hair well-groomed, as it usually is, his jaw sporting a bit of scruff.

"Torturing myself with a run." She cranes her head back as he approaches, treating her to a sweet kiss.

"That's certainly saying something. You hate running."

"That's what *I* said," I offer.

"Hopefully that good sex isn't with some other man. I'm not sure I'm cut out for prison."

"No way, baby. You keep me more than satisfied." Her eyes skate over him, a devilish glint within.

"On *that* note…" I start to push out of my chair. "I'm going to head out."

"You don't have to," Chloe protests.

"It's fine. I need to run by the store anyway."

"Actually, if you have a minute, there's something I'd like to show you," Lincoln interjects.

"What is it?" I lower myself back into my chair, his serious tone giving me pause.

"One of our reporters sat down with a body language expert on an unrelated story. Decided to show her the video footage from that day at the airport to see what she could pick up from your birth mother."

"An expert in body language? Is there such a thing?"

"There's an expert in almost everything these days."

He sits in the chair beside me and pulls his laptop out of his messenger bag, setting it on the table. Chloe scoots out of her chair, heading around and peering over Lincoln's shoulder. He brings up a video file and hits the space bar.

"You've seen this before," he states as surveillance footage displays the busy terminal at JFK.

This was part of the problem investigators ran into

when they'd originally tried to figure out what happened. The sheer number of people prevented anyone from getting a clear picture.

"The first thing our expert noticed was how anxious your birth mother was." He points to the screen, and I watch a woman sit in a chair in a gate area. "Look how she repeatedly bounces her leg. She keeps her head lowered and the hood of her sweatshirt pulled up, but you can still notice her head constantly moving, as if keeping tabs on her surroundings."

"Probably to make sure no one would notice when she dumped me."

Lincoln pauses the video, blowing out a breath as he lifts his gaze to mine. "I don't think that's it. I don't think she had a choice but to leave you behind."

I furrow my brow. "I don't—"

"Look at this."

He hits play again. We watch a few more seconds, then Lincoln freezes the video again. Instead of sitting in a slumped position as she had been, her spine is straight. "Right there."

"She saw something," I murmur.

"Our expert thought so, too."

Lincoln continues the video. I can almost feel my mother's eyes darting around, although I can't make out any of her facial features with the hood pulled over her head.

"Now, watch this."

I squint, observing my birth mother remaining completely still, apart from her shoulders.

"Our expert opined she was taking several deep breaths to calm herself before making her move right…about…now."

At that instant, she gingerly raises herself from the chair, her motions slow, as if not to draw any attention.

She places a hand on my head where it stuck out from the baby carrier attached to her body, then bent over to pick up a black duffel bag.

She maneuvered through the gate area, glancing over her shoulder briefly before continuing in the opposite direction. The camera angle changes to a different view.

"So she went to the ladies' room. We knew that."

"Yes, but look at this."

I refocus my eyes on the screen as she disappears into the bathroom. Only a few seconds go by before two men dressed in black approach. They appear as if they're about to stroll right in when a member of airport security walks up to them, directing them to the men's room instead, assuming they were looking for the bathroom, not someone *inside* the bathroom. They appear to thank him, then head in the direction he pointed.

"I've seen all this before," I argue.

"I know," Lincoln says, "but stay with me on this. Trust me."

I nod, returning my attention to the screen, watching the timecode tick by. Then a figure emerges from the bathroom, the hood still hiding her face.

"We didn't pick up on this before because of how grainy the video was."

"It's still pretty grainy," Chloe comments.

"Yes, but it's a lot cleaner than it was. Watch." He points to the woman as she seems to draw in more deep breaths, as evidenced by the substantial rise and fall of her shoulders. Then she turns toward the water fountain, bending down to take a sip. "Right here." He slams down the space bar, pausing the video.

"I'm not sure I understand."

"She's not holding your head. Before, when she had

to bend to pick up that duffel bag, she made sure to support your head, even though the angle was slight. But here." He uses his finger to circle my birth mother bent over the water fountain. "She's bent even more, yet not holding on at all. And look what's missing."

"The duffel bag. That's what I was found in. Wrapped in blankets with my head peeking out. This doesn't prove anything. It could have been part of her plan all along. Maybe she stuffed a baby doll into the duffel bag to make sure I'd fit when she ditched me," I argue, although I'm less and less confident of my original belief.

"I can see why you'd think that, but keep watching." Lincoln hits the space bar again and the video resumes.

I watch as she walks away from the bathroom. When she's almost out of view, I notice her stop. I squint, seeing the two men who'd tried to walk into the bathroom approach her. She doesn't fight. Doesn't resist. Nothing. Instead, she places her hand on what I can only assume to be a doll's head, bouncing and soothing it.

"She's pretending I'm still in there," I murmur.

"It appears that way."

"So? She still dumped me in the bathroom. We're still no closer to figuring out who she was."

"No. But I think we're closer to finding out *why*. She was trying to keep you safe, Iz."

"I don't—"

"Our body language expert agreed. I think your mother was on the run, as evidenced by her obvious anxiety as she sat in the gate area. We were able to track down flight schedules for Christmas of that year. The flight leaving from that gate was headed to Toronto, Canada. It was delayed by over an hour. I think she was running from someone. Maybe an abusive boyfriend."

He narrows his gaze. "Maybe something much worse. I think she prepared for the possibility of getting caught, which was why she had that doll in her bag. Once she ditched you, it was only a matter of time until someone would alert the authorities to an abandoned baby. She had a very short window of opportunity to get herself and those two men out of the airport. Which was why she didn't fight. In fact, our expert thinks she *intentionally* let them approach, then proceeded out of the terminal with them. As you know, after that, the trail goes cold."

My brain spins as I process this story, toiling it over in my mind. "I just… It seems like a stretch. Doesn't it?" I glance over my shoulder at Chloe, who is typically the cynical one.

"Actually, he might be right. And I'm not just saying that because I'm married to him. If your birth mother didn't want you, why would she have gone through all the trouble of wrapping you in blankets? And why ditch you in an airport?"

"But the flight manifest… If Lincoln's theory is right, there should have been someone on it who forfeited her seat when she didn't board on time. That didn't happen. We've combed through the police interviews of everyone on that manifest, including those who missed the flight and forfeited their seat. Every single one checked out."

Chloe shakes her head. "It could have been tampered with."

"Would someone really do that?"

"You'd be surprised what some people would do to cover up the truth."

"But what truth?"

"That's what we're trying to find out." Lincoln squeezes my hand, giving me a reassuring look. "Trust me. There's a story here. And I won't stop until we get to the bottom of it."

Chapter Twenty-Eight

MY MIND REELS as I sift through the witness interviews that were conducted as part of the investigation into my birth mother. I've lost count of the number of times I've read these over the past several hours. I keep hoping to find something, anything that will tell me whether Lincoln is right. A part of me wants him to be. I like the idea that my birth mother didn't abandon me because she didn't want me, which is what I've told myself since I learned I was adopted. But another part of me thinks his theory is too farfetched to be real.

My phone ringing cuts through, and I tear my eyes away from the papers, Nora's name popping up on the screen.

"Hey," I answer.

"I need a date," she replies without a greeting.

"Sorry. You're not my type. And I don't put out."

"Ha. Ha. Ha. Seriously, Iz. You, me, and a new club in the Village. One of my clients is doing the PR for it. Got me on the guest list. I don't want to go alone, so I called you."

"Did you only call me because I'm single?" I prop my phone up to my ear with my shoulder, flipping through the papers in front of me, half-listening, half-reading.

"No. Well, yes, but that's not the only reason. I only have a plus one, not a plus three."

"Then shouldn't you take your plus one?"

There's a slight pause before she whines, "Come on, Iz. There are free drinks. You need a night away from trying to put together the puzzle pieces of your life. I love you, but this whole search is consuming you. Don't get me wrong. If I were trying to solve a thirty-year mystery, it would probably consume me, too. But I want some time with my friend."

I close my eyes, blowing out a long breath. Since I started down this proverbial rabbit hole, I've been obsessed with learning the truth. In a way, it helps distract me from everything else in my life, namely Asher York. Then again, I've allowed it to distract me from other parts of my life, too, like my friends. Maybe a night out is exactly what I need.

"Fine. I'll be your plus one."

"Yay," she cheers excitedly. "I'll text you the address. Meet me at eleven."

"Eleven? So late?" God, I sound old. A few months ago, I'd consider eleven early. But that was before I started working a nine-to-five job.

"Yes, Izzy. Eleven. Of our little circle, you're the last one I thought would consider that late."

"Okay, okay. I'll be there."

"You'd better. Or I'll hunt you down. I do know where you live."

"See you soon," I sing, then end the call before dragging myself into the shower.

* * *

A few minutes past eleven, my Uber pulls up in front of a nondescript brick building in Greenwich Village. A line of people waiting to get into what appears to be the newest hotspot in town snakes around the block. I step onto the sidewalk, looking up and down the street for any sign of Nora's strawberry blonde hair. It doesn't take me long to spot her as she waves me over.

"There you are!" she exclaims as I approach. "I thought you were standing me up."

"Never." We exchange hugs.

"You clean up good, Iz." She scans my fitted black dress. I figured since I spend most of my time in scrubs, may as well wear something sexy. And with the slit going up my thigh and the way the dress pushes up my chest, it definitely qualifies as sexy. "Guys won't be able to take their eyes off you."

"You're not so bad yourself," I comment, gesturing to her simple V-neck green dress she paired with leopard print heels.

"Thanks. Now, let's go drink for free." She loops her arm through mine.

"I like the sound of that."

She leads me toward a large man standing by a roped off area and gives him her name. He checks his clipboard, then pulls back the rope, allowing us to enter.

The instant we step inside, I'm taken by surprise at my surroundings. I expected a dark club with thumping music, girls wearing dresses that don't leave much to the imagination. Instead, it's more low-key and laid back. Small tables fill the area, the focal point a stage against the far wall where a small ensemble plays jazz.

"Where's Jeremy tonight?" I ask once we're shown to a table in a separate VIP area and a waitress returns with our drinks. I take a sip of my vodka tonic, lowering it when I notice Nora's hesitant expression.

"Umm…" She chews on her lower lip as she seems to look everywhere but at me.

"Nora, is—"

"He's gay," she blurts out as the song comes to an

end, silence seeming to ring through the room. Or maybe it feels that way because of my complete and utter shock.

Her admission echoes around us until the audience finally claps. I join in, albeit halfheartedly, as I lean toward her. "What do you mean? Jeremy's not gay. I have no problem with anyone who *is*, but—"

"I know. It's crazy. Especially considering how we met. Why the hell would he be on Tinder looking to hook up with a woman if he's gay?" She throws back her rocks glass filled with a dark liquid, practically finishing it before returning it to the table.

Tonight now makes sense, why she was so desperate to have me agree to come. She needed someone to talk to. Sure, she could have confided in Chloe or Evie, but they're married. There's something to be said about commiserating with single people about relationship troubles.

"I haven't felt things were right for a while. I thought it was all in my head. That it was because we were both working so much. About a month ago, I decided to surprise him when he was out of town on a business trip. Called his assistant and got all his travel information, including the hotel where he was staying. Unfortunately, I was the one who ended up being surprised when he answered the door to his room, fresh from a shower, a man in a similar state of undress sitting on the mussed-up bed."

"Oh, Nora..."

"And the funny thing? He was so sweet about it. I want to be mad at him, but I can't."

"He still lied to you. Still went behind your back."

"That's what I thought at first, too, until I put myself in his shoes. You've met his family. They're...conservative."

I snort a laugh. Calling them conservative is putting it mildly. When I went to Hawaii for their wedding, Jeremy's parents constantly asked me to clear their plates or fetch them a drink, mistaking me for the waitstaff because of the tone of my skin. It took every ounce of resolve I possessed to bite my tongue at the constant comments of "all Mexicans look the same to me". I can imagine how they'd react if they knew their son wasn't straight.

"It broke my heart to hear him talk about how miserable he'd been," Nora continues.

"But if he were miserable, why did he go on Tinder in the first place? And why would he ask you to marry him?"

"He hoped he'd get used to being with a woman. But it doesn't work that way. You can't just flip the switch."

I shift my attention forward, nodding in rhythm with the music. I'd always thought Nora and Jeremy had the perfect relationship. She was the first of our circle to get engaged, then married. They both appeared so happy. Maybe not everything is as it seems.

"What are you going to do?" I ask after a while.

"I'm filing for divorce. Jeremy is agreeable. He doesn't plan on contesting anything, so unless there are any surprises, I'll be Nora Tremblay again by Labor Day."

"I'm sorry," I offer, covering her hand with mine.

"Don't be." She smiles sadly. "It's part of life." She tilts back her glass, swallowing the last of her drink.

"Look on the bright side," I begin, my voice chipper. "Now you can enjoy all the eye candy here with me." I gesture to a couple of tall, well-dressed men standing by the bar, obviously checking us out. "Hell, you can even take one home if you really wanted."

"I'm not sure I want anyone else," Nora says. "Not

yet anyway. It's more important I fall in love with myself again."

I give her a sympathetic smile, squeezing her hand, a silent encouragement. Nora's imminent divorce from Jeremy hits me harder than it should. On the outside, they were the picture-perfect couple. I honestly thought they'd be one of those couples who died together when they were old and gray. Instead, Nora's filing for divorce before they even hit their one-year wedding anniversary. It makes me wonder whether any couple can really survive.

"Thank you," a gravelly voice comes over the speakers after the band finishes another number. It almost reminds me of Louis Armstrong. Low. Raspy. Soulful. "You're a fantastic group of people. But this party's just getting started. Next up, we have a little surprise. A last-minute addition, a man who got his start studying the blues. And you can hear it in his music to this very day. Give it up for the one, the only, Asher York!"

I stiffen, my wide eyes shooting to the stage, where I see a ruggedly handsome man emerging. He nods in acknowledgment of the warm welcome, but doesn't smile enthusiastically. That's never been his style. His stage presence is more...aloof. Mysterious. Sexy.

"Are you okay?" Nora presses, her hand covering my forearm.

I rip my gaze from the stage, meeting her curious stare. I never told her or Evie about Asher. They weren't part of my life when I was engaged to Jessie, so they'd have no reason to know about Asher. The only person who does is Chloe.

I part my lips, a deer caught in the headlights, uncertain how to explain why I'm this on edge over the fact that one of the top musical acts in the country is mere feet away from me.

"I'm fine." I plaster on a fake smile, but it doesn't assuage her suspicion. "Just surprised someone like Asher York would be here," I flounder, unable to shake the heat of Nora's stare studying my every move.

"Thank you," Asher says into the microphone. A stagehand approaches with a black acoustic-electric guitar, and Asher takes it. After slinging it over his body, he plays a quick chord to check the tuning before stepping back up to the microphone. "This is a great little club, isn't it?"

The audience erupts in cheers and whistles, except me. I remain frozen in place, soaking up every single syllable he utters.

"The owner, Guy Frederickson, has a similar club up in Boston, which is where I grew up. In Boston music circles, it is *the* club. The place you want to play if you're going to be somebody. And I desperately wanted to be somebody. I must have sent him a new demo every week, begging to play in his club. You know what he told me?" He pauses, a nostalgic smile lighting up his eyes.

I should leave before Asher realizes I'm here, but I'm transfixed, mesmerized by the way he tells a story, how comfortable he looks in front of all these people. Granted, it's not remotely close to the size of the audience he'll play in front of tomorrow night, but this place can still easily hold several hundred people. A far cry from the basement bars where drunk men shouted for his band to play "Freebird".

"He told me if I wanted to play his club, I needed to find my soul. I thought that meant playing the blues, like he does so very well. So I studied the blues. Watched the greats play. Listened to it for days, months. Wrote my own stuff.

"After a while, I was absolutely certain he'd book me. I knew the blues. Up. Down. Left. Right. Inside. Outside. Put all the elements of the quintessential blues song into my work, too. And yet…" He tilts his head, pausing briefly. "He said no." He chuckles slightly, everyone joining in. I can't help but laugh myself.

"Next time I dropped off a demo, he pulled me aside. He said, 'Kid…'" He mimics a rough voice, pretending to wrap his arm around imaginary shoulders, "'let me give you a piece of advice. You don't play the blues. The blues play you.'"

"That's right!" a man from the crowd yells in agreement.

"At first, I thought he was just a little tipsy. If any of you know Guy, you know he likes his coffee strong and his whiskey neat. Sometimes at the same time. But he went on to explain. He told me I hadn't yet mastered the blues because I'd never experienced a soul-crushing loss. Because I'd never hit rock bottom. Because I'd never experienced…love."

In an instant, the atmosphere in the room shifts. It's no longer one of nostalgia and appreciation for the man who made tonight possible. It's more solemn.

"I couldn't believe my ears. I was convinced I'd experienced all of that. I'd lost a dear friend in high school." A sad smile builds on his mouth. "I loved her like a sister. I didn't think anything could possibly top that feeling of absolute agony. When I wrote my music, I returned to that place, those memories, those feelings. But still, Guy told me it wasn't enough. I hate to say it, but he was right. Losing this friend *wasn't* the soul-crushing loss I thought it was. Since then, I've experienced another loss… A deeper loss."

A hush falls over the crowd, not so much as the clanking of ice against glass sounding in the club, everyone on the edge of their seats to learn the rest of his story.

"You'd probably think once my music got radio time and I started selling out stadiums, Guy would have no problem booking me at one of his clubs." He laughs slightly, shaking his head. "Well, you're wrong. Because he still refused, said I still hadn't found my soul. Until I sent him a demo of this song about a week ago. I guess it changed his mind because he called me up. With no greeting, he said the words I've been waiting to hear out of his mouth for over ten years. 'Son, the blues finally found you.'" He scans the crowd. I tense, worried he'll notice me, but his gaze never reaches me. "This is 'Throw Away My Love'."

He steps back from the microphone, the lights dimming on the stage, apart from a lone spotlight shining on him. I hold my breath as his fingers find their position on the frets and he brings the pic up to the strings. Then the sound of a simple, sparse melody comes forward, like a whisper at first, before it vanishes.

When his voice fills the room, there's a collective sigh as the tension rolls off everyone. I lean closer, grasping onto every single one of his beautiful lyrics. But in that beauty is pain. Is heartache. Is soul-crushing agony. He sings of being cold, despite the sunlight bathing him. Of feeling poor, despite his lavish house and furnishings. Of feeling alone, despite being surrounded by people who call him a friend. All because the woman he'd risk it all for threw away the greatest gift he could give her — his love.

I search my memory for this song being on his latest album. I was there when he penned each of them. This isn't one of them. Which can only mean one thing — he wrote it after I walked away.

"Oh god…" I cover my mouth with my hand to hide

my trembling chin as the lyrics dig their way into the very depths of my soul.

I've seen Asher perform more times than I can count. I've always found myself hypnotized by the raw emotion he's able to evoke so easily from the crowd. But I've never experienced this, like I can physically feel his heart being ripped from his chest and displayed in front of him while it still beats. I wonder if that's what it felt like when he walked into that bar and was handed an origami dove.

As the final note rings out, the entire place is still as they process the magic they just experienced. The anguish. The despair. The unmistakable heartache. Then everyone simultaneously jumps to their feet, the applause thunderous. It's true. This song is evidence of the fact that the blues found Asher.

Because of me.

I snap my eyes to Nora, frantic. "Can we go?" I ask with a quiver, tears streaming down my cheeks.

She studies me for a moment, a thousand questions swirling in her gaze. But instead of pushing the topic, she nods. "Of course."

We push through the throng of people standing and cheering. I keep my head down, not wanting to draw attention to myself. But when a heat prickles my nape, I slow my steps. Despite my brain telling my body to keep going, to not look back, I don't listen. When I glance at the stage, despondent brown eyes lock with mine. I don't know how long I stand here, unable to move. Could be hours. Could be seconds. All I know is I've never seen Asher so…lost.

Then an icy stare washes over him, sending a chill down my spine. It's unlike any look he's ever given me. I deserve it. Deserve his hatred, his animosity, his disgust. It's what I wanted. But it still hurts.

My lips parting, I shake my head, wishing he could read the warring thoughts in my mind. But he can't. So I simply mouth, *I'm sorry*, then follow Nora out of the club.

Chapter Twenty-Nine

"ARE YOU SURE you'll be okay?" Nora asks, walking me to the door of the Union Square apartment she bought with Jeremy less than a year ago. Most of his things are gone, a reminder of how fleeting everything in this world can be.

After we made our escape from the club, we came back here, where I finally told her everything. My engagement to Jessie. The reason I broke it off. My one night in Vegas with Asher. Jessie reaching out in January. His proposition. Spending two weeks with Asher up at the lake house. Why I walked away. She didn't judge, didn't tell me I made a mistake. She simply encouraged me to follow my heart.

I wish I knew which direction my heart was heading.

"I'll be fine."

"Text me when you get home?"

"I will."

I give her a hug, then make my way out of her building and emerge onto the sidewalk. As I keep an eye out for the Uber I'd ordered, I relish in the peacefulness, the streets that are normally packed with cars much less populated after two in the morning. So instead of waiting for my ride that's a few minutes away, I cancel it, taking this opportunity to walk through the city I love.

I'm not sure how much time passes as I wander aimlessly, allowing my heart to lead me in the direction

I should go. It's not until the neighborhoods transition from the frenzied atmosphere of Union Square to more residential — at least as residential as one can get in Manhattan — that I take stock of where I am. I don't need to even look at a cross street to know I'm in the Gramercy Park area, and it's not because the familiar entrance to the residents-only park is right in front of me. Only one section of this city boasts such stunning architecture, townhouses covered with ivy. As long as I can remember, it's been my dream to afford a place like this, an impossibility on a nurse's salary.

I cross the street and meander along the perimeter of the park, basking in the brisk air. Although the temperature during the day has warmed up now that it's May, nighttime can still be chilly. I run my hand along the metal fence, my fingers tracing each spike. It's oddly symbolic of life. Ups and downs. Walls keeping people out. Doors trapping people in. Outsiders wanting a taste of what it's like inside. Insiders wanting nothing more than to have the simple life of those beyond the walls. I wonder if it's possible to ever achieve true happiness. I wonder if it's possible for *me* to be happy.

As I near the gate, I continue the same up and down movement, stopping when my finger doesn't meet with metal as it should. I turn, squinting, noticing the door didn't click shut after the last person left. The practical voice in my head tells me to pull it closed and continue on my stroll through Manhattan. But I can't ignore the other voice, the one shouting at me that it's a sign, a beacon directing me forward.

I bring a hand up to the door, electricity vibrating through me the instant it lands on the metal. I pause, then push on the gate, expelling a breath when it squeaks open. I duck inside, ensuring the door is closed behind me before venturing farther into the park that's remained like a dream to me for years. Now I know why they've kept it private. It's serene, tranquil, a complete change from the rest of Manhattan, the only source of illumination that of the stars and ambient light coming from the surrounding buildings and streetlamps.

My friends would flip if they learned I was walking through a park after two in the morning. A park I'd snuck into upon noticing the door had been left ajar. I can hear their voices in my head, particularly Evie's, telling me this is how all episodes of *Criminal Minds* begin. But something calls to me to head deeper inside.

Spying a bench along a cobblestone path, I lower myself, allowing my feet a short reprieve. Allowing my brain a short reprieve, too. If I didn't think I'd get arrested for vagrancy, I'd sleep on this bench tonight. I don't want to leave this park. Don't want to go back to reality. In here, I'm in a bubble where I don't have to live with the decisions of my past or the uncertainty of my future. And I miss my bubble.

I close my eyes, leaning my head back, breathing in the city air. I imagine I'm sitting on the dock at Grams' lake house, the moon shining brightly above me, Asher strumming a sweet song on his guitar, his gentle voice lulling me to sleep. The fantasy in my mind feels so real, I expect to be met with the darkness of the lake in front of me when I open my eyes. Instead, I'm still in New York. Still unable to forget the one man I can never have. Still wishing things were different.

On a long sigh, I reluctantly raise myself from the bench, but stop when the same, melodic guitar strains filter around me. I freeze, not breathing, expecting it to go away as I return from my fantasy. But it doesn't.

My heart rate increasing, I pad on light feet along the

path and toward the music. It isn't loud by any stretch of the imagination. For anyone walking along the sidewalk abutting the park, they'd probably think it just ambient music coming from one of the many townhouses. But I'd recognize that sound anywhere. Just like you can distinguish the shuffle of a familiar pair of footsteps walking through a house, I can pick out Asher's unique pattern of strumming a guitar. I'm sure of it.

I round a bend, stopping abruptly when Asher comes into view. Sitting on a bench, one leg propped up on the other to help balance his guitar, his fingers move along the strings with dexterity and ease as he sings the same song he did earlier tonight.

Not wanting to interrupt, I remain in the darkness, falling under his spell as I admire him from afar, like I did so often when I dated Jessie. It takes every ounce of resolve I have not to break down in tears at his heartfelt lyrics, singing to the ghost of the love he once shared... With me.

When the final note rings out and a stark silence falls over us, every little sound seems amplified. The increasing inhale of my lungs. The racing beat of my heart. The gripping pain of regret.

"Why did you do it?"

My breath hitches, and I'm unsure if he's speaking to me or the metaphorical me. Then, somehow, his eyes shift to mine, our gazes locking.

On trembling legs, I step out from the shadows, walking toward him. "How did you know I was here?"

He blows out a laugh that borders on sardonic. "Don't you realize by now?"

I shake my head. "Realize what?"

"I feel you, Izzy," he admits in a choked voice. "In here." He brings his hand to his chest. "I thought I was losing my mind earlier when I walked into that club and felt a vice squeezing my heart. I was ready to have Jessie take me to the ER to see if I was having a heart attack or something. It was the same way I felt..." He trails off, but I know what he was about to say. It was what happened when he walked into that bar and realized I wouldn't be coming. "Then when I saw you, I realized *why* it felt like someone was trying to rip my damn heart out of my chest."

"Asher..." I step toward him, but he holds up his hand, stopping me.

"Just tell me why you did it."

"Did what?"

He looks at me through sad eyes. "You know what."

I ponder my response, ruminating it in my mind. I could keep lying to him, make him think what we had wasn't real in order to protect him from making a mistake he'd come to regret. But he'd never believe it. He always could see through all my lies.

"You know why." My gaze unwavering, I walk toward him once more. This time, he doesn't halt my advance.

"I do." He stands as I approach, closing the last bit of distance between us. His scent wraps around me, a rush of adrenaline running through me at the familiarity of being in his universe. "You did what you thought you had to. What you *always* do when facing a path that scares you shitless."

"And what's that?"

"You fold."

"Either way I looked at it, I had a losing hand."

He grasps my chin, lifting my eyes to his. I don't pull back from his touch. Instead, I crave it. Need it. Am desperate for it.

"Is that all I am to you? A losing hand?"

I swallow hard, the truth falling from my lips with ease. "I don't know *what* you are to me. All I know is I'll do anything to protect your relationship with your brother."

"Even if it means hurting me?" he asks in a strained voice.

"You'll find another woman. You can't find another brother."

He peers at me with intense eyes, his grip on my chin tightening to a point that's almost painful before releasing me with a strangled cry, walking away. His fingers burrow into his hair and tug at it. When he returns his gaze to me, it's fiery, animalistic. Everything that's been missing from my life for too long now.

"Do you honestly think that?"

"Jessie's your *only* brother. I—"

"Not that. Do you honestly believe I'd ever find another woman like you? That I'd ever *want* another woman who isn't you?"

He speaks with such passion, such zeal, it makes me want to lose myself in his arms. But no amount of need, of hunger, of love can rewrite the stars. No matter what, Jessie got to me first.

"I wish I could give you the answer you want, Asher. But we can't exist outside of the bubble. Our *love* can't exist outside of the bubble. You felt it in Vegas when Jessie showed up, yanking us back to reality. The same thing happened when we left the lake house. We were yanked back to the real world. We just didn't realize it at the time. Don't get me wrong. I love our bubble. I'd give anything to stay in that bubble for the rest of my days—"

"We can," he says desperately, taking my hands in his. "If you'd stop pushing me away. If you'd take a risk for once in your life."

"At what cost?" I search his eyes for an answer. Then I sigh, pulling away from him. "I love that you're a dreamer. But that's not me. My life is ruled by science, by practical considerations. It's always what has spoken to me. I like that an answer is either black or white. No in between. No gray area. That's what the bubble is. An in between. We can't live there, not without paying the price."

I turn from him and walk away, needing to get out of his presence before I allow his fantasy to consume me once more. It can't happen. Not again. I've already fallen for it twice now. I can't do it a third time.

"Do you love me?" he shouts before I can take more than a few steps.

I stop and face him, mouth agape. Why did he have to ask this question?

He strides toward me, determined, pausing when he's a few inches away, chest heaving, Adam's apple bobbing up and down. "Do you love me?" he repeats.

I avert my eyes, despite the lack of light. It's another layer of protection against the way Asher can peer straight to my soul. "I don't know why that—"

"*Goddammit*, Izzy. Just answer the question," he thunders. If there were any walls surrounding us, I imagine him punching his fist into it. "No more lies. No more games. No more making yourself unhappy just to salvage my relationship with Jessie. Do. You. Love. Me?"

I know what I want to say. What I *should* say in order to keep my distance. This is my opportunity to push him away, give him a reason to forget about me. But as I peer into his mesmerizing eyes that have always gazed upon me with more love and dedication than any other man, I'm not sure I *want* him to forget about me.

I told Chloe I needed a sign. A boomerang. Some big

265

cosmic intervention telling me it's okay. That he's worth the risk. That despite this body-crushing fear it will all end in a fiery mess, it will be worth it. Even I have to admit that running into Asher not once, but twice in less than twenty-four hours is a huge blinking sign that could rival those in Las Vegas.

"Boomerang."

He exhales, every inch of him relaxing before he returns his blazing eyes to mine. To anyone else, it would be an innocuous word, but not to us.

"When I saw you scribbled that on the origami dove you left for me at the bar back in March, I was confused. Or maybe just blinded by having my heart broken. But after a few days, I realized what you were trying to tell me. That you were scared, and if we were meant to be together, we'd find our way back to each other." He clutches my face in his hands, his hold unwavering. "Tonight is proof we have, that we'll always find our way back to each other. But I need to know. Are you still scared?"

"Fucking petrified."

"So scared that you're going to keep running, knowing this damn boomerang is real?" He adjusts his stance, our bodies moving closer to each other with every beat of our hearts. "That our love will keep finding you?"

"I'm scared of what being with you means…for you, for us. I've been drowning in my feelings for a long time now, and it terrifies me. I worry you'll eventually decide I'm not worth the risk. That's why I keep coming up for air, keep pushing you away." I smile slightly. "But the truth is I'd rather drown with you than breathe with anyone else."

"It's about damn time." His voice comes out like a growl as he presses his hand against my lower back and tugs my body against his, his jaw tightening, the promise of his kiss a heartbeat away. "Now tell me."

"Tell you what?"

"Those words. The ones I told you to keep safe until we were outside of the bubble. I'm never going back to the bubble. Not with you. I want you all the time. So if you're ready to have more than just the bubble, I need those words. Your promise. Your devotion. I need to know you're mine. That I can finally have all of you. Your body." He brings his lips to my neck, brushing the skin. "Your soul." His mouth moves to my cheek, leaving another delicate kiss. Then he frames my face once more, making it so I'm unable to escape, to hide, to run. "Your heart. I need your heart more than anything."

"You've always possessed my heart, Asher. Always." I pause, steeling myself. Then my mouth curves into a smile. "I love you."

He exhales a long breath, the strain on his muscles falling off him in waves. "You have no idea how long I've waited to hear you say those words."

"I think I do."

His fingers thread into my hair, tilting my head back. He licks his lips, his gaze trained on my mouth, desire flickering within. Finally, his lips land on mine. I sigh into our kiss, a spark shooting through me at my first taste of him after several months. I'd expected our first kiss to be an intense explosion of want, need, and lust. But it's not. It's beautiful. Respectful. Honest. Everything Asher is to me.

When he gradually pulls away, his fingers trace over the lines of my face, stopping on my lower lip and brushing the pad of his thumb over the swollen flesh. A devilish glint fills his eyes as he watches my reaction to his touch.

"Let's go home."

I smile at the meaning in his request. Most men would say "come home with me" or some other variation, simply wanting me to come to their bed for the night. Not Asher. His invitation is authentic. He wants me to come home. To him. Where I belong.

Lifting myself onto my toes, I feather my lips against his. "With you, I *am* home."

Chapter Thirty

"ASHER, SLOW DOWN," I whisper-shout as we rush out of the park. "I'm not exactly wearing the best footwear for making a mad dash up the street."

He slows his steps, focusing on my heel-clad feet. Pausing, he seems to weigh his options. Then he slings his guitar over his body, shifting the instrument so it rests against his back. Before I can react, he sweeps me into his arms in a cradle hold.

"What are you doing?" I squeal.

"I can't wait another second to have you. If this gets you into my bed quicker, then it's what I need to do."

"You act like a convict who's just been released and is about to get laid for the first time since getting locked up."

"That's exactly what I *feel* like, Iz." We turn the corner, the hotel coming into view. Placing my feet back onto the ground, he cups my cheeks. "When I walked into that bar and realized you ran from me, it felt like a prison sentence." He brings his lips toward mine, covering my mouth, his kiss sweet but brief. "And when you refused to answer any of my calls, texts, emails, it felt like the judge had handed down the most inhumane sentence possible. Life without you is the worst punishment imaginable. And I don't want to go back. Please...," he chokes out. "Don't make me go back to that."

My heart on the verge of bursting with love, I slam

my lips against his, desperate for everything he'll give me. His pleasure. His pain. His devotion. His fear. His fury. His love.

A heady groan ripping from his throat, he pushes me against the brick townhouse we're standing in front of, pressing his hips into me. I gasp, an unquenchable thirst filling me. Sensing my need, he lifts me up, forcing my legs around his midsection as he tears his lips from my mouth, nipping and sucking his way along my jawline, throat, collarbone. I throw my head back, surrendering to his touch, his warmth, his everything.

"Inside. Now," he growls as he pulls back, chest heaving, eyes frantic. He helps me find my footing, then clasps my hand in his.

I start toward the hotel, but he yanks me in the opposite direction. "Asher, wha—"

"I'm not staying at that hotel."

"Where *are* you staying? It had better not be a long cab ride."

"Not at all. In fact, it's within walking distance." He smirks.

"Then lead the way."

"Gladly." Squeezing my hand, he turns toward the townhouse beside us, ascending the steps.

"Here? Is this an Airbnb or something?"

"Or something." With a chuckle, he punches a code into the keyless lock. When the door buzzes, he opens it, leading me inside.

A dozen questions swirl in my mind as I marvel at the posh surroundings of the Gramercy Park townhome. I can only imagine what this place costs a night. It seems a bit much for one person, but I guess when you're Asher York, whose latest album has remained on top of the charts for over a month, you can spend money on stuff like staying in a ridiculously expensive townhouse.

A hand on the small of my back, he steers me up a short flight of steps. My feet scream for relief, and I kick off my heels, dropping my purse onto the floor beside them.

When I finally pause long enough to take in the living space, my jaw drops. Not at the gorgeous built-in bookcases surrounding an inviting fireplace with reading chairs placed in front of it. Not at the stunning chandelier hanging from the ornate ceiling. And not at the large screen TV mounted over the fireplace playing *The Sound of Music* at a low volume.

Instead, I'm taken aback by the baby grand piano sitting in the center of the room. To most, it would just be a piano. Something one would expect to see in a townhome in such an exclusive area of the city. But I recognize this piano, each scratch, each nick, each worn-out key.

"Asher…," I exhale, my eyes searching his.

He lifts the guitar over his head, propping it up against a couch. "I told you. I wanted to take you home. This is my home."

I arch a disbelieving brow. "*This* is your home?"

He nods. "Closed on it a few weeks ago."

"What about LA?"

He palms my lower back, dragging my body against his. "It wasn't where my heart was. It was here. Still is." He touches his lips to mine in a beautiful kiss, the gesture causing my body to flood with warmth.

"I'm surprised Grams didn't mind parting with this piano," I murmur when he pulls away.

"Let's just say I made her an offer she couldn't refuse."

"Is that right?" I ask breathily.

"Not really." He winks. "I asked. She agreed."

271

I roll my eyes. "You certainly drive a...hard bargain."

"Oh, darlin'..." He presses his body against mine. "You have no idea how...hard I can drive."

Laughter consumes me. "Oh, darlin'..." I imitate him to the best of my ability, but I still can't quite copy the amount of soul he exudes. I bring my mouth to his, nibbling on his bottom lip. "I have a pretty good idea," I murmur. "But maybe you should give me a reminder of exactly how...hard you can drive."

He thrusts his pelvis against me so I can feel how much he wants me. "As incredible as that sounds, I'll have to take a raincheck. Because we're going slow tonight."

"Slow?"

He nods as he angles toward me. When his lips land on the sensitive flesh of my neck, I moan, my eyes fluttering closed.

"Yes, Isabella. Slow. Torturously so. I need to worship you. Take my time with you. Make love to you." His tongue traces a line up to my earlobe, swirling a circle before he nibbles. "Dine on you as if you're the finest delicacy known to man." When he pulls back, intense brown eyes meet mine as he holds my face in his firm grip. "Because to me, that's what you are, a rare treat men would travel miles just to have one sample of. Yet you're all mine."

"Yours," I murmur as his mouth finds mine. "Always."

He breathes into me, causing a flicker in my chest. This isn't the first time we've kissed, yet that's what it feels like. I've let go of my fears. My inadequacies. My apprehensions. Grams was right. True love has a way of finding you, regardless of how far you run. I'm glad it finally found me, knocked some sense into me, made me open my eyes and allow this man to want me, love me...*choose* me.

"Hold on," he whispers against my mouth.

With a smile, I wrap my arms around his neck. He picks me up, carrying me up two flights of narrow stairs. When we cross the threshold into the master suite, he sets me down, ensuring I have my footing. I float my gaze around my surroundings, which are in a bit of disarray, as I predicted them to be.

"Sorry," he offers as he rushes around the room, picking up discarded clothes and tossing them into the hamper in the far corner. "I hadn't expected company." He takes a guitar off the impressive four-poster bed, a view of Gramercy Park out of the bay windows directly in front of it. "And my cleaner hasn't been here yet this week. I think she's coming Monday."

In a flurry, he straightens the lines of the duvet, smoothing out the impression from where I imagine he'd lain earlier, strumming his guitar. He shuffles sheets of lined staff paper together, assembling them into a pile, then tosses them onto a nearby reading chair.

"If you'd rather, we can go to one of the guest rooms. Or I'll book us a suite at whatever hotel you'd like. I—"

I place my hand on his bicep, stopping him from fussing. "It's fine. Actually, it's perfect. Messy and chaotic. Like you."

He blows out a breath. "I guess I..." He licks his lips. "I guess I'm a little nervous. Is that stupid?"

I swallow hard. "I'm nervous, too."

"It feels different, doesn't it?" He laughs shakily. "It's not like either one of us hasn't had sex before. It's not like we haven't had sex with *each other*. But this time..."

I lift myself onto my toes, attempting to ease his trepidation with a kiss. "It feels different for me, too. It feels…"

"Right."

"Yeah." I smile. "Like all the pieces have snapped into place."

"And this time, I hope the pieces stay where they belong. I hope *you* stay where you belong."

"And where's that?" I ask playfully.

"Here. With me. Always and forever."

"Always and forever," I exhale, sealing our promise to each other.

He digs his hands into my hair, holding my head in place, consuming me. The instant his tongue sweeps against mine, I moan, lightheaded. I fist his t-shirt, yanking him as close to me as possible, but it's not enough, our clothes an unwelcome barrier.

He tears his mouth from mine, wild eyes staring down at me. "I need to get you out of this dress."

"I think that can be arranged." I step back, about to reach behind me to lower the zipper when Asher grabs my arm.

"Wait."

I peer at him, panicked over the idea he's changed his mind. Then his expression softens and he waggles his brows.

"I'd like the pleasure of undressing you."

"Is that right?"

He slowly nods, dropping his hold on me. "That's right."

Giving him a flirtatious grin, I face away from him. "Get on with it then."

I stare ahead, expecting to feel him work the zipper within seconds. But I don't. There's nothing, the anticipation causing my heart to pound, breathing to increase, muscles to tighten.

Finally, his fingers brush along my nape, pushing my

hair over my shoulder. I remain still, waiting for his next touch. It comes in mere seconds, his hand palming my stomach and pulling me into him. I moan as he grinds against me, teasing. The heat of him so close is sweet agony. Blissful torture. Perfect affliction.

"Something wrong?" he asks in a coy voice.

"No," I exhale, my breathing ragged. I squeeze my thighs together, trying to dull the ache building inside. "Quite the opposite actually."

"Oh really?" He circles his hips with more intensity, causing me to whimper.

"Really."

"Good."

He removes his hand from my stomach, gripping the zipper. His motions languid, he lowers it, each second painful in its anticipation. I'm ready to rip the damn thing off, desperate to feel Asher again. But just when I don't think I can take it any longer, a chill whispers from my neck all the way down to the top of my panties.

"Turn around."

I take several measured steps, my heart thundering when my eyes meet his. He pushes my dress down my arms, allowing the material to pool at my feet before I step out of it. Despite the fact I'm standing in front of him in a black, lacy bra and matching panties, his gaze never strays from mine.

"Your turn," he murmurs.

The heat in his sensual stare prickling along my skin, I reach for the hem of his t-shirt, lifting it over his head. Dropping it to the floor, I take the opportunity to admire his body. I run my hand along the grooves of the tattoo that extends from his back, over his shoulders, and onto his chest.

My fingers continue down his torso, his shoulders rising and falling in a quicker rhythm as I near his waist.

I loosen his belt and unbutton his jeans, lowering the zipper. Returning my eyes to his, I push his jeans down his legs, noticing he's not wearing any briefs.

I quirk a brow. "Commando?"

"Came in useful tonight, didn't it?"

I palm his erection. "I'd say."

With a growl, his mouth clamps over mine, his hand forcefully gripping my hip as he backs me against the bed, his kiss leaving me breathless, thoughtless, soulless. He lowers me onto the mattress, his kiss turning from ravenous and eager to respectful and loving.

He cups my cheek in his calloused hand, a stark contradiction to the desperation with which he just kissed me. But this is what I need from him. This is *who* he is. Gentle, compassionate, benevolent. But also hungry, passionate, salacious. And I'm the lucky woman who gets to experience the many sides of Asher York. And not the Asher York the public fawns and screams over on a nightly basis as he entertains the masses. But *my* Asher York.

The same Asher York who built a snowman with me when we were snowed in. The same Asher York whose eyes grew so fevered, so impassioned as I watched him teach a classroom full of at-risk children about the fundamentals of music, his excitement matching their own when they grasped a concept. The same Asher York whose mere smile in the early mornings at Grams' lake house lit me on fire more than the most intimate of Jessie's touches. That should have been the only clue I needed to know I was with the wrong man. Then again, maybe this is the path we needed to take. Maybe our journey needed to be fraught with turmoil, heartache, and anguish so when we finally found our way to each other, we wouldn't take it for granted.

"Make love to me," I whisper.

"Gladly." His husky voice hits me deep in my core, my skin tingling with the promise of his touch. And if I know Asher, he won't leave a single inch of me unexplored. He'll make love to my mind, my body, my soul, ruining me for any other man. But there isn't any other man for me.

He swiftly pushes my panties down my legs and drops them on the floor. Hovering over me, his eyes lock with mine. There's something so vulnerable about his expression. So different from the confident and assured man who takes the stage nearly every night. He brushes a tendril of hair behind my ear, admiring my complexion.

"I love you, Isabella."

"And I love you."

He exhales, briefly hanging his head, allowing my words to bathe him in comfort. Then he seals my mouth with his as he brings his arousal up to me and pushes inside.

I close my eyes, reveling in this sensation of fullness. Asher's always had a unique ability to push my body higher than I thought possible, to make me feel more complete than I thought possible. But that's nothing compared to the absolute perfection washing over me as he moves so gently, so tenderly, so lovingly.

"I love you," I repeat, wrapping my arms and legs around his body as he buries his head in the crook of my neck, each thrust hitting me deeper than the last, each push propelling me higher. "I love you. I love you. I love you."

With each declaration, my heart swells, my body shivers, my eyes spill over with more tears, this moment bigger than I imagined. No matter what happens, one thing is certain. This is where I belong.

Asher is where I belong.

Chapter Thirty-One

SUNLIGHT FILTERS THROUGH the bay windows of the luxurious master suite. I sigh, melting farther into the arm draped along my body. When warm lips land on my exposed nape, I moan.

"I can get used to this."

"Me, too." Asher circles his hips against me. "Waking up next to a beautiful woman can certainly prove useful. I won't have to jerk off first thing in the morning anymore."

I turn over, resting my chin on his chest and peering into his eyes. "You jerk off first thing in the morning?"

"What guy doesn't? Morning wood isn't a myth. It's a real thing." He waggles his brows, slyly nodding toward his waist.

"Hmm…" I give him a playful smile. "I've been working in the science field all my professional life." I trail my hand down his chest, toying with a few tufts of hair as I revel in the feel of his firm, toned muscles. "Do you want to know one of the things people ingrained into my head?"

"What's that?"

"To never take anyone's word without testing. Without running my own…experiments." I slither down his frame, his pupils dilating as I near his waist.

"And what experiments are you hoping to run?"

"A scientist never reveals her method." I pause, frowning. "Actually, she does, but that's irrelevant.

Suffice it to say, you don't need to worry about what experiments I'll run." My voice becomes breathy as I shift the duvet covering our bodies, revealing his hard arousal. "I'm confident you'll find them rather...pleasurable."

I wrap my fingers around his girth, his throat vibrating with a heady moan. Lowering my lips to him, I trace a circle around his tip with my tongue, and his body jerks.

"Goddamn, baby..."

I peek up, his stomach rolling with his labored breaths.

"You're killing me."

"That's the point." I slacken my jaw, about to take him into my mouth when the faint echo of a door opening and closing sounds from downstairs, followed by a familiar voice.

"Asher? You up? It's me."

"Shit." A rush of adrenaline shoots through me, my eyes widening, heart pounding. I roll off him, grabbing the duvet to cover my body. If there were a time I wished I had an invisibility cloak like Harry Potter, it's now.

I look at Asher, expecting him to be as panicked as me. But he's as cool as a cucumber.

"Asher," I whisper-shout. "What are you doing? Your brother."

"What about him?" A smirk tugs on his lips as he leans against the headboard, finding amusement in the anxiety coursing through me.

"He's downstairs. What if he comes up here?"

"He won't."

"You don't know that."

"You may not have grown up with siblings, but it's an unwritten rule. Never walk into a room, especially a bedroom, unless you're prepared to witness kinky-ass sex."

"But still…" I nervously glance at the door, then Asher, then back again. "What if—"

On a long sigh, he presses his lips to mine, stealing my protest. "I'll go talk to him so he leaves. Okay?" He arches a brow.

I exhale, anxiety rolling off me. "Thank you."

When he drags his body from the bed, I can't help but admire how stunning, how breathtaking he is. And he's all mine.

"There's just one thing you have to do for me."

I snap my head up, his eyes dancing with amusement after having caught me ogling his physique. He grabs his jeans and tugs them up his legs.

"What's that?"

He approaches, his firm grip on my nape forcing my lips to his. The way he holds me so possessively causes my pulse to spike, a delicious shiver trickling down my spine. When he speaks, his tone is seductive, wanton, needy.

"When I get back, I expect you to suck me off. Got it?"

His words are a magic bullet straight to my core, moisture pooling between my legs. "Anything for you," I answer huskily.

"Ash? You here?" Jessie's voice cuts through, getting closer.

We both look to the door, staring at it for several seconds. Then Asher crushes his lips to mine, his kiss bruising and scraping. "God, I love this fucking mouth. I'm coming back for it." He steals one last kiss before slipping out of the bedroom and making his way down the stairs.

I pull my legs into my body, taking a few moments to

process the past twenty-four hours. It seems like a dream, like I'll wake up and be back in my lonely apartment, not in a Gramercy Park townhouse Asher bought to be near me.

"Did you bring a girl home?"

Jessie's question tears me out of my thoughts. I look up, noticing the door is slightly ajar. I slide off the bed, grabbing Asher's t-shirt off the floor and tugging it over my body, tiptoeing toward the gap.

"What makes you ask?"

"I could be wrong, but I've never known you to wear size eight black heels or carry a Michael Kors bag."

"Shit," I curse under my breath, heat rushing over my face.

"I met a girl at the club last night," Asher answers nonchalantly, as if he had that excuse on the tip of his tongue. It's not a complete lie. We *did* see each other at the club. "We had a few drinks and hit it off, so I asked her to come home with me."

"You can't bring home random girls. There's more to consider now. You're no longer a nobody. You're somebody. A very big somebody. You need to start acting like it. What if some paparazzi figured out you bought this place and were waiting outside?"

"Judging by the fact you didn't know I'd brought home a girl until now, I assume that isn't the case."

"It's not just the paparazzi. How do you know——"

"There won't be any PR issues, if that's what you're worried about," Asher interrupts. "She's discreet. So, if you're done trying to intervene and dictate my personal life, is there a reason you stopped by?"

When he doesn't immediately respond, I inch closer to the gap between the door and frame, wishing I could be a fly on the wall in the living room right now. I've never heard Asher talk to Jessie this way. Not with this amount of irritation. Sure, they've fought, and I've witnessed my fair share of their disagreements, but there's something else in Asher's tone.

"I get paid to manage you. That includes your personal life," Jessie says finally. "You weren't answering your phone." His voice lightens. "Now I understand why. As you know, Ma, Dad, and Grams are in town for tonight's gig. They hoped to do a late lunch before soundcheck. Would that work?"

"Sure. Of course," Asher replies evenly.

"Okay." I expect to hear Jessie's footsteps as he retreats. Instead, he speaks again. "Grams asked if I wouldn't mind inviting Izzy. I wanted to run it by you first."

I blink, remaining completely still.

"Doesn't bother me."

"Okay. I'll call her and see if she picks up. It's been practically impossible lately, but it's worth a shot."

"Now?" Asher's voice rises in pitch.

"Why not?"

I spin around, my eyes searching the bedroom for my phone, not finding it. Then I remember my cell is currently in my purse. Which is downstairs. Which supposedly belongs to the girl Asher brought home.

Shit. Shit. Shit. Shit.

I grasp the doorjamb, feeling dizzy. Asher and I haven't discussed when we'll tell Jessie, but I'm sure he doesn't want him to find out like this.

"Wait!" Asher shouts, his demand reverberating against the walls.

"What is it?" Jessie replies.

"Uh… It's early," he stammers. "Do you really think she'll be up?"

"It's not *that* early. It's after ten. If you're up, she'll be up." He lowers his voice. "Ah, here it is."

A few excruciating seconds tick by, then Asher bellows, "Stop!"

The entire house falls eerily silent. I hold my breath, waiting for what's next, praying Jessie hasn't had a chance to press my contact.

"Why don't you want me to call Izzy?" The accusation in his tone is obvious. Asher may excel at a lot of things, but he's never been a good liar. Jessie knows that.

"I just… I don't want it to be uncomfortable for you, considering your past."

"It'll be fine. I'll compartmentalize it, even if it's still hard, knowing she'll never be mine again."

I swallow hard at the hurt that's still evident.

"Even all these years later?" Asher asks timidly.

"I'll *always* want her," Jessie answers, his voice unwavering. "Nothing will ever change that."

His words hit me hard, and I close the door as quietly as I can. My heart heavy, I make my way back to the bed, my mind a daze as I lower myself onto the mattress. Is any of this worth it, especially knowing the potential casualties? I can't see how. Asher must realize this, too. How can he not?

Minutes tick by as I remain in my trance. When I hear the familiar sound of feet striking against the stairs, I snap out of my thoughts. Ripping Asher's t-shirt off, I hurriedly collect my clothes, pulling my panties back on before securing my bra.

As I slide the sleeves of my dress over my arms, Asher barrels into the room. I briefly whip my eyes to his before looking away, doing my best to zip up my dress, despite the difficult angle.

"This is going to look horrible," I say nervously. "But it's a Saturday in Manhattan. I'm not the only one doing the walk of shame this morning."

"You overheard, didn't you?"

"It's kind of hard not to in this house." I chew on my lower lip, fidgeting with my hands.

"I'm sorry, Iz."

I force a smile. "It's okay. I get it. We've been here before."

"No."

"No?" I scrunch my brows together.

He clutches my face in his hands. "I'm sorry I wasn't truthful with him. I will be. I promise. I have every intention of telling him about us." He drops his hold on me, stepping back, dragging his hand through his wayward locks. "But there are complications. I need to call my attorney and get a new manager lined up first."

"A new manager?"

He shrugs, peering at me with sad eyes. "Not sure there's much of a choice here. Even if I'm able to convince Jessie there was no ill-intent on my part, on either of our parts, it might be an awkward working relationship. At least at first. So it's in my best interest to think worst-case scenario and have a backup ready to take over. Just in case."

I stare at the charcoal shade of the walls as I listen to him go on about the logistics of what a relationship with me means. All things I hadn't considered while we remained in our bubble. It's not just the potential severing of his life-long relationship and bond with his brother. It's also the end of Asher's professional arrangement with Jessie.

Possibly the end of Jessie's career.

"Are you sure about this? I understand if you'd—"

He's in front of me in a heartbeat, clasping my hands in his. "Yes, Izzy. I'm sure. I have been from the beginning." He angles toward me, his warm breath on my lips erasing all my fears. "Like I told you back at

Grams' lake house… I'd choose you if you'd let me. And you're finally letting me. I'm not giving this up for anything." He touches his mouth to mine, his kiss perfect in its simplicity.

"Face it, darlin'." He winks playfully. "You're stuck with me." His tone turns serious. "Even if I have to love you in the shadows for a little while longer." His shoulders fall, and he appears genuinely remorseful at the thought of having to keep me a secret. But if that's the cost to be happy, it's one I'm willing to pay.

I lift myself onto my toes, draping my arms loosely around his neck. "As much as it sucks, I kind of like the idea of you loving me in the shadows."

"Really?"

"Hell yeah." I dig my nails into his exposed chest, his muscles tensing under my touch. "Couples role-play forbidden relationships all the time, pretend to have sex in secret." My voice turns breathy and seductive as my hand travels farther and farther south. "Think how much fun we can have with this."

He lifts a single brow. "What did you have in mind?"

"I have a few ideas."

Allowing my dress to fall back to the floor, I lower myself to my knees and crane my head back, admiring the beautiful, addictive man I kneel before. The look he's giving me — the heat in his eyes, the need in his expression, the desperation in his grip on my head — is better than any aphrodisiac.

"But first…" I unbutton his jeans, then lower the zipper, my gaze never leaving his as I push them down his legs. "I believe you wanted me to suck you off."

"Oh, darlin'…"

Chapter Thirty-Two

EXCITED VOICES FILL the backstage VIP area when Chloe, Lincoln, and I arrive later in the evening. It's only been a few hours since Asher put me into a car to take me back to my apartment, but it feels like an eternity has passed. I shouldn't have come tonight, but he begged me to. Said he needed me in the audience when he stepped onto that stage as the headlining act at Madison Square Garden, something he's only dreamed of since the second he picked up his guitar as a young boy.

"Are you going to tell me what caused the sudden change of heart?" Chloe presses. "Yesterday, you were adamant about *not* coming tonight. And now?" She scans my body that's clad in a tight, black tank and fitted jeans, complete with heels. "You're all dolled up like you're fucking the lead singer."

"Chloe," I hiss as we're steered toward a line. "I'm not…" I trail off. I can't even tell her I'm not fucking the lead singer. I look up at Lincoln, who's dressed in his standard dark jeans and blazer, despite being at a rock concert. Chloe and he really are as opposite as they come. "Can you make your wife lower her voice? Maybe give her something to suck on?"

He chuckles. "Trust me. It won't work. If there's something on her mind, she'll multi-task."

"Plus, I'm more interested in what *you've* been sucking on." She leans toward me, her voice barely audible. "I spoke to Nora this morning. She mentioned you went to that club opening with her."

I avoid her eyes, holding my head high as I inch up the line. I hope there's alcohol at the end of it.

She grabs my bicep, angling closer still. "She also mentioned Asher York played a set. Said you left after a song and went back to her apartment, where you finally told her all about him."

"Your point?"

"My point is, what happened?"

I part my lips, unsure what to say. Asher and I agreed to keep this quiet for now while he speaks to his lawyer. I never considered what to tell my friends. Especially Chloe, my rather *observant* friend, who will surely figure out something's going on with little effort.

"Like Nora said, we left after one song."

"That is what she said…" Her analytical eyes study me in a way that makes me think I'm wearing a blinking neon sign announcing to the world I got laid last night. And this morning. And this afternoon. Hell, if she looks closely enough, she wouldn't need a neon sign. The teeth marks on my neck would be all the evidence she needs to prove her case. Thank God for a decent concealer. "But I think there's more to the story."

"And I think you're fishing for something that's not real."

"Not real, you say?"

"Exactly. There's—"

"Then why is Asher York currently eye-fucking the shit out of you?" She nods toward the front of the line.

I follow her line of sight, my gaze falling on an incredibly sexy version of Asher. Granted, I've always found him sexy, but now that he's all Mr. Rock and Roll, I can't stop my heart from speeding up. His hair is mussed up, but in a way that screams "just fucked", not "just woke up". His midnight blue jeans are the perfect fit — not too baggy, not too tight. His gray V-neck t-shirt hugs every sinewy muscle of his torso, not leaving much to the imagination.

"Now, if this were the first time you were seeing him after standing him up at the bar back in March, I'm not so sure he'd be mentally undressing you like he is. Which leads me to believe you've reconnected." She rakes her analytical gaze over me. "Based on the blush building on those cheeks, I'd say several times. And it was damn good. Am I right?" She waggles her brows.

I look from her to Lincoln, who smirks, to Asher, then back to her again. "Fine," I relent. "We may have worked things out." I grip her arm, lowering my voice. "But you know what's at stake. We need to keep it quiet, just for a little while longer."

"But you're eventually going public with it, right? This is finally for real?"

I pinch my lips together, nodding as I adjust my purse on my shoulder. "Yes. It's finally for real."

Chloe squeals, throwing her arms around my neck. I struggle to retain my balance, which is a difficult feat, especially in these heels. "Oh my god! I'm so freaking happy for you."

"Miss," a voice interrupts. I snap my eyes to see the line has moved, but we haven't. "Your turn."

I furrow my brow, confused. Then I realize what this line is for — a meet and greet.

Turning to Chloe and Lincoln, I shoot them a sly wink, then saunter toward Asher, his eyes heating.

"Hey, darlin'," he murmurs in a low voice when I approach. God, that voice does things to me, especially knowing he reserves it just for me.

"Oh, my gosh. It's Asher York," I coo. "I've always wanted to meet a famous rockstar. Can you sign my boobs? Or maybe my ass?"

He chuckles as he drapes his arm around my shoulders, pulling me in close. "Just smile and think about how hard this rockstar is going to fuck you later."

My gaze widens as the photographer snaps our picture. Then Asher nods at Lincoln and Chloe, gesturing them over. After they exchange hugs, we all pose for a photo.

"Everyone say Vegas," Chloe chimes in at the last moment.

We erupt in laughter, which draws the attention of nearly all the guests in the pre-show party.

"I guess what happens in Vegas really doesn't stay there," Lincoln remarks.

"You two are living proof of that." Asher smiles at Chloe, before shifting his gaze to mine. "And so are we."

It's a simple thing, but the fact he told someone about us causes my heart to swell. Now I'm counting the days until he can tell the world. Until he can kiss me breathless in front of all his adoring fans, especially the heavily made-up women adjusting their cleavage in preparation to meet him. Until we can finally be us.

After saying our goodbyes, we join the rest of the VIP and ticket winners in the pre-show area. Several buffet tables line the far wall with all sorts of food. Chloe has no problem filling a plate with a bit of everything. I'm too on edge to think about eating, even more so when I notice Jessie walk into the room, Grams and his parents in tow. I practically down my entire glass of wine to settle my apprehension.

"Izzy!" Reagan exclaims when she notices me standing with Lincoln and Chloe. "It's so wonderful to see you. We weren't sure whether you'd be here." She hugs me before holding me at arm's length, and I bask in her motherly affection before she moves on, allowing Lincoln to kiss her cheek. "And Lincoln. I hear congratulations are in order." She looks from him to Chloe, sighing. "Isn't it amazing? A friend of Asher's marrying a friend of Izzy's. What are the chances?"

"I wondered the same thing," Grams says, her voice laden with forced astonishment. I have a feeling she knows the true story.

"Grams." I wrap my arms around her, melting into her embrace. There's always been something soothing about her hugs. No matter the troubles plaguing me, I can find solace and encouragement in her love. "I've missed you."

"And I've missed you, sweetheart." She pulls back, taking my hand between both of hers. "I trust things are…better?"

I nod slightly, not wanting anyone else to pick up on our private conversation. She squeezes my hand, a silent acknowledgment.

"How *did* you two meet?" Jessie's voice cuts through.

My body stiffens. I hadn't even pondered the consequences of Jessie realizing Chloe and Lincoln are married, especially considering their connection to Asher and me.

"We had a one-night stand in Vegas," Chloe answers nonchalantly.

"Obviously it turned into more than a one-night stand," Sean interjects jovially.

"It did indeed, Mr. York."

"It's Sean, Chloe."

"Of course, Sean." She smiles as she returns her attention to the rest of Asher's family.

I steal a glimpse at Jessie. His eyes are narrowed into slits, mouth pinched into a tight line, arms crossed over his chest.

"I was in Vegas last January for a bachelorette party. And I kept running into this guy." She jabs Lincoln playfully.

My gaze darts between the two of them, sending her silent smoke signals to keep the details out of it. Like how they were stuck at the house where Asher was staying during the blackout, then slept together after a game of Never Have I Ever got a bit risqué. Chloe never would have been at that house had it not been for me, a fact I doubt it would take Jessie long to figure out. And I can't have him figure that out. Not yet.

God, I hate this. I hate all these mini panic attacks I seem to have whenever a conversation skirts perilously close to Jessie learning the truth. I just want him to know, and he will, but I hate this place of purgatory where I'm stuck between our relationship being public and being nothing. I don't like being a secret. I don't like the gray area.

A hand links with mine, squeezing. I look to my left, meeting Chloe's eyes wordlessly telling me it'll be okay. That I'll get through it. She must know what I'm thinking. After all, she's been in a similar situation. Her relationship with Lincoln was…complicated, yet they managed to survive. I pray Asher and I will, too.

"Such a small world, isn't it?" Reagan muses.

I bring my glass to my lips. "It sure is."

Over the next few hours, we mingle and socialize. Thankfully, Jessie was only able to stay for a little while before needing to busy himself with "manager duties". The instant he left, it felt like a weight had lifted. I wasn't the only one who noticed, either. Pretty sure even his parents did, too, which surprised me.

"Okay, folks!" A rather large man with security emblazoned on the back of his shirt makes his way through the room. "Fifteen minutes until Asher York takes the stage."

"I suppose we should go see him," Grams comments, downing a large swallow of her whiskey. I still can't believe this woman is ninety years old. She doesn't look it. And she certainly doesn't act it. I've yet to meet a ninety-year-old who goes to rock concerts and drinks whiskey like she does. She always says you're only as old as you act. At the rate she's going, she's probably only in her twenties or thirties.

"I suppose we should," I respond, finishing off my wine.

As we navigate through the backstage corridors, I marvel at how busy and chaotic it seems. People with laminated passes hanging from the neck walk with purpose. Nearly every wall is lined with road cases labeled with various things — video, lighting, sound, rigging, wardrobe. Rows of guitars fill a rack, a tattooed man with camo shorts and black t-shirt checking the tuning. Excitement courses through my veins with this sneak peek into what it's like to be backstage before a show. It's not all glitz and glamour like they portray in books and movies, but nonetheless, it's still exhilarating.

The noise level increases as we're led through a maze of corridors and into the arena. In awe, I scan the massive space, every seat filled. It's not the first time I've been to a concert here, but it's a different experience to be led to a section just off the floor, surrounded by thousands of fans cheering for the man who owns my heart. And whose heart I possess, too.

When the lights go out, the decibel level grows louder still, the screams unlike anything I imagined.

"Holy shit," I murmur as cell phones flash, people cheer, and feet stomp. I knew Asher had done well, that the album was well received. But this... It puts his fame into perspective. Fame he's amassed because his music and lyrics spoke to people. A lot of people.

"I'm right there with you," Chloe mutters, just as taken aback.

Then, in the darkness, the first chord of a familiar song cuts through the cheers and the crowd goes wild. Lights fill the stage, illuminating a drummer, keyboardist, bass player, and a few backup singers. In the middle of it all is Asher York, sauntering up to the microphone, a sly smile on his face.

The band repeats the opening measures a few times, giving the audience a chance to settle down, dancing and clapping along. Then, despite the size of the arena, Asher's eyes float toward me, locking with mine.

"This one's for you."

The audience roars with excitement as he breaks into "My Favorite Almost".

But I'm not his almost anymore. I'm his always.

Chapter Thirty-Three

BLISS. THAT'S THE only way to describe this feeling, my current state of mind as I lay in my bed, my very own rockstar beside me. This sensation of being wrapped in his arms as his breath tickles my skin can't truly be put into words. Other than it's where I belong. All my life, I've searched for the missing piece in the puzzle of who I am. Not anymore. Asher's my missing piece.

"Morning," he rasps, his mouth peppering kisses against my nape.

"Morning," I sigh as he pulls me closer. "Although, based on the amount of sun streaming through the windows, it's probably closer to afternoon."

"We both needed our rest after that workout you gave me last night, you vixen." He pushes me onto my back, leaning down and nuzzling his nose into the crook of my neck.

I run my hands through his disheveled hair. "Sleeping with a rockstar has always been on my bucket list. Now I can cross it off."

"Is that the only reason you invited me over?" Eyes locking with mine, he feigns disappointment, an adorable pout pulling on his lips. "Because of a bucket list item?"

"That, and I'd hoped you'd make me sing." I waggle my brows.

"Is that so?" With slow movements, he lowers his

mouth to my chest, dragging his tongue along my flesh, my body humming with need. When he scrapes his teeth against my nipple, I moan. "And did I?"

"God yes."

He chuckles, then pulls back. "Coffee?"

"No sex?"

"Damn, darlin'. I've turned you into a fiend."

"What can I say?" I scrape my hands down his back, nails digging in. "You're my drug of choice."

He gives me a gentle kiss. "I like the sound of that, but I need a little while before I'm ready to go again. Let me make you coffee. We can spend a few minutes talking and pretend to like each other for reasons other than ridiculously hot sex."

I playfully groan. "God, that's torture. You should know I'm only using you for your body."

"Think you can survive a half hour?"

I arch a brow. "A half hour?"

"Yup."

"Fine." I push him off me. "Make me a coffee. But I'm holding you to that half hour." Rolling to my side, I grab my phone.

"Are you setting a timer?"

I type on my cell, then hold it toward him so he can see the countdown I labeled "Rockstar Sex".

His laughter fills my tiny studio apartment as he raises himself from my bed. "You're something else."

"Hopefully a good something else." I sit up, pulling my legs into my body.

He leans over the mattress and brushes his lips against mine. "A wonderful something else." He grabs his jeans from where they landed on the floor during our mad rush to disrobe each other, about to step into them.

"What do you think you're doing?"

He stops. "What does it look like?"

"It looks like you're about to put your clothes on. Seems like a waste of energy, especially considering you now have…" I glance at my phone, "twenty-eight minutes and fifty-three seconds before you need to be inside me again. I'd save your energy if I were you. You'll need it."

His laughter grows even louder, the lines around his eyes wrinkling. Before I can react, he crawls back onto the bed, his mouth capturing mine in a kiss. "God, I love you."

Three simple words, yet they turn me into complete mush. I hope they always will.

"I love you, too." I linger near his lips another moment, the warmth they give off like a magnet. "Now, if you really loved me, you'd make me a coffee." I reel back, landing a playful smack on his ass.

"Naughty girl." He winks, then pushes off the bed, padding on light feet through my apartment.

"You have no idea how naughty I can be." I chew on my lower lip, watching him make himself at home in my kitchen as he brews two cups of coffee.

When he suggested he come to my place instead of the other way around, I was hesitant. But he thought it best, just to avoid any surprise visitors. I couldn't fault him there. The likelihood of the paparazzi hanging out here is slim to none, even less chance of Jessie making an appearance.

It should seem odd to have Asher in my apartment that's probably smaller than the hotel rooms he stays in. But right now, I don't see the rockstar who played to screaming fans last night. That man vanished the second he left Madison Square Garden. Now I see my Asher.

"Oh, I think I do." He passes me a knowing look, a

single brow arched, a silent reminder of the things we did last night.

"You're right. I think you do."

Once he's finished preparing our coffees, he makes his way back to me, which only takes a total of five steps. After he hands me my mug, he places a soft kiss on my forehead.

"Twenty-four minutes and forty-seven seconds."

"You're incorrigible."

"I know."

He heads to what I now consider his side of the bed and slides under the duvet, sitting with his back against the headboard. "What is all that stuff?" He nods toward the boxes on the coffee table. "Is it related to your birth mother?"

"You saw the article?" I bring my coffee to my lips, savoring that first sip. Since we reconnected, I haven't had a chance to tell him I'd begun my search, like he encouraged me to a few months ago.

"Read it once a day every day since it was published." He smiles a small smile. "I'm proud of you. I imagine it was difficult for you to reopen those old wounds, but it's important you try to fill in the blanks."

"Actually…" I cock my head to the side. "This investigation is probably why we're together."

"I thought it was because the boomerang knocked some sense into you."

"That had something to do with it. But there's more."

"More?"

"Remember the other night when you called me out for running when I got scared?" I ask, and he nods. "You were right. Whenever something scares me, I run. I always have. I figure if I push people away first, they won't have the chance to leave me."

"A lot of the foster kids I taught had abandonment issues like that. They never let anyone get close."

"I've always assumed my birth mother didn't want me. When I started falling for you, it scared me. All my life, I've had this nagging voice in my head, telling me if things seem too good to be true, they most likely are. And that voice told me *you* were too good to be true, that you'd never choose me, that you'd always choose your brother."

He opens his mouth to protest, but I quickly hold up my hand.

"And that's okay. You *should* choose him over me."

"But it's not even a choice." He angles toward me, his lips caressing mine. "Not when it comes to you."

I sigh, basking in his heartfelt declaration.

"So what changed? What made you stop running?"

"Right." I lean back, taking another sip of my coffee. "Lincoln asked a body language expert to review the airport security camera footage from the day I was left, and some of what she said made sense."

"And what's that?"

"That I wasn't abandoned out of choice, but out of desperation. The expert believes my birth mother was on the run from someone. That her actions and the way she carried herself evidenced a high level of anxiety and fear. Based on this, Lincoln thinks when she realized she couldn't get away, she did the only thing she could in order to protect me."

He nods thoughtfully. "It makes sense. If you're going to abandon a baby, an airport terminal is the last place I'd do it." His brow scrunches. "But what was she running from?"

I shrug. "Not sure. But maybe all that stuff on the table will help."

"And what is it?"

"All the leads the tip email address has received over the past several weeks. Maybe we'll find a needle in the haystack that can help steer us in the right direction. But for now, I can find solace in the fact that my mother seemed to make the ultimate sacrifice for me."

"What kinds of tips? Anything helpful?"

"Oh, absolutely," I reply sarcastically. "So helpful. Like, for instance, it's possible my mother was abducted by aliens!" I feign excitement over the prospect. "Or she may have undergone gender transition surgery and is now living as a man in Alaska. How amazing is that? It makes perfect sense!"

Asher laughs. "What is it about a tip line that always brings out the nutjobs?"

"People just want their fifteen minutes of fame. But that's not even the craziest." I step out of bed, swiping an expandable folder off the coffee table before returning with it, crawling back under the duvet.

"What's that?"

"These are the real crazies. Most of them are religious zealots, telling me to repent for the sins of my birth mother or I'll never arrive in the Kingdom of God, or something like that."

"There *are* people who truly believe that."

"Oh, I know." I wave the stack of papers in the air. "I have proof of that."

"May I?" He arches a brow, eyes floating to the folder.

"Be my guest."

He pulls out a bunch of papers and flips through them, shaking his head more and more with each supposed lead.

"Told you. These people need to be in straitjackets, or at least a padded room."

"I can't disagree with you there."

"I particularly like the one who equated me to Jesus and believes I'm the second savior. It *would* be convenient. Then I could call up my pops and be like, 'Hey, Dad. I had some really kinky sex last night. My step-dad wants me to say a slew of Hail Marys and Our Fathers. Can't you wave your hand and forgive me?'"

Asher bursts out laughing, the deep rumble light and carefree. "Even if you *were* the result of some immaculate conception, I don't think it would matter. You'd go to hell just for saying that, for thinking that. Isn't your mom Catholic? What the hell is wrong with you?"

"A lot. You should know that by now. And it's a shame I'm not some second savior." I lean toward him, my lips poised over his.

"And why's that?"

"Because I plan to do a lot of sinning with you in approximately eighteen minutes and twelve seconds."

Laughing, he presses his mouth firmly against mine. "And damn, darlin'. I love sinning with you." He kisses me once more, then returns his attention to the papers.

"Eighteen minutes and two seconds," I murmur, more for myself than him. Asher's right. I am a fiend for him.

He shakes his head, flipping through more and more of the crazy tips. Suddenly, his body stiffens, eyes focused on the paper in front of him.

"What is it?" I run my hand along his back, a soothing gesture.

He blinks, jaw agape.

"Ash?"

He snaps out of his daze. "It's nothing."

"It's not nothing. Tell me," I push.

On a long sigh, he hands me a piece of paper. "This." I read the quote from Leviticus. *"But if in spite of all this you do not obey Me, but continue to walk in hostility toward Me, then I will act with furious rage against you, and I Myself will punish you sevenfold for your sins. You will eat the flesh of your own sons and daughters. I will destroy your high places, cut down your incense altars, and heap your dead bodies on the remains of your idols; and My soul will despise you."*

I place the paper back onto the bed. "These zealots really like Leviticus. Deuteronomy is high up there, too. It's like they get hard-ons over the concept of punishment. They're probably secretly into BDSM." I nudge him, trying to lighten his mood, but it doesn't work.

"When Emilia disappeared, I helped go through tips, since I was so close to her." He brings his eyes to mine. "We received one with this exact quote. It could be nothing, but what if the cases are related? What if the people your birth mother ran from are the same ones who took Emilia? Your mother was pregnant. So was Emilia. After she disappeared, I started researching human trafficking. Do you know what I found?"

"I'm not sure I want to know."

"When most people hear about human trafficking, they think low-income individuals who are sold into forced labor or sexual servitude. But there's another group of women who are trafficked." With each word he speaks, he becomes more and more impassioned.

"Pregnant women," I breathe, recalling all the training I'd received about looking for the signs of potential trafficking victims while attending to patients.

"Exactly. Parents who are desperate to adopt will pay a fortune for a baby. What if..." He blinks repeatedly, scrubbing a hand over his face. "What if someone is preying on pregnant girls? What if your birth mother wasn't running from an abusive partner but something bigger? What if the reason Emilia disappeared was because someone wanted her to have that baby so they could sell it?"

I stare at the wall in front of me, sorting through Asher's theory. There's no proof this happened. But there's no proof it didn't, either. This is an angle I hadn't considered. What if he's right? What if they are somehow connected? What if the answer's been sitting next to me for years, but I was too stubborn to realize it?

Chapter Thirty-Four

"THERE'S MY favorite rockstar," I exhale into my phone as I sit in a cab Thursday evening.

I hated having to say goodbye to Asher Monday, but he had to leave for Chicago to continue his tour. He'd already stayed in New York longer than he was supposed to, which didn't sit well with Jessie. Thankfully, Asher was able to use his recent purchase of the Gramercy Park townhouse as an excuse.

"There's my muse," he croons. "How was your day?"

This has become part of our routine, at least the past several days. He calls me a few minutes after five when he's finished with soundcheck. The first question out of his mouth is always how my day has been. I like that he takes an interest in what is mundane and boring, at least compared to his life.

"Good. I'm actually on my way to Lincoln's office right now."

This catches his interest. "Really?"

"Chloe called earlier. Said they may have a lead."

"Lead? What kind of lead?" The urgency is clear in his voice.

"She wouldn't say over the phone. Just that it's connected to what we theorized the other day."

Chloe was the first person I called after Asher and I made our realization about the identical tips. While she opined it could be a coincidence, much like we did, she also said anything was possible.

"You'll call me after? Let me know what she says?"

"Of course."

"Okay." He sighs loudly. I can tell he hates being away from me during all of this. I hate it, too. "I need to get ready to do this meet and greet. Hair and wardrobe are calling."

"Well, you'd better get going then. You can't disappoint your adoring fans."

"You're the only adoring fan I care about."

I close my eyes, basking in his husky voice. God, these next few weeks are going to be torture. If I weren't worried about Jessie seeing me, I'd consider flying out this weekend to surprise Asher. I'll just have to be content with the few moments we steal during the day. The good morning text messages. The five o'clock phone calls. The goodnight FaceTimes. These things will help pass the time until I can be in his arms again.

"I love you, Isabella."

"I love you, Asher. Go. Sing me a song."

"I'll sing you all the songs, darlin'."

* * *

"What's going on?" I ask as Chloe leads me from the reception area of the country's most circulated newspaper and through the newsroom that's still bustling, despite it being after five o'clock.

"You'll see."

I draw in a deep breath to settle my nerves as we maneuver past a maze of cubicles, phones ringing relentlessly, fingers typing on keyboards. Soon, we turn down a corridor, leaving the sounds of the newsroom behind, eventually stopping outside a door, the nameplate etched with Lincoln's name, Chief General Counsel below it.

Chloe faces me, grabbing my hands. "I want you to know I'm here for you. If it's too much, we can stop."

"If what's too much?"

She pauses, then continues. "We found a woman who knew your mother."

Her words all but knock the wind out of me. "Are you telling me we finally know my mother's name?"

With a smile, she nods slowly. "Sofia Castro."

I exhale a breath. For years, she was a nameless, faceless ghost haunting me. I didn't think we'd ever find out who she is... Or was.

"How does this woman know my mother?"

"It's something you should hear for yourself." She places her hand over the doorknob, then looks to me before turning it. "Ready?"

I'm unsure how to answer that. I doubt anyone is ever prepared for something like this. But when I started down this rabbit hole, all I wanted were answers. Hopefully I'm about to get some.

After I nod, she opens the door, leading me into the large corner office. My eyes fall on Lincoln as he stands from a reading chair in the sitting area. He takes several long strides toward me, offering me a comforting smile.

"Thanks for coming, Iz." He kisses my cheek, then places his hand on the middle of my back, steering me toward one of the couches. "This is Oliver Lane. He's the investigative reporter who's been looking into this."

The tall, lanky man with gray hair extends his hand toward me, and I take it. He looks like I imagined a career reporter would. Wrinkled shirt with the sleeves rolled up. Loose tie hanging around his neck. Scruff on his jaw from not shaving because he couldn't find the extra few minutes to do so. Uneven fingernails that bear the evidence of being chewed constantly, probably a bad habit picked up when he quit smoking.

"Wonderful to finally meet you," he says in a gravelly voice that confirms my suspicion he was once a smoker. "I reported on the JFK baby story when it first made headlines, so when Linc here asked if I was interested in trying to uncover your mother's identity, I jumped at the opportunity."

"Thank you. I appreciate all you've done to help."

"Certainly." He drops his hold and we all shift our attention to the other figure in the room.

In an instant, the tension spikes as I peer at the woman. She doesn't appear a day over fifty. Her dark hair is a stark contrast to her alabaster skin. She's slender, a few inches taller than my five-seven frame. And she has the most dazzling blue eyes I've ever seen, a dusting of freckles across her nose completing her unique, yet breathtaking appearance.

"This is Avery Halloran."

She steps toward me, her expression difficult to describe. Almost like awe. On a hard swallow, I extend my hand to this woman who knew my birth mother in some capacity.

"Nice to meet you."

She nears, but instead of grabbing my hand, she wraps her arms around me, taking me by surprise.

"You're alive." Her body trembles with her cries of relief. "That's all Sofia wanted. For you to be safe." She pulls back, peering at me. "You look so much like her. But she's right. You have your father's eyes."

I blink repeatedly. "My father? You know who my father is?"

Her expression falls, her gaze awash with remorse. "Was. I knew who your father was."

"Oh."

"Why don't we all have a seat?" Lincoln suggests, gesturing for me to sit on the couch across from Avery.

He retakes his position in the reading chair, while Oliver sits opposite him in another chair. Chloe lowers herself next to me, taking my hand in hers and giving it a reassuring squeeze.

"I assume you have a lot of questions," Oliver tells me. "I know I did when I met her yesterday. I can assure you, I spent all night vetting her story. As far as I can tell, what she's about to share with you is true. Be warned, though. It may not be easy for you to hear. It was difficult for me, and I don't have a horse in this race, so to speak."

"It's okay. I'll be okay. I can handle it."

"She can," Chloe adds. "She's a pediatric oncology nurse. This woman deals with kids dying on a daily basis yet still goes to work."

"You're a nurse?" Avery breathes, and we all look at her.

"I am."

"Your mother wanted to be a nurse before she…" She swallows hard. "Well, before."

"Why don't you start with where you met Sofia," Oliver suggests.

The affection in her gaze turns blank, and she stares into the distance, as if watching a movie. "In hell."

The tone of her voice causes a chill to trickle down my spine.

"It didn't seem that way at first. It seemed like it was exactly what I needed. What we were all looking for." She pulls her quivering lip between her teeth. "I couldn't have been more wrong."

"Let's start at the beginning," Lincoln offers. "I think that might help Isabella understand what we're dealing with."

Avery nods, then looks back at me, fidgeting with her hands in her lap. "When I was fifteen, I got pregnant. I was young and stupid. Grew up in a small town in Virginia where people didn't talk about sex. They pretended it didn't happen, so forget about anyone teaching teenagers how to protect themselves if they *did* have sex. My home life wasn't great. Dad drank a lot. Worked a factory job. Mom was a waitress at a diner. To say money was tight was an understatement. When I found out I was pregnant, I was terrified, had no idea what to do.

"One day, when both my parents were working, I stole twenty bucks from where I knew my father hid money to buy liquor and took a bus to a nearby city. Went to a clinic to see what my options were. All I knew was, if my father found out about my pregnancy, he'd kill me.

"As I left the clinic, a woman approached. Told me she could help if I wanted to keep the baby. I explained I couldn't. That my parents couldn't know I was pregnant. That adoption wasn't an option because they'd still find out." She blows out a laugh. "In retrospect, I should have told them. Any abuse I would have suffered at my father's hand would have been nothing compared to what I went through." Her voice is strained as she fights back a wave of tears.

"Who was the woman?" I press, angling toward her.

"I don't know. I should have asked. But this is what they did. They preyed on teenage girls who'd just found out they were pregnant. I couldn't afford to get an abortion. Plus, I was a minor. My parents would have had to give consent. This woman gave me an alternative."

"And what was that?"

"She told me she helped at a home for girls just like me. Young. Scared. Pregnant. Painted this amazing picture. How they had private tutors so we could continue our education. Offered lessons to learn various skills. Provided all the medical care and treatment. Gave us a place to live for the duration of our pregnancy. All at no cost…at least in dollars."

"What did they get out of it?" I ask, although I fear I already know the answer.

"A baby. They didn't come right out and demand we surrender our parental rights upon giving birth, but that was all part of their indoctrination. Since I didn't think I had any other option, I took this stranger up on her offer."

"What was this home like?"

"It was actually refreshing." A slight smile builds on her lips. "I had a roof over my head. I didn't have to worry about a drunk father coming home and hitting me because he felt like it. We had to go to daily religious lessons, which I could have done without, but I figured it was the least I could put up with in exchange for everything these people were doing for me."

"Did you ever talk to your parents? Tell them where you were?"

"No. I was still scared of them learning the truth. After a while, I no longer thought of my parents anymore, was convinced they didn't care about me."

"Why?"

"It started gradually, but over the length of my pregnancy, they completely indoctrinated me. Took away my ability to think freely. Convinced me I was incapable of caring for myself, so I'd never be able to care for another human. Made me believe the only thing I was good for was having babies for other valuable members of society."

"That sounds like something straight out of a dystopian novel."

"It does, but there's nothing dystopian about what I

endured for over ten years."

"You stayed even after you gave birth?"

She pulls her lower lip between her teeth to stop her chin from quivering. I'm not sure I want to know what happened in the years that followed.

"About a week after I gave birth, they'd made arrangements with another facility. They'd give me a place to stay while I got back on my feet. I didn't even consider going home. These people had me convinced my parents weren't good people, that I should cut all ties with them. So, instead of returning to a house of sin, as they referred to my old home, they drove me to what I thought would be a halfway house. But it wasn't. It was the place that would become my prison for the next decade."

"Do you remember where it was?"

She shakes her head.

"You didn't take note of any landmarks during the drive? Cities? Towns? Statues? Anything?"

"I would have, had I not fallen asleep. That was a common theme among all of us. We all fell asleep."

"They drugged you," I breathe.

"I didn't think anything of it at the time. After all, I'd just given birth. I was pretty tired."

"What was it like? This so-called halfway house?"

She looks to the ceiling, as if trying to recall the details after the passage of years. "At any given time, there were several dozen women. The conditions were so uncomfortable, you eventually began to *want* to get pregnant."

I scrunch my brows. "What? Why?"

"If you were pregnant, you got moved to a different section of the compound. They needed to make you comfortable so nothing happened to the baby. They didn't care about *your* life. But once you were pregnant, you were carrying a gift from God."

"It's like *The Handmaid's Tale*."

"It does bear a strong resemblance, but in the book, they did it to repopulate what they believed to be a dying civilization. Here, their sole motivation was greed."

"Greed?"

She nods. "Desperate parents were willing to pay twenty grand, minimum, for a baby."

"Did these parents know what was going on?" I couldn't imagine any prospective parent being okay with adopting a child born under these conditions.

"I doubt it. From what I was able to learn during my time there, all adoptions were legitimate. This was where all that brainwashing came into play. I signed away my parental rights each and every time I gave birth. I didn't think I had a choice. It took me years to realize I was more than a walking uterus. I still struggle with it, and it's been nearly twenty years."

"So they were running a baby mill? Did the first home you went to know? Or do you think they were just as blind to it as you were?"

"They knew. It's why they worked so hard to brainwash us. That way, we wouldn't put up a fight when they sold our bodies so we'd get pregnant, then when they sold the babies."

I chew on my lower lip as I consider my next question. I feel a squeeze on my hand and look to Chloe. I'd forgotten she was here, too consumed by Avery's story.

"Tell me about my mother. What was she like?"

She swipes at her cheeks, giving a small smile. "Strong. Stubborn."

I blow out a laugh. "Sounds like me."

"She had this vitality, even in our surroundings.

Always had a way of making us smile."

"How did she end up there? Did you ever talk about it?"

"Her story was much like mine. Inattentive parents. Got pregnant and was scared. Was approached by a woman who offered her a fresh start. But unlike the rest of us, I don't think they completely reprogrammed her. Because when she was pregnant with you, she began to question things. It could be because she'd fallen in love."

"With who?"

"Adam," she responds with a lift of the shoulders.

"Who was Adam?"

"One of the security guards who escorted us to see 'clients'."

"He was her *captor*?" My voice rises in pitch, my disbelief evident.

"As an outsider peering in, it's hard to understand. But Adam gave her something in that dark place. Compassion. He fell for her, too. Saw what we all saw in her."

"And she was certain he was my father?"

She nods. "Instead of taking her to a client, they spent time together. Adam paid off the clients she was supposed to see, as well as made sure the cash she was expected to earn still made it into the pool. It's why he struggled to scrape together enough money to get her out of there."

"How did she end up at JFK Airport on Christmas?"

"About a week before your due date, they move you to a different facility."

"Let me guess. Adam was to transport Sofia to this other facility."

She nods. "Yes. But they never made it."

"Where did they go?"

"He was trying to get her to Canada, but she went into labor before they made it. He tried to talk her into going to a hospital, but she refused. Didn't want to risk it. So she gave birth to you in a New Jersey motel room, your father by her side. Probably not the story you envisioned, but at least she wasn't alone." She swipes at a tear streaming down her cheek. "She had someone who loved her holding her hand and supporting her. Every time I'd given birth, that was all I wanted. So I'm glad Sofia could have that."

It's not what I'd want when giving birth, but I guess after having everything taken from you — your liberty, your autonomy, your ability to think — you hold on to what you can.

"What happened next?" I ask finally.

"It didn't take long for them to realize Adam hadn't shown up with Sofia. According to the story Sofia told, he wanted to give her time to recuperate before leaving, thought they would be okay since he made sure to pay cash for everything. But on Christmas morning, he went out to get diapers and never came back."

"So she left, too?"

Avery nods. "They had an agreement that if more than four hours passed and he hadn't returned, she'd get out of there. So she grabbed the passport and cash he'd set aside, just in case, and took a cab to JFK. Unfortunately, the flight she was able to get was delayed. And that's what got her caught. At least Adam had talked her into leaving you behind if it came to that. According to Sofia, he was pretty adamant about it. It was why he insisted she carry a baby doll around. As a decoy."

The room grows still as I stare blankly at the wall in front of me, all of Lincoln's accolades hanging on it. But I don't really see any of them. All I can think about is if my mother hadn't gone into labor, they would have been able to get to Canada and wouldn't have had to run anymore. Then again, these people may have eventually caught up with them.

"What happened next?"

Avery hangs her head, drawing her lips between her teeth. "They made an example out of them. Shot Adam in the head while we all watched, then beat Sofia. It was a warning of what would happen if we tried something like that."

"They didn't kill her?" I ask hopefully.

"She had two good ovaries and a uterus. Couldn't waste those," she shoots back sarcastically with a roll of her eyes.

"Is she…"

On a long exhale, she slowly shakes her head. "After about two years of not conceiving, they took her to a doctor on their payroll. That was the last time I saw her."

"Oh."

"Rumor was she had a prolapsed uterus. Since she could no longer conceive and had tried to escape, she was, well… Word is they killed her, but I never could confirm that."

I close my eyes, steeling myself to not break down. Once I heard the body language expert's analysis on my mother's behavior, I knew there was a chance she wouldn't be alive. I guess a part of me held on to hope she was, that she survived whatever she'd endured.

"Is that what happened to all the girls who could no longer conceive? They were killed?"

"No. Most were sold, either into sexual slavery or forced servitude. After what we'd been through, they couldn't let us walk free. We knew too much."

"How did you escape?"

She smiles. "A nurse at the hospital."

My eyes widen. "They took you to a hospital? Wouldn't that be a sure way to get caught?"

"In some situations, they had no choice if they wanted to save the baby. I'd started bleeding heavily at thirty-six weeks. They'd taken me to see the midwife who delivered all the babies, thinking I was going into labor, but I wasn't, so they took me to the hospital to make sure the baby was okay. The doctors discovered I had placenta previa, my placenta was blocking my cervix, which meant, unless my placenta shifted in the next few weeks, I'd have to have a C-section. I'd have to have the baby in a hospital, not at the birthing facility."

A contemplative look crossed her face. "It's funny. I was out in public, yet I never once thought to find out where I was. I'd been so brainwashed, it didn't even matter. There was no question in my mind I'd have the baby, then repeat the cycle."

"What changed?"

"Before the nurse signed off on my discharge papers, she asked me a question no one had in over ten years."

"What was that?"

"'Do you need help?' I almost didn't hear it at first. It was so quiet. So soft. Then I met her compassion-filled eyes. For the first time in years, I felt human, like I had worth. So I nodded. I instantly regretted it, especially when she left the room without saying a word. I was so scared she was telling someone what I'd done. Instead, she returned with a wheelchair, then pushed me down to the back loading dock and into a waiting ambulance. Told me not to look back, only forward. That looking back would only get me killed."

She smiles a small smile. "So that's what I did. The ambulance drove me to another hospital, where a woman took me to the next stop. It was like an underground railroad, which made me believe this wasn't their first rodeo. That some of those girls who'd gone to the hospital and never came back had been saved. For years, I tried to find out who it was, who saved my life, but everything from that day is a blur, apart from the woman who reminded me I was human."

"And the baby?"

She smiles, everything about her glowing. "Isn't a baby anymore. He's a sophomore at Northwestern University."

"You kept him." My words come out as more a relieved statement than a question.

"After being forced to give up so many other babies, I figured it was time I finally kept one. He became my reason for everything. Still is. And I guess that's why I never spoke up before now. I stayed quiet for him. To protect him. To keep him safe."

"And now?"

Her expression morphs into one of anger. "Now I'll do everything I can to help you find the people responsible for this."

Chapter Thirty-Five

THE INK ON the pages in front of me bleeds together, my tired eyes refusing to read anything else. I roll my neck, trying to loosen the muscles after having spent all day pouring over some of the unsolved missing person police files Lincoln was able to obtain. After listening to Avery's story, I became even more obsessed with getting to the bottom of this. So did she. She's been saddled with guilt, too. Can't shake the feeling that, had she acted sooner, maybe the police could have put the pieces together.

Thankfully, it hasn't been a total lost cause. She'd agreed to try hypnosis, hoping it would help jumpstart her memory. After several sessions over the past few weeks, she's brought forward a few memories of being in Maryland at some point. We're hopeful that, as time goes by and her hypnotherapist is able to take her deeper and deeper into her past, she'll remember more details her brain's been protecting her from.

It should be enough that I now have information on my mother. She has a name, a face. Hell, I even found out who my father was. He sacrificed everything to save my mother, to save me. But that's still not enough, not after hearing Avery's story. I've lived my professional life according to the edict, "Do no harm". I can't help but feel like I'm doing harm if I don't make sure the people behind this are no longer able to hurt anybody else.

"You should come write for the magazine," Chloe offers from across the table in her dining room, her own attention devoted to finding an anomaly that may be the break we need for this entire house of cards to come crumbling down.

"About what?" I scoff. "I studied nursing, not journalism."

"So?" She shrugs. "You have an analytical mind. That's all you need. You just need to know how to take the facts and process them."

"No thanks. I'll stick to nursing."

"Suit yourself. You could be the next Erin Brockovich."

"She was a paralegal."

"She was still a badass who refused to give up until she had all the answers. Kind of like you. You refuse to give up."

"I'm about ready to give up." I lean back in my chair and blow out a breath, defeated.

"No, you're not."

I meet Chloe's eyes. "You're right. I'm not. Even if I *am* frustrated." I return my attention to the papers, grabbing my highlighter and marking any websites in the victims' search history related to pregnancy, adoption, abortion, and the like.

As I run my highlighter along a line of text, I furrow my brow.

"What is it?" Chloe asks, noticing my expression.

"I'm not sure," I respond, my voice distant.

I grab another printout from another missing person case and flip through their search history. Finding a similarity, I place a star by that line. I do this with five more printouts, noticing five more similarities.

"Look at this." I line the papers up and push them toward her. "Each of these girls visited the same website. Faithful Living Christian Charities."

She sighs, pushing them back toward me. "That's not unusual. If you're a teenager and see two lines on that pregnancy test, the first thing you're going to do is some online searches. And I guarantee you Faithful Living will be the number one search result. They're nationwide and the top adoption agency in the country."

"That's not what's odd. It's the fact that each of these missing girls filled out an online form requesting more information about their services. This link that shows up in their search history is a form submission page."

I grab one of the boxes and yank out a folder labeled *e-mails*, flipping through the hundreds of pages, coming to an abrupt stop when I find the one I'm looking for. I do the same thing with each of the victims, finding the email containing their responses to the form.

"They each requested more info. But to do so, they filled out personal information. Name. Date of birth. Address. Phone number. Email. Parents' marital status. Income. Religious affiliation. How far along in the pregnancy." My breath hitches, mind reeling as I fumble through the papers again, scanning them. "In each case, approximately five days passed between the girls filling out this request for information and going to a clinic. What if…" I look up, but don't see anything other than a thousand puzzle pieces I can't quite put together. "What if Faithful Living gave them information about the closest clinic, then when they went, they scooped them up?"

My intense gaze pierces Chloe's stare, which is a mixture of disbelief and amusement, like she's humoring my insane theory. Then she exhales deeply, tying her blonde locks into a messy bun on top of her head.

"I understand how that might be suspicious, but Faithful Living facilitates thousands of adoptions every year, have a huge public presence. There's no way they'd be able to get away with something like this. Plus, your mother went missing in the early nineties. The internet was just starting. No websites for you to fill out a form to request information. Even if there were, it was all dial-up. Can you imagine how slow that must have been?" She snorts a laugh.

"I'd rather not. But maybe they advanced with the times. Oliver pulled phone records. My mother *did* place a call to Faithful Living, just like Avery."

"It's a huge adoption agency. Plus, you heard Avery. I think we're dealing with some extreme religious faction. That's the angle the FBI has been looking into, as well. They have their cult specialist combing through police reports in Maryland to see if anything raises red flags. They also looked into Faithful Living. There was nothing to substantiate them being involved in any way, other than the girls contacting them about their services. Like I said——"

"I know. I know." I sigh, my shoulders slumping. "Pretty much every teenage girl who unexpectedly becomes pregnant contacts them."

Chloe reaches for my hand, covering it with hers. "If I were in your shoes and had learned my mother had been through what yours had, I'd want answers, too. But you're burning yourself out. You need to give your brain a rest, think about something else."

"It's hard *not* to think about this."

Her phone buzzes and she glances at the screen, her face lighting up as she types out a quick text. Based on her expression, I can only assume it's Lincoln. She stands from the table. "Sometimes when I'm working on a story and feel like I'm missing a piece of the puzzle,

I take a break. Step away. When I return, I have a fresh set of eyes, a fresh perspective. Maybe that's what you need."

She turns, heading down the hallway toward the bathroom. When a knock echoes, I float my gaze to the front door.

"Can you get that?" Chloe shouts. "I ordered a little something for you to nibble on."

"I suppose you want me to pay for it, too."

"My wallet's on the kitchen island."

I reluctantly drag myself to my feet. Finding Chloe's wallet, I continue toward the door, pulling it open.

"How much do I owe you?" I don't even glance up as I rifle through her wallet. It would be just like her to order an obscene amount of takeout and not realize she didn't have enough money to cover it.

"I'd settle for a kiss."

I dart my eyes up, dropping the wallet. I tackle Asher as I fling my arms around him, pressing my lips against his, both of us laughing and kissing at the same time. I thread my fingers through his hair, tugging at it, eliciting a satisfied moan. God, I missed that. There's nothing sexier than that deep, guttural vibration.

"What are you doing here?" I ask once I manage to pull my lips from his.

"I have the day off." He lowers his mouth to mine once more. "And there's no one I'd rather spend it with than you."

"You flew all the way from Charleston just to spend a few hours with me?"

He shrugs. "That, and hopefully get laid." He playfully waggles his brows.

"Is that all I am?" I teasingly pout, making a show of crossing my arms in front of my chest. "A long-distance booty call?"

His eyes darkening, he grabs my ass, yanking me against him. "And what a nice booty it is." He kisses me again. I melt into him, my heart full.

"Get a room." Chloe's voice cuts through our moment.

We tear our lips from each other, but I remain in Asher's possessive hold, his hand still firmly planted on my backside.

"No need to get a room when I have an entire house." He places a kiss on my mouth, then releases me. Approaching Chloe, he hugs her, kissing her cheek. "Thanks for your help."

"Anytime. She needs a break. So go give her one."

"Yes, ma'am." Asher salutes her before turning to me, holding out his elbow. "Shall we?"

I hastily grab my cell and shove it into my purse, then loop my arm through his. "Where are we going?"

"Anywhere you want, darlin'."

Chapter Thirty-Six

"**Y**OU KNOW WHAT just occurred to me?" I ask as I lay on my back, using Asher's stomach as a pillow while he reclines in the same position.

We'd spent our day doing whatever I wanted. After a casual lunch at one of my favorite pizza places, we walked along the high line in Chelsea before heading out to Gramercy Park. As if able to read my mind, Asher grabbed a bottle of wine from his place, then took me to the residents-only park, where we've been for the past hour, watching the sky turn from blue to pink to almost black.

At first, I worried some paparazzi would appear and snap his photo, or an adoring fan would recognize him and ask for a selfie. Not because it would interfere with our time together, but because of our fear that Jessie would learn the truth before Asher had all his ducks in a row. Thankfully, that never happened, the sunglasses and baseball cap a sufficient disguise until we were safe behind the locked gates of Gramercy Park. I look forward to the day we no longer have to sneak around like this.

"What's that?" He runs his fingers through my hair, his touch light.

"This is our first official date." I adjust my position so I can peer into his eyes, resting my chin on his chest. "We've never gone out. Not like today. Until now, we've only hung out at your place or mine. Or Grams' lake house. This is the first time we've gone out in public and held hands, like real couples do."

"Huh." A furtive look momentarily crosses his brow before he floats his eyes back to mine. "Well, I hope it met all your expectations of a first date."

I inch my lips closer to his. "It did. I liked getting a taste of what it'll be like to be your official girlfriend."

"Soon, darlin'. I promise we won't have to keep it a secret much longer." He brushes his mouth against mine, treating me to a sweet kiss.

I can't remember ever being this happy, this at ease in a relationship. Sure, we still have the matter of Jessie, but Asher's handling that. His lawyer has most of the paperwork drawn up. Essentially, Asher will buy Jessie out of his contract, offering him a substantial amount of money up front that equals a large percentage of royalties on future albums. In addition, he'll retain his royalty payments on all albums already released. Of course, that all depends on how Jessie takes the news. Asher remains hopeful he'll understand. I have my doubts.

"Tell me about your first date," I murmur against his lips, then pull away.

"Ever?"

"Yeah." I hoist myself into a sitting position, pour a little more wine into both of our glasses, and hand him one. "Who was the lucky girl?"

He squints as he sits up, searching his memory. "It was probably Lauren Donovan."

"When was this?"

"Eighth grade."

"Where did you take her?"

"Mini golfing." A nostalgic smile tugs on his mouth. "I had to swallow my pride, since I'm absolutely horrible at mini golf. But that's what she wanted to do."

"What happened with you guys, other than the fact you were both only thirteen and incapable of being in a real relationship?"

"Jessie started dating her younger sister, Angela. At first, it was perfect. We were able to double date, but one day, Angela wanted to go see some chick flick and Jessie wanted to see an action movie. So they broke up."

I laugh. "If only life could be as simple as it was when we were thirteen and thought a disagreement about which movie to see was the end of the world."

"Exactly. So, since they weren't together anymore, Lauren broke up with me."

"I'm sorry."

He shrugs. "Doesn't matter. Everything in my life brought me to you. And trust me. As lovely as Lauren was, she couldn't hold a candle to you, darlin'." He digs his hand into my hair, pulling me toward him. "Have I told you today how addictive these lips of yours are?" He nibbles on the bottom one, tugging it gently.

"Yes. But you can tell me again."

"I fucking love your lips. Love the way they taste. Love the way they feel. Love the way they love." He claims my mouth with a kiss, then drops his hold on me and takes a sip of his wine. "How about you?"

"Me?" I pant, electricity humming through me, my body still on high alert from his kiss.

"Yes. Your first date." He sucks in a breath. "As long as it wasn't with Jessie. I'd rather not go there."

I roll my eyes. "I was almost nineteen when we got together. I *did* date before him."

He worries his bottom lip, and I can see the question on the tip of his tongue. "But you were a virgin, weren't you?" he asks, a hint of sadness in his voice. "That's what he... Well, he said you were."

I close my eyes, slowly nodding. I hear him expel a shaky breath.

"I'm sorry," he says, and I lift my gaze to his. "That should have been me. If I just—"

I cup his cheek. "No. Like you said, everything that's happened before now has brought us to this place." I laugh slightly before launching into my best Asher York impression, my voice turning gruff. "And as wonderful as Jessie was, he couldn't hold a candle to you, darlin'."

He sets his wine glass on the ground, then pushes me onto my back, caging me in with his arms as he hovers over me, his eyes skating over my lips. "Is that right?"

Reaching up, I scrape my fingers through his locks, relishing in his reaction as he arches into the touch. "Definitely." I grab the back of his neck, forcing his mouth to mine. He resists, a lust-filled tug-of-war as I plead for his kiss, wrapping my legs around his waist, pulsing against him.

"Goddamn, baby," he groans. "Do you have any idea how hard you're making this?"

"I believe I do." I grin coyly.

He lowers his mouth to my neck, tracing a circle with his tongue. "I've been trying to be good all day. Didn't want you to think I only came up here to have sex. Wanted to spend some time with you fully clothed for a change."

"Clothes can be overrated."

"But still." He pulls back, meeting my eyes. "I don't want you to think I'm only interested in you for sex. I'm not. I mean, I *love* the sex. The sex is fucking fantastic. But that's not why I'm with you. I'm with you because I can't breathe without you."

"It means a lot you're not only interested in sex. But right now, I'm *extremely* interested in sex. While I've enjoyed every single second of today, I need my happy ending."

He arches a brow. "Happy ending?"

"Or hole in one."

It's silent for a moment while he gives me a sideways glance. Then he laughs a full belly laugh, collapsing on top of me, his body shaking. His mood is infectious, so I join in. These are my favorite memories of us. No elaborate dinners. No designer clothes. No fancy chauffeurs. Just us. The way we began. The way I hope we'll always be.

"Come on." Asher pushes off me and climbs to his feet. He extends his hand, helping me up. I dust off my jeans as he collects the blanket and our wine. "Let's go work on that hole in one." He leans toward me, nibbling on my earlobe. "Last I checked, I had a zero handicap on that."

"That's what I'm hoping for."

Chapter Thirty-Seven

"**H**URRY," I BEG the second we're inside Asher's townhouse, both of us frantically trying to rip each other's clothes off as quickly as possible. Our kisses are interspersed with moments of heavy breathing before our need for one another gets the better of us and we return to the source of our addiction.

"I don't think I've ever been this desperate to get a woman naked."

"Bedroom. Now." My demand is an animalistic growl.

"First one there gets a spanking."

"God, I love the way your mind works." I dive in for one more kiss, then start up the stairs, my squeals echoing through the space when he lands a hard blow against my ass.

"Is that the best you've got?" I call after him as I crest the top of the first flight of stairs. "I barely felt that."

"Careful what you wish for, Isabella. When I'm done with you, that ass will be sore for days."

I squeal again, rounding the corner and about to dash up the next flight of stairs when a light snaps on in the living room, causing us to come to an abrupt stop.

Disoriented, I scan the space. The instant my eyes fall on Jessie, sitting in the reading chair, his cold eyes trained on us, my heart plummets, face burning. I part my lips, struggling to come up with something, *anything* to explain what he'd overheard. But I can't. Asher can't, either, as evidenced by his own silence.

"So it's true then, is it?" Jessie's eerily calm voice cuts through the thick tension.

"Jessie, I—"

He holds up his hand, cutting Asher off. The muscles in his face tighten in a pained expression as he looks away, almost like the sight of us makes him physically ill.

"I didn't want to believe it. Didn't want to you would do something like this." With each word he speaks, his tone becomes more hurt. More distressed. More broken. He stands and begins pacing, agitated. "I thought I must be overreacting. That there was no way my brother, my own flesh and blood, my best friend would do something so deceptive, so cruel, so insidious as to go behind my back and sleep with my ex-*fucking-fiancée!*" he roars, his voice seemingly causing the liquor bottles on the wet bar to rattle. His face reddens, his nostrils flare, his lips curl. "God!" He bends over, tugging at his hair.

My throat tightens as I watch this man I once loved break into pieces. I thought I'd seen him at the lowest of his lows when he begged me not to leave him. But that was nothing compared to this.

I open my mouth, wanting to offer him some sort of comfort, but what is there to say? Nothing can make this hurt less. When we started down this path, I knew this would happen, that Jessie would be a casualty of our love. It doesn't make this any easier, though.

"Do you want to know how I figured it out?" Jessie asks, his tone almost cruel in its severity. He pins his stare on me, the vein in his neck pulsing. "Next time you sleep around behind someone's back, make sure you don't leave your shoes and purse lying around for anyone to see, then wear those *same* shoes and purse around that person a few hours later. Chances are, they'll put two and two together."

I blink, having difficulty breathing. How could I have been so stupid? Jessie had seen my purse and shoes. Had commented on them. That hadn't even crossed my mind as I got ready for Asher's concert that night. I don't exactly have a closet full of purses and shoes. I have one purse. As far as shoes, I have a few options, but the black ones are sexy. And since I was seeing Asher, I opted for sexy.

"Jessie…" Asher steps toward him, his hands clasped in front of his chest, pleading. "We never meant to hurt you."

"*Bullshit*. Bull. Shit. You can't say that. You *did* intend to hurt me. The second you two started whatever you call this fucked-up situation, you knew the consequences. Yet you didn't care."

"It's not like that," he argues, but doesn't raise his voice. "I'll admit we hooked up last year in Vegas but we walked away from each other because we knew what pursuing anything would do to you."

Jessie blinks, processing this additional information. When he speaks again, his words are low. "It was the morning after the blackout, wasn't it? That's why you acted so weird, so off, right?"

Asher's Adam's apple bobs up and down. That's all Jessie needs to know the truth. "Like I said, we walked away with no intention of seeing each other again. Then she came to Grams' lake house with you…" He shakes his head. "I know you don't believe in such notions, but I knew fate had brought her back to me, giving us another chance. Why else would she keep walking into my life if there weren't some other reason?"

"Is that how it works? You run into a girl a few times,

call it fate, and that makes it okay to fuck her?"

"I love her."

"Oh god..." He briefly closes his eyes, the agony in his voice causing tears to spill over my eyelids. "Do you seriously think that makes this any better? That I'll suddenly be okay with this because... Oh, great! You're not just fucking the woman I wanted to marry, but you *love* her?" He bites on his fist in an attempt to control his emotions. Then he looks between us, drawing in a shaky breath. "I hope you two will be very happy." He pushes past us, hurrying down the stairs.

"Jessie, please," Asher calls after him. "Let's talk about this. Just... Just hear me out. Please."

To my surprise, he pauses, facing forward for several excruciatingly long seconds before turning. His disgusted eyes look from Asher, to me, then back again. "Actually, that's a great idea."

"It is?" Asher tilts his head, taken aback.

"Let's put it all out there. I'll start."

"You'll start?"

"Yes. It's only fair." His voice is chilling as he slowly makes his way back up the stairs. "After all, if you're going to be honest with me, I should tell you about something *I've* been keeping from you. Something Izzy's involved in."

I furrow my brow, wracking my brain for what he could be talking about. I've barely spoken more than a few words to Jessie over the past few months. The last real conversation I had with him was when he'd called for a status update on the album.

Then it hits me. The album. Our agreement.

The money.

"Jessie..." It's all I can manage, my pulse skyrocketing, a scorching heat covering me, sweat beading on my nape.

"What are you talking about?" Cautiously, Asher steps away from me, floating his gaze between Jessie and me, waiting for one of us to explain. If I only knew how to formulate the words.

"She didn't tell you?" Jessie's statement is biting in its malice.

"Tell me what?"

"The reason she came to Grams' lake house. It wasn't fate that brought her there. It was *me*," he hisses, pointing to himself. "I called her a few weeks earlier and asked for her help with a little…problem."

I stand mute, unable to find any words at this crucial moment. Instead of defending myself, I watch the train I'm on race closer and closer to the cliff.

"What was the problem?" Asher asks timidly, but he probably already knows. He increases the distance between us, crossing his arms over his chest.

"What do you think? You were blocked. I needed to do something so you'd hit your studio date. Talked with Grams about it. She suggested you come up to the lake house in the hopes it would inspire you. But she also suggested inviting Izzy. I hadn't spoken to her in nearly a decade. At the time, I didn't think *you* had, either. I thought I was lucky she even picked up the phone."

"So?" Asher shrugs. "You asked her to come help. She did."

"Do you want to know the only reason she *did* come help?"

I pull my lips between my teeth to stop my chin from quivering.

"Because I *paid* her to." Jessie leans into Asher, eyes wild, muscles tense. "Two points on an album, on one of *your* albums, is a lot of fucking money. But I knew she wouldn't see that money for several months, possibly not at all, so as an incentive, I told her she'd get a twenty grand bonus if you had songs for an album before your next studio date. Told her to do whatever it took." He turns his bitter eyes to me. "I just didn't think she'd take that to mean she should fuck you."

Tears stream down my face as I reach for Asher, hoping he'll be rational enough to know none of this matters. But he steps away, his Adam's apple bobbing up and down in a hard swallow. I've never seen him look at me this way. With such repugnance, such spite, such pure hatred.

"Is it true?" he chokes out, stance wide, eyes bulging.

"Asher, please—"

He holds up a hand, and I fall silent. "Is. It. True?" This time, his words come out louder, his expression imploring me to tell him the truth. But I still struggle, knowing once I do, that may very well be the death knell in our relationship. "It's a simple question. If Jessie hadn't paid you, would you have come to the lake house? Yes. Or. No?"

I lower my head, my voice barely more than a whisper. "No."

I can't bear to look at his reaction, but I can feel his anguish deep down in my bones. When I'd told Nora about the money, she warned me to tell him, especially once we got back together. I planned on it. I never expected this to happen, although in hindsight, I should have known Jessie would try to hurt me like I hurt him. An eye for an eye. A heart for a heart. That's how he operates.

"That night you finally came to me… Did you only do so because of the bonus? Because you saw the clock ticking and needed to do something to hurry me along?"

I rip my eyes up to his, shaking my head. "No," I answer vehemently. "Absolutely not. I came to you because I wanted to be with you. Because I *love* you. Because I finally realized you possessed every last piece of my heart. For the longest time, I thought Jessie kept a piece. But he didn't. You did. You always have. Our souls are connected. That's why we've always worked, why we feel like we've known each other so much longer than we have. Because there's something tethering us to each other. Because we're meant to be together. Please… You have to believe me."

It's silent as my confession rings between us. Then he pinches the bridge of his nose. "How can I?" He brings his eyes to mine as his glare hardens. "I don't know what's real, what's not."

"Asher, please," I beg frantically, desperation taking over. "You know me. You know how I feel about you."

"Do I?" he shoots back. "How do I know what you told me was true? How do I know *anything* you've told me is true? You could have just said it all to make sure I released my goddamn album on time." He bites his lower lip, his muscles quivering. "It was all a fucking lie, wasn't it? No wonder you didn't show up at the bar like you promised. You'd gotten paid. I'd recorded the album. No need to continue the charade, right?"

"That's not true." I rush toward him, but he avoids my touch. I've never been so desperate to feel another person's skin as I am now. "I've always loved you, Asher."

He stares at me, his reddened eyes narrowed into slits. "People who love each other don't hurt each other. Not like this."

I shake my head, struggling to say anything that will prove my feelings for him run deeper than this arrangement. That I loved him before that. That I've loved him for years.

"*You're* the reason I broke off my engagement with

Jessie," I blurt out, the words leaving my mouth before I can stop them. The entire house is still as my voice seems to echo around me.

I slowly shift my eyes toward Jessie, meeting the anguished and shocked expression on his face. I wish I could make it hurt less, but he deserves the truth. They both do.

"It's why I gave him back the ring." I turn my attention back to Asher. "Not because he brought Candace home with him. I didn't care about that. Even if he hadn't brought her home, I had to walk away. Do you know why?"

I approach Asher. This time, he doesn't retreat. Simply stares down at me in silence.

"Because I loved you. Even back then. I couldn't stay with Jessie knowing you possessed a piece of my heart. At the time, I convinced myself I had no choice but to walk away from you, too. Convinced myself you'd never choose me over Jessie. When we saw each other again in Vegas, I wondered if maybe our story wasn't over yet. If we could finally have the chance we both deserved. But then Jessie showed up, and I got scared. Not of being caught, but because of how strongly I felt toward you. Just like when I left all those years ago." Relentless tears fall from my eyes, obscuring my vision, as I beg for Asher to believe me, to trust me, to *choose* me.

I wipe my cheeks. "Okay? That's the truth. The only truth I know. That I love you. That I'm absolutely petrified of the way I feel about you. That I know there will never be anyone who possesses every last part of me like you do. Like you *always* will."

My chest heaves as I stand before him, pleading for him to understand, to realize any agreement I made with Jessie doesn't matter. That the only thing that does is this once-in-a-lifetime love we've miraculously found in one another.

"If that's true, why didn't you tell me when I shared *my* truth about that night?" He pulls his lips between his teeth, shaking his head. "This is just too little, too late. One final act of desperation." He lifts his eyes to mine, not a single hint of emotion within. "You know where the door is."

His words are a knife to my already ruptured heart. I don't know how I'd feel if the shoe were on the other foot. If I'd learned I'd fallen in love with someone who was only with me in the beginning because he'd been paid to be there. I'd probably question whether any of it was real, too.

"Is this want you want? To throw away everything we have?"

"There's nothing *to* throw away. Apparently, there never was."

His shoulders slumping, he turns toward the stairs leading up to the bedrooms, pushing past Jessie, who looks on with sadness, the self-satisfied smirk he wore minutes ago gone. It's almost as if he's realized exactly what he's done.

I want to go after Asher, shake some sense into him, force him to see the truth behind the lies. But I have nothing left. I'm drained. Defeated. Shattered.

I shuffle down the stairs, then glance over my shoulder as he's about to disappear from view. "I'm sorry I broke you."

He pauses, not moving for several long seconds. Then I make out his faint voice. "You don't get to take credit for that. I broke myself when I made the mistake of believing in something that isn't real."

Chapter Thirty-Eight

"A RE YOU SURE about this?" Nora asks as she grabs the roll of packing tape and slides it across the top of a box labeled *kitchen*, sealing it. She adds it to a stack that's begun accumulating over the past week. "I told you that you can stay with me. The other girls have offered, too."

I stand from where I've been wrapping up various framed photos and other keepsakes. Dusting off my shorts, I use my arm to swipe away a few beads of sweat from my brow, then make my way toward her. "And I appreciate that." I place my hand over hers. "It means a lot. But I think getting out of the city for a while is exactly what I need. What was it you said at that blues club?"

I force a smile to hide the pain from the memory of the night that changed everything, as I've done so often these past several weeks whenever anyone asks how I'm holding up. At this point, my responses are second nature, having repeated them so many times. But anyone can hear the lack of conviction in my voice when I say I'm fine. That it doesn't matter. That when you think about it, Asher and I were only together a few weeks, even if our hearts have belonged to each other much longer. I'll move on. I have to.

"That I need to learn to fall in love with myself before I can fall in love with another person," Nora recites with a sigh.

"So that's what I'm doing. I need to learn to love myself again. And I don't think I can do that in this city." I move past her, wrapping a wine glass in bubble wrap, then inserting it into a box of glassware. "Plus, I got a new job in the pediatric oncology unit at the hospital in Stamford. There's no reason for me to commute. My parents live the next town over. It just…works."

"You're really okay moving back in with your parents?"

"It's not permanent. Just long enough for me to get back on my feet."

"You wouldn't have to if you keep the money from the album," Nora sings as she edges in beside me, wrapping my dishes, then placing them in another box.

"You know why I can't do that," I remind her in a low voice.

"I know." She gives me a sad smile. "I'm just going to miss having you in the city."

"Like I told Chloe and Evie, I'll have Sundays and Mondays off. We can meet for brunch every Sunday. You're all making it sound like I'm moving to the opposite part of the world. I'm not. I'm going to Greenwich."

"That place *is* a different part of the world," she mutters.

"It's… What? An hour by train? I'm barely over the state line. It's not a big deal. I just…" I set a wine glass on the counter, drawing in a breath. "I need to leave this place. Need to go somewhere else. I can't be here anymore." I lift my pleading eyes to her, a heaviness in my chest, an ache in my heart.

She runs her hands down my arms, her soft expression full of sympathy. "I get it. Doesn't mean I'll miss you any less." She pulls me against her, hugging me tightly.

"I'll miss you, too," I manage to say, struggling to keep my tears from spilling over. I knew this move would be draining on my already overwrought emotions. I didn't realize it would be this difficult.

I faintly make out the sound of the door opening and closing, then two additional pairs of arms surround us.

"We need in on this, too," Chloe says.

"Think if I keep my arms around Izzy she won't leave?" Evie quips after a few seconds.

"Maybe," Nora responds. "You can try it."

"No, you can't," I answer. "You guys will never last."

"How do you know?" Evie asks.

"All your bladders are tiny. I swear, you three pee every few minutes. I guarantee Chloe already needs to."

I sense her shift on her feet. "Now that you mention it..." There's a pause, then Chloe drops her hold. "Okay. You win. I really have to pee."

We all break apart, laughing, watching as she makes a mad dash to the bathroom.

When she returns a minute later, I nod at a small gift bag on the kitchen counter. "What's that?"

"A little house-chilling gift," Evie responds.

"House...chilling?" I cross my arms over my chest, a single brow arched.

"You get a house-warming gift when you move in to a new place. We decided to get you a few things you might find useful now that you'll be living with your parents."

I pinch my lips together, observing my friends' amused expressions. I'll probably regret this, but I reach for the bag and shift through the tissue paper, pulling out a small box. "Ear plugs?"

Chloe shrugs. "I've seen the way your dad looks at

your mom. Trust me. You'll need those."

"Oh, my god! Those are my parents!" I toss the box onto the counter as if it holds some infectious disease. "I'm scared to see what else is in here."

"You should be," Evie states.

"But I'm also curious." Reaching in, I pull out a hardcover book. "*The Complete Grimm Brothers Fairy Tales*?"

Nora giggles. "Look inside."

I crack open the cover, then slam it shut when I catch a glimpse of what's hidden within the pages.

"You can't leave sex toys out in the open anymore," Evie explains. "No one would ever open a book looking for your private things."

"My parents won't be treating me like a teenager. I doubt they'll snoop through any of my stuff." I wave the book with the vibrator hiding inside. "But this certainly gives new meaning to a fairy-tale ending."

Our giggles echo against the empty walls of my once lived-in apartment. Then I pull the final item out of the bag. It seems innocent enough. But I know my friends. There's no way this is just a t-shirt. Unfolding it, I read the bold text and roll my eyes.

With a smirk, I hold it up to my body. "*I still live with my parents*?"

"I had to have them make it special," Chloe explains. "It normally only comes in baby and toddler sizes."

"Great. Way to make me feel good about this."

She winks. "You know I love you."

"I know."

She faces me, grasps my shoulders, and holds me at arm's length. "Do you really think this is the right move? You don't think—"

"What? That Asher will change his mind?"

"You never know. This is about the same amount of

time it took Lincoln to come around after I pushed *him* away."

"That's different," I argue.

"Not really. I pretended I didn't love him. Same thing Asher did to you."

"There's no pretending. I hurt him."

I spin on my heels, heading in search of the package I received yesterday. When I find it by my bed, I bring it back to the kitchen and dump the contents onto the counter.

"Pretty sure this is all the evidence I need that Asher wants nothing to do with me."

"What is this?" Nora asks, picking up one of the folded pieces of paper, examining it with her scrupulous gaze.

"When Jessie and I dated, Asher and I spent a fair bit of time together. We had our disagreements. Usually over stupid stuff. But after every single one, we'd apologize by leaving the other an origami dove, our peace offering. No matter what, all would be forgiven."

I swallow hard through the lump in my throat. For the past month, I'd found solace in the idea that he held onto these doves. But the second I opened this box, all hope of him forgiving me evaporated.

"Asher had given me a copy of his tour book. It has all his travel information. Hotels where they're staying. Production office address of each venue. So every day this past month, I've sent him an origami dove, hoping it would be the day he realized how long I've loved him, that the money didn't change anything, that it was just something that got me to where I was meant to be. So the fact he sent these back..." I shake my head, biting on my lower lip to stop my chin from quivering, the ache of losing him settling deep in my marrow. "There's no forgiveness coming. He's done."

All my friends' expressions fall. Evie's own chin quivers. Nora clutches her heart. And Chloe wraps her arms around me, kissing my temple. "Don't forget what Grams told you." She meets my eyes.

"What's that?"

"True love has a habit of coming back." She gives me a hopeful smile.

I wish I could find even an ounce of hope in my situation. A year ago, I would have been the one instilling hope in her. Hell, I *was* the one instilling hope in her. Now, I don't see any way I can make this right. I've betrayed Asher's trust in a way I doubt he'll ever move past. Without trust, we're nothing. And now, we *are* nothing.

"The only thing coming back for me is a lot of lonely nights." I gesture to all the origami doves.

"I never knew you to give up so easily," Nora states.

"What choice do I have? I can't chase after a broken dream."

"Can't? Or won't?"

Chapter Thirty-Nine

"HOW WAS IT, *mi amor*?" Mama asks as I remove my napkin from my lap, placing it on top of my empty plate.

"You know I love your lasagna. And I told you. You don't have to cook for me."

She pushes back from the table, waving me off. "Hush. You're my daughter."

"I can cook, too."

"Don't even worry about it," Papa interjects in his deep, booming voice. "Your mother and I are retired. We have nothing but free time on our hands. You work fifty hours a week. Let us take care of you again."

"I hate depending on you guys."

"You're not," Mama insists. "You're *familia*."

"Plus, you know how your mother is. She doesn't know how to cook for just two people. You're doing me a favor by living here and eating all the food she makes." He pats his stomach, but he's still in as great a shape as he's always been, despite the passing of years.

I must admit, it's been refreshing to be back with my parents these past several weeks. I'm sure the novelty will wear off soon. Hopefully I'll be in a better place financially by then. My plan is to save everything I can over the next few months, then return every cent I received from Jessie. I'm not doing it to earn Asher's favor. That ship has sailed. I need to clear my conscience. Then I can finally start my next chapter.

"Since you put it that way, I'm more than happy to help you out, Papa." I wink.

"I knew I could count on you, Isabella."

"What are daughters for?"

There's a brief pause at the table before he says, "Speaking of which... Any more news on figuring out who was behind your birth mother's disappearance?"

I shake my head. "The FBI had to move resources away from this and to more pressing matters. Ones with more concrete evidence."

"How did Avery take the news?"

Ever since I announced I wanted to find my birth mother, my parents have supported me completely. More so once I found out her identity and shifted my attention to solving the mystery behind her disappearance.

"She wishes she had come forward sooner with what she knew. She can't help but think how many girls she could have saved if she had."

"She had more than just herself to think about. Trust me." He covers my hand with his. "When you have a child, your focus shifts. You make your decisions with one purpose in mind. Protecting them. If I were in her shoes, I would have done the same thing. As an outsider faced with the decision to save one hundred lives or one, you'd no doubt opt to save a hundred. But when that one life is your child..." His eyes well with tears as he squeezes my hand. "Well, that life is more valuable than even a hundred thousand lives. And I'll forever be grateful your birth mother thought so, too."

I stand and walk over to the head of the table, wrapping my arms around him from behind. "Thanks for choosing me."

"It was never a choice. The second we arrived at the hospital to pick up our new foster and I saw your mother's eyes light up, I knew you'd never be leaving us."

The doorbell rings, and I release my hold on him, allowing him to stand to answer the door. He leans down, kissing my temple. "Love you, butterfly."

"Love you, Papa."

I watch as he leaves the dining room, then gather the plates together and carry them into the kitchen. "Mama, stop. I'll clean up," I say, nudging her away from the sink.

"I can do it."

"I know you can, but you should go relax with Papa." I turn on the faucet, rinsing off a dish.

"Isabella, there's someone here to see you."

My father's voice makes me turn and I stiffen, inhaling a sharp breath, the shock of the man standing there causing me to drop the wine glass in my hand, which shatters the second it hits the floor.

"Crap. I'm sorry." Jessie reacts quickly, lowering himself to his knees to help pick up the shards surrounding my bare feet.

"Don't you worry about any of this, Jessie dear," Mama says.

I should hate her use of that term of endearment toward him, especially after I told her everything that transpired between Asher, Jessie, and me. But Mama was always a practical person, able to see both sides of a story with clarity. While she may not have liked how Jessie handled the situation, we *did* hurt him. We all hurt each other. Every single one of us carries blame with this mess.

Mama shoos him away with the dustpan, and he straightens once he's certain all the glass has been cleared.

"Do you..." He scrubs a hand through his hair. "Can

we talk?"

"Talk?" I cross my arms over my chest. "You did more than enough talking the last time we saw each other, don't you think?"

"Please, Izzy," he implores.

I take a minute to survey him. The confident, composed man is nowhere to be seen. Sure, he still wears an impeccable three-piece suit, but he doesn't carry it as he usually does. There are a few wrinkles in the fabric, his tie loosened. His eyes are bloodshot, dark circles around them. His hair has grown out more than I ever recall him wearing it, and the beginning of a five o'clock shadow is visible along his jawline. This isn't the same Jessie I dated. Hell, this isn't even the same Jessie who destroyed everything mere weeks ago.

"You have every right to kick me out. After what I did, I deserve it. I just... I can't sleep." He raises his red-rimmed eyes to mine. "I need to make this right."

I glower at him, wanting to refuse, but I know how it feels. I've been in this same place myself these past several weeks. It's a kind of purgatory I'd never wish on my worst enemies. The only thing that's kept me from having a breakdown has been the hope that someday Asher York will be no more than someone I used to know. That there won't be this heart-crushing ache consuming every inch of my body. I have to believe I'll find my own version of happiness, even if it won't hold a torch to what I felt with Asher.

"Okay," I agree reluctantly, then walk through the living room and out the front door, Jessie following close behind.

A gust of wind hits me, splatter from the rain steadily falling dotting my bare arms, causing a shiver to roll through me. It's not bitter cold, considering it *is* July, but the rain causes a damp chill to run through me that my tank top doesn't do much to protect me from. I head to the far end of the covered porch and lower myself onto the swing. Jessie starts to sit beside me, but before he does, he shrugs out of his suit jacket, draping it around my shoulders.

"Same Jessie. Always offering the shirt off your back to a girl in need."

He smiles a sad smile. "Same Isabella. Never dressing appropriately for the weather."

I pull my lips between my teeth, a myriad of emotions filling me. Rage. Frustration. Betrayal. Sadness. But also love. Despite it all, I still love Jessie, just not the way I once thought I did.

"Izzy, I—"

"Listen, Jessie," I say at the same time.

We both pause, then laugh.

"Normally, I'd be all chivalrous and say ladies first, but I can't do that this time. I need to get this off my chest."

I give him a subtle nod. He shifts his gaze forward, pulling his lip between his teeth. He doesn't say anything for several moments, the summer downpour the only sound.

"I fucked up."

"No," I interject vehemently. "*We* did. We never—"

He holds up his hand, cutting me off. "I'm not talking about that. I'm talking about when we first met."

"When we first met? I—"

"Do you know why I first approached you?" He runs his hands along his pants, something I've rarely seen him do, if ever.

"Because you saw me at a party."

"That's only *half* true. I *did* see you at that party. But that was after Asher had already told me about you."

"About me?"

"Not by name, but he'd mentioned a girl who'd been at a few of his gigs. Asked me to come down to the club one night as moral support. That he was going to perform a song he'd written for this girl who'd caught his eye." He chuckles slightly as his gaze shines with nostalgia. "Said he hadn't even spoken to her. Didn't even know her name. I thought he was crazy, thought no one in their right mind would go through all that trouble for someone they'd never spoken to." He swallows hard, turning his head toward me. "When I saw the look on Asher's face as he admired you that first time he performed 'Amante', I knew he wasn't just a horny twenty-something-year-old who wrote a song to impress a girl in the hopes of getting laid. It was more than that, deeper than that. But that still didn't stop me."

"Stop you from what?" I ask timidly.

He hangs his head, his shoulders falling. Then he returns his eyes to mine. "Seeking you out. At first, I was more curious than anything. But... I don't know..." The corners of his mouth curve into a smile. "I saw you sitting all alone outside the rugby house in forty-degree weather and couldn't *not* offer you my jacket. So I did. Then I—"

"Asked why I wasn't inside partaking in drunken debauchery like everyone else."

He nods. "To which you responded you had absolutely no desire to be around hormone-crazed teenagers who concocted some strange variation of Never Have I Ever and Spin the Bottle as an excuse to hook up." He chuckles. "You went on this whole tirade. How if you were interested in someone, you wouldn't go through the trouble of making up some game so you could get laid. That you'd approach them and tell them."

Laughter rolls through me as I peer into the distance, recalling that night. "You sat with me for hours. When my roommate finally reappeared from whatever room she'd been hooking up in, you refused to let me get into the car with her. Offered to drive us back to the dorm."

"I almost didn't," he confesses. "I knew I should walk away right then and there. Knew what I was about to do would kill Asher if he found out. Granted, he'd never pointed you out to me, but I knew you were the one he wrote about. I saw the way he looked at you. So I kept telling myself it was just a ride home."

"And it was. You were a complete gentleman."

"Nothing I did was something a gentleman would do. Asher and I have always had a standing agreement. Never fall for the same girl. If we learned we thought the same girl was hot, we'd both walk away. Made a promise to each other that our relationship was more important than any piece of ass. No offense."

"None taken."

"Despite that promise, do you know what I did?"

Remaining mute, I shake my head.

"I told him not to talk to you yet."

"And your reason for that?" My words come out shaky.

He lifts his remorseful gaze to mine, his lips a tight line. "To give me more time with you. I wasn't stupid. I'm still not. I couldn't compete with Asher. I've never been able to. Once girls realized he played guitar and could sing, I was no longer of any interest. Just once, I wanted the girl. It sounds immature now, but all my life, I've felt like I was living in Asher's shadow. Mom and Dad always told everyone how gifted he was with his music. Then there was me. What could they say? 'Oh, Jessie. He really knows how to punch those numbers into a calculator'?"

"Is that why you never wanted to go to the club with me? Because Asher would see us together?"

He slowly nods. "And why I waited to introduce you to my family. But I figured our annual Thanksgiving dinner up at Grams' place would be the perfect way to do that. I'd have a buffer between Asher and me in case he realized what I'd done."

I stare forward, seeing that first Thanksgiving through a different lens now that I know the truth. That he only started dating me as some adolescent competition with his brother.

"That night…," I murmur, then look at Jessie. "Do you remember what you told me right before we went inside?"

He licks his lips, exhaling deeply. "That I loved you."

"Did you mean it? Or did you only say that because of what you knew was about to happen?"

"I wish I could tell you I love you more fiercely than I've ever loved anyone, but I can't. I did love you, still do, but my love has never measured up to what you deserve. It's juvenile. I see that now. But all I cared about was finally having something Asher didn't. Something I knew he wanted."

I nod, swallowing hard through the thickness in my throat. "And when you proposed?"

This shouldn't matter. But it's not me I hurt for. It's Asher. This doesn't sound like the actions of the man I promised to marry. Jessie always seemed mature beyond his years. I knew him to be somewhat manipulative, but I'd written that off as him being a great negotiator. I never could have imagined he'd be capable of this level of deception. And to his own brother.

"I only did that because you two were spending so much time together at Grams' lake house. You didn't even come up to bed with me. You stayed up all night with Asher. You guys had a bond, a connection. I saw it the first time I brought you home and introduced you to him. But that summer, I felt you slipping farther and farther away. Toward him. So I proposed."

"Even though you didn't love me like you should have."

He nods. "Even though I didn't love you like I should have," he repeats. "And I'm so sorry. I lied to you for years."

"I lied to you, too. I made you think you broke my heart, that it was your fault we broke up, when in reality..."

"You were in love with Asher."

"Nothing you said or did would have kept me yours," I explain.

"I think we both know you were never mine." He pinches his lips into a tight line. "And that's why I'm here. To fix this."

"I'm not sure anything can ever fix this," I exhale.

"I need to at least try."

"What do you mean?"

He stands, then smiles down at me. "There are a couple backstage passes in the inside pocket." He nods to the jacket he draped around my shoulders. "We're playing up in Boston tomorrow night. I penciled in a fifteen-minute interview with a member of the 'press'," he explains, using air quotes.

Pulling back the jacket, I reach into the inside pocket. Sure enough, there are two laminated passes. I raise myself to my feet, brows scrunched. "I don't understand. You *want* me to talk to Asher? After everything, I thought you'd be happy if I never saw him again."

He threads his fingers through his hair, then looks up

at the night sky before returning his eyes to mine. "At first, I was. But my happiness came at the price of Asher's."

"Does he know?" I ask in a quiet voice. "The truth about how you met me?"

"He does now. The guilt ate away at me. So, after watching him mope around for a week, I finally told him."

I expel a breath. "Yet he still sent back the origami doves."

"I think he's confused. And hurt. Maybe…" He sucks in his lower lip. "Maybe he needs to see you again. The choice is yours, Iz. I wanted to give you the opportunity. What you do with it is up to you."

"So are you guys… Are you okay?"

"Asher and me?"

I nod.

"We'll be okay. It's not the same, but we're sorting it out."

"You're still his manager?"

"He said it was up to me. But we both know there's no one else out there who cares about him like I do." He lowers his voice. "Except for you."

I force a smile, straightening my spine. "I'm glad you were able to work things out."

"We were. We are. Now I need to fix us." He gestures between our bodies. "And the two of you. Hopefully it's not too late for that."

Chapter Forty

"NERVOUS?" NORA ASKS as we make our way through the arena in Boston, following the directions Jessie gave me toward the backstage dressing room area. I'm not sure I would have done this if she hadn't agreed to come with me as moral support.

The pounding of my heart fights for attention with the drummer of the opening act currently on stage, and I nod quickly. I can still back out, approach Asher somewhere else. Somewhere on neutral ground. But he needs to know I'll do whatever it takes to win him back, even if that means showing up backstage at one of his concerts.

"You have no idea."

We skirt past roadies wearing headsets, one of them carrying what I recognize to be one of Asher's black acoustic guitars. Just knowing it's recently been strapped to Asher's body, my fingers long to reach out and touch it.

"What are you going to say to him?" Nora's question snaps my attention back to her.

"I'm not sure. I want him to know I'll always love him. That I always *have* loved him. That I also love him enough to let him go, if that's what he truly wants."

"Hopefully it won't come to that."

"I hope so, too," I say as Jessie rounds the corner with a man of average height and build, sporting what I've learned to be the unspoken uniform of roadies — dark t-shirt, cargo shorts, and heavy work boots.

"Oh, good. You found it," Jessie begins, then turns to the man at his side. "Izzy, this is Tom, the production manager. Tom, this is Isabella Nolan. She's scheduled for a brief meeting with Mr. York. He's expecting her." Then he looks at me. "He'll show you where you need to go while I give Nora a tour." He holds his elbow out to her.

"You got this." She squeezes my bicep, then loops her arm through Jessie's.

"This way." Tom continues through the corridors. This time, I don't marvel at the excitement of being backstage at a concert. My focus is on one thing and one thing only. Asher.

He leads me down another hallway, this one much quieter, the floor carpeted instead of being bare cement. Every door is marked with names of the bands I recognize to be Asher's opening acts. Finally, we approach the end of the hallway, the door labeled "Asher York". Butterflies flap in my stomach when Tom brings his hand up and knocks lightly.

"Mr. York, your interview is here."

I hold my breath, my limbs jittery. It's been six weeks since I've last seen him and he peered upon me with utter disgust and animosity. Am I ready for him to look upon me with the same distaste? As much as I'm desperate to see the love he once had for me, I need to do this, need to put it all on the line.

"Send them in."

Not her. Not him. Makes me think Asher isn't exactly expecting *me*. A fact I confirm when Tom opens the door and I step inside, meeting Asher's eyes. He stiffens in surprise. But thankfully, he doesn't kick me out. Just stares, mouth agape, chest rising and falling in a faster pattern.

"Call if you need anything."

I lift my pleading gaze to Asher, bracing myself for him to tell Tom to get me out of here, that I'm not welcome. But he doesn't, and Tom retreats, closing the door behind him.

I don't move, just study him. His eyes are duller than they were last time I saw him. His hair and unshaven jaw coupled with his fitted t-shirt and torn jeans give him that same seductive, disheveled look, making him appear sexy as hell. But there's something missing. *My* Asher is missing.

"I'm probably the last person you want to see," I begin in a soft voice.

"You've got that right." He leans his acoustic guitar against the wall beside him and crosses his arms over his chest, defensive, making no move to offer me the chance to sit beside him on the leather couch.

"And I don't blame you for hating me. I hate me for what I've done, too. Which is why I moved back into my parents' house and am saving every penny so I can return the money to Jessie."

"Still doesn't make what you did okay."

"You're right. It doesn't. But you want to know the truth?"

He stays silent.

"I don't regret anything that happened," I declare passionately. "I don't regret dating Jessie first. Don't regret agreeing to marry him. Don't regret walking away from both of you. Don't regret sleeping with you in Vegas."

I swipe at the tears spilling over my eyes. I tried to remain strong, to remain in control of my emotions, but I can't. Not when a future with Asher is on the line.

"And I certainly do *not* regret accepting Jessie's offer. Because if I hadn't, I never would have seen you again.

After Vegas, I didn't *want* to see you again. Didn't want to put my heart through the wringer again. But those days at Grams' lake house made me realize something."

He uncrosses his arms, his expression softening. "What's that?"

A sad smile tugs on my lips. "That I'd gladly suffer through the worst pain imaginable every day for the rest of my life if it meant I got just one more minute with you. Despite everything, I still love you. I have since the moment I laid eyes on you in the dingy club in Boston. And I'll continue to love you even after I draw my last breath. The fact I may have had an agreement with Jessie doesn't change anything. It doesn't change who we are, what we felt for each other."

"How could it not?" Jumping to his feet, he advances toward me, stopping a breath away.

I inhale sharply, his familiar scent wrapping around me. God, I hope this isn't the last time I'll savor in his woodsy aroma that reminds me of late nights at Grams' lake house, building a snowman, cooking dinner together.

"You were paid to make me believe in something that wasn't there," he chokes out, his own eyes red with emotion. He turns from me, pacing, tugging on his hair.

"No, I wasn't." My voice is strong, determined, the vein in my neck tight. "I was paid to be there. That's it. Everything we shared was real. *Everything*. My feelings were real. My *love* was real. And it still is. So much so that I'm willing to walk away."

He stills, looking at me, brows furrowed. "You are?"

I nod, swiping away more tears. "If you truly believe none of it was real, if you truly believe all the time we spent together was only an illusion, nothing I say or do will convince you otherwise. After all these years, I'm fully aware of how stubborn you are."

The tension loosens momentarily as he cracks a light smile.

I slowly walk toward him. "But if even a small part of you thinks it might have been real..." I come to a stop in front of him, grateful when he doesn't retreat, "then let's start over. From the beginning."

"The beginning?"

"Exactly. At Sammy's."

He closes his eyes as realization washes over him. The club where we first saw each other.

I grasp his hands, a spark shooting through me when I feel his calloused skin against mine after so long. "If you still feel the connection I know you did that very first time our eyes met, come there after your show tonight."

He seems to assess my proposal. "And if I don't?"

"Then I'll walk away." I drop my hold on him, taking a step back. "That's how much I love you, Asher. I love you enough to let you go."

Closing the distance between us, he peers deep into my gaze, the intensity in his stare stripping me bare, exposing all my secrets, lies, truths. He brings a hand up to my cheek, but doesn't touch me. I can see indecision plaguing him, a tumultuous game of tug-of-war raging within his mind.

"I..." He licks his lips, chest heaving, eyes raking over my face.

"Yes?" I silently implore him to remember everything we've been through. To realize we can have that again. To realize we can have more than that if he'd just give me another chance.

"I..." He inches closer, focusing on my lips.

"Yes..."

"I have to get on stage."

The buzz instantly disappears, and I whirl around, watching as he opens the door.

"You can see yourself out."

My shoulders fall, a vice squeezing my heart. When he steps into the hallway, he pauses, and I perk up, willing him to look back at me. To rush to me and sweep me into his arms. To forgive me.

Instead, he shakes his head and walks away.

* * *

My knee bounces as I sit in the corner booth of the club I once frequented during my college days. Not much has changed. The bartenders still serve watered-down drinks. The floor is still sticky with spilled beverages. College students still fill the place as they dance to the music being performed by the latest trend in Boston music.

I check the time, just as I've done every few minutes for the past several hours. When eleven o'clock rolled around and I knew the concert should be ending, hope grew inside of me. Every time I noticed the doors open, my eyes darted in their direction, only to be disappointed when it wasn't the man I hoped it would be.

"Last call," our server says as she approaches. "Want anything else?"

"I'm fine," Nora states before looking at me with sad eyes.

She's been incredibly supportive all night, cracking jokes to help keep my mind off the likelihood that Asher won't be coming. If it weren't for her, I'd be a complete mess by now. She's kept me grounded, optimistic. But now, that optimism is slowly waning. Maybe I should have pushed harder, thrown myself at Asher's feet, begged for forgiveness. Not given him a way out, a clean slate.

"Nothing for me, either," I answer with a sigh.

"Enjoy your evening."

When the lights snap on and the bouncers usher everyone outside, I stand and scoot out of the booth, pretending my heart isn't breaking with each step I take out of the club. Nora and I wait a few minutes for our Uber to arrive, which gives Asher a little longer to show up.

He never does.

Chapter Forty-One

THE SUN BEAMS through the open curtains of our hotel room in the Copley Square area of Boston, but it does nothing to boost my melancholy mood. I barely slept last night. I'd hoped the threat of me walking away was enough for Asher to realize what was at stake. Maybe he truly does hate me like I feared.

"I think the Sox are in town. We can try to find some tickets," Nora suggests as she flips through tourist brochures about Boston.

I grit out a small smile. I'd normally jump at the opportunity to see a game, but going to Fenway will only remind me of Asher, considering how much he loves the Sox.

"I'm not in the mood."

"Fine." She tosses the brochures to the side. "Maybe we should just get raging drunk and pass out before three o'clock in the afternoon. How does that sound?"

"It's Sunday. You can't get alcohol before noon. Obviously the fucking Puritans didn't think people would suffer a broken heart in the morning." I flop onto the bed, expelling a long breath. I stare at the ceiling, wishing I hadn't planned to stay in Boston through Monday.

"We can go home," Nora offers, her voice filled with compassion. "Switch our flight to leave today instead of tomorrow."

"No," I sigh. "You've never spent any time up here.

You should at least decide which place has the better cannoli — Mike's or Modern."

She scrunches her nose. "Is that supposed to make sense?"

"It will soon." I raise myself to sit. "I'll shower and we'll go do something." I drag myself off my bed and head toward the bathroom when my cell rings. I decide to let it go to voicemail, thinking it's Chloe or Evie to offer me words of encouragement.

"It's Jessie," Nora sings.

I pause, glancing over my shoulder at her. "Jessie?"

"That's what the caller ID says."

My pulse gradually increases as I return to the bed, grabbing my cell. I consider sending him to voicemail, too, but something makes me answer.

"Hey, Jessie."

"Izzy…" The kindness in his tone is all the evidence I need to know Asher must have told him what happened. "How are you?"

I force a smile, if only for myself. "I'm fine."

"Are you?"

"I will be. I have to be. It's time to move on. I can't keep putting myself through this."

He exhales deeply. "I can't fault you there. I just… I was hoping you'd do me a favor. Before you move on."

"What's that?"

"I was talking to Grams this morning. I sort of let it slip you were in town. She'd like to see you. Do you mind suffering through another three-hour car ride with me up to the lake house? It would mean a lot to her. Don't worry," he adds quickly. "It'll just be us."

I pull my bottom lip between my teeth. "I'd have to talk to Nora."

Her hand wraps around my forearm, and I dart my eyes to hers. By her response, I can only assume she's able to overhear my conversation. "Go," she whispers. "I'll be fine."

I cover the microphone. "Are you sure?" I murmur.

"Of course. You should spend some time with Grams. You'll regret it if you don't."

I pinch my lips into a tight line, then sigh before returning my attention to my phone. "Okay. I'll go."

"Great!" Jessie's voice brightens. "I'll pick you up in an hour."

"Looking forward to it."

When Jessie pulls his rented SUV onto the unpaved path leading up to Grams' lake house hours later, I can't help but marvel at how different it is from the last time I was here. The trees lining the property are no longer barren but filled with leaves and pine needles, offering plenty of cover against the hot summer sun. There are a few clouds, but instead of the sky being a desolate gray, it's a gorgeous shade of blue.

Jessie kills the ignition, then steals a glance at me. I meet his sad eyes, a half-hearted smile crossing his mouth. "Let me win one?"

I furrow my brows, confused, before the meaning of his question sinks in. Our game of who can get to my door faster. "Of course."

He holds my gaze for a beat, then ducks out of the car, making his way to the passenger door and opening it for me. He offers his hand and helps me down. This moment is bittersweet. I promised I'd move on, but it's still painful to know this is one of the last times Jessie will open the door for me.

He rests his palm on my back and steers me up the walkway. I swallow hard as we pass the tree with our initials still carved in the bark. They've faded over the years, but it serves as a reminder. Of what, though? It's not love. I know the truth now. Maybe friendship? Despite everything, Jessie was always good to me. He always treated me with respect, with decency, apart from the lies. But we all told lies. We all hid secrets. We all buried our truths. Hopefully we'll find the strength to move forward and learn from our mistakes.

"Grams?" Jessie calls out when we step over the threshold and into the foyer. "Where are you?" He walks into the living room, but there's no sign of her. No sign of anyone. "She might be out back. You know how much she loves lying in that hammock during the summer."

"That I do," I say as a lazy smile pulls on my mouth. I'd lost count of the number of times I walked past her as she snored on the hammock, an open book resting on her face, an empty whiskey glass on the ground below her.

I follow Jessie through the quiet house and onto the back deck. My steps are slow as I descend the stairs into the large yard, ghosts of my past dancing before me. Playing volleyball with the entire family. Lying on the grass beside Jessie. Building a snowman with Asher. This place holds some of my fondest memories. And some of my most painful ones.

As we approach the hammock hanging between two mature oak trees, Jessie comes to a stop. "She's not here, either."

"Would she have gone to run some errands?"

He scrunches his brow. "I texted her when we rolled into town. She would have said something. Maybe she's in the music room. She's taken to listening to Asher's album with her headphones on and the music cranked up while she plays air guitar."

My eyes bulge. "She does not."

"She does."

I burst out laughing at the image he painted. As crazy as it sounds, I absolutely believe it.

"I'll take another look through the house. Why don't you stay out here?" He gestures toward the lake. "I know how much you love this place."

I'm about to tell him I'll come with him. The sooner I see Grams, the sooner we can leave and I can move on with my life. But as I stand beneath the towering trees with the view of the lake just beyond, a calm I've been searching for washes over me.

"Okay."

He nods. "Okay." With a sad smile, he leans down, kissing my forehead, a finality in his gesture.

When he pulls away, he locks his gaze with mine for a brief moment before he turns, his steps sluggish as he heads up to the house. I watch until he disappears, then exhale a long breath and slowly make my way down to the dock, the wood creaking under my weight as I walk toward the far end.

I lower myself, allowing my feet to dangle off the edge, the roar of a boat motor audible in the distance. Waves lap over the rocky shoreline, dragonflies skimming along the water's surface. I close my eyes, savoring the fresh air that can only be described as wet earth. For two years of my life, this spot was my heaven. All because of the man who often sat by my side.

Opening my eyes, I smile as I glance to my side at the space I left for Asher out of habit. Then I notice something that wasn't there when I sat down mere moments ago. With shaky hands, I reach for it, almost certain it's a hallucination, a vibrant memory of a past I'd give anything to return to. But when the roughness of the folded-up staff paper in the shape of an origami dove touches my skin, my throat closes up.

"That's not from me."

I jump at the familiar voice, my breath catching as I look around. When my gaze falls on Asher's silhouette standing a few yards away, I swallow hard. He looks different than he did last night. His eyes are no longer cold and broken. Instead, they peer at me with longing.

"It's not?" I stand on shaky legs.

"No." He shoves his hands into the pockets of his cargo shorts, advancing toward me with measured steps. With each inch he erases, my heartbeat increases. "That one's from Jessie."

"Jessie?"

He nods, coming to a stop less than a foot away. I focus on his dark eyes, a myriad of emotions swirling within. "An apology for lying to you."

"About what?"

"Today." He briefly looks away, shrugging, the confident man who dismissed me so easily last night nowhere to be found. "I asked him to set this up."

"Why? I thought—"

He holds up his hand, cutting me off. "I need to ask you something. And I need you to be completely honest."

"Okay...," I answer in a drawn-out voice.

"Did you do it?"

My brows scrunch together. "Do what?"

"What you said you would last night?" On a hard swallow, he closes the final bit of space between us, his eyes softening as they skate over my features. "Did you let me go?" he chokes out.

Hearing the pain in his voice causes the dam to break, tears spilling over my eyelids. I bite my lower lip to stop my chin from quivering. "I could no sooner let go of you than I could breathe without lungs or live without a heart."

He hangs his head, processing my response for a moment, probably assessing whether any of it holds even a hint of truth. I can't make him believe it. All I can do is hope he does.

When he lifts his gaze, it's fiery, impassioned, wild. Before I can react, he clutches my cheeks in his hands and crushes his lips to mine, his tongue firm and demanding as it slides against mine, leaving no doubt in my mind that this is real, that Asher's here, that he's finally kissing me.

Grabbing the back of his head, I deepen the kiss, tugging his body even closer to mine. I need more of him, all of him. I can't let him go, *refuse* to let him go. Never again. Our kiss is passionate, yet reserved. Lust-filled, yet serene. Reckless, yet unhurried.

"Goddamn, darlin'," he groans after he tears his lips from mine. "Do you have any idea how long I've thirsted for your kiss?" His hands continue to frame my face as he touches his forehead to mine, both of us struggling to get our breathing under control, our shaky inhales echoing around us.

"Then why didn't you come to me last night?" I sob. "Why did you make me think you didn't care, that you'd already let me go?"

He brings his thumbs underneath my eyes, swiping away the tears that fall. "Like I could ever let you go. Your soul is permanently etched on mine. It always will be."

"But—"

"I was fucking scared, Iz." He steps back and paces, digging his hands through his hair as he attempts to find the words he needs. "And upset. And irrational. And insecure. And ignorant. And probably a thousand other things." He stops, facing me. "I messed up. This is on me," he declares passionately. "All of it. I just…" He licks his lips, then draws in a breath. The intensity in his expression dissipates. "I just hope you'll accept this as a token of how sorry I am."

He reaches into the front pocket of his shorts and pulls out a small, black velvet box. My eyes widen, probably bordering on horror at what it could contain.

"Don't worry." His chuckles hit me deep in my core. God, I've missed this man's laugh. His smile. His everything. "It's not *that*. I figure we'll cross one bridge at a time."

I blow out a breath as I take the velvet box and slowly open it, gasping when I see the contents. "Asher, I..." I shake my head as I admire the stunning platinum necklace. But it's not just any necklace. At the end is an origami dove pendant, tiny diamonds sparkling under the sunlight.

"May I?" He arches a brow, eyes pleading with me to allow him to do this, to accept this gift, to accept this apology. If my time with Asher has taught me anything, it's to finally take a risk. And I'm willing to bet it all on him.

"Yes."

His shoulders relax as he takes the necklace from me, shoving the box into his pocket. When he steps behind me to secure it, his hands smooth my hair over my shoulder, the gentle brush of his flesh on mine sending electricity coursing through my veins.

Once the necklace is secure around my neck, he spins me so he can admire the pendant sitting just above my cleavage.

"Look at the inside of the wing," he instructs.

Curious, I do as he says, squinting when I notice an inscription. "My...Favorite..."

"Always," he finishes.

"Not almost?"

"Never again. I'm a complete fool, Izzy. I lost sight of the most important thing."

"And what's that?"

"That regardless of what brought you up here this winter in the first place, you said those three little words to me *outside* our bubble." He cups my cheeks once more. "So, let me ask you." He licks his lips. "Do you still love me?"

I cover his hands with mine as he holds my face, my eyes locking with his. "Boomerang." Between us, no other word is needed.

Tension vanishes from his body as he expels a long breath. "Boomerang." His grip on me tightens as he seals his devotion with a kiss — consuming, captivating, hypnotizing.

When Jessie called to ask if I'd pay Grams a visit before I went home, I never could have imagined this would be the result. What if I hadn't agreed to come with him?

"So this was your plan all along? Bringing me up here?" I ask once our kiss comes to an end.

He shrugs. "More or less."

"What if I refused to come when Jessie asked?" Stepping away, I cross my arms over my chest, giving him a playful look. "I very well could have."

"That's true." He palms my back and tugs me against him. "But I know you, Iz. You'd do anything for Grams."

"And how would Grams like it if she found out you used her to get back together with me?"

"She'd endorse it one hundred percent," a familiar voice calls out.

I pull away from Asher, looking at where the dock meets the grass, Grams and Jessie standing together.

"Grams," I exhale, walking into her outstretched

arms.

"Glad you three worked things out," she whispers, kissing my cheek.

"Thank you." I squeeze her, then drop my hold, glancing nervously between Asher and Jessie. But any apprehension disappears the instant Jessie beams, giving Asher a heartfelt hug.

"Glad you finally got the girl," he says.

"Thanks, man," Asher responds. "For everything."

"Anything for you. You know that."

Asher steps back, draping his arm around my shoulders. "I do now."

"We'll give you two some privacy," Grams announces, then turns to Jessie. "Come on. There's a church a few towns over I'd like to check out."

We all erupt in laughter at the memory of how Asher and I finally reconnected. It was all because of Grams...and her Sunday morning booty call.

"You don't have to make up some elaborate scheme to get me out of the house anymore," Jessie remarks, taking Grams' hand and leading her back toward the house, Asher and I following close behind. "Plus, it's after three in the afternoon. Isn't church more a Sunday morning kind of thing?"

"How would I know?" Grams shoots back. "The only time I've felt close to God has been when I've screamed out—"

"And that's enough!" Jessie exclaims, the tips of his ears turning red. "No more."

"Oh, there will be plenty more," Grams reminds him as we step into the house, navigating toward the living room. "You're stuck with me for three hours while you drive me back to your parents' house. The best thing about being my age is when I speak my mind, people just think I'm some crazy old coot."

Jessie gives Asher a look of feigned annoyance as we approach the front door. "You owe me for this."

"Oh, I know." Asher pulls my body tighter against his. "More than you realize."

We all say our goodbyes. But unlike before, this isn't actually goodbye. I'll see them again, probably very soon. And surprisingly, it doesn't feel awkward to hug Jessie. I can honestly say he doesn't hold a grudge. Not anymore.

Once we're alone, I turn to Asher, biting my lower lip. For years, I've masked my love for this man. I'm not sure what to do now that I no longer have to hide it.

"Do you think it's strange, too?" he asks, looking down at me in awe.

"A little, but it's a good strange."

"Yes, it is." He loops an arm around me, pulling my body into his.

"So, what should we do?"

"I have a few ideas."

"Oh really?"

His pupils dilate as he gradually lowers his mouth back to mine. "Really," he murmurs, a spark shooting through me when his lips feather against mine.

"And what would that be?" I ask in a husky voice.

"Don't worry, darlin'. We've got forever to find out."

I melt into his kiss. "I like the sound of that…darlin'."

Chapter Forty-Two

IPEER OUT the window of the hotel room, the Washington Monument visible in the distance, the bright white of it stark against the blackness of night. Soft lips feather along my shoulder blades, and I moan.

"Are you seriously ready to go again?" I murmur, peeking one eye at my cell on the nightstand. "You do have twenty-two minutes and thirteen seconds."

Asher's raspy chuckles surround me. "I need to make sure I keep my woman satisfied." He kisses my neck, then pushes me onto my back, hovering over me. I reach up, pushing a few strands of hair out of his eyes. "How did you like the show tonight?"

After getting out of work earlier, I hopped on a flight and came down to catch Asher's concert. It's the first one I've been to since we reconnected a few weeks ago. And the first one that he's publicly announced me as his girlfriend. He offered to keep it quiet for my own privacy, but after being forced to love each other in secret for so long, I want the world to know, regardless of the scathing comments I'm sure will be left all over social media by the time we wake up in the morning. Hell, they're probably already there.

"You were as sexy as ever." I rake my fingers down his back, my lips seeking his. "I didn't realize my pass came with preferential treatment by the star of the show himself."

"Oh, but it does."

He lowers his mouth to my neck, and I tilt my head, surrendering to his addictive touch. I don't know how I survived as long as I did without the warmth of his lips on me. It's something I don't wish to endure again.

"I needed to give you the full Asher York treatment."

"Is that what you're calling it these days?" I exhale as he slithers down my body, his tongue flicking my nipple. "The Asher York treatment?"

"Mmm-hmm," he moans. "I hear it's quite the experience."

I moan, digging my fingers into his scalp as he bares his teeth, tugging slightly on my sensitive bud. "Oh god, it is."

My eyes flutter closed, the world disappearing as I succumb to his talented mouth. Suddenly, the jarring sound of his phone ringing cuts through, breaking the moment.

He pauses, not moving, his tongue pressed against my chest.

"You should get that," I whisper. "Pretty sure any phone call after midnight is probably an emergency."

"Jessie thinks *everything's* an emergency."

"He's getting better." I push against him, forcing him off me. "How about this? You talk to Jessie. I'll order a ridiculously expensive bottle of Champagne and we can drink it off each other's bodies." I go to stand, but he wraps an arm around my waist, pulling me back onto the bed.

"I like how your mind works." He covers my mouth, his kiss brief, yet still toe-curling. "But see if they can send up an ice cream sundae, too. With all the fixings on the side."

I arch a brow. "On the side?"

He nods slowly, eyes darkening. "Because I'm going to create my own dessert out of you."

A quiver trickles through me, moisture pooling between my thighs. I almost want to tell him to forget about Jessie's phone call, but as I've learned, sometimes delayed gratification is worth it.

"Be right back." He presses his lips to mine once more, then rolls off the bed, grabbing his phone and padding into the living area of the suite. I pull my legs into my body, unable to stop myself from admiring Asher's naked physique as he stands by the window, focused intently on his conversation with Jessie. But as beautiful as he is on the outside, he's even more gorgeous on the inside.

Sighing, I look away, grabbing the room phone to put in our order, hoping they'll still be able to cater to our…unique request this late at night. Just as I'm about to press the button for room service, Asher dashes back into the room, eyes wide, expression panicked as he makes a beeline for the remote, turning the TV to a news station.

"What's going on?" I ask, returning the phone to the cradle, staring at the screen that displays what appears to be aerial footage of a warehouse-sized building set on a large expanse of land. When I read the caption on the banner, it sucks the air from my lungs.

Dozens Arrested In Human Trafficking Ring.

"Did they…," I begin, cut off when a reporter's voice comes over the footage.

"*Earlier today, the FBI arrested David Jordan, renowned televangelist, founder of the Faithful Living Church, and president of Faithful Living Christian Charities.*"

I blink, raising myself from the bed and stepping toward the TV, my heart hammering in my chest.

"*This is an ongoing investigation, but the FBI has confirmed Jordan was arrested in connection with what they're calling one of the largest human trafficking rings in the history of this country.*"

A raid late tonight led to the discovery of multiple properties where women were imprisoned, at the direction of Mr. Jordan. These women were forced to get pregnant, the product of these pregnancies then sold to unsuspecting couples who had reached out to his charity's adoption agency. The FBI states it could take months or years to fully understand the scope of how massive this so-called baby mill operation was, but early guesses estimate thousands of adoptions could be affected."

"Holy shit," I breathe just as my cell rings, startling me. I whirl around, dashing toward it. When I see Chloe's name on the screen, I quickly answer.

"Are you watching the news?" she asks breathlessly.

"Yes."

"Isn't it magnificent? You were right!"

"I don't... I can't believe it. How... I thought the FBI moved on to other cases."

"They did. But Oliver refused to give up. He started looking at areas that had an above average birth ratio."

"Didn't the FBI already investigate that?"

"They did. Based on the areas in question, they explained the variance as being those associated with the Amish or Mennonites."

"Which would make sense."

"Or it would be a great cover."

"What are you saying?"

"Oliver narrowed it down to about a dozen areas, mostly in Maryland, Ohio, and Pennsylvania. He went to each of these locations himself. Looked for anything suspicious. Asked locals if they knew of any out-of-the-way properties, most likely fenced in, where they didn't see a lot of activity. It took about a month, but he was able to provide the FBI a list of addresses."

"What did they find?"

"They pulled property transfer records. They discovered that every property in question was actually owned by a member of one of the many branches of Faithful Living Church. That's a bit suspicious, but still not a smoking gun, right?"

"Right…"

"What would you say if I told you each of these so-called property owners was actually deceased?"

My eyes widen. "Deceased?"

"Looks like they used private information belonging to a variety of their church members to buy property in the hopes of not raising any suspicion or connecting the dots back to Jordan. If Oliver hadn't gone that extra step to look into the background of who owned each property and realized they were actually dead when the property was transferred to them, he probably would have gotten away with it."

"Didn't anyone in the recorder's office question it?"

"If they did, I'm sure they were paid to look the other way."

"Wow…" I shake my head as I lower myself onto the mattress, staring at the TV, seeing an overhead shot of an enormous house, blue and red lights flashing as police swarm the property.

An arm drapes along my shoulders, and I lift my eyes to Asher. He smiles down at me, the pride in his gaze making my heart swell. If it weren't for him, I never would have taken the first step to find out the truth about my birth mother. I owe it all to him. All the girls who no longer have to live in fear owe it all to him.

"The girls," I say excitedly, mind racing. "What about them? Any names?"

Chloe blows out a long breath. "They aren't releasing any information until family members are notified. There were several dozen girls at each property. You can imagine the amount of paperwork this number of missing people is going to cause."

I rest my hand on Asher's arm when he hangs his head. I can finally find comfort in my past, knowing I did something to bring those responsible for my mother's disappearance to justice. But what about Asher and Jessie? Will they ever get answers about Emilia? Will they ever find closure?

"Hey, listen, I've got to go," Chloe's voice interrupts my thoughts. "This is causing quite the stir at Lincoln's paper. Not to mention, some chick showed up as Asher York's girlfriend at his concert tonight, so the entire single female population of this country is up in arms, causing the gossip mills to work on overdrive. I'm trying to track down who this person is, since the new gossip columnist at the magazine still leaves a bit to be desired."

I laugh slightly, a welcome break in the tension. "No one will ever be as good at getting them to talk as you were."

"Don't I know it," she groans. "But I'm happy for you. You deserve this."

"Thanks, Chloe. For everything. I…" I trail off, collecting my thoughts. "Thanks for believing in me."

"I love you, Iz. Now go. Spend some time with that rockstar boyfriend of yours and enjoy this."

"I will. Love you, too."

I linger on the line a moment longer, then end the call, staring into space as I process this turn of events. In truth, once I heard the FBI wasn't putting forward many resources on this, despite Avery's statement, I gave up hope anything would come of it. I certainly hadn't expected anything like this.

"You did it, Iz." Asher grips my face, the way he holds me all-consuming. This man has never had a problem showing his emotions, but I've never seen him so overwhelmed, so moved, so…proud.

"I didn't do anything," I insist.

"Yes, you did. You refused to give up. Saw something no one else wanted to. If you hadn't found the courage to search for your birth mother, none of this would have been possible."

"I only found that courage because of you. You gave me the strength to confront my past, not run from it and pretend it doesn't exist."

His lips brush tenderly against mine, and I sigh, the touch perfect in its simplicity. "No more running." His words come out as a cross between a plea and a demand.

"No more running."

"Good."

My cell chimes and I rip my eyes away, grabbing it off the mattress. When I realize it's not another phone call but my alarm, I smirk, displaying the screen for Asher.

"Looks like break time's over."

He gently pushes me back onto the bed, climbing on top of me. "You love cracking that whip, don't you?"

"God yes," I giggle as he buries his head in the crook of my neck.

Chapter Forty-Three

"I APPRECIATE YOUR time," an FBI agent says, standing from behind his desk. I meet his gray eyes that match the shade of his hair, his no-nonsense demeanor making me think he's been in law enforcement most of his professional life. "I'm sorry it wasn't under better circumstances."

"It's okay." I swallow hard through the lump in my throat as Asher helps me to my feet, his hand placed firmly on my back. "I knew this was a strong probability. A part of me held out hope she hadn't been killed, but at least I have closure about what happened to her."

The agent nods solemnly. I shudder to think how many more of these conversations he'll have over the next few days.

After the raid, not only did they find several dozen women being imprisoned, but they also uncovered what can only be described as a burial ground containing the remains of dozens of women in various stages of decomposition. The authorities estimated some had been dead as long as forty years, others only a week at most.

In the days that followed the news of what David Jordan had been doing, I dashed to my phone anytime it rang, waiting for word about the names of the victims who were found alive. Unfortunately, not one bore the name Emilia Morgan. When I got the call asking me to come down to the Maryland FBI office, I hoped they'd also have information on Emilia, if just to give Asher and Jessie closure. They didn't. But they did confirm my birth mother's remains were found.

Needless to say, this story shocked the country. They've interviewed hundreds of people who knew David Jordan, many of whom were members of his church. Every single one of them appeared stunned that he could have been involved in something like this. It still boggles my mind he got away with this as long as he did.

However, throughout the course of the ongoing investigation, it was revealed that many local and even federal law enforcement officials were involved, that David Jordan offered many of them huge sums of money to keep quiet. Anyone who looked into reports about suspicious activity taking place around his properties soon met dead end after dead end. Had their efforts not been thwarted by someone receiving kickbacks, they would have uncovered exactly what was going on much sooner.

The FBI is still investigating to determine how long he's been running this baby mill operation. As far as they can tell, it started out as a legitimate adoption agency. Then he must have seen how lucrative the adoption industry could be. At first, he had his staff use methods of persuasion to convince young, naïve, scared women to give up their baby for adoption. But once Roe v. Wade legalized abortion, his pool of babies dwindled, forcing him to find another way to make the same amount of money. When I think of how a man who'd appeared so devout, so humble, so compassionate could have been the mastermind behind something so depraved, so evil, so malicious, it makes my stomach churn.

The number of victims is mind-boggling. Not only were the women abused, treated as nothing more than a pair of ovaries and uterus, but thousands upon thousands of adoptions have also been drawn into question. While I can't imagine going through what these women did, what my mother endured, my heart also goes out to the parents who adopted these children. However, in the absence of wrongdoing by the parents, Child Services advised the adoptions be upheld. All in all, thousands of lives have been uprooted because of this one man who deserves nothing less than to be treated the same way he treated all these women for decades.

"You'll keep us posted?" Asher presses. "If you're able to identify any additional remains?"

The agent gives him a sympathetic smile. "Absolutely."

"Thank you." He reaches across the desk and the two men shake hands. I do the same, then Asher ushers me out of the office, returning his baseball cap and sunglasses to his head in an attempt to mask who he is.

A melancholy silence stretches between us as we make our way through the corridors and into the reception area, the chairs filled with people from all walks of life. Some of them stare blankly into space, eyes red from tears. Others bounce a leg, a sense of hope filling them. I wonder how many of these people will receive the same news I just did. That they found the remains of their loved one.

"It's okay." I face Asher once we're outside. "Maybe Emilia's disappearance wasn't connected to this. We'll go through all the records from when she went missing and see what we find."

He blows out a sigh. "Or maybe it's time I let Emilia go. Let her live on in my memory. Maybe there's a different reason she disappeared. Maybe she disappeared so we'd somehow connect the dots in your mother's case."

"Do you really believe that?" I crane my head back.

"I have to." He shrugs. "If she hadn't gone missing, if I hadn't offered to help the police comb through tips they received, we never would have come up with the theory that something bigger was at play than your mother running from an abusive partner." The corners of his lips curve into a small smile. "I wish I knew for certain what happened to her, but for now, I can find comfort in the fact that it gave you the closure you needed. As long as you're happy, I'm happy. That's the most important thing in the world to me. Everything else is just...gravy."

"But you love gravy."

"I do. But I love you more."

"And I love you... Boomerang."

"Boomerang," he murmurs, his lips skimming mine, neither one of us caring that we're standing on the steps of the FBI office building.

When he pulls back, it looks like a weight has lifted off him. "Come on." He nods toward the parking lot, draping his arm over my shoulders. "Let's go home."

"I like the sound of that." I melt into him, allowing him to lead me toward his SUV.

"So, let me get this straight," a scratchy voice cuts through.

We both stop in our tracks. I expel a long breath, steeling myself to deal with another crazy zealot who doesn't believe David Jordan did anything wrong, that he was doing God's work in making sure babies who were the result of sin grew up in a good, wholesome family. This isn't the first person who has approached us since our involvement in this case was made public.

I doubt it'll be the last.

"They actually gave you a record deal?"

This catches our attention and we whirl around. I peer at the woman, estimating her to be only a few years older than me, although she's much shorter, probably only five-one. Her blonde hair has a slight wave to it, dark sunglasses covering her eyes. Her ripped jeans and Queen t-shirt don't make her look like the typical fanatic who's been protesting many of the funerals of Jordan's victims. Based on her statement directed toward Asher, I get the feeling she's not a zealot at all.

"Do I—" Asher begins, his brows scrunched.

"Jennifer Neil." She thrusts her hand out, and Asher grabs onto it, shaking it warily.

The name sounds familiar, and I search my memory. I've heard more names these past few weeks than I have in my life. From the dozens of women who were rescued from the baby mills and are now going through the process of readjusting to life again. To the even more women whose bodies were found buried on David Jordan's property. To the people who've come forward to share their own stories of escaping his baby mill and living to tell about it. To the network of Good Samaritans who helped rescue as many girls as possible, often putting their own lives at risk.

"Jennifer Neil…," I murmur. Then it hits me. "You helped them. You helped some of the girls escape."

"Wish I could have done more."

She refocuses her attention on Asher. "Of course, you may remember me by another name." Her chin quivers as her lips lift slightly in the corners, her voice strained. She removes her sunglasses, revealing dazzling blue eyes.

His body stiffens as he inhales a sharp breath. "Em?"

She smiles. "It's me."

"Oh, my god. You're alive."

Asher immediately drops his hold on me, not hesitating for an instant, hugging her tightly. I observe their interaction, my heart nearly bursting at this unexpected turn of events.

He pulls back, holding her at arm's length. "Where? Wha—" Licking his lips, he shakes his head, then crushes her body back against his, as if scared this is a trick, a figment of his imagination, a manifestation of his deepest desires. When he angles away once more, he stares at her, his mouth agape, a thousand questions on the tip of his tongue. I have a thousand questions on the tip of mine, too.

She touches her hand to his arm. "I'll tell you everything, but you need to answer my question first." She smirks. "They *really* gave you a record deal?"

Asher's laughter echoes against the buildings surrounding us as he hugs her again. "Like you always said, record labels have shit taste in music."

"They do." She lifts her eyes to his. "But I'm glad they finally smartened up."

* * *

"So, you escaped?" Jessie presses as we all sit in the living area of our Baltimore hotel suite. The second Asher called him about Emilia, Jessie jumped on the first flight from LA and was here the following day.

"I did." She brings her eyes to mine. "Much the same way it appears your friend, Avery, escaped."

"But if you escaped, why didn't you—"

"Come home?" she interrupts Jessie.

"You know how much I cared about you." The muscles in his face tense as he struggles to understand why she didn't return to her family, why she started over. If I hadn't been living and breathing this case for the past several months, I'd question it, too. But it all makes sense.

"I couldn't. I refused to do anything that could put my life in jeopardy…" She meets his sad eyes. "Put my daughter's life in jeopardy."

He expels a breath. "You have a daughter?"

Her lips pinched, she slowly nods. "Julianne."

"How old?"

"She'll be eight this October."

"Is she…" He trails off, unable to finish his question.

"She's the product of what I went through, but I don't care about that. I love her just the same. I don't see the man who raped me when I look at her. I see a strong girl I'd do anything to protect. She's why I decided to finally do something."

"How did you get involved in helping these women?" I ask.

"About two years ago, I found myself outside of Portland, Maine, for work."

"What is it you do?" Jessie asks.

She smiles, meeting my eyes. "I'm a nurse."

He laughs slightly as he glances at Asher. "We just can't get away from it, can we?"

"Nurses really are the best people," I remind him.

"I know." He returns his attention to Emilia. "So, what's significant about being in Portland?"

"It was the end of the line for me."

He scrunches his brows together. "End of the line?"

"There's an entire network made up of people who help women who are in the same position I was. A girl shows up at a hospital, pregnant and distant. The nurse tries to ascertain their mental state. If they make any mention of needing help or not being okay, we put the wheels in motion. One person takes the girl only so far before she's handed off to someone else. I was being held somewhere in upstate New York. This network got me all the way to Portland, at which point they handed me an envelope with my new life. New ID. New social security number. And enough cash to get me started."

"But if it's a nurse, why don't they just report it to the authorities?"

"They did at one point." She shakes her head. "Nothing ever got done. A nurse would report it. An officer would show up to take her to a shelter, but guess where they took her?"

"Back to Jordan's property," I exhale.

She nods. "Precisely. Where they'd remind you of your place."

"Remind you?" Jessie swallows hard. "How?"

She raises her left hand, revealing where her pinky was removed at the metacarpal. "The staff at the hospital noticed the same women returning and decided to stop involving the police. They took matters into their own hands and successfully saved dozens of women, myself included. So, when I was in Portland, I stopped by the address where I remember spending the night before going on my way. At first, it was just to see it, to remind myself of how far I'd come. When I saw the woman who helped me, I went up to her. I don't know what came over me, but I begged her to let me help. I'd been living in New Hampshire, close to the route I was sure they'd been using. They initially refused because of who I was, but they eventually relented."

"What did you do?" I ask.

"Every few days, I'd get a message on a burner phone with an address and a time. I'd go, pick up the girl, then transport her to the next waypoint."

Jessie leans back, processing this story. "And they were all from one of Jordan's properties?"

"Some of them were, but we also helped other human trafficking victims. Anyone who came to a hospital in our network and exhibited any of the signs — poor mental health, abnormal behavior, quiet, bruises, sexual abuse — we'd attempt to intervene and get them away from their captor."

"And you never went to the police?" His voice is strained. I can hear the hurt, the pain, the years of not knowing whether she was still alive. "You never tried to get in touch with me? With Asher? Tell us you were okay?"

She covers his hand with hers. "I would have loved to reach out to let you know I was okay. But one of the things they'd ingrained into me, into all of us when we were given that new life, was not to look back, to only look forward. That looking back might help them find me again. It wasn't just me I had to think about. I had to think about my daughter, too."

She swipes at her tears. "I'd been living as Jennifer Neil so long, I almost didn't say anything when I saw Asher walk out of the lobby of the FBI building." She shifts her attention across the coffee table to Asher. "But I decided it was time to give you the answers you deserved." She floats her gaze back to Jessie. Her expression softens, a flicker of something in her eyes. "That you deserved, too."

It's silent for a moment as Jessie pinches the bridge of his nose, pulling his lip between his teeth. Then he exhales, wrapping an arm across her shoulders, drawing her closer. "I'm so fucking glad you're okay."

She pushes out a laugh. "Asher said the same thing. Good to know some things never change. That despite your differences, you still have the same reaction to a situation."

"That's right!" I exclaim excitedly, flinging my mischievous gaze toward Emilia. "You knew them when they were younger. Tell me…" I lower my voice. "What were they like in middle school?"

"Oh boy, do I have stories. There was this one time at a dance——"

"Stop!" both men shout simultaneously, their eyes bulging out of their sockets.

Emilia's laughter fills the room, light and carefree. "I'll tell you later." She winks.

"Why do I have a feeling I'm going to regret the fact you finally came back into our lives?" Jessie jokes.

"You don't." She playfully jabs him. "Admit how much you missed me and my twisted sense of humor."

He kisses the top of her head. "You have no idea."

Chapter Forty-Four

"I'M SO HAPPY you both finally got your shit together," Chloe announces as we lounge in the rooftop garden of Asher's Gramercy Park townhouse, several dozen of our closest friends and family congregating for our house-warming party. This time, there were no earplugs, hidden vibrators, or t-shirts announcing I still lived with my parents. No. My friends went above and beyond. Handcuffs. Blindfolds. Even a pair of sexy dice.

"Is that right?" Asher muses, bringing his scotch to his lips as the sun sets behind him.

"I mean, I'm happy you're finally together. But mostly, I'm thrilled Izzy's back in the city. It was pure torture when she lived in Greenwich."

"Again…," I begin with a roll of my eyes, "you act like I moved to the other side of the world. I was right over the state line. I could practically spit on New York from there. Not exactly an arduous journey."

"Anything outside of Manhattan is an arduous journey," she responds.

"Typical New Yorker," Lincoln quips, draping his arm along Chloe's shoulders, kissing her temple. "Which is why I love ya, babe."

"You're not so bad yourself." She winks.

I smile at them, then shift my attention to Nora, who gazes into the distance. I know how she feels right now. She's the last single woman in our little circle. Granted,

Asher and I are only dating, but this relationship is different from any of my previous ones. Which was why I didn't hesitate when he asked me to move in...officially.

"What time does your flight leave tomorrow?" I ask, getting Nora's attention.

She tears her eyes toward us, forcing a smile. "Eight a.m."

"So you're really doing it...," Chloe muses.

"Why not? Like you guys encouraged me at my Ding Dong Divorced party a few weeks ago, I deserve to take some me time. Mark this next step in my life with an adventure. What better adventure is there than driving Route 66?"

"Well, I know this is a party for Izzy and Asher," Evie announces, retrieving a gift bag from beneath the patio table, "but we all chipped in and got you a little something for your trip."

Nora hesitantly takes it. "I've seen the gifts you guys give. I'm not sure I want it."

"You're probably right," Chloe interjects. "But it may come in useful."

"Is it safe to open up here?" She glances over her shoulder toward where Grams socializes with my parents, Jessie and Emilia laughing at something she just said, Emilia's daughter giggling next to her.

Ever since Emilia appeared out of nowhere, Jessie has been up in New Hampshire every chance he gets. While I haven't seen anything overtly amorous between them, I sense it's headed that way. I'd hoped Avery would be able to make it today, if for no other reason than to meet Emilia, but her son is moving back into his dorm at Northwestern this weekend. Regardless, we've stayed in touch. In a way, it feels like I did find my mother, especially when she tells me stories about her.

"Trust me. Grams has seen much worse." Asher takes a sip of his drink. "She probably *owns* much worse," he mutters.

"Your Grams is a rockstar," Evie states. "When I'm ninety, I want to be like her."

"Don't we all," I remark.

"Okay." Nora exhales deeply. "Here goes nothing." She rummages through the bag and pulls out the first gift, scrunching her nose. "Maps? What did you hide inside?" She flips the slim package around, scrutinizing it to figure out what kind of kinky gift we disguised within its pages. "Butt plugs?"

"Nope." Evie holds her head high. "They're just maps. Complete with turn-by-turn directions of Route 66. We were reading up and found out a lot of the route isn't marked. So those maps will help you stay on the old road as much as possible."

"There's an app you can download, too," Chloe adds. "But since you're going old school with driving Route 66, we figured maybe you'd like something tangible to hold on to."

"This is perfect." Nora beams, clutching them to her chest. Then she reaches into the bag, pulling out a leather-bound journal. Her fingers trace the grooves of the words embossed in gold on the front — *Let the Adventure Begin.*

"We thought you'd like to journal along the way. Might help with some self-introspection," Evie offers.

"I love it," Nora breathes, examining the pages. "This is gorgeous. And it's the perfect journal for this trip." She smiles at all of us, then ruffles through the tissue in the bag. When she takes out the final gift, she bursts out laughing, her face turning red as she holds up the vibrator. "And there it is."

"What did you expect from us?" I suggest. "For those lonely nights when you're staying in a sketchy motel room. Trust me. That thing will make you forget your name."

"It's true," Asher offers. "Izzy tested out dozens to find the best one before ordering that for you. We ran a series of experiments. It was a grueling few days."

"Oh, I'm sure it was absolutely torture for you," Nora quips, and we all erupt in laughter. Then she stands, giving each of us a hug. "You girls are the best friends anyone could ask for. I don't know how I would have survived these past few months without you."

"We didn't do anything." Evie rests her hand on Nora's bicep.

"You were there," she replies in earnest.

"And we always will be." Chloe wraps an arm around her, and the four of us hug, leaving our guys out of this special moment.

It doesn't matter what we go through, what disagreements we may have. We'll always be there for each other. I suppose that's all anyone can ask for.

* * *

"I'm not cleaning a damn thing tonight," I moan as I flop onto the couch in the living room after all our guests are gone. "I'm rethinking this whole homeownership thing. I don't like entertaining."

Asher lifts my legs, then sits next to me, setting my feet on his lap. "Then we'll pay someone to entertain for us."

"I like the sound of that."

"And don't worry about cleaning. I have a crew booked for tomorrow. Actually, Jessie booked them, but I'm going to take credit for it."

I laugh, then whimper when he rubs the arch of my

foot, flexing the muscle, savoring in his touch. I could probably die happy right now. There's something incredibly orgasmic about him rubbing my feet.

"He's always good like that," I murmur, closing my eyes. "You'd be lost without him."

"No question about that."

Despite all the lies and truths that were revealed over these past several months, Jessie and Asher came out the other side strong. Maybe even stronger, especially now that Jessie found Emilia. There's no doubt in my mind he never truly loved me. Not when I see the unequivocal devotion in his eyes whenever he catches a glimpse of Emilia. Not to mention how fantastic he is with her daughter. I never took Jessie for the type who'd want kids. I figured the second they spilled something on his suit, he'd flip out. Again, I was wrong about him.

Or maybe I was wrong *for* him.

"So where are you off to next week?" I ask, cutting through the comfortable silence.

"Somewhere in the middle of the country. I've lost track at this point. All I know is I have a car coming for me at ten Friday morning and I'm flying to Dallas."

"Oh, Texas. I bet those Texas girls are going to love them some Asher York."

He flashes me that same panty-dropping smile that had me wanting to drop *my* panties the first time I saw him. "Perhaps, but there's only one woman I care about loving me." He leans toward me, his lips hovering close to mine. "And that's you."

"You know I love you. But not Asher York."

He angles away. "What do you mean?"

"I know the real Asher. And that's the man I fell in love with. This whole music thing is a nice bonus."

"So you'd still love me even if I never wrote another song for you?"

"Why do you ask?" I playfully bat my lashes. "Did you write me a song?"

"You should know by now, Izzy. They're *all* for you." His lips touch mine in a soft kiss before he pulls back. "But I'd like your opinion on something I've been working on."

"Okay." As much as I'd love to lounge on the couch as he rubs my feet, I can't resist when he sits at the piano or strums the guitar. I love watching him perform. And I'm lucky enough to be treated to a private concert anytime I want.

"Okay." He places a kiss on my nose, then stands. I sit up as he pads toward one of his guitars, grabbing it before returning to the couch. He checks the tuning and makes a few adjustments. Drawing a deep breath, he positions his fingers on the frets, then a slow, lilting melody fills the room. I relax into the cushions, the sound of Asher's voice putting me at ease.

> "I can't promise it will be easy
> Or that we'll never fight.
> I can't promise dark clouds will stay away
> Or that it will only be blue skies and smooth sailing.
>
> But I can promise my undying love,
> An eternity of devotion, a lifetime of passion.
> I promise I'll always be by your side through any
>   crisis
> If you'll be my boomerang, my always...my wife."

I shoot up, spine straight, jaw dropping, eyes widening as his words ring around me. I almost want to ask him to sing that again. There's no way he just said that, is there? He continues the next verse, but I don't hear it, can't register the lyrics. The smirk on his face tells me he finds amusement in my reaction. When he reaches the last line of the chorus once more, he leans into me, lips brushing against mine.

"I promise to be your friend, your family, your life.
Please, be my wife."

"Did you really just say that?" I ask when he doesn't say anything further.

Pulling back, he sets the guitar beside the couch. When he gets down on one knee in front of me, there's no longer a question in my mind about whether those lyrics were there on purpose.

"Isabella Delaney Nolan…" He takes my left hand in his, everything about him sincere. "When I saw you from across the room at a dirty club in Boston, it felt like I was listening to a song for the first time and knew it would always be my favorite. And that's what you've become to me over the years. My favorite kiss. My favorite good morning. My favorite sunrise. My favorite person. My favorite goodnight." His Adam's apple bobs as he licks his lips. "But there's one thing I no longer want you to be my favorite."

"What's that?" My voice trembles.

He frames my face in his hands, his grasp determined. "I don't want you to be my favorite almost. There's nothing almost about you, about us. Not anymore. From this day forward, I want you to be my favorite always. Officially."

He reaches into his pocket and withdraws a black velvet box. He flips it open to reveal a stunning princess cut diamond flanked on either side by smaller stones, then even more diamonds inlaid into the band.

"It's so shiny," I laugh through my tears.

"That's what I told the jeweler when I picked it out. Told them I needed the shiniest setting."

I roll my eyes. "No, you didn't."

"You're right. I didn't have to. I knew exactly what you wanted. So, what do you say? Will you be my muse for the rest of my life?"

I nod quickly, touching my lips to his. "Yes," I say against his mouth. "I'll be your forever muse. Your favorite always." I swallow hard. "Your favorite wife."

His muscles relax as he kisses me with even more determination, taking my left hand in his and slipping on the ring, not tearing his lips from me. His tongue swipes mine, and I tug him on top of me as I lower myself to my back. When he grinds his hips, I moan.

"Wait." He pulls back. I dart my eyes open, meeting his, my brows pulled in. Then a salacious smile crosses his mouth as he waggles his brows. "There are a few things I should mention. Job requirements if you're to be my full-time muse. A few things Jessie must have left off the last time you accepted employment for this position."

I pinch my lips together, giving him a playful look. "Is that right?"

He erases the distance between us, covering my mouth with his. "I'll need you to lay on the couch after you come home from a long day at work while I rub all your sore muscles."

"That sounds exhausting, but I'll do my best." I breathe deeply as he makes his way to my neck, his scruff grazing my skin.

"Every morning, you'll need to rest in bed while I bring you breakfast."

"Now you're getting demanding." I throw my head back as he continues slithering down my body, lifting the hem of my shirt, peppering kisses along my stomach.

"And if we ever have children, you'll need to take some time for yourself while I change their diapers, read to them, and rock them to sleep."

"You're an absolute slave driver," I groan as he trails his tongue just above the waistband of my jeans, then dipping into my belly button. "But I must say, the employment package is rather…enticing."

He breaks into a throaty laugh. I can't help but join in, everything about this moment exactly as I imagined it would be.

"God, I love you." He lifts his eyes to mine.

"And I love you."

A breathtaking smile builds at the declaration he's heard hundreds of times by now. But there's something different in his gaze this time. It's a look of peace unlike any I've seen. It's the same look I always noticed crawl across my father's face whenever he walked into the house and saw my mother. She'd always go to him and give him a kiss that may have bordered on inappropriate as she welcomed him home. Even if they weren't physically in the house I grew up in, she'd still greet him the same way.

Home isn't four walls and a door. It's a feeling.

It's *this* feeling.

Sure, we'll have fights. We'll get mad. We'll have moments when we'll want to throw in the towel. But at the end of the day, we'll always have our love, a boomerang, and an origami dove.

"Welcome home, Asher," I murmur as I grab the back of his neck and bring his lips to mine.

"Welcome home, Isabella."

The End

Thank you so much for reading *Dangerous Games*! I hope you enjoyed Asher and Izzy's story! Want a little bit more of them? Sign up for my mailing list to get a bonus chapter from Asher's point of view. Trust me... You don't want to miss this.

www.tkleighauthor.com/mailing-list-sign-up-dangerousgames

Royal Games

Every girl dreams of falling in love with a prince.

When I met Jeremy, I thought he *was* my prince.

Caring. Compassionate. Sensitive.

And, unfortunately for me… Not attracted to women.

So here I am, thirty years old and divorced when most of my friends are just getting married. In desperate need of a restart, I set off on a road trip to learn how to love myself again.

The last thing I expected was to meet *him*.

Anderson North.

Mysterious. Enigmatic. Sexy as hell.

And, after a malfunction with my rental car, my new road companion.

As we travel Route 66, I find myself experiencing a connection I never have. We share our truths, our secrets, our fears.

Can I give this man a piece of my heart after having it broken?

Can I learn to trust again after having that trust betrayed?

When he reveals his deepest secret, can I look beyond the lies and toward the only thing that matters?

I've always dreamed of finding my very own Prince Charming. Maybe my prince is Anderson North.

www.tkleighauthor.com/royal-games

Playlist

You Were Good to Me - Jeremy Zucker
Can I Be Him - James Arthur
I Can't Fall in Love Without You - Zara Larsson
Lately - RuthAnne
Place We Were Made - Maisie Peters
If The World Was Ending - JP Saxe with Julia Michaels
Acoustic - Billy Raffoul
Satisfy Me - Anderson East
Put Me Back Together - Caitlyn Smith
What Would It Take - Anderson East
Can I Stay - Ray Lamontagne
Love of my Life - Queen
Favorite Part of Me - Astrid S
All On My Mind - Anderson East
Wasn't Expecting That - Jamie Lawson
Never Really Over - Katy Perry
Break My Heart Right - James Bay
I Fell in Love with the Devil - Avril Lavigne
Grow as we Go - Ben Platt
Slide - James Bay
Dancing with Your Ghost - Sasha Sloan
Lying in Her Arms - Anderson East
Lie to Me - 5 Seconds of Summer with Julia Michaels
Rush - Lewis Capaldi with Jessie Reyez
Rewrite the Stars - James Arthur & Anne-Marie
You Say - Lauren Daigle
Light As the Breeze - Leonard Cohen & Billy Joel

Girlfriend - Anderson East
Incredible - James TW
Love Like This - Ben Rector
Careless - Amos Lee
BRKN - Madison Ryann Ward
Just Your Memory - Johnnyswim with Penny and Sparrow
Let It All Go - Birdy with RHODES
A Safe Place to Land - Sara Bareilles with John Legend
I Get To Love You – Ruelle

Acknowledgments

I always said I'd never write a rockstar romance. Well, I should know after 6 years in this industry to never say never. My husband actually works in the rock n' roll industry. Well, technically, he's a producer / director, but he's spent the past twenty years of his life touring with a very well known musician. So yes. I married a roadie. I've been backstage at more concerts than I can count and I swore I'd never write in this particular genre because it hits a little too close to home.

And then Asher York made his appearance in Wicked Games, and I knew I had to write my first rockstar romance.

But I wanted to do something different with mine. I didn't want Asher's status as this incredible musician who rose to the top of the charts to define who he was. He's more than that. Too many people define who they are based on what their profession is instead of their relationships with other people. I didn't want that to be the case with Asher and Izzy.

A big thanks to my hubby, Stan, for marrying me. LOL. In all seriousness, my time spent backstage in video world, on tour buses, and at pre-show parties really helped me paint the picture I needed. (And I almost put in the necessary union blackout you all complain about when you play MSG. It was tempting.) On that same note, a huge thanks to my amazing nannies, Karissa and Bree, who come to play with little Harper Leigh so I can have time to write.

There's only one woman I trust with my babies and that's Kim Young. She's an incredible editor who somehow knows exactly what I'm trying to say when my brain refused to fire on all cylinders, which is common. Thank you for all your hard work and for accommodating my crazy schedule.

Another huge thanks to the Thelma to my Louise, my PA, Melissa Crump. I couldn't do any of this without you taking the initiative and doing whatever needs to be done without me asking you. You've made my life infinitely easier this past year.

To Emily and the girls at Social Butterfly - thanks for all your hard work and expertise in this release!

To my beta readers - Vicky, Lin, Stacy, Sylvia, and Joelle. Thank you so much for your patience! You finally got your Asher York! Thanks so much for all your feedback on this book. And for agreeing not to read Mind Games until I finished Dangerous Games. I value your honesty and encouragement.

To my fabulous admins… Vicky, Lea, and Joelle. Thanks for keeping everything under control while I hide away and write.

To my review group — thank you so much for taking the time and reading all my books before release. I am truly humbled by all the support you've shown me over the years.

Last but not least, thanks to you for picking up this book and taking a chance on me. Whether you've been with me since I published A Beautiful Mess back in 2013 or if this is your first book of mine, I'm so thrilled your love of reading led you to me.

Buckle up! We're about to hit the road with Nora's story in *Royal Games*!

Peace & love,

~ T.K.

Books by T.K. Leigh

ROMANTIC SUSPENSE
The Beautiful Mess Series
A Beautiful Mess
A Tragic Wreck
Gorgeous Chaos
Chasing the Dragon (Deception Duet #1)
Slaying the Dragon (Deception Duet #2)
Vanished: A Beautiful Mess Series Novel

The Vault
Inferno

Heart of Light

CONTEMPORARY ROMANCE
The Redemption Series
Promise: A Redemption Series Prologue
Commitment
Redemption

The Dating Games Series
Dating Games
Wicked Games
Mind Games
Dangerous Games
Royal Games

ROMANTIC COMEDY
The Book Boyfriend Chronicles
The Other Side of Someday
Writing Mr. Right

MATURE YOUNG ADULT
Heart of Marley

For more information on any of these titles and upcoming releases, please visit T.K.'s website:
www.tkleighauthor.com

About the Author

T.K. Leigh, otherwise known as Tracy Leigh Kellam, is the *USA Today* Bestselling author of the Beautiful Mess series, in addition to several other works ranging from sexy and sinful to fun and flirty. Originally from New England, she now resides in sunny Southern California with her husband, beautiful daughter, and three cats. When she's not planted in front of her computer, writing away, she can be found training for her next marathon (of which she has run over twenty fulls and far too many halfs to recall) or chasing her daughter around the house.

T.K. Leigh is represented by Jane Dystel of Dystel, Goderich & Bourret Literary Management. All publishing inquiries, including audio, foreign, and film rights, should be directed to her.